Canda

Thank you for your support!

Unexplained
Behavior

Madame Pink

c. Jan 2016

Madame Pink

"Hey Sara, I took a phone call earlier and it was a guy asking about assistance with new accounts. I told him to come by at 12:30, but I just got an email from one of my HUGE account holders! I must do some work for him, he's a big spender with me! Can you help this new guy? Please?"
I hated doing favors for Freddy. He always wanted a piece of the pie; having done absolutely no work to assist with the sale. The last time we had this issue, it cost me a huge client. That was probably the client he was speaking about. This client was a major investor. He was a big business owner in the United States and in numerous countries overseas. Freddy was very lazy. I wondered if he knew anything about the new client. His track record made me say no. However, I was long overdue for a surprise from him. In the same regard, I was prepared to have to start from scratch and build rapport; I was good at it, but for once, I didn't want to.
"What can you tell me about said new client?"
"He's an investor. Apparently, he's a wealthy small business owner. He's got a financial advisor that he is trying to replace. He heard great things about our office and I suggested he come by. He said he had an hour at 12:30 and the rest of the meeting would have to be handled via Face-Time. I have an Android."
"Hmm, What's his name? Where's he from?"
"You want his damn blood type also?!?!!! Here..."
He handed me a poorly written note. I envisioned his large self leaning all the way back in his chair while he was on the phone, scribbling this note. I was certain he was spinning. The poor chair was probably squeaking just enough to sound like a small child whimpering. Freddy was the awkward 5yr old that goes to the nail salon with his mother, and the entire time she's getting her manicure; her child is running all over the salon, touching toenails and tearing up the magazines. He was the child that you asked a million times to stop doing that same annoying thing, and the entire time this annoying child was repeating the words coming out of your mouth, instead of listening to them. Obviously, Freddy was my least favorite co-worker.
"I will take care of the new client, only because I do not have anything scheduled until 2:30. But DO NOT come to me after the deal is completed looking for a hand out. It's not happening. Got it!?"
"OK. I promise. He's your new client."
As promised, he walked in at 12:30pm on the dot! This man was prompt

& professional. Immediately, I was pleased. The tall, wide glass door that lead into the bright foyer of our office opened and a handsome man entered. He was tall with fair, smooth skin, slim build with muscular upper body. He was like a Greek God! His arms, like Tarzan. Slender features; thin nose, pointy, and behind a thin pair of silver wire frame glasses, were big beautiful blue eyes and long dark eyelashes. I briefly imagined those eyes on a beautiful biracial baby girl. I smiled. Those eyes; they were the doors to his soul. He had a full head of dark, healthy hair. He was wearing a pair of black linen pants that held his waistline to perfection, a semi-tight, white Burberry button up shirt, and a pair of white Sperry's. Fresh! It was a beautiful day for the outfit. He was carrying an iPad and a single key. I spotted the key immediately. Porsche. He looked like a Porsche driver.

"Hello. Welcome to Bradley and Associates. My name is Sara Bashir. You must be Jackson Ellis. I received a note that you would be coming in at 12:30. I'm glad you made it." I extended my hand. He shook, delightedly.

"I-I-I, yes, I am Jackson Ellis. You may call me Jax."

"Jax, sweet! May I get you any coffee, tea, water?"

"Jameson."

"Straight? Or on the rocks?" We both laughed. Oh, even his laugh was beautiful. It was the perfect laugh! It made me smile. I was glad to know he was a whiskey drinker. I was sure he picked up the innuendo that I too, was a whiskey drinker. I was giggling like a schoolgirl, but I managed to speak behind my laugh.

"Please, follow me." I walked ahead of him slightly. We walked through a second set of tall, glass doors. This time we walked down a very long, well-lit corridor. Along each side of us were an array of trees, plants, and flowers. They were maintained by building staff. My favorite spot in the entire setup were the beautiful, white calla lilies and baby's breath entwined with ivy vines. At the end of the corridor, we made a right and walked down a narrower, curvy hallway. There were offices on both sides. We got to the end and I opened another set of tall, wide, glass doors. These lead to my office. My office suite was a pure indication that I was a big deal around here and Jackson picked up on it. His eyes became very bright when he walked in past me. He was looking around the room, reading the credentials on my walls. He smelled so good.

Fresh; like he had just gotten out of the shower.

"Jax, please, have a seat."
He did. I walked around my desk and sat across from him.
"I see you went to NYU. I went to NYU Medical."
"It is always a pleasure to meet alumni. I went to NYU and received a Bachelor's in Finance. If you look that way, you will see I received my MBA from North Carolina A&T."
I laughed at the differences in my schools, the locations, and I decided to continue talking to explain. "While I was in high school, I went on a black college tour. I had a ball! I was certain that when it came time to apply, I was going to an HBCU. I started filling out applications and applying for scholarships and I decided to apply to NYU on a whim. Not only did they accept me, they gave me a scholarship. That was when my college search came to an end. I did very well at NYU. When it came time to explore my options for graduate school, I was DETERMINED to go to a black college. I went on a new tour; It was different this time, I was looking at the program with a different pair of eyes. And...well, there you have it." I realized I may have been rambling, so I stopped speaking. Jackson tilted his neck back slightly and grinned. He sat upright and spoke; on cue.
"I went to UConn and received my Bachelor's in Biology. I worked in a lab for 2 years because I thought my brain needed a rest from school. My father sat me down and basically threatened my life if I didn't go to medical school. Everyone in my family is a doctor. I am the oldest, a neurologist. I have 2 younger brothers; 1 an endocrinologist and the other an orthopedic surgeon. My sister is a cardiologist. Mom and dad ran an office for damn near 50 years! She, an obstetrician and he, a gynecologist. Anyway, I bartended while I was in medical school. I did it for fun; I thought it would be a great way to meet girls. It was an epic fail!" He laughed. And it made me smile, again. "And...well, there you have it!" The infectious laughter erupted from his belly this time. It was wonderful! We laughed. I liked that we laughed. I glanced at my watch and wound the laughter down again.
"What can I do for you, Jackson?"
I liked saying his name. Funny, I think he liked hearing me say it also. He leaned back in his chair and perched his right ankle on his left knee. Hmm, he was getting comfortable. I guess I had that effect on gorgeous, business men.
"I am currently operating out of 2 offices and I need to begin merging into

one office; I own a medical office building that I finally decided to move my practice into. I also own some rental real estate property, commercial property, an auto body shop and a car wash. All of which are individual businesses, with individual accounts. I fired my financial advisor. There were some funds missing at the end of the last fiscal year. He couldn't account for them, so I fired his ass. He was lucky that was all I did. I need to give access to my finances to one person that I can trust. I know that if they are a part of a firm, they will be less likely to make an idiotic move like that because they are a part of a firm that will not take the fall for their idiotic moment. I need someone who can make all of this under one LLC and begin making me an enterprise. Can you help me?" I heard what he said, and I could help him; in fact, I was practically dying to help him! I had the ability to make his name an enterprise. I was a genius with skills and connections. I handle multi-million dollar companies and accounts. I handled anything. However, I was not sure if I could handle the barrage of feelings that I was feeling for this man so early. While he was speaking, I fixated my attention on his accent. It was mild, low. Perhaps he had been in the United States for some time and its beginning to fade. Is that possible? Who knew, but it was sexy. Is he an Aussie? I imagined him calling my name...snap out of it, Sara! I had to snap out of it because the thoughts were about to get very naughty!

"Yes, I, Yes. I can help you. By any chance, do you have copies of your most recent financial statement from each of your venues? I'll need a breakdown of what each piece of your pie is constructed with. I'll also need a spending report. If you don't have one, I can make one. I usually take 3 months to set everything up, and then I trust that the system can maintain itself consistently. But just in case, your financial statement will be available to me via remote access 24/7. If something requires my immediate attention, I can take care of it. If something requires yours and my attention, you will be notified." He seemed pleased with my presentation. He sat with me for almost 2 hours. We discussed his business financial plans. He told me his financial goal and asked me to assist his companies with that goal. He hired me to be his full time financial advisor for his entire company. This was a BIG deal! Ha! "In your face, lazy Freddy!"

It took me a couple of days, but I drew a contract and called him back into my office so could collect his signature. He called ahead and said he was in a hurry and asked me to meet him in the foyer with the contract. As per his request, I was standing front and center waiting for his arrival;

contract and pen in hand!

"Hello Sara. You look very nice!" The rain came with a brisk breeze today, so I dressed accordingly. I wore black riding pants; form fitting, of course, and a black tweed blazer on top of a white, T-shirt. I wore black leather ankle booties and my hair was pulled back in a ponytail. I felt that I was a tad bit too casual for a Tuesday, but it was raining and it's a wonder I came in today anyway. "I ain't come here to work!" I said to myself, with attitude when I walked in the building at 9:02am.

"Thank you, Jackson, I wasn't even trying this morning!" He laughed again, and I smiled again.

"You don't need to try, darling. Where do I sign?"

Well just turn me to chocolate pudding why don't you. He signed very quickly. I handed him a copy and just like that he was gone. I worked on Jackson Ellis' financial reports, billing statements, spending accounts, and bank accounts for each part of his business. I was finally able to make one umbrella with various chairs under it. He got an enterprise; an LLC, just like he asked. It took me a bit longer than I expected. This dude was wealthier than I thought. He was pleased, I was pleased that he was pleased.

Ring Ring Ring.

"Sara speaking..."

"Hello Sara, Jackson Ellis here. How are you? Did I catch ya at a bad time?"

"Hello Jackson, Jax, it's not a bad time. I am well. How are you? Are you keeping your finances in order?"

"No babe. That's what I hired you for! But I'm busy as always, hungry as always. Hahaha! I have a business idea that came across my desk and I was wondering if I could pick your brain about it. Would you like to join me for dinner? I know a great place not too far from your office?"

OMG! I had a mini nervous breakdown sitting at my desk. I wondered if he heard me breathing. I thought I was breathing like a fire dragon! Of course, I was going to meet him for dinner! I would've been a damn fool not too!

"I think I can break away for a moment. Which place were you thinking about?"

"Baang! It's Asian fusion. Do you eat Asian fusion?"

"I am familiar with Baang, and yes, I do eat Asian fusion."
"Great! It's a date! Let's say, how's 6:30?"
"I'll see you then!"
As I hung up the phone, I felt the smile come across my face. It was like I was in high school, speaking to my crush for the first time. I was so excited and anxious to share this with my girls. I picked my cell phone up and began a text message thread to Daniela and Arianna. They were my best friends, since childhood. We grew up together; same elementary, middle and high schools. Separate colleges and grad schools; but we always stayed close. We were sisters.

Me: So y'all remember dude I was telling you about; Jackson? Well, I just agreed to have dinner with him and I am so EXCITED!!
Daniela: Isn't he your client? Is it a good idea to date your client?
Arianna: Did you know that Keith has been asking about you? He wants to know if you are coming to his 4th of July shindig

Keith was my ex. Arianna went to college with him. She introduced us over spring break during our junior year. He was sweet, but when I decided I was going to get my MBA and I wouldn't be moving back home with him, he got mad and broke up with me. Arianna wished that our relationship would work out and I was totally cool with all of us being friends. She deemed it necessary to tell me when she spoke to him. I often thought she was waiting for one of his stories to sound amazing to me and I would be so inclined to take him back. Yea, that wasn't happening. Keith was a great guy, but I didn't go backwards. It was a rule of mine.

Me: Blah. I don't want to talk about Keith. Oh, and I'm not going to his shindig. I'll be out of town.
Daniela: Uhm, where are you going?!?

I could hear her playful attitude in her voice as I read that text. It made me giggle.

Me: Relax your attitude over there miss lady. Remember, I have a client that does that 4th of July boat ride thing. This year, it isn't a boat ride. It's a party on Miami Beach. I'm out!

Daniela: Can you bring a plus one?

Me: Unfortunately, no.

Daniela: Can I come anyway?

Me: I'm sure you can come to Miami, you're grown. LOL. But the party on the beach is private.

Daniela: Damn! Well, alright! We can plan a girl trip for another weekend.

Me: Sounds good to me. Did Ari die? Hahahaha!!

Arianna: Na, I'm here wench. I was just reading, and waiting for someone to say my name. Hahahaha!!!! Where's dude taking you for dinner?

Me: A place up here in CT.

Arianna: Oh, ok cool. Have fun. I want the details. You should come over after dinner.

Me: Ok. I'll txt when dinner is done and make sure you heifers are still awake.

Daniela: I will be. I'm off tomorrow.

Arianna: I'm not off tomorrow, but I wanna hear about the date and we haven't seen you since 99, so I'll be up!

Me: 99 though?! Hahaha!! I saw you 2 weeks ago. Anyway, I'll come over after dinner. I'll txt before I come.

"Ugh, this day is a drag!"

I was sitting at my desk, anxious and waiting for the clock to say 6pm so I can freshen up and head to dinner. "Come on Sara, you only have 1hr and 42mins. You can do it!" My legs were falling asleep so I stood and did some leg stretches.

"I should be going to the gym tonight, since I didn't go last night, but I am really excited about dinner with Jackson." It had been a few weeks since he first walked into my office. We only spoke when it was business related, so him wanting to meet for dinner was a bit out of the norm. Then again, he did say a business idea came across his desk.

"Hey Sara, you remember that dude that came in a few months back? Jackson something; anyway, did you complete that project? Whatever happened with that?"

I knew Freddy was going to roll himself in here looking for a piece of the pie. I wanted to make a run for it.

"The Jackson Ellis project has been completed. In fact, I have already been paid on that project. By the way, did I tell you that I bought a new car?"

That was low blow because 3 or 4 weeks ago, Freddy came in here complaining that he needed a new car but he still owed too much money on his current car and the new car took him out of his price range and blah, blah, blah. I couldn't understand how someone with so many clients and so many opportunities to make so much money, didn't have enough money to buy a new car. But then again, I did not care.

"Uh. Yea, I thought you were, you know, gonna hook me up, break me off a piece of that pie!"
He attempted to fist bump me. I just stared.
"Don't you think you've had enough pie, Freddy?"
"Was that a fat joke?"
"Did it feel like a fat joke?"
"Listen! If it wasn't for me..."
"STOP!"
I cut him off. I knew exactly what he was about to say and I was not in the mood to have that conversation yet again with this fool! "I remember telling you that I was NOT going to give you any cuts from this deal. Let's not mention the HARD WORK that I DID for this project; it wasn't easy. I didn't just smile and gain a client and then smile and close a deal. I worked! And that is something that you know nothing about because you don't do any work! Now, take your lazy, begging, annoying, loathing self down the hall and bother someone else. Make sure you close my door behind you." That's exactly what he did. I did not play when it came to my money and he always thought he can pull a fast one on me. Not me!
"Well that took up some time. Now I only have 1hr and 20mins. AHHH! I'm going to go take a walk."
I rose from my desk and stretched again. I approached the large glass doors, pulled, and walked through. I heard a commotion as I glided down the hallway. I was walking at a slow pace because I had no destination in mind. But the commotion was getting louder and louder. I turned the corner and was coming toward the corridor with the plants and flowers. Freddy was standing in the middle of the hallway with the president of the company, Brian.
"Freddy, I asked you for the notes from this meeting 3 weeks ago!! Do you know where I found them?!? I found them on your desk, in an

envelope, underneath 2 bags of chips! It's ridiculous. Do you know what happened because of me not having those meeting notes? I lost the deal! I lost the deal because when it came time for the conference call, I was not prepared! Do you know why I was not prepared?!? Because I allowed my idiot son to take meeting notes at a meeting that he begged me to go to because he's 'mature now'. I don't care what you think you are! Do you know why? It's because you will always find a way to mess something up!"

"Aw man! I don't think anyone knew I'm your son. I was trying to keep it a secret."

"You don't do any work! Even if no one heard us clarify it, they knew, because otherwise there will be no reason for you to still have a job here. And I am tempted to fire you right now but I'm not. I'm sending my personal assistant on vacation. You are going to run my errands and run around the block. You could care to shed a few pounds and I hope you can manage grocery shopping, picking up dry cleaning and taking the cars for service appointments. That's all your worthy of doing. Now get out of my sight!"

Today was just not Freddy's day. I chuckled to myself as I watched the crowd disperse. As my eyes skimmed the room, I looked past the crowd to the front desk. Keith was standing at the front desk asking the receptionist if I was available. I quickly dipped around the corner into an empty cubicle. Thank goodness, this cubicle had a phone on the desk. I dialed the receptionists' extension...

"Front desk, Jenna speaking."
"Jenna! It's Sara. I do not want to see the man that is standing in front of you asking where I am. Do not let him know I am in the building. In fact, tell him that I am in meetings for the duration of the day. I'm leaving at 6 and I will not be back until Monday at noon."
"Ok. Will do."
"I'm sorry sir. That was Sara's assistant. Sara is in meetings for the duration of the day. She is leaving at 6 this evening and she will be back in on Monday at noon. Would you like to leave a message for her?"
"No thanks, I have her cell number, I'll send her a text. Thanks, miss."
"You're welcome sir, thanks, you too!" I gave Jenna a few minutes before I called to make sure he was really gone.
"Front desk, Jenna speaking."

"It's Sara. Is he gone?"

"Yes ma'am, he is."

This was a strange day. Arianna was just talking about this fool, now he was standing in my office suite. I decided to go back to my office before anymore strange shit happens. As I enter my office, I hear my cell phone ringing. I had no idea where it was and couldn't locate it before it stops. It rang again. Immediately, as if the person on the other end put their finger on the receiver, picked it up and it hit redial. Finally, I found it in my bag. I was not surprised. It was Keith; and he called right back.

"Hello..."

"I saw you and then I didn't see you and then the receptionist says you're in meetings for the rest of the day. Then I call your cell phone and you don't answer. Are you avoiding me?"

"I answered the phone. I can hear your voice. I didn't answer it fast enough for you. That's what you mean, right? And no, I am not avoiding you. I am working. But..." I looked at the clock. I had 55mins. I entertained Keith for 20 of those minutes.

"I have about 14 minutes that I can spare. How may I be of assistance to you?"

"I met someone. And now she's pregnant. I'm getting married. I need your financial assistance."

"Wow! Congrats! What kind of assistance do you need?"

"I need a prenuptial agreement. I made 6 million dollars last fiscal year. I just want to be on the safe side."

"You need a lawyer."

"Aren't you a lawyer and a financial planner?!?"

"I'm a notary and a financial advisor. Call my brother. If he cannot help you, he will point you in the right direction." My brother was a lawyer. He was an ADA in Boston. I was 75% sure he couldn't help Keith, but, I enjoyed making him jump through hoops because I knew he would.

"You ok with me getting married and being a father? I know that you wanted that family thing with me." I was not surprised that Keith made that statement. He really wanted me to break down and beg him not to move on with his life. He got a rush from needy chicks needing him. Well, that was not me.

"Yea, no, I didn't. But if you love it, I like it. Is that all you need? I have things to do."

"Oh, Sara Karina, we all know that you're rich but do not do any work!"
"Work smart, not hard. I'll talk to you later."
"Peace out cub scout!"
I wondered if that was what Ari was going to say about Keith when she mentioned him. I meant that though. If he was happy, I was happy. Keith was a good guy. He just wasn't a good guy for me. There was nothing wrong with realizing you do not have chemistry with someone. I was glad that he found someone to be happy with.

I loved Baang. It was the first restaurant that I tried when I moved to CT. I no longer lived around the corner from it, so it had been a while since I had been. As I pulled into the parking lot, I realized that I had no idea what he was driving. I parked and proceeded to go inside and grab a table. Dr. Sir Handsome face was already there. When I walked through the door, I saw him sitting in a corner towards the back of the restaurant. I walked towards him. He rose from his chair and greeted me with a hug and kiss on the cheek.

"Hello Sara. You are beautiful. How are you? It's so good to see you.
"Hi Doc! Thank you. How are…"
"Hello, Welcome to Baang. My name is Nick and I will be your waiter this evening. May I start you with a drink?"
"Jameson!" We both bellowed out of turn to the waiter.
"Hahaha! Ok. Great! For the lady, how would you like your Jameson?"
"I prefer it chilled; straight."
"Ok. Got it. And you sir?"
"I'll have mine with a splash of ginger ale." The waiter smiled and walked away.
"Jameson and ginger ale…sounds good. Have you ever tried Jameson straight?" The contagious laughter began.
"I like that you make me laugh, Sara. You're funny. I do drink Jameson straight, after the first one that I have with ginger ale. It's a drinking tradition that I do with myself. I'm not sure why, but it's what I do."
"Hahaha! I'm cool with that! Drink to your hearts content." I smiled. The waiter approached with our drinks.
"So, tell me about this business idea that you want to run by me."
"Would you be mad if I said that I didn't have one and that was my awkward way of asking you to dinner?"

"I'm flattered that you like me. I'm not sure of how I feel about you using business to get me to have dinner with you; but, no, I'm not mad. So, tell me about you. What should I know about you?" His big blue eyes dropped as if I stabbed him in the heart with that question. I wasn't expecting the answer.

"Well, you know that I am a doctor. I love cars and high fashion. I love jewelry. I like to travel. I love football. I work out 5 times a week. In addition to Jameson, I also drink Kettle One, or Merlot. I have 2 kids; boys. They are fraternal twins. They are 7. And… I am in an unhappy marriage." I sat still like stone. I had been all warm and tingly for this man since we met. The anticipation of our dinner date tonight was practically killing me. And of course, it was my wonderful luck that Dr. Mr. I Smell good was married. I was going to make the best of this night. It will probably our last.

"Bad things happen sometimes, right!? I am not judging you; however, I hope you did not seek me out to be a part of your love triangle that she doesn't know about. I do not do drama."

"I felt a connection to you when we first met. It was a real connection. I know you felt it also. I have absolutely no plan in play. Let's just see what happens." I was normally all for 'see what happens', but I never dealt with it at this magnitude.

"How long have you been unhappy?"

"10yrs."

"How long have you been married?"

"9yrs. don't ask."

"Don't worry, I won't. I know when to change the subject. Where are you from?"

"I was born in Copenhagen. I moved to NY when I was 12. I've been here since the early 90s. I did my residency at Yale Medical. What about you?"

"I was born in Cairo. My parents are Egyptian, but I was raised in NY. They were simply visiting home in Cairo. My mother says that I wanted to see the land. I was born 3 weeks early. When my brother went to college, my parents moved us to CT."

"Do you speak Arabic?"

"I do, with my family only; and usually I am listening to Arabic and answering in English. My father hates that I do that. But technically, I am American. They boarded a plane back to NY when I was 3 days old, however, I have dual residency. They spoke Arabic at home, but my mom also spoke English at home."

"That's interesting. I speak Danish and German. I speak to my children in German. My wife is German, but she was born and raised in New Jersey. Her German is horrible. And of course, it's a world war when/ if I correct her grammar. So, I no longer fight it. I told her to speak to the children in English and I will speak German."

"Ha! How's that working out?"

"Well the boys are getting older and they recognize that her German sucks so they tell her also. To answer your question, it works! So, I know where you were born. I know where you went to school and what you do for a living. What does Sara like to do for fun?"

"My idea of fun is sleeping late on a Saturday, drinking a pot of coffee while smoking a blunt and online shopping!" He laughed. Good, because otherwise that would've been awkward.

"I own a bed and breakfast in Newport, RI. I drive up there often during the summers. I swim, Jet Ski, parasail, raft, canoe and hang glide. I also own a cabin in Bar Harbor, ME. In the winters, I go there and ski, snowboard and sled. I have a timeshare in Tahiti that I visit twice a year and then I attend various annual events hosted by clients. I also own a car collection. I drive at Lime Rock a few times a year. I attend dealer day at the NY Auto Show every year. I used to write a blog for Motor Trend, so they keep me hooked up pretty well."

I smiled and he smiled back.

"So, those are some of my 'fun' things to do. You?" Jackson's mouth was perched open ever so slightly. I wanted to jump across the table and passionately kiss him. I did it in my mind. It made me blush a bit. I wondered if he noticed.

"Wow! I don't mean to stare but I think that you stopped my heart for a moment. I dreamed of meeting someone that shared some of my common interests. I gave up. No one likes what I like, but then here you are. For example; you have a winter cabin in Bar Harbor, mine is in Portland. You have a timeshare in Tahiti, mine is in Santorini. I have a car collection that I haven't added to in a while. I ski, but not very well; I go to Geneva for the Auto show. You are beautiful, funny, wealthy, adventurous, smart, talented, just simply amazing. Why are you single?" That was the million-dollar question that I wish I had the answer to.

"I'm single because I refuse to settle. I need a full package person, because I am a full package person. I also don't trust very easily. I would imagine that plus; I'm just not looking for anyone. I figure if I'm designed to be single, I will be and if I am designed to be with someone, I will be."

"What's in your car collection?"

"Oh. My collection is huge! It's best to show you one day."

"I can only wish."

As the night carried on, we conversed about so many different things. Not once did he mention his wife, but he had good stories about his kids, his mother & father, siblings and friends. He asked about my family and friends. He wanted to know my dreams, hopes, fears, goals and aspirations. He and I laughed so much. We had so much in common; down to the news shows that we watched. I couldn't imagine being married to this man and not wanting to do absolutely everything in my power to make sure he was 100% happy always. Then again, not everyone was meant for everyone. What I didn't understand, and I wouldn't dare ask, was how does someone remain married to someone that they were unhappy with? Was that what marriage all about? I wouldn't dare bare children knowing that I was in an unhappy marriage. He said they've been married for 10 years, but he had been unhappy for 9 years. The boys were 7. That math didn't add up to me. And now, here I was the most amazing person he claims that he had ever met. Was that good or bad? Did I want this man to enjoy my amazing personality?! I liked him though. I know that I said this will be our first and only time out but I have this feeling that we won't walk away from each other right away. Before we both knew it, it was 10pm. I knew he had to go. He was ignoring phone calls and txt messages for about 20 minutes. He signaled to Nick, the waiter, and asked for the check. I excused myself to the rest room. When I returned, the bill had been paid and Dr. Wonderful face was waiting for me at the door.

"Shall we go Madame?"

"We shall sir, thank you." He assisted me into my jacket like a gentleman. He held the door open as I walked past him. It was a beautiful, calm evening. The air was crisp and clean. We walked side by side into the parking lot. He looked around.

"Which marvel are you driving this evening?"

I took my key out of my handbag and pushed the unlock button on my key fob. The lights flashed on my 2012 VW EOS.

"An EOS?! Really?" Jackson laughed. It was infectious, so I laughed too. Hard.

"It is the only convertible in the world with a sunroof!" I was laughing so hard, but I managed to stop and catch my breath.

"In all honesty, someone owed me money after I did some financial work for them. He refused to pay me so I showed up outside of his daughter's high school. When she came out of the building, I addressed her by name and told her that her father asked me to take her home. She handed me her key and I hopped in on the driver side. When we reached her home, her father knew exactly what was going on. He instructed her to get out and go inside. I allowed her to take her girly, cheerleading stuff out of the back. I looked at her pops and said 'when I get my money, she can have her car back. Now go get me the title!' He pouted; probably ashamed of how he got his daughters car snatched. He grabbed the title and handed it to me. I got in the EOS and I drove away. 3 weeks later, I returned his plates and I haven't heard from him since. That was last year, November."

"WOW! So, the closet mob boss in you showed up at Greenwich High School to repo a 16yr old's car! That's classic! I'll make sure your bill is paid always. No worries here!"

That was when the infectious laughter took over again. This time, he stood in close to me. He's taller than me, so I had to hold my head back slightly. As I did, he cuffed my face in his hands, pulled me in and kissed me softly.

"Thank you for dining with me, Ms. Bashir. It was my pleasure. Get home safely and I'll call you tomorrow."

He watched as I got into my car, started it, and lowered the top. It was a nice enough evening for a drop top ride. Even though I moved, I, still was not far from Baang. I figured I would be home before the real chill hit anyway. I made it all the way home. Parked my EOS, made it inside and took off one shoe when I remembered I was supposed to go to Dani and Ari's house after dinner. I decided to pick up the phone and call them.

Ring Ring Ring

"Home of the whopper, what's ya beef!?"

Crazy Ari answered the house phone and it sounded like they were having a street fair in the living room.

"Hi it's me. I don't know how many Jameson's I had at dinner, but I'm home and a tad tipsy. Can I come over tomorrow?"

"How about we come to you in the morning and have brunch?"

"That works! A que hora?"

"DANIIIIIIII SARA SAID WHAT TIME FOR BRUNCH?!?!" I had to take my ear away from the phone when she began hollering.

"How about we pick her up at 11?"

"Didya hear that?"

"Yup. I'll see y'all at 11. Call me when you wake and wake me too."

"Ok. Sleep tight, drunkie!" As I hung up the phone, I received a text message.

Jax: Miss Gotti. Again, it was a pleasure. I enjoy your company. I would like to take you out again. May I?

Me: Ah look at you...giving me an offer I can't refuse. When? Where?

Jax: I didn't want this evening to end. The annual Greenwich Auto show is Sunday. All classic cars. It starts at 10.

Me: Can we meet at Starbucks first?

Jax: LMAO!! I am not surprised that you are a coffee girl. I am a coffee guy. I will be glad to meet you for coffee and then take you to the show.

Me: AWESOME!!!!

Jax: Yes! Sweet dreams dear and I shall see you Sunday.

Me: My dreams are always sweet and now yours will be too! Good night Doc!

<u>Chapter 2…</u>

I woke up to the sun shining through my bedroom window. It was blinding already and it was only 8:15. That meant today was going to be hot and sunny! I'll take it! I loved spring and summer. I grabbed my cell and checked to see if I had messages or email. I did. I had a missed call from my mom at 7:30am. I called her immediately.

"Hi Mom. How are you?"
"I called you at 7:30! I'm glad I was not dying."
"Mom, its Saturday. I always sleep in on Saturday."
"You call 8:15 sleeping in?! Anyway, your brother and his family will be coming into town next weekend. They would like to see you."
"Ok. I'll be around. I'll come by. Why didn't he call me himself?"
"Because he is a Bashir man, and they are cut from a different cloth. The cloth that all the women in their lives will gather the family members. He will call you when he has financial questions, you know that."
"Uh huh…I know."
I rolled a blunt while we were speaking. My family hated that I smoked weed but since I always did in the privacy of my own home, they dealt with it. They would prefer that I smoke hookah but hookah makes me sick. So, while they are all being Egyptian and smoking hookah at family functions, I was smoking weed.
"What are you doing? Smoking?!?" How'd she know?
"Yes I am. I am home and this is what I do sometimes when I'm home."
"It will kill you."
"Not faster than hookah will kill the others. I love you mom. I should get ready. The girls are coming for brunch. Call me on my cell if you need me, otherwise I will see you when Hosni comes to town."
"I love you too. Come have Sunday dinner with us. Your Aunt and Uncle will be here around 6."
"Ok. Mama. I'll see you Sunday for dinner." Dani and Ari arrived promptly at 11. They were already high, so I did not feel bad about my morning coffee/weed fix. We arrived at Sunset Cove shortly after 11:30. We had a regular waitress here because we are here at least 3 times a month. Once we were seated, she immediately brought over a pitcher of mimosas and 3 glasses.

"Hello ladies. Welcome. Shall I let you marinate or would you like to order?"

"MARINATE!" We sat outside and enjoyed the view. This restaurant overlooked the sound and the bridge. It was such a beautiful day. I was soaking it all in. I was also extremely tipsy by the time the food arrived. I ate. It was necessary.

"So, you must have had a wonderful evening. How many drinks did you have?" Ari hadn't forgotten that I went on a date. I was kind of hoping she would. Once I found out he was married, I immediately wanted us to be a secret. Ah and it sucked because I tell my girls everything, but this would put some distance between us. Arianna was a product of an affair. Her father cheated on his wife at the time with her mother. He promised her that he would be there for her and the baby, but when his wife found out, she wouldn't let him leave her. Ari didn't know her father. She had one though. Her mother met and married a wonderful man when Ari was 2. He raised her as his own.

"Oh, I don't know. We were having such a good time speaking and getting to know each other, that I never counted my drinks. I just drank them!"

"That's a first. You always know how many you had. Let me find out Sara found a man!" She and Dani high fived!

"Oh, no boo! I do NOT have a man!"

"What does he do for a living? Is he financially stable? Does he know the magnitude of your wealth? You have a track record of scaring guys who's salary is subpar in comparison to yours."

Ari knew me well. She was right about that. I once dated a guy for 3 months before he decided that I made too much money. He had the audacity to tell me he preferred his women middle class so that he could take care of them. It made him feel like a man; uhm, WHAT?! Or how about the guy that I dated, then stopped dating, allowed him to still be my friend on Facebook and then he called me to tell me I spend too much money when I bought my house. 'What do I have to bring to the table? Boy I bought this table!' The dating scene sucked and sometimes it required too much energy. Therefore, I relaxed, kicked up my heels and indulged in the activities that I loved. If I met someone, great, if not, oh well. Just when I finally accepted this theory, Jackson walked into my office and the butterflies immediately erupted from within. It was like lava rushing out of a volcano. It hadn't stopped flowing. Naturally, I wanted to see how far this would go. I was taking a serious risk and it was completely out of my norm. I was raised better than to play with someone else's husband. However, someone else's husband never wanted me until now. 33 years on this earth and this was my first encounter with a man I couldn't have.

"He's a doctor. He is also a small business owner. He has quite a few endeavors on his plate."

"That's right up your alley, Miss 'I want to own a little bit of everything'. Maybe you can go into business together. It would be cute!"

"I don't do 'cute' in the business world." I laughed.

"Why do I feel like you are being vague?"

Bingo! I knew it. Dani always knew when I wasn't saying something. No matter how hard I tried, she always figured me out.

"I'm not. He's new to me; therefore, I have not established anything in my mind. It was only dinner. I'm sure I won't see him again anytime soon. We are too busy for that."

Did she buy it?

"I'm not buying it. But I will let you do your thing for now. You will tell more when you're ready. Or when he finally pisses you off."

We all burst into laughter and we sat there for the entire afternoon; 5 pitchers of mimosas later. It was a great day. While we were sitting outside, we discussed a new business venture. Arianna was a beautician and was paying entirely too much money for the chair that she was renting in a salon that wasn't good enough for her. Arianna had been in business for a very long time and had a book of business that was heavier than the dictionary. She found a retail space that was available and she wanted help acquiring it.

"Absolutely! I am more than happy to do this with you. In all honesty, I will buy the space and you can move in. I want your business to boom! I am not planning on collecting rent from you. I will send my contractor over there to inspect the space. Once he reports back to me, I will reach out to the agent that owns the space. I'll work on it first thing Monday."

"Oh thank you so much! I cannot wait to have my own salon! And then I can rent out chairs in the salon for a ridiculous price!"

In fact, Arianna didn't mean a word of that. Revenge was not in her nature. I was the one who set the price of chairs that she rented out. Had it been up to her, she wouldn't have made any money.

"You in a giving mood today, what can I have?"

"What do you need, Dani?"

"Nothing. I was just asking."

Daniela wouldn't ask me for anything even if she did need something. She always said she didn't want to give me anything to hold over her head. She felt that way about everything with everyone. Whenever I bought gifts for her, she fussed. When she fussed, I laughed.

"I bet she wants a house."

Arianna moved in with Daniela last year, when she and her boyfriend broke up. They were together for 4 years. They moved in together after the first year and half. At the beginning of year 4, he decided she had to pay rent in the apartment. Meanwhile, he convinced her to move in the first place because he was paying the rent so she 'didn't have an additional bill'. The entire setup was weird. It was supposed to be temporary, but Dani loved having Ari there, so she told her she didn't have to move if she didn't want to. Recently, Arianna confided in me that she felt like a burden to Dani. She said, "Dani deserves to have her home back."

"I do want a house; but not yet, and when I get one, I want it to be because my husband and I are purchasing it together. I love you and I appreciate all that you do for me, but Sara, I don't want you to buy me a house."

"Ok. I won't."

That was how we left that. It was 5:44 when I finally got home that day. I was exhausted and it was because I sat in the sun and drank champagne like a fish in water. I took a hot bath to relax. I slipped into the tub and the water was nice and warm. I had candles lit around the bathroom and soft jazz was playing from the Sonos speaker in my bedroom. The only thing missing was Jackson.

"SARA! STOP thinking about him!"

I talked to myself...all the time. I had to snap out of the hypnosis that my brain was trying to put me under. I laid there for a moment, just soaking my skin. Jackson was on my mind. I was looking in his eyes again. I closed my eyes and I felt his kiss on my lips. I heard him say my name and I got excited.

My heart fluttered... I wanted this man so badly!

...the next day...

Ring Ring Ring
Ring Ring Ring
Ring Ring Ri…

"HELLO!!!"
"Sara? It's Jackson. You alright?"
"Ah yes. Hi Jackson! I was running from the other room!"
"Ok. I'll add marathon runner to your description. I would like to pick you up today. What's your address?"
"Uh, 3200 Meadow Lane, Greenwich."
"I am familiar with the area. Is it off Lake?"
"Yes, it's a left off Lake onto Harley, then a left off Harley onto Meadow. My house is the very last one on the block. It is the back of the cul-de-sac."
"Awesome. I'm headed that way. I live on the other side, off Stanwich. Do you need more time?"
"I'm fine. I'll be ready when you get here."
Let the freak out begin! I couldn't believe he was coming to my house! I couldn't believe he was going to pick me up!! I waited outside. While I was standing on my large front porch, I paced and picked at the pedals that fell from my cherry blossom tree. I looked down and needed a broom. Jackson was going to pull up and I was going to be out here in an apron; sweeping! However, those were thoughts. I stopped and turned around; in a nick of time! I saw a car coming up the road and I knew it was him. "What's he driving?" Was that…? Yup! He pulled up in a white, 1968 Shelby GT. "Seriously!?!?"
I bellowed to him as he pulled into the driveway and got out of the car. He looked fantastic! He was wearing white linen pants; very much like the pair he wore to my office. This pair had cargo pockets though. He was wearing a fitted white tee shirt and today he was wearing Louis Vuitton flops! I love it! Oh, and he has pretty feet!
"What?! Wiow!! He must have liked my outfit as well. He licked his lips slightly. I saw it! I was wearing a loose fitted one-piece jumpsuit; Michael Kors. It was pink. And I was wearing gold MK flops. I guess we were feeling "floppy" today.
"Come with me." I extended my hand to chauffeur him around my property. I walked Jackson down my long driveway and around the corner to a garage door. The setup looked as if I had a driveway that pulled up

to a 4-car garage. When the garage doors opened, they revealed a motor car showroom. Along the far-right side of the garage sat all the daily cars. Along the back wall were 4 platform lifts; they each held a classic car. Along the left side were the remaining classic cars. When I opened the door, and flipped the light switch, Jackson's eyes lit up like a kid in a candy store. I pointed to the middle platform lift where my 1968 Shelby GT sat. Mine was grey. He walked in and his eyes followed my finger. He quickly spun around, grabbed and kissed me. This kiss was a bit rougher than the one prior. It was intense and passionate. I felt so much emotion in a millisecond of a moment.

"You are my match made in heaven. You have no idea what seeing that car sitting there has done to me. It's my favorite car ever! My dad had one when he was a kid. Then he bought another. He gave me one for my 16th birthday. I left it home when I went away to college and my brother decided he was going for a joyride. He came home, and my car did not. I beat him bloody. Then, dad sent me this one right before the movie came out."

"Gone in 60 seconds."

I whispered it to him while he stood towering me and telling me his story. Those eyes were looking at my soul. I had to break the mood.

"Come on! I need coffee. Shall we go?" He walked out ahead of me but stood still on the opposite side of the garage door. I turned off the lights and pushed the button.

"Your home is beautiful, and that collection is killer!"

"Thank you very much. I've only been in this house for a year. I lived in a townhouse prior. I now rent the townhouse out. In fact, one of my good friends from grad school lives there now, Javier. Last year he got a job offer from UBS, so he packed his things and needed a place to live. No questions asked he was renting my place."

"You're good to your friends and family. I like that. You have a big heart."

"I do have a big heart. I am humbled by my wealth. I know that it is a blessing so when someone is in need, I share my blessings. I could only hope it helps make them better."

The midmorning rush met us at Starbucks. I didn't mind. I was long overdue for a cup and I really should've changed my panties after the garage kiss. I was still kissing him in my mind while we were standing in line. He was speaking to me and I was not very coherent.

"Sara...babe...helloooo"

He lightly tapped my arm.

"Hey, sorry. I'll have a Grande, soy, caramel macchiato."

"Where did you go that quickly?"

He giggled; man, even his giggle was sexy! I smiled before I answered.

"Back to my garage." We walked from Starbucks to the auto show. It was in the park about a mile or so away. It was a nice day for a walk and we took the route that allowed us to pass some shops. My eyes widened as we approached a small consignment shop. I had to go inside.

"Oh, I have a shopper girl, huh?"

"I do love to shop!"

We walked around the shop very quietly. Not many words were spoken, as if he wanted me to concentrate. I was concentrating on a set of pink Queen Anne chairs. They had Rose Gold arms, legs and base, but the silk was a beautiful pale pink that was perfect for my master bedroom suite. I was still designing some rooms in my home. I wasn't rushing to complete the task, simply doing so as I found the pieces. I walked over and sat in one. It was the most comfortable chair ever! I had to have them!

"Well, you look stunning sitting in that chair."

Jackson came around a corner and he was carrying a set of Rose Gold and pink furniture handles.

"Do you have any furniture that needs handles? I noticed you like pink."

"Hmmm, well, there's a chest of drawers in my bedroom and I'm not too fond of the handles. The piece matches these chairs and those handles match everything!" He found a young man to assist me with my purchase. He purchased the handles even though I insisted he not. He insisted he did. He won. The gentleman in the store said they would deliver my chairs on Monday morning. Awesome! My lateness would've been forgiven; I was sure of that. The auto show wasn't all that great this year. Not as many cars as years prior and the ones that were there weren't very impressive. We did more people watching than car watching. We conversed and he asked questions. I did more talking than he did.

"How are you feeling? Shall we have lunch?"

I remember Jackson said he liked to eat. In fact, I think his exact words were "I'm always hungry!" But, before I could answer the question, his phone rang.

Ring Ring Ring Ring Ring Ringgggggg!!

The ringtone on Dr. Sir Yum lips' phone was loud and long.

"Guten Tag."

"What's wrong?!"

"Where are you?" His German sounded like poetry, and that wasn't easy to do. German always sounded like a harsh language. His lips moved so swiftly while he spoke. He stared off while he was listening, then he paced. I couldn't imagine who he had been speaking to. He looked...confused, maybe. Anyway, I had this feeling that our date was ending.

"I'm sorry beautiful. My mother needs me. I must cut our date short. I promise I will make it up to you."

"It's quite alright. If your mother called and you didn't run to be by her side, I would question your integrity as a human." I giggled, but I really meant it. I didn't play around when it came to the treatment of mothers. My mother had a tendency to get on my nerves, but she never wanted or needed anything, ever!

"Mothers are touchy subjects to me too. Come on. Let me take you home."

When we arrived to my street, it was to my surprise that a handful of my best friends were sitting on my porch.

"OH NO!! What are they all doing here?!"

I freaked out. I didn't want them to meet him or him meet them.

"Those are your friends, I assume."

"Yea, they are. It's ok. You can stop here and let me out. It's like a 5-minute walk up to my door."

"You don't want me to meet your friends, huh?"

"Not that I don't want you too, but they are nosey and you are new to me. It's just better this way for now. Is that ok?"

"Absolutely! I'll call you later." He kissed me on my cheek. As I was walking up the block, I heard a commotion on my porch and it made me upset. What the heck was going on?! As I got closer, I saw Arianna, Daniela, Patrick and Rena. Patrick and Rena were our married friends. They were originally friends of Hosni's. I couldn't recall who we met first or how, but they had been around for years. They lived nearby. Patrick was short; extremely short, and insanely muscular. He was Nigerian. His skin was very smooth and very dark in complexion. He looked like tar. Rena was taller than Patrick, but she was not very tall. Her nationality was unknown. She was adopted at birth and never cared to search for her biological parents; her adopted parents treated her like a princess. She had a caramel complexion. Her skin was smooth also. She had freckles, green eyes, and wild red hair. They were beautiful people; inside and out.

"What's going on?!"

"Well, Patrick is upset because your date didn't drop you off at the door. I told him that this is literally date #2; unless you are keeping secrets, and you probably are not sure if he is going to stick around, so there was no need to do the introduction shit. Am I right?"

Daniela scored again!

"She's right. Listen, he is new and I am not sure what we will be; if anything at all, but I think it's too soon for him to meet family and friends. You will be ok. So, what brings you all to me?"

"Ari and I were in the Stamford Mall and we ran into the love birds. They asked where you were and we didn't know because we haven't heard from you so we all decided to ride over and see you. SUPRISE!!!"

"I am quite surprised! Thank you all for coming. Come inside. Let's eat and drink."

I lead the way into the house and to the kitchen. I had bar stools on the opposite side of the island. That's where everyone sat. I walked over to the bar on the other side of the wall and I poured Kettle One on the rocks with a splash of cranberry; that was for Rena. I walked over to the fridge and grabbed a corona for Patrick. I had a chilled, walk in wine cellar. I went in there and pulled a bottle of Riesling off the shelf for Ari, Dani and me. I reached into the fridge a second time and pulled a meat and cheese platter. I sat down with my friends and the good times rolled. But Jackson was on my mind.

"So, Rena, I heard briefly that you are going to be doing an exhibit at MOMA. Are you excited? When is it? I would love to be there." Rena was a phenomenal artist. She drew the NYC skyline looking at Cairo's skyline for my home office. She said it was a constant reminder of what I am made of. It was my favorite piece of art work and I own pieces by Monet and Van Gough. I was very proud that her work is going in the best art museum in the country.

"My show will not open until January. It is my first time working with sculptures, so I am taking my time. I want to make sure all of them are beyond perfect, and I have a 2-year-old!" She laughed. We all laughed.

"I love my baby, but it's not easy balancing her and sculpting art during the day. I work while she naps and sleeps."

"I'm sure it is going to be amazing and it is going to add to your success. I am proud! Will I allowed to buy a sculpture and are any of them pink?!"

"That's not the only color in existence, contrary to what you believe. But it is all recycled metal. Maybe not anything for your home, but you may find something you like for the new salon!!"

"YESSSSSSSS!!!!!!!!!" My friends were very important to me and I was glad I had them, but it was time to send them home. I wanted to strip and walk around nude while drinking yet another glass of wine. They all gathered themselves and their belongings and exited the kitchen.

"Would you like some help cleaning?" Rena was like that. She always wanted to clean after our visits.

"You all are guests and guests don't clean. Get out! It's not a problem. Trust me." We all laughed. It was a pleasure having them visit.

"I love you all. Thank you for coming. I was pleasantly surprised. I'll do a dinner party once I complete the entertainment section of the house. It will be done within the next 2 months. Just in time for summer."

"Uh-huh and you and Dr. Secret should be well established by then. Make sure he's on the guest list!"

Rena was pushing for this harder than Arianna was. "I'll see you later." I walked back inside and immediately took my jumpsuit off. "Whew!" I felt so much better. It was getting later in the day and the sun was setting. I walked around and closed shades and curtains on all my windows. I had floor to ceiling windows, so they were covered by shades that opened and closed with the push of a button. "I should've gotten a remote for these things."

Ring Ring Ring Ring

"Hello."

"Sara! It's Sunday! Where are you?!?" OH! I forgot dinner at moms...

"Hey Ma. Well you called my house phone. I'm sorry. I lost track of time. When I came home, my friends were here and they literally just left."

"It's ok if you are ok. I heard nothing, so I was just making sure you were not dead. It's fine that you didn't come. Your Aunt and Uncle hate your father and me again. Something about not coming to an event or something. I don't know. Well anyway, they are finally settling down but it was tense in here before."

"Well we go through this all the time! Thank goodness, I missed it this time."

"Have you eaten?"

"Of course, I have. I've also had an entire bottle of wine!"

"Hahaha!! You are such a wonderful person. I love that you tell me everything. Your brother doesn't tell me anything! I must talk to his wife; I hate his wife."

"Didn't you teach me NOT to hate?"

"Shut up girl! Ok, I dislike the wife. A lot! Speaking of which, when are you getting married? Are you dating?"

"Hahaha! Married! I'm not getting married until I find a guy and I haven't found one yet."

"Ok. Ok. Ok. I will not stress it. If it is meant to be, it will be. I must go now. Apparently, I am being rude to guests that don't want to be in my home; she's such a wench. I will let you know when Hosni and wife come. You better not miss that visit!"

"Yes ma'am! I love you."

"Love you too!" Before I could hang up the phone, my doorbell rang.

"What the hell tonight with the interruptions?! Now I have to find a robe!" While I was talking to my mom, I wandered upstairs and took the handles off my chest of drawers; preparing to install the new ones. I put on a long, sheer, black robe and a pair of pink ballet slippers and pushed the view button on my security camera. OMG IT WAS JACKSON!

"What is he doing here?!" Quickly, I gathered myself and sashayed down the steps nonchalantly to the front door. I peeked through the peep hole.

"Are you selling Girl Scout cookies?!"

"I've got Bison burger sliders, fries, caprese salad and a bottle of Jameson."

"Hahaha! That beats a dozen Girl Scout cookies any day!" I opened the door. He followed me into the kitchen and sat his bags down on the counter. He stood back and looked around.

"This is beautiful!"

"Thanks. Would you like a tour?"

"Yes. Please."

We walked around from room to room. I told him stories about the furniture, pictures and artwork; where it originated, how I found it, why I put it where it was. He loved every minute of it. He said his favorite part was the front porch that wrapped around the entire house. The kitchen, living room and dining room had French doors that opened onto the porch. There was a fireplace in my living room and on the opposite side was an outdoor fireplace.

"Does that work?" He asked as he pointed.

"Yup! I sit out here on chilly nights. I turn it on and read, or drink a glass of wine, or smoke a blunt."

"I like you. Do you know that? I like everything about you. I'm addicted to you. I'm here because I couldn't deal with the idea of an incomplete date. I had to finish it."

"I knew that you would make it up to me. You said so, but you didn't have to come back tonight."

"Yes, I did. I couldn't get you out of my head."

"What about your family? Where do they think, you are?"

"It's ok. Trust me. When I am with you, I am with you."

"Yea but who is that fair to? You're the only one that benefits."

"How so, Sara?"

"You get to spend time with me, leave and go home and spend time with your beautiful family. I am home alone at night."

"I'm alone at night. You have no idea."

Those blue craters fell again. As if his own statement stabbed him in the heart. What the hell?! He was clearly keeping some type of secret and not just me, from his wife too. There was something else going on with this man and I was dying to know what; but I knew that if I pushed it, he could possibly walk away, and I didn't want that either. I never wanted to make him or see him mad. It was better to just change the subject. I was getting good at that!

"Come. I should probably eat that burger. I drank an entire bottle of Riesling. Well, Ari and Dani helped me, but I poured into a bigger glass for myself!"

We laughed; that infectious laughter like always. I liked his consistecy. He followed me to the kitchen; the kitchen was my meeting place. I loved my kitchen. The kitchen, the porch and the garage were why I bought this house. He seemed to like the outdoor seating area around the fireplace. When I joined him outside, I flipped a switch and the fireplace ignited. I liked flipping switches.

"So, these are electric fireplaces? Nice! You cannot tell."

"Well only the outside one is electric. They are running on separate channels."

"Did you build this?"

"Not technically. It was newly built when I first found it. I walked around and was like 'a lot of this is wrong, but enough of it is right', so I bought it, I tweaked it and I moved in and that is why some of the rooms are still incomplete."

"What made you fall in love with it?"

"My parent's home is a Victorian, so naturally, I was like 'this is a modern version of mom and dad's house'. When I walked the wrap around porch I saw all the parties and entertaining that I can do here. I love to host, but the master bedroom suite is what did it for me; to answer your question."

"Aw man, the things I could do to you in a bedroom..."

Wow! It pleased me to find out he had the same sensual thoughts about us as I did. Although part of me felt as if he said the quiet part loud and the loud part quiet.

"I'm sorry. I guess I'm getting comfortable with you."

"No need to apologize. We would be upstairs if you weren't..."

Before I could complete the sentence, he cuffed my face and softly kissed my lips. I melted into his arms...

Chapter 3

I woke up on another rainy Monday, to the sound of a truck backing up into my driveway. "OH NO!! The chairs" Also, I decided that I was going to dedicate my week to Arianna's salon, so I called Brian at my office and took some time off.

"I think that's a great idea! You have been putting in a ton of hours here. I am more than happy to grant you some personal time. Let me know when you are ready to come back."

It paid to be a dedicated employee. I put on an Adidas track suit and matching pair of sneakers. I went outside to meet the movers.

"Oh. I only purchased chairs Hun. What's the rest of this stuff?"

"These items were added to your order this morning. They were paid by, uh...here." He handed me a receipt.

"Ellis and Associates" I rolled my eyes and smiled.

"Ok. Thank you. Let me show you where it all belongs." As the movers were unloading the truck, I saw my beautiful chairs and everything else was bundled well. I directed them to the master bedroom and they did their thing. Meanwhile, I went on a hunt for a telephone. I needed to call Dr. Action Jackson.

"Hi. It's me; Sara. I, just received some additional items with my chairs. Thank you very much. However, I am not sure why you purchased more items for me. You really didn't have to. Anyway, I decided to take some personal time from work, so I am home today, and tomorrow. I'm going to start this project for Ari. I'm sure that you are busy, but call me when you have a moment. Have a great day!"

I hated leaving messages because I didn't like how my voice sounded recorded. But when I had something to say, I said it. The movers were done unloading the truck. I headed upstairs to see what had been done. They put the chairs in opposite corners of the room, just as I asked. At the foot of my bed, they placed an elongated ottoman that was covered in the same pale pink silk as the chairs. It also had Rose Gold feet and base. There was also a floor to ceiling mirror whose frame was very thin Rose Gold. "Wow, this man!" I stood there amazed at how those 2 additional items completed my master bedroom suite. Along with the Rose Gold and pink handles affixed to the chest of drawers, I had a pink and rose gold fort inside of my single woman mansion. It was surreal. I rolled a celebratory blunt.

Ring Ring Ring

"Bonjour Dr. Sexy face!"

"Well good morning beautiful. How did you sleep?"

"I slept well, thanks. How about you?"

"Would've been better if you fell asleep and woke up in my arms. Nonetheless, it was sleep!"

"About as normal as can be expected, huh?"

"Yup! So, what's that master suite look like now?"

"Oh, babe, it's amazing, really! Thank you so much! So, you went back this morning?"

"I did. The consignment shop is near the Starbucks and that's where I get my morning coffee. The shop was opening when I left, so I took another look around. The same gentleman that assisted you was there and he remembered me. Said he had a few pieces that 'my girlfriend' may be interested in, so, he showed me."

"Uh huh. Did you correct the girlfriend reference?"

"No. Because you are my girl."

"Oh, am I?"

"Well, I would like you to be. When you're ready, so I am just getting prepared."

"Uh huh..." I was really at a loss for words at this point. This time, he picked up on the need to change the subject and he did just that.

"So, you took some personal time? Is everything ok?"

"Oh yea, all is well. I think this may be the beginning to me venturing into my own financial firm. I haven't decided yet, but I do need to focus on the salon for Ari. I am going to have her up and running by the beginning of next month. I have 27 days." I giggled.

"I know you can do it. I love what you are doing for Arianna. She deserves it, I'm sure."

"Oh, you have no idea."

"I want to see you again. Am I smothering?"

"You are not smothering. You are ignoring."

"I beg your pardon."

"I've seen you every day since Friday. Doesn't your family need your attention?"

"Not yet. As long as they are not in need, I will be with you. If you have any regrets or hesitations, speak now."

"You're a grown man. Who am I to question how you spend your time, right?"

"I would like to go back to Baang tonight. Let's say 8? What do you think?"

"I'll meet you there at 8; I have a lot to do today. I've got to go; have a good day ok?"

"You too. I'll see you later."

I spent the duration of the day on the phone with the realtor that was offering the space for the salon. She was acting very snide and for the life of me I couldn't figure out why. While she was speaking, I was thinking she needed to check her attitude. I was praying for her, that the attitude was gone by the time I arrived. We agreed to a selling price and I told her I would be there within the hour. I jumped up, grabbed my Celine bag and ran out to the garage. I grabbed a set of keys off the key wall, pushed the button, jumped in my 2014 TDI Touareg and drove like a bat out of hell down to the bank to acquire a certified bank check for the realtor. I made it to her office in under an hour. She looked happier than she sounded when we were on the phone. She greeted me with a smile and a cup of coffee.

"What are you converting this space to?"

"A beauty salon. Hair, nails, waxing, makeup and in due time, Botox."

"That sounds fantastic, and we could use a full service, high class salon over here."

"That's exactly why it's going here. I did my research."

"But I thought you were a financial advisor."

"I am. This is an investment. Arianna is the stylist and my best friend and in due time, we will hire."

"Fantastic. Just so you know, technically this is 2 units, so ideally, you can split this into 2 different salons as opposed to one big one. It's up to you. Both spaces will be yours. Come let me show you what I mean."

She walked me around the facility and my imagination was spiraling out of control with ideas. I envisioned the placement of everything, down to the coffee station. I had to remember, this technically wasn't my project. I was simply funding it. I hated thinking of it like that but in layman's terms, that was what I was. I couldn't wait to tell Arianna and Daniela about the space. I opened that same txt message thread.

Me: Guess what I just bought?!

Dani: Birth control!

Me: Huh? NO! The space for the salon!!

Dani: Wow, that was fast! We only had the conversation on Saturday.

Me: I know but I couldn't wait any longer. You know what happens when I get fixated on an idea.

Ari: YAY!!!!! THANK YOU SO MUCH!!!!!! When can we begin setting up? Did you buy it just now? Aren't you working?

Me: You're welcome. I've got the contractor, electrician, and plumber over there now making sure everything works. As soon as we get the green light from them, we can set up. I took some time off from work. I want to focus on this project. The new month begins in 27 days, which means we have 36 days to get you out of that expensive, crappy salon that you are currently in. I do not want you to give them another red cent for rent!

Dani: You never lie! Girl, I hate this salon she's in. I want her to run them totally out of business.

Me: And she will! I gotta go. I'll talk to y'all later.

I was busy with my day. Who knew what I was doing exactly, but I was late to Baang. When I arrived, Dr. Mr. Bought my furniture was already seated and waiting for me.

"I am so sorry! I was busier today than I thought I was going to be."

"No need to apologize, but I do want to spank you!" OHHH!!! The kinkiness of that statement made my nipples hard; which sucked because I wasn't wearing a bra. Tonight's dress was a halter and a bra wouldn't go with it properly, and when the rain stopped, it became humid so extra clothing was not an option.

"As long as that spanking is accompanied by you from behind..." He had no idea how freaky I could be.

"Hi guys! Welcome back! Jameson?" Nick was our waiter again. I wasn't sure if he came at a good time or a bad time.

"Hi Nick. Tonight, I would like a glass of wine. Shiraz please?"

"That sounds good. We'll take a bottle."

Of course, he ordered a bottle.

"Great. I'll be back."

Nick was gone. Jackson went back to our conversation.

"So, I'll assume 'from behind' is your favorite position. What else pleases you sexually?"

"Ha! I don't 'kiss and tell'. When the time is right, you will know." I winked at him and he blushed.

"Well then, I will tell you this, I enjoy the female body; a beautiful female body. I am a firm believer in tasting the woman, especially if she means the world to you. I believe in making love when in love. There is no need for me to pound you hard; unless you like it that way."

"Make love to me until I tell you to pound me and then pound me until I cum." I did NOT mean to say that.

"Oh babe, I could make love to you all night!"

"I'm sure I would wear you out." He laughed. That same contagious laugh.

"Here you go!"

Nick was back. This time with the wine and 2 glasses. He popped the bottle and poured. Immediately, I picked my glass up and guzzled. I was beyond hot!

"Thanks Nick. I think my lady needs a moment before we order, but if you could bring us a calamari appetizer, that would be great."

"Absolutely!" He smiled and walked away.

"You think you could wear me out huh? Do I really seem to be that old?"

We laughed, but the thought instantly popped into my mind. How old was he?

"Wait, huh? How old are you?" He laughed again. I giggled lightly this time, but the laugh was still an infectious one.

"I will be 50 in January. That reminds me, when is your birthday?"

"August 18th. I'll be 34."

"Am I too old for you?"

"Absolutely! Am I too young for you?"

"Yup!"

The infectious laughter broke out and we disturbed a couple of tables around us.

"In all honesty, I like older men. Seriously though, I assumed you were closer to my age. You look amazing for 50!"

"Sara Bashir, Thank you. I appreciate your verbal compliment and the compliment of you on my arm."

"You're welcome Dr. Amazing!"

We were out until midnight. This time his phone didn't ring at all. Strange, but I refused to give it a second thought. He walked me to my car, like a gentleman. When we got to my driver side, he stood in front of me and gave me the tightest, strongest hug I'd ever received. I melted again. The power he had over me was insane. He drove me insane! (In a great way!) He pulled me away, cuffed my face and kissed. This must've been his style. I loved it! Cuff my face, kiss my lips, turn me around and smack my bootie! Instead, I got in my car and while he watched, I drove away. Our conversations were becoming more intense and our dates were becoming more frequent. It made me wonder, did he even have a wife, but who would lie about being married if they weren't married? Javier was sitting in a hammock chair on my front porch when I pulled into the driveway. 'Wait, I don't own a hammock chair.' I said to myself while I parked my car.

"Happy housewarming!"

"JAVYYYY HIIIIII!!!!! You're sitting in a hammock chair!"

"SARAAAAA, yes, I am!" We both laughed. I sat down next to him.

"Most people explain at this point."

"Oh yea! I had a boyfriend for about 4 months. I was just enjoying the fact that he cooked, cleaned and gave great head!"

"OMG! TMI!" I had no problem with Javier being gay, but the gay sex references made me squirm.

"Ok. Sorry, so, we broke up because I really do not want to be in a relationship right now. While we were together, he insisted on having this monstrosity and squeezed it onto the back deck. Now he's gone and he said he doesn't want the chair because it reminds him of me. I don't know why, I didn't even like the thing! Never sat in it! He left it and you are the only person I know with a porch large enough for this thing, so, here ya go!" This story made me burst out in laughter. He laughed also. He knew it sounded silly.

"Ok. I guess I have a hammock chair now. Rollup! I gotta tell you a story." That's exactly what happened. Javier rolled the biggest blunt and we sat there on the hammock chair and I proceed to tell him every single detail of my brewing relationship with Dr. I want to lick you.

"You should google him. I'm sure if he murdered his wife or if she went missing or anything along those lines, those stories will popup. What do you say?"

"No. I am perfectly fine with thinking he's got a wife at home that he is legitimately not happy with and he is out doing his thing, waiting for her to get tired of his indiscretion." I rolled my eyes and hung my head.

"Seriously!? I mean, if that's what you want. May I see your bedroom?"

That was Javier's way of noticing I wanted to change the subject. Javier and I went in the house. I dug my phone out of my bag. I had 5 text messages from Jackson.

Jax: Hey babe. Did you make it home safely?
Jax: Listen, it was a pleasure seeing you this evening. I'm thinking of our table talk and...
Jax: Are you asleep? Or perhaps you are in a different room than your phone?
Jax: Wow! 20 mins and no answer. Should I worry? Na...no worries. I'm sure you are asleep.
Jax: Ok. I'm coming over....
Me: Hey, I'm sorry. I'm ok. My phone was in my bag and I was talking. Javier is here
Jax: Oh, thank goodness!
Jax: I still want to come over though. May I?
Me: May I rain check? I haven't seen Javier in a while, even though he lives in my townhouse.
Jax: Completely understood. Absence makes the heart grow fonder.
Jax: Have a good night and sweet dreams.
Me: Good night Dr. Sweetness

I grabbed a Corona out of the fridge; Javier wasn't a liquor drinker.

"You want water or something?"
"Oh! I drank Pinot Noir for the first time. Not bad!"
"I've got an amazing bottle of Pinot Noir. Would you like to drink some with me?"
"Sure. Why not?!" HMMM, would you look at that?! Javier became a wine drinker. We went upstairs to my master bedroom suite. We got to the top of the stairs, made a right, walked down the hall and got to the French doors. They still had no curtains.
"What the hell? Why don't these doors have curtains?!?"
"I don't know. I haven't purchased any yet."
"Dr. Hot pants can buy you furniture handles but no curtains?"
"He's never been in this room. In fact, he's only walked around the bottom of the house, and the garage."
"Oh well, that's good. That means you haven't spread your legs."
"Duh. He's married!"

"Oh baby, that don't mean a thing; let me tell you! When he wants you bad enough, and y'all are getting hot and heavy, you will let him. I can tell by the way you talk about him. I'm not saying it's right, but you cannot help who you fall in love with."

"Love?! No, we're not in love."

"It sounds like love to me. You guys didn't confront it yet. It's ok. It happens."

When did Javier become a love guru?! Love? Was I in love with him? Did he love me? I didn't think so. Javier was a great friend. I missed him so much. It was good to have that time to catch up. He was the busiest person I knew. I woke up around 3am and Javier was gone. He left a note on my nightstand saying that he loved me, it was great seeing me and he was going home to go to bed. He had a spare key to my house, so he locked up. I laid in my bed, staring at the ceiling. The only thing I could think about was Jackson. I wasn't wondering if he was thinking about me. Instead I was thinking "what happened when he came home from our late dates? Did his wife get mad? Did it start a fight?" I never called or texted him first. Was it because he didn't give me a chance to or was I subconsciously not texting him? Was all of this moving too fast? Was I thinking too much into it? I guess so because I dozed off shortly after. I had no problem falling asleep when I was comfortable; and comfortable was an understatement for how I was feeling. I was high and slightly inebriated. The next morning came with a bright glimmer of sun. I smiled, then I frowned. My thoughts picked up where they left off the night prior. Whether my mind was sober, an unfinished thought always attempted to be finished.

"Sara, get it together! You took all this time off work; do something productive and make some money!" I had to give myself a pep talk with my morning cup of Joe. I decided to go for a run. I needed to do some cardio and what better cardio than running? I dressed in a pair of black Nike running tights, a sports bra and a fitted Nike track jacket. I laced up a pair of black and pink Air Maxes, put my iPod on shuffle, put my Fitbit watch on and went for a run. No cell phone. Just my music and a great pair of running shoes! I ran 10 miles. After my shower, I walked around my closet trying to decide where I was going and what I was going to wear.

"I need to go check on the salon."

I put on a pair of jeans, a white wife beater and a pair of pink platform pumps. I grabbed a pink blazer, just in case. I switched to a pink, MK hobo bag and walked out to the garage.

"What am I going to drive today? Maybe the Shelby." I never drove the Shelby, but seeing Jax in his made me reconsider. As my eyes scanned the garage, my cell phone rang.

"Hello."

"Hi. It's me. How are you?"

"Dr. Me. I am well, thanks. How are you?"

"Busy at work as always. Missing you like crazy. I'm sorry I haven't reach out since our last date. I started moving into the new office and nothing is working properly in the new location. Anyway, I didn't call to be a bore. Do you think you can get away for a late lunch today?"

"A late lunch, hmm..."

I wasn't sure how I felt about him not reaching out to me and then mentioning it. Did I believe the reason? Under normal circumstances, I would have, but for the life of me I couldn't help but think that his wife was bitching that he wasn't spending enough time with her.

"Sara, I promise, I'm telling you the truth about my office. Please. Meet me for lunch."

How the hell did he know what I was thinking?!? I guess because I was so silent. I wasn't ready to speak yet. He knew it, so, he held the phone.

"I'm headed to the salon today. I'm not sure how long I will be, but it is the only thing on my agenda. I'll call you back once I have an idea of what my day will look like. Which car should I drive today?"

Random, but I wanted to know what he would say.

"Drive the Shelby."

Seriously?! I couldn't take him in my head anymore. Can he see me?

"Had the same thought. Thanks. I'll call you later."

Immediately, I hung up the phone. I felt the tears build up in my eyes. But why? "Snap out of this, Sara and go make some money!" I wiped my eyes and grabbed the keys. Damn right I drove the Shelby! I felt the need to shift gears and speed. It completed the pep talk. When I arrived to the 'soon to be salon', the contractor, electrician and plumber were already there and working.

"How's it going guys?!!?"

"Hey Sara!" They answered in unison. John, the contractor came over to speak to me first.

"The structure is good. All the walls are sturdy. No asbestos, no lead, no mold, mildew, nothing. This place was well maintained."

"Good. That's what I like to hear. And the flooring?"

"Floors are good too!"

"All the pipe lines are clear and safe and you have clean, running water. Once you know what the setup will be, I can get and install the sinks within a couple of hours."

"Ok. Cool. Thanks Mike."

"Ben. How's my electrical system?"

"It's fine now. I had to split the lines apart, otherwise you would be in here blowing fuses all day. You said a salon, right? Yea...you need strong electricity for the hair dryers and such. But you're all set. The way we see it, you can start setting up!"

"Awesome. Thank you, gentleman. I guess I should pay you now, huh?" I wrote some pretty fat daddy checks, but every dime was worth it. Once they were all gone, I walked around. The bathrooms were well put together and the space was well lit. I am pleased with the work that they did for me. I needed Arianna to be pleased. "Let me call her."

Ring Rin...

"Thank goodness you called. I am about to slap this insipid, horrible woman!" She answered on the first ring.

"What woman? What happened?"

"Jen. My boss. I have a client scheduled for 12:30. A walk-in came in at 12:20. I told Jen I cannot take her; I have a client coming at 12:30. Ok. No problem. My client was late. Granted, she sent me a text, but I didn't broadcast it because I didn't feel I needed to. Jen looked up and realized the woman hadn't been seated, so she sat her in my chair. Just then my client walked in, so I nicely asked the woman to get up because my appointment was here. Jen says 'oh no! Your appointment was late, she lost her turn. This is my salon, my rules!' So, my client says to me 'no problem, come to my house tonight and I'll pay you double.' She turned to Jen and told her she lacks professionalism. I am so over this place!!!"

"Good. Walk out! Pack your station; grab your chair and leave. I am standing in your new salon and it is ready for you to come setup, open and make a ton of money! Are you ready!?!?"

"OH MY GOD!!! SERIOUSLY!? I LOVE YOU SOOOOO MUCH!!!!! Legit? I can leave?"

"Please do. I'm here now waiting for you."

"Ok. I'll be there in 20 minutes!" She was so excited. While I waited, I opened my iPad and set up things like cable, lights, internet; all in my name because we hadn't named the salon yet. I suggested we do that when she arrived. I looked up and realized I had no TVs for the cable I turned on. I called Best Buy to see what they had in stock that they could deliver and install. They sounded excited to get this sale.

"Helloooo!!!! OH, MY GAWWWWDDD!!!!! I really have a salon?!?!"

Ari was so excited; she didn't even realize we were dressed alike. The only difference was she was wearing yellow Louboutin pumps and carrying a yellow Celine bag.

"It's really yours! Get the gawk out now. We have a lot of work to do!"

"Sir, yes, sir!"

She saluted me and laughed. I was happy that she was happy. She opened her MacBook and began researching salon setups; sinks, counters, chairs, tables, everything. She started making phone calls and placing orders. I was impressed.

Me: Dani. You gotta see this!

I sent her a picture of the busy bee at work; setting up her salon. Dani: What's she doing?

Me: She's working on her salon, in her salon.

Dani: SWEET!!! You there now? I'm coming by.

Me: Sweet! We're here.

"Sara, did you order TVs?" Best Buy arrived.

"I sure did! I have no clue where we will put them, but I ordered phone, internet and cable. I need TVs here when they come install."

"Touché. I think they should hang back to back in the center. This way they can be seen at every station."

"Whatever you want darling. This is all yours. I'm going to get coffee. You want?"

"No thanks."

I stepped outside and the wind was blowing ever so lightly. I felt good. I felt good because my darling best friend was happy and it was because I was helping her make her dream come true. I made it to Starbucks and the line was out the door. The door shut behind me and I heard my name, really?!

"Sara, Bashir, right?!" I looked up and I saw a man that I didn't recognize.

"Uhm, yes."

"Hahaha! Do you remember me; Justin Taylor? You put me out of your office last year." He amused himself and laughed from his gut.

"Ah yes, you were not prepared for a meeting that you rescheduled twice. Have you gotten yourself and your schedule in order since we last spoke?"

"I see you really didn't forget. Well, yes, I am in a better position schedule wise. I would love to sit with you over dinner and discuss some business plans."

I rolled my eyes and thought to myself, 'Was he hitting on me? Eww!'

"I don't do business at dinner. I took some time off. I'll let you know when I'm back in my office and we can schedule a meeting."

"Na, that's not gonna work for me! I want to go out with you. Meet me for dinner tonight!"

"UHHHH, NO! I'm not interested and your approach is offensive and rude. Now please, get out of my way."

He rolled his eyes, sucked his teeth and stepped aside. That annoyed me. I couldn't believe he had the audacity to address me in such manner. This was what I meant about the dating scene and why it was so terrible. Was he serious? Was that how men were asking women out? Really?!? He was uncouth. I hoped he wasn't expecting to find the love of his life with that opening statement. Maybe he's looking to just gain another notch on his belt. I remember that was a thing when I was in college; 'how many girls can you have sex with?' Guys were horrible back then also. I hope he was single, however, I wouldn't have been surprised if he wasn't single. He lacked professionalism in the business world, that too, was a major turn off. How good of a date could he be if he wasn't a good business man? It was finally my turn at the Starbucks counter. I ordered my usual, Grande Sara drink. When I got my cup my name was misspelled. Too bad, I wasn't surprised. It could blame the way I pronounced it, but I vaguely remember reading a news article stating it's done on purpose for the social media likes and discussios. Therefore, I never took pictures of the intentionally misspelled version of my name. I headed back to the salon and checked on Ari.

"Hey girl!"

Daniela arrived. She hugged and kissed me on my cheek. She was wearing a long, free flowing, floral maxi dress. Her hair was neatly combed in a bun on the top of her head. She looked amazing! She was glowing! Before I had a chance to acknowledge her glow, I heard what sounded like my Shelby and I got nervous. I turned around and to my surprise...

"Is that?"

Daniela knew it was him. By this time, I was standing there looking stupid and he was practically standing on my toes.

"Hello ladies. My name is Jackson Ellis. You must be Daniela, yes?"

"Hello Jackson; I am, and that's Arianna."

"It's a pleasure to meet you both. Hello Sara."

"Dr. reads my mind. What brings you here?"

"You know why I'm here. I wanted to see you for lunch."

"Go ahead, girl. We will be fine here."

I rolled my eyes and reluctantly walked out. Well, not as reluctantly as I wanted to believe. I was feeling in control today, so we hopped in my Shelby.

"Wow! Yours is stick shift. Impressive!

"Thanks. I learned how to drive on a stick. I was 15 and Hosni; my older brother, had a stick shift Corolla. It was raggedy, but it ran. We ran it into the ground." I smiled as I walked toward the car. The doors unlocked with a key, so naturally, I let myself in first.

"Where are we headed?"

He looked so good as he climbed into the passenger seat of my classic car. He was dressed for the office; navy blue dress slacks, a crisp white button up shirt, and a red and blue stripped tie. Very presidential.

"I feel like eating shrimp. How much time do you have?"

"My afternoon is yours."

"Good."

I turned the Shelby on and she growled. I put her in gear and away we went. I had a friend that owned a restaurant on South Street Seaport. That's where I went for excellent, succulent shrimp. They were endless and were available in 100 different flavor combinations. I never called ahead, I just showed up. She was always there. When we arrived, I pulled into the valet section and told the valet that he wasn't allowed to park my car. Instead, I made him get in on the passenger side and he directed me to the absolute most desolate parking spot in the entire area. He looked at me as if I were uglier than Medusa. I loved every minute of it. When we walked into the restaurant, the hostess recognized me.

"Hi Sara! It's been so long. You look great! How's everything?" For the life of me, I couldn't remember her name, and of course she was not wearing a name tag.

"Thank you. I am well, thanks. Is my favorite table available, and is Rita around?"

"Yes, and yes. Please come this way."

We followed the hostess around the bottom of the restaurant to a spiral staircase. At the top was another room full of tables and a bar. Along the far, back wall was a collection of glass sliding doors that led out to a veranda style seating area. The furniture up here was wicker. She walked us over to a quiet table in the back. I liked this table because it was rather large for a 2-person table and it had a perfect view of the city. They added a water fountain since the last time I was here. It was a bit tacky, but nonetheless, it was there. I could hear Rita walking across the room. She was a petite woman with a big walk. She sounded like a herd of elephants wearing high heel ankle booties. She literally wore ankle booties every day of the year. She had them in various colors, prints, fabrics, heel size; you name it. I met Rita at my bed and breakfast in Newport. She was there as a guest and while she was out in town, her car was stolen. The police brought her back to my B&B and asked if I had any riffraff come through during the day. She was devastated and need-ed to get back to the city. The police told her they would let her know if they find her car. I asked her where she was headed and offered to give her a ride. She was so grateful and we have been friends ever since. She opened her restaurant during restaurant week back in 2008. People said she was crazy to open during one of the busiest times in the restaurant business and during a recession. She told everyone what they could kiss and where they could go and she opened the doors. She was successful from day one. I was on her side when she told me her plans. It was her dream, not mine. Who was I to say she couldn't do it. When she did do it, I threw her a party with the help of her staff. She told me 'honey, as long as you have air in your lungs and a hunger in your belly, you can eat at my restaurant; free of charge.' I always left a hefty tip on the table and I donated to a charity of her choice every year.

"SARA DARLING!!!! It's been too long! I can't believe you haven't been hungry in a year!" We both laughed. Jackson chuckled and it triggered her to check him out.

"Wow! Who...is...this...?" She gawked.

"Down girl! He's mine! Jackson Ellis, Rita Stanton, Rita, Jackson."

"Pleasure." Jackson stood and extended his hand.

"The pleasure is all mine. Please, take your seat. Do you mind if I stare for a moment? I've never seen Sara with a respectable gentleman. In fact, I've never seen Sara with a gentleman."

"Rita. The restaurant looks great, but what's up with this unnecessary fountain?"

"Whaaaat?!?! You don't like my fountain?!? Listen, I go to a psychic and she told me that water helps me keep my focus. She suggested that I put fountains and water streams in my daily environment and it will help me think clearer." I looked at Jackson and Jackson looked at me and we laughed our typical, infectious laugh. Rita looked at us like we were crazy.

"Aww and you're in love. Only people in love laugh together like that. Tell me, where did you meet? How long have you been together?"

"All of this is new, and we laughed because really? You're seeing a psychic? Do you need something to spend your money on? I can think of a million business ideas for you!"

"Oh, speaking of which, do you still love cars?"

"That's not something you out grow. Yes, I do. Why? Did you buy me a car?"

"No, but I know a guy that owns an auto group that he wants to sell. Do you think you be interested?"

"Hmm, I never thought of owning an auto group."

"I'll be right back. I have the info in my office. Did you order yet?"

"Not yet."

"I'll send you a waitress. It's not intentional, but my entire staff is female right now. All these little wenches get their periods together and they fight each other like sisters. It's annoying! If you know any diligent, hard, working men that are in the restaurant business; please send them my way."

Rita took off quickly and just as quickly, a waitress appeared.

"Hello. Welcome. May I start you with a beverage?"

"Jackson. Do you drink Sangria?"

"Yes, I do."

"We will have a pitcher of sangria. The peach one."

"Ok. I'll bring that right out. Do you need a moment with the menu?"

"Yes, but in the meantime, may we have a grilled shrimp shish kabob appetizer please?"

"Absolutely."

Jackson looked so good. I wanted to undress him and expose his penis. I imagined him sitting in the pink chair in my bedroom and me on my knees in front of him, ingesting every inch of him; and he was moaning ever so softly...

"Sara, what are you thinking about?"

"You, naked."

"Good. Because I was thinking the same."

I licked my lips. He licked his. Then our sangria arrived. Our waitress poured our glasses and sat the pitcher on the table. We spoke no words until she walked away.

"I dreamt of you last night. I was very excited. You have no idea what you do to me."

"Enlighten me doc."

"Didn't you say you don't kiss and tell? Well I don't.... dream and tell?" I laughed at the sound of the statement being a question.

"Touché."

"I like this place. This was a nice surprise. Thank you."

"You're welcome."

"Are you really going to consider owning an auto group?"

"I would have to look at the financials and speak to the owner. I need to know what he's selling and why. It would also depend on the manufacturers that make up the auto group. I do not want to own a Kia store."

"KIAs are good looking cars, right?"

"Dude, I have no idea! All I know is Toyota, Honda, everybody else; then luxury!" Rita returned with a folder. She handed it to me. The contents were the manufacturers, the location, and the presidents contact information. I adjusted my position in my chair and read aloud.

"BMW and Mini of Henderson Hill" Jackson looked at me over the top rim of his glasses. He sat up tall and smiled.

"Thanks Ri. I'll consider it."

Our afternoon was wonderful. We had lunch and then we went for a walk around the city. We talked and Jackson gave me his input about me owning the auto group. By the time, we got back to the car, rush hour traffic was well underway. Jackson offered to drive because I drank way more sangria than he did. Also, I was fatigued from walking in an intoxicated state. When we arrived back to the parking lot, I allowed the valet driver to bring the Shelby to us. I made him promise to be beyond careful and threatened his job if he wasn't careful. His cautiousness motioned me to tip him. Jackson opened the passenger side door. I climbed in. Jackson climbed in on the driver side and away we went. I was very relaxed and totally comfortable with him driving my car. I asked some questions.

"How old were you when you lost your virginity?"

"Hmm...I think I was 15. You?"

"19"

"Really?!?" He sounded surprised. The people that knew that about me, were still surprised.

"Are you surprised?"

"No. Well, maybe a little. I didn't think you were fast, I just wasn't thinking after high school."

"I was determined to graduate high school a virgin because none of the other girls were, but then I got caught up in college life and I basically forgot; if that makes any sense. Also, I didn't want random, or planned. In my opinion, sex is paired with a relationship; commitment. What's the worse place you ever had sex?"

"In the bathroom at a family party. My girlfriend at the time was addicted to sex. She had to have sex all the time. We were at my parents wedding anniversary party and she pushed me into the bathroom. We got caught because there was a line of people waiting when we came out. You?"

"I've always had sex in a bed."

"Really!?! OMG! I gotta change that!"

He blushed. He meant it and I knew it.

Chapter 4

Finally, it was the grand opening of 'Total Image Salon'. Arianna worked very hard on this project and I was proud of her. She hired a receptionist/greeter and 2 shampoo girls. She rented booths to 3 nail techs, 3 beauticians and an eyebrow thread artist. She was still looking for 2 makeup artists. In the meantime, she handled all makeup appointments. The beauticians, nail techs and tread artist had their own book of business, plus they all accepted walk-ins. Arianna was collecting $850 a month from each person. It was her startup fee. She let all parties know that as time went on, the prices of rent will go up. They had a full week ahead of them and they extended salon hours. Tues-Sat 8am-8pm, closed Sun & Mon. I was pleased with that. Once I made sure everything was up and running smoothly, I retreated home. I wanted to spend the rest of the day in my house. While sitting on my sofa, I planned a celebration for Arianna's grand opening with a dinner at the Benjamin Steak House. I called and made reservations for Sunday night and I sent out a mass text message.

Me: hey all. I made dinner reservations for Sunday night at 6. We will be dining at the Benjamin in White Plains. We are celebrating the grand opening of Arianna's salon. Please respond with regrets only. See you Sunday!

I called my mom to see how she was doing since Hosni's wife called to reschedule their dinner visit. My mom was pissed off. "She has such a nasty attitude! She said she's starting a new, 60-day diet and cannot eat any traditional food. Who calls their mother in law and says that?! Ok, no problem, so, I say send the kids! She says no because the kids have lessons that they cannot miss! My kids had lessons and they saw family; she has no idea who she's messing with! So, I am going to drive to Boston and see them myself."
"WOW! Well, I agree that was rude. I also think that maybe a visit would be nice, but do not go alone, and do not go because you are upset with her. Go because you miss the kids and Hosni and you would like to see them."
"Where did you get your peace?"
"Weed, and Bob Marley."
"I hate you!"
"No, you don't. Have you spoken to Hosni at all?"
"Yea. He calls me from his office. He said she's been very difficult lately

and he has no idea why. He doesn't want to leave her, but he's getting sick of the random attitude. He had no idea that she rescheduled our visit until she called him and said 'Hi, I just rescheduled our visit'."

"Hmm, maybe he's cheating on her, she knows it, and she's making him miserable because of it. But he's a man, he thinks he's covering his tracks, but his wife is a woman and women have a pretty powerful intuition."

"Uhm, what the??? Is that really where your mind went when I told you that story? What are you going through?"

"Oh, nothing mama. I'm just shooting out an idea. I'm sorry. I didn't mean to freak you out."

Beep Beep...

"Hold on ma, my phone is beeping." I pulled my phone away from my face to read the caller ID. It was Jax.

"Hey Ma, may I call you back?"

"Sure baby. Love you."

"Love you too!"

"Dr. Disappear, hello"

"Hi babe. I know, it's been a few days. I'm sorry."

"Oh, no office excuse?"

"No excuse. I legitimately have no reason for my absence."

"I could think of 3 reasons." Silence. Oops, did I cross a line with that remark?

"I miss you." I held the phone for a few moments. Finally, I vomited "I miss you too."

"Have you gone back to work yet?"

"No, I think I am done with the firm. I don't hate it but I don't love it anymore. I like being a 100% independent business."

"Wow! I admire that! Congrats! What's the next move?"

"I'm meeting with the auto group's current owner next week. We are going to talk and I am going to evaluate. In my mind, that is my next project."

"Bravo! Bravo! I am totally impressed! We must celebrate..."

"What kind of celebration do you have in mind?"

"I have a friend that throws this ridiculously amazing 4th of July party every year. I never go because it's usually a boat ride; I hate boat rides. The idea of possibly getting stuck in the sea freaks me out. Anyway, this year's party is on Miami Beach. I cannot wait and I would love to have your beautiful, chocolate body on the beach by my side. What do you say? It's next weekend, so."

I was so quiet that I wasn't sure if I was still breathing. Was this for real?!? The coincidences that we shared were frightening. I jumped up and ran down the hall into my home office. I had to find that invite.

"Sara. How do I always seem to render you speechless?"

"I don't know but you do; hold on."

I put the phone down and dug through stacks of paperwork like a mad woman!

"What's your friend's name?"

"Avery Anderson McBride. The President and CEO of McBride Recycling Corp. Do you know him?"

"I do. He's one of my clients." Jackson laughed. Wholeheartedly laughed from the bottom of his gut. "Why is that funny?"

"He is who referred me to your company. Trust me, I had no idea that he was your client. He never told me who he worked with. Confidential, I guess. I swear."

"It's ok. I am not mad. How would this work? I have my own invite to Sir McBride's awesome beach party! How do you know him?"

"We grew up together. Literally. His father is my God father."

"Wow! It's a small world."

"It is it is."

"Well, we can fly together; first class. Did you already book a room?"

"Babe. I'm prompt. I've had a room and flight booked for 2 months. I need this weekend away!"

"Alright. Then I will meet you on the beach. In the meantime, I need to kiss those lips again. When can I see you?"

"Would you like to come over for dinner tonight?"

"Do you cook babe?"

"I do; quite well, if I do say so myself."

"I would love to come over for dinner. Should I bring anything?"

"Just you, and your appetite."

"I can do that. Wie viel Uhr?" I did not, under any circumstances speak German. However, I had common sense...

"Uhm, how about 7pm?" He and I laughed together.

"You are so smart. Teaching you to speak German will be easier than I thought. Anyway, I have a patient. I must go. Enjoy the rest of your day and I will see you at 7."

I walked down the steps and entered my kitchen. I opened my freezer and my fridge to see what I had versus what I needed for my meal. I had nothing; just like I thought. I looked at my watch and it was 1:30. I needed to hit the grocery store. I grabbed some reusable bags from my pantry, placed them on the back of the stool and scribbled a grocery list.

-rack of lamb
-red potatoes
-green beans
-lettuce, tomatoes, cucumbers
-herbs

I grabbed my purse, stuffed the list inside, grabbed the reusable, shopping bags, and headed to the garage. Grocery shopping always started with a short list and then before I knew it, I spent $200. Grocery shopping also always required me to drive a SUV. I grabbed a set of keys off the wall and pushed the unlock button on the key fob. I opted to drive the 2014 Porsche Macan. I liked this gas guzzler! Hosni gave it to me for Christmas. I gave him a Tesla. We gave ridiculously lavish gifts to each other. I couldn't tell you why, but I was certain it was just because we could.

I despised grocery shopping. I loved food, but I would prefer it just appear in my kitchen. Someone suggested I use Peapod; the service that grocery shops for you and delivers to your home. It was a great idea; however, I didn't want someone else picking out my produce. So, I sucked it up and did my own shopping. I went to Whole Foods on this shopping mission. I enjoyed being in Whole Foods. While walking around, I decided to turn my regular tossed salad into a Greek salad. I walked over to the olive bar and dug in. After that, I went to the cheese bar; I walked over to the meat and fish department. I knew lamb was on my list, but the Sea Bass looked so fresh and amazing! I had to get it. I walked around for almost an hour, just picking up stuff. "Let me get out of here!" I said to myself as I sped towards the front of the store. I made it to the register and drumroll please. $189.92. I retreated to my car!

I couldn't decide if I was going to get dressed up for dinner or if I was going to be comfortable. After all, I was home. I spent 2 hours in the kitchen, preparing a feast fit for a king. My meal looked great and I couldn't wait for Jackson to try everything. I hopped in the shower and got dolled up for our dinner date. I stood in the middle of my huge closet trying to decide what to wear. I picked out a fitted, knee length skirt. It was very much like wearing leggings. Stretchy and soft. I put on a pale pink fitted tee shirt and tucked it into my skirt. I was home so I walked around barefoot. My floors were clean. I didn't do anything special with my hair. I made sure I combed all the tangles out and left it to hang freely. I was gawking at myself in the mirror and before I knew it was 6:40.

"Crap! I gotta set the table." I ran downstairs and looked around.
"I wonder what it feels like outside."
I went out the French doors in the dining room and stepped onto the porch. The dark mahogany wood was warm beneath my feet. I hadn't set any furniture out here yet. I quickly shuffled into the shed in my garage and pulled out a tall round table and matching bar stools. I set the table and chairs up with time to spare. It was 6:50. Jackson was always prompt. I knew he was going to arrive promptly at 7. I turned my plain table and chairs into a romantic eating nook. It looked so peaceful when I was finished. There was dim lighting overhead and a speaker outside. I turned Sirius radio to channel 34 'classic vinyl'. I like rock, but I will change it if I need to. I could see into the driveway from where I was standing. I watched Jackson pull into the driveway, park and get out of the car. There was a short flight of steps in front of me. I stood at the top and watched Jackson walk around his car and towards me. He was so damn sexy! He was wearing skinny jeans that hugged his firm ass perfectly, and a grey tee shirt.
"Wow! Babe, this is nice, really, nice! Did this take you all day to put together?
"I will never tell my secrets! Would you like a drink?"
"Yes please. Gin & Tonic." That was a first.
"I hope you like Bombay, because that's what I've got."
"Bombay is the best."
I walked over to the bar and assembled his drink. I heard his footsteps behind me and I anticipated him touching me. He walked up behind me and put his arms around my waist. He hugged me tight. Then, he gathered my hair and nicely tossed it over my right shoulder. He began kissing me down my neck. His touch is so light and gentle. I was getting excited. He moved his hands down my sides and grazed my legs. His arms scaled back up my body, to my waist and this time he spun me

slowly to face him.

"Do you trust me Sara?"
"Do I have a reason not too?"
"Do you always answer a question with a question?"
"Not always, but when I do, it's because I want to know your answer before I give an answer." Jackson's stomach growled. I giggled.
"I guess you're hungry, huh?"
"Yea, I haven't eaten all day. You told me to bring my appetite."
"I'm glad you listened to me."
I went into the kitchen and made a plate for Jackson. Grilled Sea Bass, steamed green beans, wild rice, a side of Greek salad and fresh ciabatta rolls. None of which, was on my original menu. We sat at the high table outside; eating and drinking. I heard one of my favorite songs playing on the speaker. Forgetting the company, I was keeping, I sang...

"Sing with me, sing for the years
Sing for the laughter, sing for the tears
sing it with me, just for today
maybe tomorrow, the good Lord will take you away..."

Jackson clapped. Seriously!?! I could not sing so if he complimented that...
"Wow! You should definitely stay in the business world."
He laughed. I laughed too; a bit harder.
"Oh yea, I know, but I can dance."
"That means you have rhythm. We should dance after dinner."
"Come on let's dance!" I sung. I ran inside and switched the station to 'smooth R & B'

"Oooh baby. I'm hot just like an oven
I need some lovin'
and baby; I can't hold it much longer
It's getting stronger and stronger..."

It was the perfect song. I walked back outside and Jackson extended his hand to me. He pulled me in close and we swayed to the beautiful sound of Marvin Gaye's voice.
"I'm falling in love with you. That was the reason for my absence."
"How does love make you disappear?"

"I fell in love with you too quickly."

"Since when is there a time limit on falling in love?"

"Do you love me?"

"I haven't successfully become acquainted with that emotion. I found it pointless to explore..."

"Why?"

"Why else?"

I dropped my eyes. I felt them fill up, so I turned away and guzzled the drops of Bombay that were in his glass.

"Come here, Sara. I'm sorry. I didn't mean to make you upset. I know that this relationship is difficult because of the terms that it must happen. Trust me, I know that isn't fair to you. But tell me something, why do you still see me if it bothers you so?"

"Because I love you too."

I whispered, I turned around and walked away. I needed to smoke. I went upstairs and instead of heading towards my bedroom suite, I made a left at the top of the stairs. At the end of the hallway, there was a narrow set of steps that lead to a hidden bedroom. That was my woman cave. It was a long, deep room with limited headroom in the doorway. I usually crawled into the room and stood once I was inside. This room had wall to wall black, shag carpet. There were pillows instead of furniture in this room. This was my lounge space. Jackson found me.

"This house really is amazing." I said nothing and he could tell that I was perturbed.

"I have questions. I would like some answers, and this cannot go any further until I get them."

"I know you have questions. I wish I had the answers. Please babe, don't think about it. Just live freely with me; like you have been. I love you. You love me. It will fall into place perfectly the way it should."

He leaned in and kissed me. We were sitting on the floor, so he laid me down. I melted into his arms. This time there was no waiter or glasses of wine between us. We kissed intensely and he caressed my body. He slipped his hands into the sides of my skirt and slowly pulled it down. Once removed, he tossed it. He moved over, sat me up, removed my shirt and then my bra. The kissing commenced and I pulled his shirt over his head. He laid my body down again and kissed everywhere; down my neck and my chest. His tongue slowly caressed my nipple and it rose immediately. He sucked it. It was gentle. I was getting excited. He sucked one nipple, while gently tugging on the other. He kissed down my stomach and licked my belly button. It tickled. I giggled. He kissed between my thighs. He separated my legs slightly to reveal my juicy, wet pussy. He grazed it with his tongue. I moaned quietly. Before I could regroup myself, his tongue was licking vigorously on my clit. I was getting louder. He sucked. He licked. It was perfect. He knew exactly what he was doing with his tongue. He never lost his stride and before I knew it, he was inside of me.

"OHHHHH BABE!!!"
I bellowed out loud and quickly covered my face. He moved my hand.
"Don't hold back. Let me hear you."
He pushed himself deeper inside of me and I wrapped my legs around his waist. I moaned. He fit perfectly. He had perfect rhythm. He flipped me over and I was straddled on top of him. I rode him. He stopped and turned me round. I dipped low and arched my back.
"Remember to spank me...!"

I woke up the next morning in my bed. It was very quiet in my house but I could smell food. For some reason, I was not in a rush to move. I was hoping Jackson was in my kitchen and he was. Shortly, he walked into my bedroom.

"Good morning beautiful."
"How are you still here?"
"I should've handed you this before I spoke." He handed me a very hot cup of coffee.
"I'm sorry...Good morning Dr. Makes me cum. What are you doing here?"
"I slept with a beautiful woman last night. And when I sleep with a beautiful woman that I love, I make her breakfast and I bring it to her."
"You know what I mean."
I rolled my eyes and bit into a cantaloupe chunk.
"My family is out of town. So, no one knows that I am here."
"Hmm, so this can't happen again? Is that what you're saying?"
"Are you sprung already, Ms. Bashir?"
"I've been sprung since the moment you walked out of my office."
"What are your plans for today?"
"I don't know." My mouth was full. I finished chewing and swallowed.
"I think I am going to go to Bradley and speak to Brian about me giving

up my office. It is to my knowledge that I get to keep my clients."
"Are you going to start your own financial business?"
"I'm going to continue the work that I do for the clients that I have. I don't plan on taking any new clients."
"Would you do business out of your home office?"
"I hadn't thought about it. Why?"
"I was just curious. I know that you entertain here, I was just wondering if you would work here also."
"I guess I would have to for a while. I don't own an office building; did you carry me to bed?"
"I did. I put you to sleep. I wasn't going to leave you in the dark alley room." We laughed.
"Get out of my house!"
"Luckily for you, I do have to go. I've got to get to the office, but I have to stop home and get a suit."
"When can I see you again?"
"So, I had to vigourously make you cum repeatedly in order to get you to ask me out first?"
"Hahahaha! Shut up!"
"Can I call you later and let you know? I would like to take you somewhere special tonight. I need to make sure we can do the activity."
"See, why didn't you just say, 'I'll let you know what time', because now, I'm going to be thinking about the mystery date all day." I pouted. He kissed my bottom lip.
"You have work to do today. You are going to speak to Brian and then you are going to begin looking for office space!"
"Look at you, planning my day!"
"Will you come walk me out?"
Finally, I got out of the bed; I was nude. I giggled. I walked into the master bathroom and grabbed a robe from behind the door. I put on pink slippers and walked my man down the steps. When we reached the lower level, I noticed how clean it was.
"Did you clean up?"
"I've only been here a couple of times, but I've never seen anything out of place. It was only right that I straighten up. I just hope everything is in the right spot."
"Wow! Thank you very much!"
"Oh, and I envisioned that mirror on the ceiling."

"Who's putting it there? You?"

"I can. I saw a pink tool box in your garage, didn't I?"

"You did."

"Ok. So, the next time you invite me over, I'll hang it for you."

He kissed me, turned around and walked out. I stood in my kitchen with my cup of coffee; my 2nd cup of coffee. I realized that I still hadn't smoked. I went to the stash and rolled up. Then I remembered I had no idea where my cell phone was, so I went looking for that. I found it! Dr. Sleeps at his mistress's house plugged it in for me. It was on my night-stand. There I was with my coffee and my blunt and something didn't feel quite right, but I ignored my intuition.

Ring Ri…

"Hello."

"It didn't even ring, woman!!"

"It was in my hand. Hey Javi. What's up?"

"Nothing special is up, what's up with you?"

"Not much. I'm chillen."

"Why aren't you working? Did you get fired?" I laughed.

"No, I think I am going to quit my job and fully go into business for my-self."

"I love that idea!"

"Really?"

"Were you waiting for someone to tell you otherwise?"

"Absolutely, not."

"Good, so, how's your married boyfriend?"

"I think I will refer to him as my Beau, and he's fine I guess. I'm keeping my distance." I totally lied.

"Oh. That's good, you still didn't google him huh?"

"Nope and I'm not going to. What are you doing today?"

"Girl, it's Wednesday. I am at work until 6:30. You are the only one for-tunate enough to take 3 weeks off from work before quitting!"

"Blah! Ok, are you coming to the Benjamin on Sunday?"

"Yes I am. Is this dinner on you? Or are we doing the individual bill non-sense."

"We will not do that at the Benjamin! I have no problem paying to keep from being embarrassed. Listen, let me go. I am dragging out quitting my job. I'll call you later."

"Peace, love and hair grease."

It took me an additional 2 hours to leave my house. I was not in the mood to deal with people, so, I had to sit still until I was. Brian said he will be available at noon. I arrived at noon. I walked down the long corridor and there were no plants. There were signs on the wall that read 'Please pardon our appearance. We are getting a makeover'. Seriously!?! I turned the corner and there was Sir lazy fatness.

"Hey, I thought you quit."

"Hey, I thought you were on a diet." That was mean but I said I didn't want to deal with people.

"Whatever! If you do quit, can I have your clients?"

"My clients won't work with you. They are coming with me."

"Ah Ha! So, you are quitting?!?"

I rolled my eyes and walked away. I could careless to be bothered with Fredrick Winslow Harz-Bradley today. When I approached Brian's door, he was on the phone. I entered and sat down quietly. I was looking around and noticed a stack of paperwork on Brian's desk. The page on the top had Jackson's name on it. I became intrigued. I was going to grab it, but Brian hung up and was focused on me.

"Sara, are you leaving me?"

"I think it's time Brian. Remember when I first came on board I told you it would be temporary."

"I know but it's been 12 years. You are my best advisor. What can I do to make you stay?"

"It's not you, it's me. I want to dedicate my time to becoming my own business mogul. It's time."

"I guess that's understandable. As per our contract, you may take any clients that you have done 3 or more projects for. Everyone else must remain a part of the firm database." Then I realized, that's why Jackson's name was on that page. Technically, I only did one project for him. Even though it was a big project, it was only once. The only way to be my client outside of this firm was if we canceled the project I did and redo it. I was not doing that, but Jackson wasn't going to work with anyone else.

"I have to take Jackson Ellis' project with me. I understand that it's a new project, but he isn't going to work with anyone else at the firm."

"Is that so, and why is that, Sara?"

"I did an excellent job on that project, and in a timely manner. I doubt anyone else can even handle what I did for that client." Brian rolled his eyes and leaned back in his chair. I wasn't expecting his next remark. "Stay. I will sign the entire firm over to you."

"I'm sorry, what?!"

"I'm getting old. In fact, I'm dying; ALS. Freddy is my only child and he is not mine. I raised him because I married his mother when he was just an infant. I wouldn't leave my company to him anyway. He has proven to me that he cannot handle it. You are good at this; great at this. You could run this company in your sleep. The building that this office is in is mine also. Well, it would be yours if you say yes. You would be the sole proprietor of everything. The only thing it will cost you is your signature. That's it! What do you say?" I was drooling. Was this really happening? I went there to quit so that I could begin my own financial company. Brian was liter-ally going to hand me his financial company. Insane! I was always up for a challenge and I could use something to occupy my time. I could not be home all day making dinner for Jackson.

"Where do I sign?"

Brian and I spent the duration of the afternoon on the phone with his law-yer and mine. We discussed the specific information about the company, finances, what to expect, and they drew contracts. This building had 500 offices in it; doctor's offices, a lab, a few insurance companies have offic-es here, a law office and a pharmacy; over 5.5 million dollars in monthly revenue. Plus, in the financial office, as the President of the company, I re-ceived 10 ½% of the profit made by each deal closed by an advisor. This was liquid gold; I was sitting on gold. We agreed that the merge would begin at the beginning of the following month. Happy birthday to me! Bri-an also suggested I find something else for Freddy to do in the company. He was not working out as an advisor, but Brian doesn't have the heart to fire him. "I'll see what I can do" was my answer. In my mind I was thinking, "take that sorry fool with you!" It was 5:20 when I finally left the office. I sat in my car and took a deep breath. I dug my phone out of my bag. I had a ton of missed calls and text messages.

Javier: When you're done, call me.

Daniela: Hi...are you alive?

Arianna: You cannot help me start my dream and then fall off the earth. Call me.

Hosni: Hey boo...I miss you. I was thinking we should go to Cairo for your birthday. Call me and let me know what you think.

Hosni: Just the 2 of us though.... I need a home visit with my sis.

Missed call: Mom
Missed call: Jax
Missed call: Jax

I called Jax back first.
"Hello beautiful. I was beginning to worry. How did it go?"
"August 2, I will be the sole proprietor of Bradley & Associates, as well as 5210 W. Broad St."
"Wait, what?" I laughed.
"I went in there to quit and Brian offered me the entire company and ownership of the office building. I didn't even know he owned the building."
"That is wonderful! You took 3 weeks off from work. You now own a Salon, an office building, a financial company and you could possibly be an auto group owner. WOW! You're making me hard!" I admitted that he was becoming more and more comfortable with me. I smiled to myself.
"You called me before, I'm returning your call."
"Yes. I want to work out the specifics for our special mystery date."
"I'm listening. This was your date idea, remember?"
"Yes. I remember. Well it can't happen today because your meeting ran longer than I expected. No worries. We can do it tomorrow. Are you available?"
"I can be. What time?"
"Can I pick you up at 4?"
"Yes. How should I dress?"
"You've never asked me that before. I'm not sure how to answer." He laughed.
"Surprise!" I laughed.
"Yes. It is a surprise. I like that, surprise me. Just make sure you are comfortable. Preferably no platform pumps, shorty!" Again, we both laughed.

"Ok. I will see you then. I have other calls to return. May I call you later?"
"Please. In fact, meet me at Baang at 7."

Chapter 5...

It felt like it took a million years to get to Sunday. I couldn't wait to get to the Benjamin. In addition to wanting a good steak, I was looking forward to the fellowship. I put on a little black dress and gold gladiator sandals. I put on a chunky gold necklace, bracelet and watch and I braided my hair into a French braid. No big bag tonight, instead I carried a soft, gold clutch. I looked at myself in the mirror and said "Yea, I would hit this!" When I got to the garage, I decided it was a convertible night. A year prior, I bought a Porsche 911 Targa. I drove it once and that was home from the dealer. It had 7 miles on it. Targa night arrived. I got in and pushed the button to open the T-top and away I went. I arrived and pulled into the line for the valet. Ahead of my car was Arianna, and Javier's cars. The valet came over and opened my door. I stepped out. Arianna, Javier and Daniela were standing at the entrance.

"Wow! You look amazing! I thought this was Arianna's dinner?"
Leave it to Javier to assume I was trying to outdo someone. He didn't say it, but it was implied by his tone.
"I thought I was dressed rather simple for the evening; thanks though. Hiiiii ARIIIIII!!!!!! HI DANIIIII!!!!"
Arianna lightly jogged over and leapt into my arms. Daniela came over and politely waited her turn before she hugged me and kissed me on my cheek.
"Hiiii I am sooo excited and I'm high and I'm hungry. Thank you so much for planning this." She said. I laughed.
"Hi. I see, you're high. You're welcome." Arianna looked nice this evening. She was wearing all white. A white A- line skirt, a white blouse with big sleeves, and a pair of white platform pumps.
"Is anyone else here?"
"I think it's just us so far."
We all walked inside. I told the hostess my name and she agreed to seat us even though we were waiting for others. I loved this place. The classic style atmosphere, the loaded bar, the food, the staff, everything was perfect here. She sat us at a large, round table in a room to the right of the entrance. We sat in various seats around the table and slowly but surely, the rest of the guests arrived. Drinks arrived at the table first; followed by the appetizers, salad, main course and dessert. We were having a great conversation and enjoying the evening. Arianna picked up her glass and tapped it lightly with her fork.
"May I have your attention please? I would like to take a moment to thank you Sara for everything that you helped me do. If it wasn't for you and your tenacity, I would not have a salon to call my own. In fact, as I look at

who's here, we all have Sara to thank for a lot of things in our lives. You are a true friend to me, to us and I appreciate you. Thank you, thank you! Here's to Sara!" Everyone raised their glasses.

"HERE HERE!!" I was flattered but this wasn't about me.

"Guys, Ari, thank you, but this isn't about me. It's about Arianna. It's about all of you helping her business. That's what I want. Send business her way. We all know someone in need of her service. This dinner was to celebrate the hard work that she did. All I did was write a check. The real work was done by Arianna and she deserves the praise and the recognition. This dinner was also a chance for all of us to fellowship. There's too many years of friendship at this table and I felt like it had been too long since we all gathered. I love you all."

"WE LOVE YOU TOO!!" I felt good. This was nice. I appreciated my friends and moments like these are rare. I was gloating; to myself, in my mind, but Rena didn't let me continue enjoying this montage.

"So, Sara, we know what Ariana has been doing, business wise, what are you doing business wise?" Rena was sitting the furthest from me. She and I didn't usually talk about business, so I was a bit reluctant to answer the question.

"Oh. I am doing what I do, you know, financial stuff." I was being vague because I wanted to see where she was going with this.

"Is that what you call taking a company right from under a good, dying old man?" What the hell was she talking about?

"Uh. I don't think I follow."

"My mother's best friend is Anne Harz-Bradley. She told my mother that the younger woman that works for her husband, TOOK HIS MULTI MILLION DOLLAR COMPANY AWAY FROM HIM. How and why did you do that?! Don't you have enough?!"

I had no idea that Brian's wife knew Rena's mother. It really was a small world. I was beginning to get some glares as my eyes scanned the table. I needed to say something quickly because they were all beginning to judge me. I didn't want to talk about this until the merge was completed, but I did just say these were my best friends... and this needed to be clarified.

"First, now was not the right time, nor was this the right place to bring this up, and your tone, as a grown woman, Rena, I am a bit disappointed in you. Second, I don't normally discuss my business deals with my friends because I prefer my time spent with my friends to not include my work life; but I guess I merged that with the salon. Here's the deal. I walked into Bradley & Associates earlier this week with the intent to quit, gather my files, leave and begin my own firm with the clients that I already have. Brian had a different idea. When I sat down and gave him my verbal resignation, he countered with the opportunity to take over the company. I did not TAKE anything from anyone, it was GIVEN and that is because I gave that firm 12 long, hard working, years that equated to millions of dollars in revenue. Of the staff that remains, I've been there the longest; longer than his not-son, son. I have what I have because I worked hard for it!" The table was completely silent. I signaled to the waitress. She came over. I reached in my clutch and handed her my Amex.

"Please close this tab."
"Yes ma'am."
I was livid. This was not what I had in mind for a night with friends. I was insulted knowing that Rena was offended by my business deals. The nerve of that woman! The waitress returned with the receipt, my card and a pen. I placed my card back in my bag and pulled out $150 in cash and left it as a tip for our waitress.
"Thank you everyone for coming. I am excusing myself from the table."
I felt the tears build up in my eyes as I approached my car. I got in and sat still for a moment, trying to gather my thoughts. I opened my recent call list in my cell phone and touched Jackson's name. The phone barely rang before he answered.
"I was just thinking about you." The sound of his voice was so calm and soothing to me. Who knew why, but it made the tears fall. I sobbed.
"Baby, what's wrong? Where are you? What can I do?"
I sniffled and gathered myself so that I could speak coherent English.
"You, can you meet me at my house in 20 minutes?"
"Of course, I will!"
I couldn't get home fast enough. I couldn't leave the restaurant fast enough. The entire time I was driving, Rena was calling my phone. I was sending her to voicemail. I didn't care to hear what she had to say. I needed to talk to Jackson. I pulled into the driveway and parked in the garage. By the time, I made it to the front door, Jackson was pulling into the driveway. He threw his car into park, the driver side door flew open and he came running towards me. He put his arms around me and hugged me tight. I sobbed into his chest. I couldn't believe all the emotion that was coming over me. Jackson scooped me up into his arms and walked toward

the front door. My keys were in my hand. He took them and unlocked the door. When we got inside, he sat me down on the sofa and proceeded to the bar to pour us both a drink. I guzzled it. He poured another. I guzzled that one. He didn't pour a third. He took the glass and sat it on the table. I reached my hand out.

"Speak first. Then I'll pour another."

I took a deep breath and picked my head up. He looked so yummy. I wanted to jump him right there. He was wearing sweatpants and a pair of Jordan's. I was surprised. It made me look at my watch. It was 11:15. Jackson sat waiting patiently for me to tell my story. "Dinner was nice. Ari was thankful and appreciative for all that I've helped her do. Then Rena deemed it necessary to question me about the deal with Brian Bradley. But it was her tone; her verb choice. She basically accused me of stealing the company from a dying old man."

"Wow! What made her do that?"

"I have no idea. My anger is for a couple of reasons. First, during Ari's speech, she mentioned how I have helped everyone at the table at some point in life and she appreciates me as her friend. That was lovely. Then I spoke after and I probably shouldn't have said 'all I did was write a check' but it's true. Arianna did all the work. But then Rena speaks and she's like 'oh so I heard you took the company from Brian Bradley. Don't you have enough stuff?'"

"I am not passing judgment, but it sounds to me like Rena is a little bit jealous."

"I'm not sure why. Do you know how much artwork I purchased from that girl?! I'm pissed and I told her so, at how she chose the wrong moment and the wrong place to have that discussion with me."

"I agree. What are you going to do?"

"I'm not going do 1. THING! I cried. Now I will drink and then I will make love to my man and not care about Rena and her jealousy."

Jackson moved over closer to me. He cuffed my face in his hands and kissed me gently. I melted into his arms. He picked me up and placed me on his lap. I straddled him and kissed him harder. The little black dress that I wore was asymmetrical. It zipped up the back. Jackson unzipped my dress and exposed my breasts. He fondled my nipples with his fingers. I ran my hands under his tee shirt and fondled his nipples too. His shirt was in my way. I pulled it off over his head. The freaky girl came out of me and I stood up. I bent over slightly and put my hands on either side of his hips. I tugged at his waistline. He lifted his lower body up to assist me with pant removal. He was slightly erect inside a pair of royal blue boxer briefs. They were sexy. The last time he was wearing boxers. Too bad these were in my way. They had to go. I pulled them down, and there was his manhood; staring at me. I got down on my knees and ingested him; all of him. He moaned and that turned me on so I sucked harder. I slobbered up and down in a swift motion and my mouth salivated. I cuffed his balls in my hand and rotated them while I sucked his shaft.

"OH!! BABE!" His excitement fueled me. I loved every minute of it. He tasted so good. He smelled so good. The more I sucked, the more he moaned and before I knew it, I made myself cum. I stood and the trail of juice slid down my inner thigh. Jackson noticed and he leaned in and licked it up. He licked all the way up my leg, and lightly grazed my exposed clit. He picked me up and carried me upstairs. When we reached my bedroom, he laid me on my bed and began kissing me. He kissed down my neck and sucked my nipples. I moaned. We shared so much sexual chemistry. His touch made me cum all night long. I looked at the clock and it said 3:03. Jackson was lying beside me. He was asleep on his back. The sheet was draped over his lower body and his arm was across his stomach. I rolled over and watched him sleep for a moment. I couldn't take it anymore. I slowly raised the top of the sheet and slid under. I picked his manhood up and placed it in my mouth. I took all of him in my mouth and sucked; slowly. He began to wake up.

"Oh, I could soooooooooo get used to th--!" He couldn't contain himself. He moaned and I enjoyed giving him head. His reaction was all I needed. He climaxed quicker this time. I didn't mind. He went to the bathroom and cleaned up. When he came out, I was standing in the bedroom looking at the mirror that he purchased for me.

"When I bought that mirror, I had no idea if I was ever going to see it in your home. I thought it was beautiful and I wanted you to have it."

"I love it. I stand in front of it every day and I admire what I see." I giggled.

"Jackson, "

He must have known what I was going to say because he cut me off.

"Miami is this weekend coming. Are you ready?"

"I am. Is your family still out of town? Where are they going to be when you are in Miami? My invite doesn't include a plus one. Does yours?"

"My family is out of town; Copenhagen for the summer. No one's invite includes a plus one. It's Avery's signature. He believes that he knows enough people that people can come alone, meet new people and develop new friendships."

"Uh huh."

I was done speculating and asking questions. I knew that this wonderful, sexy, fun loving man belonged to another. I was preparing myself for the day when he decided to cut me and all of this off.

"Sara."

"Jackson."

DING DONG!

"What time is it? Who is ringing my doorbell?!?"

I was dumbfounded. Jackson and I both walked downstairs. I got to the door first. It was Rena. I opened it and stood, surprised.

"I'm sorry. I know it's late, but I couldn't sleep."

Rena was talking to me through the glass door. I was hesitant to let her in. I turned around and Jackson wasn't standing nearby, so I opened it.

"You deserve great things. You are the best person to ever exist. I'm sorry that I accused you of taking the company from Brian. Anne, his wife, is upset because he didn't leave the company to her son. She was livid when she told my mother and my mother was livid when she told me. I carried the anger over to you and that wasn't fair. I'm sorry. Please forgive me."

"Rena, I love you. You are a good friend. We've known each other for years, but I thought you knew me better than that."

"I do. I swear."

"Good. Then make that the last time you EVER ACCUSE me of something in a negative manner amongst others. That conversation should've been between us and behind closed doors."

"Absolutely. You're right. I owe you and Arianna a do over."

"Yep! You do. I love you. It's late, or early; depends on who you ask. Get out of my house!" Rena laughed, hugged me and walked away. I closed and locked the door behind her.

"Jackson!"

"Sara!"

"That was good. I'm glad she came to make peace. Can I make love to you now?"

I woke up around 11am the next morning. Jackson was already gone. I figured he would be because it was Monday and we were up all night and he had an office to report to. I enjoyed making love to him. He was a beautiful man. While I was lying there thinking about Dr. Mr. Sex, I replayed the conversation that I had with Javier. 'Are you gonna google him?' Should I google him? I grabbed my cell phone from the nightstand. I opened Safari and typed . Just as the page loaded, my phone rang. It was Daniela. I answered with a smile.

"Hey Dani baby!"

"What's up love? How are you today?"

"I'm well thanks, how are you?"

"I'm ok. I thought I should check on you after last night. When you left, I tore Rena a new asshole. That's why she was blowing your phone up. I told her 'I don't care how she does business, she is our friend and you do not ever judge her!'"

"Thanks Dan. I appreciate it. She came to my house at 6:15 this am."

"Wow! Now that's nuts! Do you think she's jealous of you?"

"I don't think she has a reason to be. I think it was just a misinterpretation of what really happened. You know how the game telephone works."

"Well you are in wonderful spirits for someone that paid $500 to be insulted."

"$850"

"HA!!! Rena should reimburse you."

"It's water under the bridge boo. So, what's up? What are you doing? You wanna go shopping today?"

"Wench! I am at work! You need a regular 9-5."

"Whatever you're working on is not important. Come on! Go home early today!" Daniela was a graphic designer. She was an illustrator for a kid's magazine.

"You're a bad influence. Lucky for you, I was planning on leaving early today anyway. Where are we shopping?"

"I need to go to Lord & Taylor and I would like to go to the Hermes store on Greenwich Ave. I need a new duffle and don't want another Louis duffle."

"Oh, are you going away?"

"Yeah, Miami this weekend."

"Oh yea. I forgot. Ok. The earliest that I can leave work is 2. It's 11 now. There's enough time for you to shower, get dressed and get your luggage. I will meet you at Lord & Taylor."

"Ok. That works. I will see you later. What time?"
"Yes. Around 2:30. I'll meet you in the shoe department."
"Awesome."

When I hung up, the google page reloaded. I closed the safari app and put my phone back on the nightstand. I didn't google him because I didn't want to see what the results were. I headed to the kitchen and brewed a single serve iced coffee on my Keurig machine. I rolled a blunt and headed to the bathroom. I took a bath. I needed to relax. The tension from dinner and the wonderful sex wore my body out. I wanted to know how Jackson's day was going but I didn't want to bother him. I wanted him to focus on his work because I was only half ass focused on mine. My meeting with the auto group owner was scheduled for Thursday morning. I was scheduled to leave town Thursday night. I wasn't doing any work on that project until after Monday. I began as President of the financial firm August 2, so that gave me a month to kick it with my feet up; at least that was what I planned to do. This weekend was Miami. I considered driving Jackson up to my bed and breakfast. There was a reggae festival on the beach that I've attended in the past. I stepped out of the bath and put on a robe; realizing I hadn't checked the weather. There was a balcony in my master suite, so I opened the French door and stepped outside. It was chilly. I returned to the closet and pulled out a pair of black leggings. I also pulled out a long, white button up shirt with side pockets. It was fitted in the middle and flared out slightly under my booty. I laced up a pair of red Giuseppe Zanotti ankle booties and switched to a red leather handbag. I looked at the clock. 12:50. "AHH!! I gotta go!" That's what I got for looking in the mirror. I ran to the garage and grabbed the keys to my Touareg. Jumped in, turned it on and peeled out of my driveway. When I walked into the Hermes store, I was greeted by a younger gentleman. He looked like a 12-year-old!

"Hello Ma'am. Welcome to Hermes. May I assist you with a purchase today?"
"Hello, you may, but you cannot call me 'ma'am'. Understood? The young man was tall and thin. He wasn't attractive at all but he was polite. He smiled.
"Understood. So, what brings you in today?"
"I need a new duffle. What's your name?"
"Roger. And you are?"

"Sara. It's a pleasure." I extended my hand. We shook.

"Roger, I am replacing a duffle. The handle finally gave out on me. I would like a medium sized, black leather or brown leather bag."

"Sure. Please, follow me."

When I knew what I was looking for, shopping was a breeze. But when I had no idea, or if I was shopping to deal with an emotion, you can forget it! I'll be in the store for hours! I completed this task and had enough time to drive across two cities to meet Daniela at Lord & Taylor. I parked on the side closest to the shoe department, since that's where we were meeting. I saw Daniela's car while I was walking towards the door. I entered and saw Daniela looking at a pair of boots.

"Please don't buy riding boots. You are indicating that summer is going to be over soon and we will need to wear these." I hated winter.

"Exactly. That's why we should buy them now, so, we don't have to worry about it later."

"Eh."

Daniela and I walked aimlessly around Lord & Taylor. I bought something from every department. We laughed and we talked about a ton of different things. I already confided in Javier about my relationship with Jackson, but I wanted and needed a female opinion. Daniela listened to the handful of Jackson stories I was willing to share. She didn't judge me. She just listened. When I was finished speaking, she looked at me. The silence was simply that. Silence. It wasn't awkward. There was no tension, just silence.

"Some people are meant to fall in love with each other, but are not meant to be together." I looked at Daniela and looked away. I didn't want to believe that he was placed in my life for me to love and love only from a distance.

"I want to buy jewelry. Let's go to Tiffany & Co."

I was 100% destructive to money when my emotions were running on full throttle.

"I think you've spent enough money today. I am not counting your stacks, but you started your day at Hermes and I'm sure you bought more than a bag. We have been in here for almost 2 hours. You bought shoes, perfume, a bag, a watch, a dress and a pair of jeans. Go home. Pour a glass of wine and pack your weekend bag."

Daniela always knew how to talk me down. She was right. I spent well over three thousand dollars today and had only been out of the house for 4 hours. Just like that, our shopping date ended. I got home a few minutes after 6.

Ring Ring. It was Hosni. I forgot to text him back.
"What's up brother?!"
"Whew! I thought you were mad at me."
"Why would I be mad at you?"
"Mom and Monica have been fighting so much lately. I assumed you were being the good daughter and taking mom's side."
"It's not a matter of taking sides, but if I were, I wouldn't be on Monica's side. I don't like how she speaks to my mother."
"Monica swears that our family doesn't like her. She didn't want to go to dinner because mom always critiques how she and I raise our kids."
"Monica should understand that it's not personal. Mom is a hot-headed person and she's unpredictable. She cussed when I was on the phone with her a few moments ago. I was shocked. She also has a strong opinion of how children should be raised. Monica needs to let mom know nicely that she will ask for her opinion on the kids when she deems it necessary. Otherwise, please let us raise our children. On the flip side, mom has to understand that those are your children and you are raising them the way you want."
"Where do you get your knowledge and peace?" That was funny because mom asked me a similar question. My answer was the same.
"Weed, and Bob Marley."
"Did you get my text or are you completely avoiding me?"
"I got your text. The last few weeks have been pure insanity for me. I took some time off from work and bought a salon for Arianna. She opened last week. I saw Rita after almost a year, and she hooked me up with someone selling an auto group, so I set that up. We'll see what happens, and when I decided I was leaving Bradley & Assoc., Brian offered to sign the entire company over to me. So, to answer your question, I would love to go to Cairo for my birthday, but I will just be going back to work and as an owner."
"WOW!!!! I am extremely impressed. You always do miraculous things! I love that you helped Arianna. Lately, she didn't have the best of luck. I should've married her."
Hosni and Arianna messed around briefly in between undergrad and graduate school. Hosni was looking for a wife and Arianna was not ready for a relationship, nonetheless marriage, so they "broke up" and decided to

remain friends.

"Yea, let's not go back down memory lane with the shoulda, coulda, woulda's. Please miss me with all of that. Oh, and no lavish gifts this year ok?"

"What?! Lavish is what WE do, Sara. Besides, it's too late, I already purchased your lavish birthday and Christmas gifts."

"Oh! Damn, man! So, you bought a gift and were gonna take me to Cairo?"

"I was but you said no to Cairo. We can go next year. Anyway, I worked the nonsense out with mom and my wife. We will be there on Friday, for the weekend. See you Saturday?"

"I'll come to Boston before August. I'll be in Miami this weekend."

"UGH! McBride's thing, right?"

"Yup. You know he gets this weekend from me every year."

"Alright kid, call me when you get back in town and we will plan a visit. The kids will be excited."

"Will do. Love you."

"Love you too, SK."

Chapter 6

"NOW BOARDING, AT GATE 10, US AIRWAYS FLIGHT 1404 TO MIAMI IN-
TERNATIONAL..."

It was 7am and I was finally boarding this much needed flight. I
was excited about this vacation. Avery McBride always threw a pretty kick
ass party. This was the first one on a beach and I couldn't wait to see the
setup. I was staying at a Sheraton Hotel near Miami Beach. I figured anything within walking distance to the beach was good. I didn't like to fly.
In all honesty, the only form of travel that I tolerated was driving. That
was simply because I controlled the car and avoided the non-driving ass
people when necessary. To fly in peace, I had to be intoxicated. I called
a car service to chauffeur me to the airport. I smoked a fat blunt before I
left the house and I had a couple of vodka shots at the airport bar. I slept
from takeoff to landing.

It had been a few days since I last saw Jackson. He suggested we
not see each other until we got to the beach party. "Absence makes the
heart grow fonder, Sara." Whatever! The pit of my stomach was in knots.
I felt like I was sitting on Kingda-Ka at Six Flags; waiting for the roller
coaster car to speed rapidly down a metal hill at 200mph. It was a great
feeling. I never felt like this about a man. I desperately needed to find the
switch on my feelings and flip it! Summer was over soon and summer ending meant Jackson's family will be back from Copenhagen, and then my
summer love would be ending, right? My flight was just shy of 3hrs. When
I arrived in Miami, I couldn't stand the heat. I was wearing a pair of loose
fitted linen shorts. They were short shorts and I was wearing a tank top.
I was tempted to not wear panties or a bra, so instead I put on a yellow
string bikini. I had a car service take me to my hotel and when I walked in
the lobby, there was Jackson.

"Whaaaat?!?!" I was so excited! "What are you doing here? I thought you
were coming tonight?"
"Well when you told me that you were coming early, I couldn't dare think
of you enjoying the sunshine without me admiring. So, I changed my
flight. I came in last night."
"Look at you...full of surprises. What room are you in?"
"808. You?"
"1210. I like heights." I winked and smiled. He smiled.

"After you." Jackson extended his arm so I could take the lead. I walked past him and headed toward the elevator. He spanked my ass! "Those shorts, Sara." He made a motion with his hand as if he was trying to cool himself off with a fan.

"Wait until you see my party outfit."

The elevator doors closed and Jackson grabbed me. He pushed my back to the elevator wall and kissed me. It was one of our rough, intense make out sessions and I didn't want it to end. The elevator doors opened on the 12th floor. Jackson let me go and picked up one of my bags. He stepped off the elevator and read the number signs so we knew where to head.

"1210. Here it is." I swiped the key card and the door unlatched.

"WOW!" In unison; we were both amazed. The room was spacious and bright. There was a balcony that had an amazing view of the beach. When I stepped outside, there were 2 lounge chairs and one card.

"Sara Bashir, Welcome to Miami Beach." It was a very nice touch from Avery. I continued to walk around the room and got comfortable. I removed my linen shorts and tank top to reveal my yellow bikini. I was tempted to take that off too.

"We should take a trip to Hedonism so I can walk around fully nude."

I made a face when I made the statement because as the words were falling off my tongue, I realized that I didn't have a normal boyfriend and couldn't just plan a weekend getaway with him. This freaking trip was circumstantial, coincidental at best. Jackson walked toward me. I didn't want to look at him so I turned my back. He placed his hands on my shoulders and massaged nicely.

"There's a pamphlet on your nightstand that will allow you to order a masseuse. Would you like me to order a masseuse for you?" His accent made the word 'masseuse' turn me on!

"I would like you to be my masseuse." I couldn't contain the freaky girl.

"Ah Ha!" He exclaimed. I giggled. I didn't know what that meant, but before I could ask, Dr. Damnit kissed me and picked me up. He pushed my back on the wall again and untied the top to my bikini. I loved it when he sucked on my nipples and he knew it. Immediately, he cupped a breast and placed my nipple in his mouth. I moaned out loud, and he kept sucking. I had my arms wrapped around his neck and my legs wrapped around his waist. He unzipped his pants and they hit the floor. His erection made me wet. He could tell and before I knew it, he was inside of me. I took control of the motion this time; bouncing swiftly up and down. Technically I was on top even though he was standing. Sexy! I woke up nude in the hotel bed. The bed was very comfortable; even though it freaked me out a bit to be nude in a universal bed. I got up quickly and headed to the bathroom. I took a shower and got dressed because I wanted to walk the strip and do some shopping. While I was getting dressed, I could see Jackson sitting on the balcony in a lounge chair. He was on the phone. I couldn't hear the conversation but he was doing more listening than talking. I put on a long, white maxi dress with spaghetti straps and a pair of gold sandals. I opened the screen door to the balcony and walked outside.

"Hello beautiful. Are you ready to tour the city?"

"Hello, I am ready. Can we begin with food?"

"You are a woman after my heart!" He kissed my cheek. As we walked back through the hotel room, I picked up a gold clutch. This one had a wrist strap so I didn't have to hold it. We approached the elevator and he pushed the button.

"Going down?" There was a very tall man standing in the elevator when we stepped in.

"Yes. Please. The lobby." Jackson answered.

"Newlyweds?" The man looked at Jackson.

"Not yet!"

Jackson laughed and looked at me. I rolled my eyes. The elevator doors opened. We all stepped off.

"Wish you the best. Take care!"

When we stepped out of the hotel doors, the sun was beaming and hit me right in the eyes. I fumbled and found my cat eyed sunglasses on the top of my head. We walked a few blocks and stumbled upon a Trattoria. It looked good so we walked in. The hostess met us at the door. We requested an outside table and she walked us to one that was equipped with an umbrella. He and I sat across from each other. He was so sexy. He must've been the sexiest man in existence and I was lucky enough to be enjoying his sexual stamina. I was staring at him; the kind of stare you gave your favorite sweet treat when you were on a diet. It was the kind of stare that clearly indicated infatuation. I was surprised that I wasn't drooling, or maybe I was.

"Hey. You ok babe? Where'd you go?"

"Hey, I'm fine, I'm happy." I smiled. I was truly happy.

"That's good to hear. I'm happy too." He smiled.

"It's funny how I didn't realize anything was missing from my life until I met you."

"My life was over until I met you and you brought me back to life." He reached across the table and grabbed my hand.

"Well, everything happens for a reason, right?"

I gave him a look. It was enough to end the conversation. We finished lunch and continued our walk along the beach. I enjoyed people watching. There were men dressed in drag. Women wearing bells and sashes. We walked by mimes, magicians and fortune tellers.

"Do you believe in tarot readings and fortunes?" I was curious. Jackson gave me a look that I couldn't describe.

"I don't believe that a person can read another person's life through cards and palm readings. What exactly are they looking at?" I laughed.

"I believe a person can read another via their aurora. For example, there's something about you that you're not telling me. I can feel it. I'm just not able to pinpoint exactly what it is."

"You know all that I am able to tell." I had to take that for what it was. I left it alone and Jackson did as well. We spent the entire day out, in the sun, on the beach. I was exhausted. It was almost 11 when we finally made it back to the hotel. We walked arm and arm slowly through the main entrance of the hotel. There was music coming from the bar. I perked up a little bit; mainly because I was being nosey and I followed the sound of the beat. As I walked around the corner, the bar was filled with people. People were sitting at tables, standing in corners; it mocked a serious club setting. There was a stage, a monitor and a microphone. There was a sign on an easel that read "Karaoke Night 11pm-2am". "Oh, that's interesting", I thought to myself. I wondered if Jackson would be interested in making a total fool of himself with me for the love of Karaoke Night. I turned around to see if he was still standing where I left him.

"Jackson."

"Sara, let me guess, you want to participate in karaoke night?!"

"Absolutely! Will you make a fool of yourself with me?"

"Anything for you, Sara"

He kissed me on my hand. We walked over to view the list of songs. The list was subpar, at best. No duets; no problem. We made a duet. We chose "I don't know why" by Stevie Wonder. When the music came on, we danced and warmed the crowd up. Neither of us could sing, which made it even more fun. We made it a party and before we knew it, we had a crowd of people standing and cheering for us. It was a blast.

"Wow! Look at that. We can't sing, but we just became famous in the world of terrible karaoke singers." Jackson and I laughed. You know, that infectious laughter that we shared from the beginning.

"Oh, you guys were great! You must do another!" The woman that stumbled to us was intoxicated. Jackson wasn't paying attention to her. He was looking over his shoulder.

"I'm done pretending to be a singer. It's your turn!"

"OKAY! SEE YOU!" Just like that, she was gone, bothering someone else. Jackson and I continued our path to the elevator. When the doors opened, we stepped inside. Jackson pushed both the 8th floor and the 12th floor buttons.

"I will let you sleep alone tonight, Ms. Bashir."

"Really?!? Why?"

"Because I paid for a room and I would like to sleep in it once during this trip."

"You can sleep in it for the duration of the trip, how's that!?" I stuck my tongue out at him.

"Sweet dreams babe. I'll wake you for breakfast."

"Sweet dreams to you too. I'm sure I'll be awake already." He stepped off the elevator and walked down the hall to his room. When the elevator doors opened on my floor, I stepped off and glided to my room. When I reached, there was an envelope on the floor in front of my door. I reached down and picked it up. There was a note inside. "Make sure you know who you are dealing with." That's all it said and there was no signature. Freaky. I folded the paper and placed it in my clutch. I walked through the door and undressed. I had no idea what that note meant and I wasn't going to wrack my brain about it right now. I was too tired. I got in the bed and slept like a fat, breastfed baby. There was a knock at my door the next morning. I was asleep, so it took me a moment to wake up and realize where I was. I finally made it to the door. It was Jackson and he was pushing a cart.

"So, you work in the hotel now?" I stepped aside and let him in.

"Good morning beautiful! I attacked a server in the hallway and took his cart."

"If there's no coffee on that cart, get out!" He laughed. He was dressed already. Not for the party but for the day. He was wearing a pair of skinny khakis and a thin white tee shirt. I wanted to jump him right there, but I regained control.

"Of course, there's coffee. There's also pancakes, bacon and cantaloupe."

"Sounds like the perfect Sara/Jackson breakfast. Shall we dine outside?"

"Oh, we shall." We walked outside and sat on the balcony. The weather was perfect! Once we finished eating, I rolled a blunt.

"Do you travel with weed or did you find that here?"

"If I tell you, I'd have to kill you!" I winked at him. "Have you ever smoked?"

"Never. Not even a cigarette." He paused and looked over his shoulder. "Ok, I tried weed once when I was in high school. My dad could smell it on me when I got home. He beat me for 2 days."

"Oh! That's unfortunate!"

"Let me hit that!" I tilted my head and looked at him over my shades; this pair was huge and round. They literally covered my entire face.

"I will not be responsible for you having a fit or becoming addicted." I put the blunt in the ashtray on the table that sat between us.

"If you pick it up and smoke it on your own, you're on your own." I laughed. He picked it up, lit it and puffed.

"Aww man! That felt great!"

"You sure you only tried it once? You look like you know what you're do-." Before I could finish that sentence, Dr. I want to smoke with my girlfriend, choked. I laughed hard!

"Would you like some water?"

"Na, I'm good." He was wheezing and giggling at the same time. He handed the blunt back to me. I finished it while we sat and talked.

"There was a note under my door when I got in last night."

"Under what door?" I laughed.

"You're that high already!? My hotel room door, silly face!"

"Let me see." I went inside, grabbed the clutch and took the note out. I went back outside and handed it to Jackson. He read and refolded it and handed it back to me.

"Hmm, that's weird." Those were the only words spoken about the note. I wondered, for a moment, if he knew who sent it, but I couldn't be bothered. I went inside and got dressed. Jackson and I toured the art deco district. I was super excited. I loved old architecture and I wanted some ideas for the office building. It needed some renovation. I knew I could replace boring doorways with elaborate ones. We toured the older part of the city for most of the afternoon. The structures were amazing, electrifying. I couldn't believe I was in Miami. I was hoping there were art deco stores around so I could've made an art purchase, but there weren't. I took pictures and made a note to do some extensive research when I returned to Connecticut. I needed some of that artwork! Jackson was a gentleman. Art was not his thing, but he was quiet and allowed me to gawk as we walked. He said he enjoyed seeing me enjoy things that I loved.

"You get so excited about things that you love and I love to see that look on your face. We can do whatever you want, whenever you want."

How did I get this lucky? Was I lucky? In all honesty, I knew it was temporary and I couldn't help but wonder what was I going to do when it ended? Was I going to ever find another man like Jackson? Is there anyone else on the planet that I can mesh well with and that will love me for who I really am? It was hard to believe there could be, because it took me nearly 33 years to find Jackson. Why is he married? Why didn't I say no when he first asked me to dinner? Had I said no and still come to the party, would I have met him? Would he be down here if he didn't meet me? He said he never attended an Avery party. I had been going to Avery parties for years, at least 6, and I never saw Jackson. Even though I wasn't looking for a man period, I would've remembered his eyes. His eyes were unique. I had never seen a blue eye like the blue eyes that Jackson had. They were rich in blue color; bright on the outside and husky in the middle. They brightened when he wore bright colors and they darkened when he wore dark colors. They magnified when he got excited and they toned themselves down when he became sad. I would've remember those eyes. I had to stop thinking so much and just live since that was what he asked me to do, even though the mystery of him was killing me. We got back to the hotel a little after 3pm. The party started at 6. It was a red, white and blue affair, so the guests were asked to wear one or all 3 colors. Jackson went to his room and I went to mine. We decided we would meet at the party. I needed a nap. Jackson was wide awake. I'm not sure how. I laid down for 35 minutes. It was the best nap ever! I rose and approached the mini bar in my room. I made myself a vodka tonic and got ready. I wore makeup this evening; not too much, just a little mascara and I covered my lips in red lipstick. "I should wear lipstick more often" I looked in the mirror with such awe. I couldn't believe who I was seeing. It made me giggle. I was wearing a white jumpsuit. This one was cut very low in the front; V shape. It was form fitted with long sleeves. It was "separated" with a wide red leather belt. It was skinny legged and I was wearing a pair of red Louboutin stilettos. I brushed all my hair up to the top of my head and secured it into a bun. "My bun is poppin!" Self-confidence was the only confidence one needed. I put on a watch with a blue band, a pair of sapphire earrings and a sapphire around my neck. There was my red, white and blue, all in one outfit; and I didn't have to shop for it. These items were already in my wardrobe. I walked out of the hotel and down to the beach. The party space was setup and it was beautiful. They laid a makeshift hard wood floor and put it together on the sand. There was enough space to dance. There were round, 2 person tables all around the perimeter of the makeshift floor. There were longer, rectangular shaped tables in various locations; they were the food tables. I saw one with meat and cheese, one with fruit, one with fresh carved pork, a bread table, a salad bar, a fresh sushi bar, and a granola bar. There were 3 bars and a ton of waitresses wearing practically nothing, carrying trays of champagne glasses. I was impressed. Avery out did himself this year. The guests were gathering and I grabbed a drink and a piece of pork. I didn't really recognize anyone, but that was the point of the party. I looked up and saw Avery sitting at a table. He was talking to Jackson.

"Avery man...it's been too long!"
"Yea. If you didn't show up tonight, I was going right to your doorstep when I returned home. What's going on with you man?!"
"Not much. You know me, I'm doing my doctor thing, running my businesses. How's everything with you? This party is, wow! You must've made good money this year." I approached Jackson and Avery. I had to say hello.
"Avery Anderson! Amazing party! You must've made serious cheddar last year!"
"What the hell!? Sara! It's so good to see you!" Avery hugged me and kissed me on my cheek. Jackson looked at me and licked his lips.
"Oh, I'm being rude. Sara Bashir, Jackson Ellis." I smiled.
"We know each other Avery. Hey Dr. looks good in blue." Jackson blushed.
"Uh, yes. I took your financial advice and called Bradley & Associates. I made an appointment and when I walked in, this Egyptian goddess assisted me."

"Egyptian goddess?! I mean, yes, she's beautiful, but you were supposed to get assistance with your finances, not find a girlfriend."

"Sara, please pardon Avery's rudeness." Jackson seemed annoyed by Avery's tone.

"Sara and I are friends. We go back. Not as far back as you and I, but she knows my comments are harmless. She's not offended."

"I'm not...at all. Avery knows I can touch a button and detonate his entire company." We laughed in unison. Avery took a step back.

"Did you two fall in love? What am I missing here?"

"You're not missing a damn thing, apparently."

"SARA! Sara Bashir! Is that you!?!"

I turned around and saw Avery's sister Megan walking toward me. I assisted Megan with her finances after I assisted Avery. Her company was very small and only required my assistance per diem. I hadn't seen her in years. I stepped away from the guys and greeted her with a hug. She and I walked in a separate direction from them and had our own conversation. We stayed within eyesight of the guys, but I couldn't hear what was being said.

"So, Jackson, how serious have you gotten with Sara?"

"Why does it concern you?"

"It's been years since we spoke...I tried to help... and showed love to you and I haven't heard from you in over a year. You never come to my 4th of July parties and then when you show up... Listen, I'm glad you came, and I love you man, you're my best friend. We grew up together. There's a picture of us from the 3rd grade on the mantelpiece in my home, but you are being vague on a new level right now."

"Avery. I met Sara in a business setting. She completed my project and I asked her out on a date 6 months later. It wasn't planned, but we went from 0-1000 in milliseconds and she is the best thing that has ever happened to me. I'm happy brother."

"Mazel tov! Really, I'm glad that you're happy. Sara is a good friend of mine and her best interest means a lot to me. If she is unstable, my company affairs are at risk; believe it or not; yours too. We must make sure she remains stress free."

"Do you think I'm not in her best interest?"

"You're not if you're lying to her."

"I'm not lying to her. She knows I have a family."

"Does she KNOW your family situation?"

"Not exactly. Listen. I will tell her what she needs to know when I think she needs to know it. I love her, I need her; but I must make sure it's real. You know?"

"I hear you brother. I'm not saying a word. My loyalty is to you first, but I am loyal to her also. I'm having a Christmas party this year. I will be inviting you both; with individual invites, of course. If she doesn't know by then, I will tell her."

"No need for threats. Oh, that reminds me. Someone slipped a note under the door in her hotel. Was it you?"

"No."

"Hmm, ok. It's strange. Anyway...look at her. She's beautiful."

"Yea, she is."

Jackson made his way to me and asked to dance. We walked out to the dance floor while Ordinary People was playing. The DJ was exceptional! He kept the hits playing all night and we danced for hours! It was a perfect evening. Around 9pm, Avery took a microphone from the DJ and walked to the center of the faux floor. A light shinned bright on him as he gathered everyone's attention. "Good evening. I'm not putting you all out; I just want to say a few words before I get too drunk." The crowd laughed. "I throw these parties every year because I want to give all of my friends a chance to gather and enjoy eating and drinking my money." The crowd laughed some more. "In all seriousness, I appreciate every single person under the sound of my voice. I have benefitted from everyone in this room, at some point in my life and this is my way of saying Thank you. Thank you for coming. I hope everyone is having a good time. There will be fireworks at 9:30; oh, and don't be shy, please eat all the food and drink all the liquor! Cheers!"

"CHEERS!" The crowd roared. The DJ played "We will rock you!" Everyone was shouting and cheering. Jackson grabbed my hand and led me for a walk. We walked down the beach, away from the party. Since we were walking on sand, I stopped to take off my shoes. He offered to carry them. I giggled.

"Whew! I wanted a moment with you, away from the crowd. Is that ok?"

"Absolutely."

"How's Megan?"

"She's Megan. She hasn't changed a bit, but I like her."

"I haven't seen her in ages. I almost didn't recognize her when I first got here."

"How's Avery? I haven't had a chance to speak to him. He's Mr. Social butterfly this evening." Jackson smiled and huffed slightly.

"Avery is Avery. I haven't seen him in well over a year and he reamed me about it."

"As he should, how do you not see your best friend in a year?"

"Ha! I know it's hard for you to fathom, since you see your best friends almost every day, but there's no real reason; we're both busy as all." Jackson hung his head a bit, as if there was more to this story. I wish I knew what he and Avery were really speaking about.

"I guess. You guys also live in different parts of the state. I can understand that. I don't see Hosni that often because he lives in Boston."

"Exactly, you understand."

"Somewhat." We stopped walking and I was staring up at the sky. It was a clear evening. The moon was full. Usually when there's a full moon, things happen. Not good or bad things, just things; things out of the ordinary. I had a feeling tonight was going to be one of those nights. Jackson got quiet. I looked over my shoulder and he was sitting in the sand. He had a sad look on his face, while he was fumbling with a shell.

"What ya thinking about?" I asked as I was taking a seat next to him.

"Oh, nothing babe. I'm fine." He looked at his watch. "Let's head back so we can watch the fireworks."

We got back to the party location just in time. The venue had been changed slightly. The staff removed all the tables and replaced them with 2-person wicker chairs; love seats. Jackson and I took a seat on one. People were beginning to fill into the seats around us, and the wait staff was walking around with dessert.

"Would you care for dessert?"

A waitress walked over to us. She was carrying a tray with a piece of tiramisu, a piece of chocolate cake, a piece of red velvet cake, apple pie, and a piece of festive cake. It was red, white and blue. I opted for tiramisu and Jackson took chocolate cake. A waiter followed the waitress. His tray had glasses of champagne. We each took one. We sat there with our dessert and our champagne, watching the fireworks. It was magical. I couldn't have been happier. The firework show lasted a little over an hour. I was getting tired, so it was a good thing that the party was winding down. I spotted Avery and he was finally standing alone.

"Wow. I thought I wasn't gonna get a chance to speak to you this evening. Hey man!"

"Sara! What's up woman!? Are you enjoying yourself?"

"I am, I am. Thank you for inviting me. I appreciate it."

"I appreciate you coming. I also appreciate you being the reason Jackson came. It sounds sucky, but I think if it weren't for you, he wouldn't be here."

"Oh? Why is that?"

"Well you know, Jackson is weird; to me. He may be normal to you but he's weird with me. He's never been to any of my parties. He always squealed about them being boat rides. He hates boats, so I decided this year to do something different, and boom, here's Jackson!"

"See, silly, it's not me. Your venue is the reason why he came."

"No, I wish you knew; I'm sure you are the reason he's here. Thank you. I appreciate it. I missed my best friend. I was his best man at his wedding you know?"

"I knew you were close, but I didn't know that."

"Yup. I liked, like his wife."

"Hey. What are you guys talking about?"

UGH, the one time I did not want to see Jackson. I swore I was going to get something good out of Avery.

"Oh, I was thanking Sara for you being at my party brother."

"What?"

"He swears that I am the reason why you finally made it to a party. I told him it's because he changed the venue."

"Exactly. You know I hate boats, brother. Anyway, Sara, may I walk you to your room?"

Jackson was standing next to me and cuffed my ass in his hand.

"Sure. Hey Ave, I'll catch you later."

"Good night guys."

Jackson put his arm around my waist and pulled me close to him while we were walking back to our hotel. I was trying not to think about my conversation with Avery, but I couldn't help it. Jackson was becoming more and more of a mystery to me and I was getting suspicious. I didn't want to ruin our otherwise wonderful trip with insipid questions. I left it alone. I was hoping by the time we got home, I would be so busy that it wouldn't take up space in my mind. We made it back to the hotel, into the lobby and to the elevator doors. Jackson pushed the up button and the doors opened immediately, as if they knew we were ready to go up.

"My room or yours?" He was so sexy.

"Yours. Since I don't get to see your house."

That was a low blow; it knew it, he knew it.

"I'll let that remark slide because I am pretty sure you're drunk." He pushed 8.

"I am drunk. But that doesn't change the fact tha-."

Before I could finish speaking, Jackson grabbed and kissed me. He knew how to shut me up and change a subject. If this relationship continued past the summer, that had to change. The doors opened on the 8ᵗʰ floor. Jackson picked me up and carried me to his room. He swiped his key card and walked us inside. His room appeared to be bigger than mine. I was jealous. Jackson picked me up and sat down on the bed. I was straddled on his lap. I stood and unlatched my belt buckle. I slowly peeled myself out of the jumpsuit and let it hit the ground. I bent down and kissed him, turned around and walked toward the bathroom.

"Wait. Where ya going babe?"

"Shower. I'm sweaty, are you coming or are you gonna sit there and wait until I'm done?"

Jackson jumped up and followed me to the bathroom. He was undressing as he walked. I made it to the bathroom, turned on the shower and hopped in. The water felt so crisp and clean running down my back. Jackson climbed in behind me.

"You are so beautiful." He cuffed my face and kissed me softly. The water was running down our faces while we kissed passionately. He ran his hand up my thigh and placed two fingers inside of me. I moaned through the kisses and he pushed them in further. The motion became consistent and my moans got louder. He whispered in my ear. "Cum for me babe." I moaned louder. He penetrated with his fingers deeper. I was in pure bliss. I couldn't contain myself anymore. "OH BABE, I'm CUMMING!" But he didn't stop there. He picked me up and now his erection was inside of me. He was pumping me deeply and quickly. It was so intense. I could feel the cum building up inside of me and it kept gushing out. I moaned and yelled over and over. "Oh, babe!!!" He stopped and stepped out of the shower. He turned me around and I put my hands on the sink. He inserted himself from behind and began to pump me full of him again. "Oh! Babe, spank me!" And he did. He smacked my ass repeatedly while he was pumping me in a quick, consistent motion. We both climaxed at the same time. He smacked my ass one more time while I walked out of the bathroom past him.

"Babe, you ok?"

"You sexed me to sleep and that's where I'm going."

I got in his bed and went to sleep; with a smile on my face. I woke up in Jackson's arms. He was so sexy. His arms were so strong and powerful. I daydreamed of him holding me up against a wall, penetrating me. I got excited. I began kissing his neck and down his chest. He squirmed and began waking up.

"Mmm, good morning."

He moaned. I continued kissing him; I never broke my stride, not even to answer him. He was nude so it made easy for me to grab him. I did. With my mouth. I ingested him deeply and sucked quickly and swiftly. My mouth salivated intensely. He moaned, loudly. I loved hearing him moan and scream my name. I couldn't wait for him to say my name. I was too excited. I quickly climbed on his lap and rode him swiftly.

"Oh Sara! You ride me so well, mama. You are amazing!" I cuffed his face and kissed him. He sat up and I repositioned myself so my legs were now around his back. He was deep inside of me. I could feel his penis in the pit of my stomach. I cried out. I was so overwhelmed with emotion, I cried lightly.

"Oh babe. I hope those are tears of joy."

"Ah yes babe! I'm so happy. You feel so good inside me."

"Oooooh babe! I love you baby. I love you so much!!"

I continued my stride and Jackson broke it. He threw me down on my back and kissed my body. He cuffed a breast and put it in his mouth. He cuffed the other one with his hand. Immediately, he sucked one nipple and vigorously fondled the other. It felt so good. He kissed down my stomach and down toward my clitoris. He sucked gently and I cried out in excitement. He continued licking and sucking me. I was holding his head and screaming out with excitement as I climaxed. He rose from below my stomach and laid his body on top of mine. I could feel his erection drag up my leg. He inserted himself and I cried out again. This time his stride was consistent and slow. I thought I was going to die. He was amazing! I couldn't contain myself. The cum escaped my body repeatedly. I screamed and cried and he held my body in his arms while I shook with excitement; with contentment; with joy. I was 100% in love with this man and my body loved him too. We were made for each other.

"We have an excellent sex life. Would you agree?" I was worn out and he wanted to talk...

"I definitely agree. It's surreal." I was whispering.

"I mean it when I tell you that I love you. Do you believe me?"

"I must take your word for it, yes?"

"I hope you would take my word for it. You truly are amazing and you really did save my life. There's more to me than you know. I trust that I can trust you and you can trust me. Your body tells me you trust me. I can't imagine you would express yourself in such a way if I didn't mean something to you. You may not be ready to tell me you love me, but I feel it. It's there."

He was right about all of that. I didn't want to tell him that though. I wanted to continue trying to play hard to get. It wasn't working. He really did have a spell on me. I wanted to know everything about him. I wanted to know his dark secrets and his aspirations. I also wanted to have sex with him constantly. I wanted his tongue between my legs again, so I climbed on his chest and turned my body around. I sat my vagina in his face and he moaned. He immediately began sucking my clit and I immediately began to wail. He licked and sucked in a constant motion. I was so excited. He was so excited. I adjusted a final time and slid my lips down his shaft. He moaned out. I sucked. He sucked. We both sucked each other. He tasted so good. We both climaxed together. I rolled over and Jackson began rubbing my feet; they were now in his face.

"Ma'am. I hate to be the mood breaker, but what time is your flight?"

"Oh! It's at 2pm. What time is it?"

"Oh, you have time. It's 9:40."

"Ok. Good. I need one more round before I go back to my room. I'm addicted to you."

Jackson laughed. He grabbed me, cuffed my face and kissed me. This time he was gentle with me. He caressed and kissed me softly. He was handling me with such care and concern. He slid easier into me this time. I moaned. He kissed and sucked my ear.

"I want to whisper to you; while I'm digging deep inside of you. Your body feels like pure gold. I want you to cum for me, baby. Cum for me."

A tear slowly fell down my face. I was sprung. I couldn't have enough of this man. I loved the way he made me cum. No one had done that for me; not like that. I was in love. That was the only way I could describe it. I sprinted, up the steps to my hotel room. I couldn't be bothered waiting for the elevator. It was almost 12:30. I had to get to the airport ASAP!

When I reached my door, there was another envelope. "Again?!" I really didn't have time to be slowed down by a mystical messenger, so I threw the envelope in my duffle and proceeded packing my belongings. I had stuff all over the room, but I got it all cleaned up in record time. "12:47. Nice!" I proceeded out of the door, to the elevator and down to the lobby.

"Oh Sara, I'm glad I caught you." It was Avery.
"What's up man?"
"Are you headed to the airport?"
"I am."
"Here, let's take my car. My flight is at 2:30." We walked outside and hopped in a limo.
"Is Jackson gone already?"
"I'm not sure. We didn't fly together."
"Oh. Is he keeping you at arm's length?"
"Possibly; I'm not sure."
"Are you having second thoughts?"
"Not exactly. I just feel as if there is something he isn't telling me."
"I'm sure there is, but when/if you find out what it is, be patient and understanding. Jackson is very vague with people."
"Are you saying I should be grateful for what I already know about him?"
"I'm saying." Avery's eyes shifted. "Oh. I almost forgot. Here's your thank you gift." He handed me an envelope.
"What's with all the envelopes, Ave?"
"Huh? What do you mean?"
"There was an envelope at my door this am. Was that from you?"
"Nope, this is the only envelope I'm handing out. Where's the other one?"
"Oh, I tossed it in my big bag. I guess I'll open it when I reach home."
"Jackson mentioned you received a note?"
"Yea, was that from you?"
"It wasn't, but when you get home and open the envelope, call me. I may have an idea what's going on."

Everything was eerie, but whatever, I couldn't do anything about it right then. We arrived at the airport. The driver parked the limo in the unloading zone, opened the doors and let us climb out. He walked around to the rear of the car, opened the trunk and put our luggage on a carry cart. Avery wasn't done traveling. His birthday was the following week, so he decided to take a trip to the Bahamas. He said he had a native hottie waiting for him in the sun. I laughed. "Whatever helps you sleep at night!" We laughed together. He hugged me and I walked away. It felt like I was only in the airport for minutes before my flight was called to board. I stepped on the plane and realized that I didn't have enough time to get intoxicated before this flight. As the stewardess approached with the drink cart, I asked her for 2 drinks.

"Flying freaks me out. I didn't have time to sit at the bar." She reached in the cart and handed me 2 small bottles of vodka. She put ice in a cup and asked if I wanted juice. I opted for cranberry, even though I knew I wasn't going to mix my liquor with it. I relaxed and fell asleep while the plane traveled back to reality. That's how it felt when I was on vacation and then had to go back home. It wasn't home, it was reality. I wondered what type of foolishness was going to greet me when I got home. I had to put my game face on this week. I couldn't allow myself to fall into the pit of love and lust. I had to fight my Jackson temptations off and focus. I was a big-time business owner now. I was embarking on the biggest business venture of my entire career. When the flight landed, I stepped off and made my way to baggage claim. My phone was vibrating in my bag. I finally dug it out and I was receiving text messages.

Javier: Hey girl. Let me know when you land. I'm here to pick you up.
Javier: I'm in the pickup line outside of your gate. Whenever you are ready…
Jax: Hello beautiful. Did you land yet?
I gathered my bags and walked outside. It was beginning to drizzle. I approached Javier's car and to my surprise, he had Arianna and Daniela with him.

"Heyyyyyyyy girllll!!!" They all bellowed together.
"Hiiii guysss!! What a nice surprise!"
"I hope you're hungry."
"I am and slightly inebriated."
"Intoxicated flight?" Daniela knew me well. I smiled.
"So, we have to hear all about the trip. How was this year's party?"
"The party was very nice. Avery out did himself. I should get you all together so you can meet. You must make it on the invite list."
"I googled him, Avery McBride, he's well established, and he's single, apparently. How come you never mentioned him as a potential husband

for me?" Arianna had been expecting me to find her a suitor since her last relationship flopped.

"I never mentioned him because as long as I've known him, he never seemed like he was interested in settling down. He's often off to play with a 'hottie' as he calls them."

"I'm a hottie."

"Aw you are honey, but she means, well, he means, sluts, and you are definitely not a slut."

Javier pretty much hit the nail on the head with that comment. I loved having a gay friend. He was the best of both worlds; male perspective but understood a female point of view. I giggled.

"What are you laughing at over there?"

"Nothing, that was just a funny statement. What are we eating? I'm famished."

"Famished? You're embellishing."

"Could be."

"There's a new tapas bar near my house. Want to try it out?"

Javier lived in an awesome section of Westchester County. I did a great job when I selected the location when I originally lived here. It was suburban, yet city. A nice, eclectic blend of people and food. I was glad I kept that place. Javier loved it up here. He was born and raised in North Carolina. He moved here from D.C. This area fit his lifestyle, his demeanor; it's classy, and professional. That's exactly what Javier was; classy and professional. I was blessed to have him as a friend. I was blessed to have all of my friends.

"Sure, I like tapas. I could go for another drink also."

I remembered that I didn't answer Jackson's text. I dug my phone out of my bag and scrolled to his text message thread.

Me: Hiiii I landed! Javier, Arianna & Daniela picked me up from the airport and now we're headed to eat tapas. Where are you?

Jax: Hey sexy lady, I was just about to call you. I am headed home. I just left the airport.

Me: Are you driving?

Jax: No. A car service is taking me.

Jax: I want to see you tonight. Am I smothering?

Me: No...you're not smothering. What did you have in mind?

Jax: Well...I never took you on the mystery date. My apologies. We can still do it but this is the last night. What do you say?

Me: I say ok! What time?
Jax: I'll pick you up at 7
Me: Ok. I'll see you then

      We arrived at the tapas restaurant and when we walked in, the place was empty. A hostess met us at the door and explained that they just opened for the evening and we were the first guests to arrive. We didn't mind. She allowed us to select our own table and we chose one in the front by a huge window. An older gentleman; a manager, walked over and opened the large window. Now our table was half inside and half outside. It was a nice setup. I liked the atmosphere. It was a darker room; dim lighting, mahogany wood floors and the tables were large and rectangular. There was artwork everywhere. I saw a few Frida Kahlo pieces hanging. There were tall plants in corners. There was a small chandelier over our table which provided sufficient lighting for reading the one page menu. We ordered 4 small plates and a pitcher of sangria. We laughed and talked. I told them about the party, but I left Jackson out of the story. I was still trying to process our time spent and I knew if I brought him up, it would bring about a dozen questions; questions I was unprepared to answer. I was getting excited about our date. I looked at my watch and it was 6:15.

"I hate to break up the party, but I have to head home."
"Whaaaat?!?"
"I have a date with Jackson."
"Ooooh la la. Are things getting serious over there?"
"I'm not sure yet. I'm just taking it day by day."
When the waitress brought the bill over, I opted to pay it. I figured I should've since I was ending the evening early and they did me the favor of picking me up at the airport. I assumed it was fine, but when I pulled my Amex out of my wallet, Daniela thought otherwise.
"Why do you always feel the need to always pick up the bill?"
"Uh, I, well I figured since I was ending the date early and you guys picked me up, it's the least I can do."
"It's not just today. It's every time we are out. You always pay. You pay for coffee, food, you buy gifts, and you are always spending your money. Do you think we're broke?"
"Uh, no, it's just what I do. It's what I've always done. I grew up like this. When I go out with my parents and Hosni, it's 20 minutes back and forth of who's paying and who's not. It's just what I do. I pay. I will gladly place

my American Express card back in my wallet if you deem it necessary. I swiped it enough this past weekend anyway."

"Yes. I would like to pay for this meal, don't worry about the pickup. We wanted to do that."

Javier drove like a bat out of hell. He got me home with minutes to spare. I emptied my mailbox when I approached the front door. It was a bunch of nonsense fliers and such. Although, I did notice one from CVS. "Paper towels are on sale." I proceeded into the house and kind of wished I had a man and a child to greet me at the door. I walked around just to make sure everything was where I left it. It was. I walked into my master suite, freshened up and changed my clothes. I remember Jax telling me to be comfortable when this date was supposed to happen originally. I walked into the closet and pulled out a cotton, polo dress. It was fitted and stopped just above my knee. It was white and the polo horse in the corner was blue. I laced up a pair of blue and white Chuck Taylor's and proceeded down the steps toward my front door. Jackson was pulling into the driveway as I was walking out of the house. This time, he was driving a Porsche Cayenne.

"Hello again." He said with a huge smile. He stepped out of the car, walked around to the other side and opened the passenger door for me. "Hello; thank you." When I got in, a song was playing that I never heard. I thought I knew every song ever written. A beautiful sultry voice belted out notes in perfect pitch.

> "What is love? If you're not here with me?
> "What is love? If it's not guaranteed?
> "What is love? If just ups and leaves?

"This song is beautiful. Who is it?"

"Someone new, I assume. I've never heard of her. This is satellite radio. You look nice and comfortable; I'm glad you remembered." I smiled.

"I remember everything." We rode for approximately 25 minutes. Jackson drove as smooth as he was. It could've also been the fine engineering of his SUV. "I should've gotten the Cayenne diesel instead of the Touareg TDI."

"Essentially you did. You just spent $14K less than I did."

"Probably more like $20K less."

"You can't out do me."

"I can match you." Jackson laughed. The laughter came from his gut. I burst out in laughter also.

"Your laughter is contagious."

"So, when you're laughing, it's because my laughter made you laugh? Am I in fact not funny?" At this point he was practically crying because he was laughing so hard.

"It's all funny. You, the laugh." I couldn't contain my laughter. It hurt.

"Stop! Stop! I'm gonna tinkle!"

"TINKLE!?!?! What the hell is that!?!" Now he was hysterical.

"Tinkle, you know; wee wee."

"Oh!! You mean pee? Piss? You're laughing so hard, ya gonna piss!?" His accent was so sexy; He made the word 'piss' sound sexy.

"Ok. Ok. I'll stop. I won't tease you and your 'tinkle'".

We arrived at a park; hopped out of the truck and walked toward an entrance. It was a carnival; how did he know I liked carnivals? My eyes lit up as we walked around. We walked over to a ticket booth and Jackson handed a kid a $5 bill. He handed him a roll of tickets. Thus, began our carnival date. We played games and won prizes. We ate corn dogs and funnel cake and purchased candy apples.

"Wanna get on the Ferris wheel?" I remember being a kid and thinking Ferris wheels were boring. As I got older, I thought differently.

"Sure."

We walked up to the Ferris wheel and we were one of maybe 3 couples attempting to ride. We left our souvenirs down below on the deck of the Ferris wheel and climbed into a 2-person carriage.

"It turned out to be a nice night. It was sprinkling when I got off the plane."

"Yea. I was worried that we were going to miss this."

"How did you hear about this place?"

"Oh, through friends. I used to come here every year. Then I got busy and missed a year and once you miss one, it's hard to get back on track."

"Did you bring your kids here?"

"Only once. Turns out my kids don't like carnivals or amusement parks. If it wasn't for the eyes, I wouldn't think they were mine." He giggled. "May I see a picture?"

"I wish I had one." Jackson hung his head. I assumed that was my queue to change the subject and I did.

"This was the perfect way to end the perfect weekend. Thank you, Dr. I amaze Sara daily." He laughed.

"I appreciate having you to spend perfect weekends with."

Our Ferris wheel ride came to an end. It was almost 10 when we headed toward the exit. I was in awe of the amazing things that were happening thus far, but I had to get ready for my work week. As badly as I wanted Jackson to spend the night with me, I decided against it because I really needed sleep. Not 'fucked you to sleep' sleep, but real sleep.

"Thank you, Jax. It was a pleasure."

"The pleasure was all mine, Ms. Bashir. Are you going to be ok to sleep alone?"

"Yes. I think I can manage."

Jackson kissed me on my cheek and I got out of the car. He waited until I was inside before he drove away. I sat my souvenirs on the table in the living room and headed to the kitchen. I ate so much crap this weekend, so I brewed a cup of cleansing tea. I took my cup, picked up the souvenirs and headed upstairs. "I need to unpack". I walked into my closet and placed my duffle on the dresser that sat in the middle of the room. It was more like an island for a closet. It was very long and had multiple drawers. I unzipped the bag and the envelope was right on top. That reminds me. I never opened the one that Avery handed me. I went back in to the bedroom and opened my handbag. I took the envelope and my cell phone out, just in case I needed to call Avery. The envelope that Avery handed me contained a thank you card and gift card to Nordstrom. "Aw that's nice." Now the moment of truth; to open the mystery envelope from the mystery sender.

"ASK HIM QUESTIONS"

Immediately I folded the paper up. I grabbed the clutch that I carried the night I found the other note and pulled it out. The handwriting appeared to be the same. Was it really or did I want it to be? I folded them up, walked out of the closet, out of the room and down the hall to my office. I opened the desk drawer and put the notes inside. As I was walking down the hall, I could hear my house phone ringing.

"Hello."

"You travel and return and not once do you call your mother. Who are you?"

"Hi mama! I'm sorry. How are you?"

"I am fine now that I know you are breathing. What's going on, woman, did you find a man?!?"

"Huh?"

"That is the only excuse for your lack of memory. A man, preferably a good looking one, I need cute grandkids. Hosni's children are beginning to look like aliens. That's because Monica is funny looking!" As mean as it was, I had to admit it was funny. I laughed out loud.

"Ma! That's not nice! Don't talk about people's children?"

"Why not? The superstition is that if you talk about people's children, your children will be ugly. Well mine are grown and gorgeous."

"Tis true. So, what's up woman?! How was your weekend?"

"It was ok. Your father and I went car shopping."

"Oh really? What did you look at?"

"We went to BMW store in Greenwich. I drove 750LI"

"Ma! You're 4'10. Why do you need a 750LI?"

"Have you seen it? It's nice!!" Not sure why, but she whispered; I laughed.

"Ok ma. If that's what you like."

"Well we haven't decided yet. Do you own a BMW?"

"I do. I have an M4 convertible."

"Oh. Why didn't I know that?"

"Not sure ma. So, Ma, I did meet someone. I met him months ago. I didn't say anything because I wasn't sure what it was or where it was headed. But I think I'm in love with him. He's good to me."

"IS HE GOOD LOOKING!?! Because if he's not, love doesn't matter. Ok, I don't really mean that, but for the love of God!"

"WOMAN!?! Focus!"

"Not until you answer the question."

"Yes. He's beautiful. Tall, slim figure, big arms, blue eyes, dark hair. He's a dream."

"Did you have sex yet?"

"MA!"

"You're 33. You think I don't know you have sex!?"

"OH, MY GOD! I cannot believe you right now."

"What!? You are your father's minion. I bet you have his sex drive. The man is almost 75 years old and still horny as when he was 30."

"Good night, Annabelle Bashir. I cannot deal with you right now."

"I love you. Listen to your heart; but also pay attention to your brain; your intuition. Those things have to tell you yes. If there is hesitation, there could be a problem. I am sure you will be fine. When you're ready, I need to meet Mr. Wonderful."

"I love you too, ma. Thank you. Oh, and he's Dr. Wonderful"
I smiled and hung up the phone.

Chapter 7

I woke up refreshed and ready to embark on my new journey as President and CEO of Bradley & Associates. I went to the kitchen, put on a pot of coffee and turned on the morning news. There was some political non-sense on the screen so, I proceeded with my morning routine. I made a cup of coffee and headed back upstairs to take a shower. It seemed to be a nice day out; I didn't go outside, but the windows in my bed room were open and I could feel a warm breeze. I stood in the closet trying to decide what type of statement I was going to make today. It was summer time and I liked to wear white in the summer, so I put on a white skirt suit and a pair of nude pumps. I had time to do my hair, so I spiral curled it and let it hang to my shoulders. I grabbed a nude leather medicine style handbag off the shelf and loaded it with my crap. I called a car service. Why not pull up like a CEO? When the car arrived at my house, I walked outside and the driver opened the rear passenger side door. I slid in. I scribbled a few notes on a piece of paper that I found in my bag. I had to address the entire company and I had a few points I needed to touch on. When the car pulled up in front of the office building that was officially mine, I exhaled. I said a quick prayer; mainly of thanks and got out of the car. As I walked through the building doors, people waved and said hello. I heard various snickers as I walked through the halls. Nothing bad, just a lot of "there she is." "That's her." I walked through the large glass doors that opened into the receptionist area of Bradley & Associates.

"Welcome back, Sara." Jenna was sitting at her post with a smile as usual. I liked Jenna. I reviewed her pay plan and gave her a raise.
"Thank you. Good morning Jenna."
"The entire company is in the conference room awaiting your arrival; whenever you're ready ma'am."
"Thanks Jenna. Do me a favor, please, drop the ma'am."
The office looked fantastic. I walked down the long corridor and all the plants and flowers had been replenished. I walked to what used to be my office. It was empty because they moved my stuff to the bigger office at the other end of the hallway. I walked the long way around all the offices and cubicles. I was admiring what was mine. I also made mental notes of things I wanted to change. As I approached the glass doors that led to my office, I noticed a gold plaque on the wall opposite the door.
SARA BASHIR

PRESIDENT AND CEO

      I admitted, that looked pretty good. My cell phone was in my hand, so I snapped a picture and sent it as a picture message to my mom, Jax, Hosni, Arianna, Daniela and Javier. Immediately, I received responses.
Jax: CONGRATS BEAUTIFUL!! Knock 'em dead!"
Javier: Yaass!!! When's the celebration!?!?
Daniela: OMG! That looks so good! Congrats girl! I'm proud of you.
Mom: Aww my baby, I am proud. I cannot wait to show your father.

Hosni: (clapping hands) we're coming there this weekend, btw. See you Saturday!

      Arianna didn't respond. It was early on a Monday; I was willing to bet she was still asleep. I placed my cell on the hostler on my desk, grabbed my iPad and proceeded down the hall to the conference room. When I opened the door, everyone stood. As I descended the ramp, everyone clapped. I smiled. It felt good being there I climbed 4 steps and stood onto a stage, at a podium. I adjusted the microphone and spoke.

"Thank you. Thank you. Good morning everyone."
"GOOD MORNING SARA" The crowd roared. There was at least 250 people in the room. I blushed.
"Well there goes my introducing myself." They laughed. "Just in case, my name is Sara Bashir. I am the new president and CEO of Bradley & Associates. Thank you all for being here bright and early this morning. Since I requested your presence early, you all are dismissed early today, if all projects are completed. I don't plan on changing much about the way we do business. I don't think many changes are needed. Everyone in here is diligent and hard working. I appreciate that. I looked at finances; revenue, and everyone is headed in the right direction. I think we successfully weeded out the weak and weary over the years. However, I am open to suggestions. I have an open-door policy; if my door is open, you are welcome to come in and chat. I want to know all of you individually. I will be sitting with everyone, one on one and we are going to chat. What are your goals? What are your fears? What do you need help with? If you don't have any goals, or any fears and if you think you don't need any help, this is no longer the place for you. No one is perfect. I am not perfect. I have, however, mastered this industry; hence why I stand before you today. I want to help make you presidential material. This is

the beginning of our next quarter. We must hit the ground running and continue our path to success. The financial world is constantly changing. You must be abreast with what is going on. Read articles. Do research. Maximize your potential. This way your client's potential is maximized. The more money they make, the more money you make; so, on and so forth. We are the number one company in financial advising. We are a household name. That didn't happen overnight and it didn't happen with lazy people. Let's continue great things! I am opening the floor for questions. Please raise your hand. When I address you, please stand and give me your name prior to asking your question. Any questions? Yes, you sir." I pointed to a gentleman on the front row.

"Hello. I am Jason Wallace. Are you going to become a sole overseer or are you going to continue working with your book of business?"
"Hello Jason." I typed his name and his question on the iPad in front of me. "I am going to continue working with my current clients. I will no longer be taking on new clients." I pointed to another hand that shot up.
"Hello. I am Melissa Beddingfield. I am new to the company. This is my 3rd week. What is going to happen with my training schedule?"
"Hello Melissa. What department are you in?"
"New accounts."
"Melissa, I'm not sure if you realize what type of company we are. Training never ends. You will have a training schedule for the duration of your time spent here. We want to make sure that our advisors are well equipped; well versed. Your current training schedule will continue as is."
One more front row hand shot up. It was Freddy.
"Why don't you explain to everyone why you were chosen to stand before us as president. What did you do for the old man?!"
Immediately, I started sweating. I envisioned myself leaping off the stage and attacking Freddy. I was punching, kicking and scratching him. He was such a spoiled rotten child. I wanted to obliterate him!
"Hard work, determination and perseverance is all one needs to succeed in life. Nothing is going to be handed to us, not even our jobs. We all must work hard for it. Freddy, thank you for your arrogant question. You are officially on 60-day probation. You have 60 days to impress me, or you will be without a job. I promised your step father that I wouldn't get rid of you, but clearly you have no problem getting rid of yourself. Does anyone else have a problem with me standing before you as President of this company?"

"No!" The crowd answered. A man stood, and I pointed to him

"I am Peter Silverman. I am also in the new accounts department. I would like to say, I think it's a great thing that you are now in charge. We all have a lot to learn and I am glad that we will be learning it from you. I have been here 2 years and your name was at the top of the high earnings list every time we printed it. You have the most, new accounts to date. Freddy is just jealous." The crowd laughed.

"Thank you, Peter. Listen, I am not a brash person. I worked hard. Brian Bradley saw good in me that I didn't even see in me. I am honored to stand before you all. Anyway. I have taken enough of your time. Thank you all for coming. Happy selling and investing. Have a great day. If you need me, I am in Brian's former office and my extension is 1175."

The crowd clapped as I trotted down the steps and up the ramp. A few people patted me on my back as I passed. I was feeling too good. When I arrived back to my office, the madness of the day and my new position began. I had a ton of messages, clients that needed advising. I had financial statements piled up on my desk and the billing manager was calling asking for assistance with commissions. The day flew by! Before I knew it, it was 4:30. My desk phone rang. It was Jenna.

"Hello Sara. Your driver is here waiting for you. Did you forget you didn't drive today?"

"Oh, I sure did! Thanks. Will you let him know I will be out in 7 minutes?"

"Will do."

I was cleaning off my desk and sorting paperwork. I never took work home. I always sit in to do piles for the next day. I shut my desktop down and was closing the curtains when Freddy entered my office.

"Do you have a minute?"

"I can give you 3. Please, have a seat."

He plopped down in one the chairs opposite my chair at my desk. The chair squeaked. I rolled my eyes and thought to myself, "he better not break my chair".

"I just want you to know that I am not happy that I have to work for you now. I wanted to run this company and my mother promised me I would, but then he had other plans. I took it out on you but it's really him that I'm mad at. He raised me as his son only to dislike me in my adult years. He told me that I am spoiled and arrogant and that's why I couldn't have the company. He always compared me to you; in the privacy of our conversations. I think he wished he raised you instead of me. I must excel and do well. I must prove to him that I am not a waste. I know I cannot get the company from him, but in due time, I will get it from you."

Did he just insinuate that he was going to do good solely to "take" the company from me?

"What exactly are you saying, Freddy?"

"I am saying that this is only temporary. You will not have this office next year. I will be here because I am going to prove to my stepdad that making you president and CEO was a bad idea!" I laughed. This conversation was bringing me pure joy.

"Do you know the particulars of our contract?"

"I don't care to concern myself with it. I am just focused on running you out." I cleared my throat while I leaned back in my chair and crossed my legs. The contract was in my bag because Brian left a copy of it in his/ my desk drawer. I pulled it out and read;"Fredrick, Winslow, Harz-Bradley" I laugh at the fact that he even allowed you to have his name. "The terms of our contract regarding the company is as follows. I, Brian Michael Bradley, sign over 100% ownership of the company, Bradley & Associates, including its staff, its financial clients, its financial contracts, and the building in which it sits to Sara Karina Bashir. I, Brian Michael Bradley fully sign over 100% of the earnings and assets of this company. All bank accounts and dollar amounts are now 100% full ownership to Sara Karina Bashir. All previous debts have been settled. Sara Karina Bashir may do whatever she deems necessary for the success of what is now her company. I, Brian Michael Bradley also sign over 100% full ownership of the name Bradley & Associates. In the event, Sara Karina Bashir decides to change the name of the company, she must discuss with Brian Michael Bradley. The two will decide what is best. If I, Brian Michael Bradley, shall die, the last statement becomes void." Freddy had a blank expression on his face.

"In other words, Freddy. There is nothing you can do to me. You cannot get this company from me. Now that I know that you have a motive... you're fired! Remove yourself from my building immediately. Do not return tomorrow. If you do, I will have you arrested. You just threatened the wrong person. Man up, get up, go home and tell your mother and step father what you've just done."

He sat for a moment. Slowly, he got up and left my office. I jumped up and followed. I wanted to make sure he was leaving. He did. He walked out past the front desk. I ran back into my office, grabbed my things and headed to the door.

"Sara. You ok?" Jenna was still sitting at her post.

"Huh? Oh yea, I'm fine."

"Ok. Your driver is out front. Have a good evening."

"Thanks Jenna, you too." The driver pulled up to my front door shortly after 6pm. I had a long ass day! I took the mail out of the mailbox and walked inside. I got an envelope from Avery McBride. I opened it.

SARA BASHIR; YOU ARE CORDIALLY INVITED TO CELEBRATE THE CHRIST-MAS SEASON WITH AVERY ANDERSON MCBRIDE
12-5-15 6PM-UNTIL 2288 GRAND CHAMPION BLVD. MILFORD, CT 06460

I laughed to myself when I opened the envelope. I couldn't believe this fool was planning his Christmas party so early. I grabbed my cell and scrolled to Jackson's name in my recent call list.

"So, how was day 1 as CEO?"

"I had to fire Freddy."

"The old man's sort of kid?"

"Yup. He threatened to sabotage and take the business from me. He thought Brian still had a say so in the company's future and who's hands it was in."

"Oh wow, the nerve of that kid. Goes to show you, spoiling children isn't always a good idea."

"Eh. Anyway, I just opened an invite to a Christmas party."

"Oh. I'm still at the office. Let me guess, Avery?"

"Uh Huh." My response was muffled because I was rolling a blunt.

"What you doing? Rolling up?" How did he know?

"Am I that predictable?"

"It's not bad. I'm sure today was a bit long and a tad stressful. Isn't weed how you unwind?"

"Yea today was long and stressful. Mr. plump and spoiled started with me in this morning's meeting. I addressed the entire firm and opened the floor for questions. He stood and proceeded to ask me how did I acquire the company. I had to maintain composure, anyway, how much longer are you going to be in the office?"

"Why? Do you miss me?"

"Yup."

"I miss you too; I could be done now."

"Could you be? I could use male company."

"Oh, is that so? Should I bring food?"

"OH, MY GOD, COULD YOU!?!" Jackson laughed.

"Absolutely. What would you like?"

"I don't know, surprise me."

"Will do. I'll see you in about 30 minutes."

He hung up the phone. I took the invite and proceeded upstairs to my office. I pinned it to the pin board on the wall and walked out. I headed to the balcony in the master suite and finished my blunt. It was a nice evening. I sat there thinking about the day and the weeks ahead of me. My birthday was coming and almost immediately after, summer always ends. I thought about the note that I received at the hotel. "ASK HIM QUESTIONS". Who was taunting me and why? What kind of questions was I supposed to ask him? Was I supposed to pry about his family? Was there really something I needed to know? I picked up my cell, scrolled through the contacts and touched Avery McBride. It rang...

"Sara Bashir, to what do I owe the, oh, you must've opened the note?"

"Hey Avery. How's everything?"

"I'm good. How are you?"

"I'm good, I started as CEO and President of Bradley & Associates today."

"Congrats! I read an article about the takeover prior to my party, but I was utterly distracted and forgot to mention it when I saw you."

"Distracted, how so?"

"Oh, you know, by you, by Jackson; the sight of the 2 of you. You clearly look like you've fallen in love."

"The note said I should ask him questions. Who's the mystery mailman?"

Avery laughed. I wasn't sure what he found funny and of course I didn't ask. I looked up and saw Jackson's Cayenne pull into my driveway.

"Hey Ave, I have to go. Jackson just pulled into my driveway."

"Ok. Oh, but don't ask him any questions. If he's not ready to answer them, he won't and then you will get frustrated and it's not worth it. Trust me. He will tell you all you need to know. Hopefully he will prior to the Christmas party, otherwise I will." That was all he had to say; he hung up the phone.

"What does that mean!?" I was annoyed and muttered to myself as I stood and walked back through the house. I lightly sprinted down the stairs and to the front door. I opened it and stood, waiting for Jackson to approach me. "Hello beautiful."

"Hiiii..." I waved and stepped aside so he could walk in the house.

"I brought sushi, edamame, brown rice and sesame chicken."

"Hmm, sounds good." Jackson walked in the house and sat the bags of food on the counters in my kitchen. I walked through the kitchen and into in the wine cellar.

"Oh wow! I never noticed that."

"I don't think you've had wine here before."

"I can't say that I have. What you got in there?"

"Anything you can think of. What would you like?"

"Hmmm, I bet you don't have Gewürztraminer? It pairs well with Asian food." I said nothing and walked into the wine cellar. I stood there for a few minutes reading, because I couldn't remember what shelf I put it on. "Ah ha!"

"No way! No way!" I walked out and sat the bottle on the table in front of Dr. Knows his wine.

"Sara, Are you kidding me?!?! Blown! My mind is absolutely blown! Where did you get this?"

"I know my wine!" I smiled.

"I have a client that is a wine vendor. Every time he goes somewhere and picks up a bottle, he picks up 2. I get the other. He sent this to me last year after a trip to Germany."

"Wow! I am impressed. May I have a bottle opener? Or do your bottles magically open on their own!?" He laughed. I opened a drawer on the opposite side of the kitchen. I handed him a manual wine bottle opener and an electric one.

"Take your pick." My doorbell rang.

"Hmm, I have no idea who that is. I'll be right back."

I walked to the door. It was Brian Bradley. I hesitated. Then, I opened the door. "Hey Brian. To what do I owe this surprise visit?"

"Hey Sara. I'm sorry to bother you at home. May I come in?"

"Please do. Come in. Have a seat. May I get you a beverage?"

"Jameson." I walked to the bar and poured him a double shot. Jackson came out of the kitchen. The sound of a man's voice startled him.

"Brian, this is my beau, Jackson Ellis. Jackson, Brian Bradley."

"Pleasure is mine, sir." Jackson was so polite. He extended his hand. "Do you mind if I stay?"

"Not at all." We all took a seat.

"Sara. Can you tell me what happened when Freddy walked into your office today?"

"Sure. It began in this morning's meeting when I addressed the company. Freddy raised his hand and asked me how did I manage to get the company from you. I answered as professional as possible. Instead of using it as an opportunity to bash him, I answered in a manner and tone that addressed everyone. I mentioned that hard work, diligence and perseverance is how you get ahead with anything that you do. I publicly placed him on a probation. Peter, in new accounts, stood and reassured me that Freddy was the only one with negative feelings toward me being in the hot seat. We all went back to work and at the end of the day, Freddy walked into my office and told me that he was going to do what he could to take the company from me. He was under the impression that I was holding your place. I nicely read the part of our contract where it basically states that it's all mine; staff, the building, etc. I fired him. I don't want to come to work every day anticipating a fight with Freddy. I definitely did not sign up for that." Brian sat still for a moment. A tear ran down his face. My mind was blown. What in the WORLD was going on? Was he taking the company back from me? In the 30 seconds that it took him to answer, my mind ran through a thousand possibilities, but I certainly was NOT prepared for what he said next.

"Freddy came home this evening and sat down in my study. He looked at me and said 'how come you love her more than you love me? I know I'm not yours biologically, but you are MY father! You married MY mother!' I had no idea who he was talking about. He told me exactly what you just told me. I fussed at him. I told him 'I can't believe you said those things to her. I can't believe you acted like that. She was going to let you keep your job and your clients. All you had to do was work, but no! You want EVERYTHING handed to you. I don't love her more than I love you; but I respect her! I respect her hard work and dedication. You can learn from her! Beg her for your job back and work hard like your mother and I tried to teach you.' I guess that wasn't what he was expecting me to say; it wasn't enough for him. It wasn't what he wanted to hear. He wanted me to take the company away from you and give it to him. He looked at me and said, 'tell my mother this was your fault, Dad.' He took a pistol out of a holster on his belt, held it to his head and pulled the trigger. His mother heard the shot and came running down the hall. I was motionless. She screamed so loud, it was piercing. I-I didn't know what to do; what to say."
My body shook. I couldn't fathom the words that came out of Brian's mouth. Immediately, I sobbed. Jackson held me close to him and I sobbed

in his arms.

"Sir. I'm sorry for your loss. Please, don't blame her. She had no idea how adamantly he felt about her taking over." Jackson was consoling. It was nice.

"Jackson, is it?"

"Yes sir."

"Jackson, I do not blame Sara. I just had to be the one to come and tell her. I didn't mean to ruin your evening, but that selfish boy ruined his mother. What am I going to do? I'm dying, he's dead. She's never going to be the same."

"Sir. I know that I don't know you, but I suffered great loss once in my life. You must pray. Bradley is Irish, yes? Was your father catholic?"

"Aye. He was. I am too."

"Then you know God does not give you more than you can bear. Pray. Be there for your wife, even if she fights you. The two of you need each other more now than ever."

I was still crying. I felt terrible, but I knew it wasn't my fault. Sitting there listening to Jackson give comfort to Brian warmed my heart. Jackson offered Brian a chance to stay and have dinner with us. He declined but he thanked Jackson for the invite. I was calming down after a while and we all stood. I walked Brian to the door. He turned and hugged me. "I don't regret the decision that I made giving you my company. You are the best man for the job." I smiled.

"Please do not let my family tragedy keep you from excelling. Hold your head up high and lead that office to financial greatness. I believe you can do it. I have faith in you. Oh, and Jackson is a good fellow. Someone raised him well. Keep him in your life." He turned and walked away. I closed and locked the door behind him.

"JACKSON! I CANNOT DEAL!! Please, open that bottle of wine."

I was numb. Jackson opened the wine, grabbed 2 glasses and we sat down in the living room. I didn't have much of an appetite anymore. All I wanted to do was drink. That's exactly what we did. Jackson and I sat there and drank the entire bottle of Gewürztraminer. After that, we drank Jameson. He insisted I eat something. "Otherwise you will be sick in the morning." He was right, so I ate the plate of rice and chicken that he fixed for me. It was almost 10pm when I was ready to smoke again. I got up from the sofa. Jackson dozed off while we were watching TV. I made my way to my stash and rolled a blunt. I stepped out of the French doors in the living room and walked out on to the porch. I sat down on the hammock chair that Javier left. I had my cell phone in my hand. I scrolled through the contact list and touched Rena's name. The phone rang...

"Hey Sara. What's up mamas?"

"Hey, how are you?"

"I'm good. I just put Julissa down. She hasn't been feeling well. A mother's work is never done." I was silent.

"Sara, what's wrong Hun?"

"Uhm, Freddy shot himself this evening. You may want to call Anne and check on her."

"Oh, my goodness. I mean, we all knew he was crazy, but, oh no! Did Anne blame you? I am so sorry!"

"I'm not sure. I spoke to Brian. He came to my house this evening. He made very little mention of Anne. I just figured since she was friends with your mother, I would tell you."

"Would you like some company?"

"Oh. No thanks Hun. Well, Jackson is here. I think I am ok for now."

"Jackson? Oh, so you decided to get serious and you didn't tell me?"

"I haven't shared much about him. Nothing personal. I am just feeling it all out."

"Ok. I am sure you know what you're doing. Call me if you need me."

"Thanks Hun."

We hung up the phone. I sat there on that very comfortable hammock chair. I hadn't sat there since the night Javier left it there. I had so many thoughts running through my head. I was thinking about Anne and how devastated she must have been; I had Jenna send a floral arrangement to her home. I was thinking about my company and how I had to go in there and dampen the mood. There was no easy or nice way to share that someone committed suicide. I was thinking about Brian and how he had to fight ALS with the vision of his stepson shooting himself. I was thinking about Avery. I was certain that whatever it was I was supposed to find out, I wasn't going to find out until Christmas. Do I dare wrack my brain about it then? I was thinking about Jackson. What great loss did he suffer? Was his wife dead? No, if she were dead, why would that be a secret? Maybe the kids were dead. He didn't have a picture of them. Who didn't have a picture of their kids? I woke up the next morning and I was in my bed. Jackson was sitting on the edge of my bed looking at me when

I opened my eyes.

"Did you sit there all night?"

"Pretty much. I woke up around 2. I was frantic. I had no idea where you were. I found you asleep on the hammock chair. I picked you up and put you in the bed. I undressed you. You sleep like you're dead, so I sat here."

"I'm devastated. I'm angry. Why would Freddy do that to his mother? Hast thou had no care for anyone besides himself!?"

"It's something we will never know the answer to; I'm sorry. I wish I could tell you why."

"It is what it is. Bastard! I didn't like him anyway. He forced my hand!" I got out of the bed. I was nude. I stayed that way, proceeded downstairs and made coffee. It brewed and I poured my first cup. I stood in the middle of the kitchen and said a quiet prayer. I felt release when I said Amen. God whispered in my ear that "it is well, it is well, with, my soul." I smiled. I walked back upstairs and Jackson was in the shower. I climbed in behind him. I hugged his waist and he turned around. His face was red. Was he crying? He hugged me back and that's how we stood as the water poured down our bodies.

Chapter 8

A few weeks passed and things were moving swiftly. The funeral service for Freddy was very nice. Anne pulled me aside and thanked me for always trying to push Freddy to do his best. She knew he was spoiled and she knew he was sick. "I don't blame you darling, he always had issues." She also apologized for her outrageous game of telephone that had me wanting to punch Rena in her face. "Rena's mother is very outlandish". Anyway, as the world turned, it was all water under the bridge. Hosni canceled his visit; some nonsense about his wife being sick. "Oh please, it's July. She is not sick; she just doesn't want to come." God forbid Hosni came home without his wife that he didn't meet here anyway. It was time to sit down with Hiro Matsumaura, the President and CEO of BMW and Mini of Henderson Hill. This was the first time we met. Our discussions were via email. I didn't even know what his voice sounded like. His wife was ill and they were moving back to Japan. He was a mogul, so, to him, selling an auto group was the equivalent to selling skittles in a bodega. The man was disgustingly wealthy. I was sure his net worth trumped mine and Jackson's combined. He decided to come to my office because the quarter was off to a busy start and I needed to be able to multi task. He said he understood when I explained via email.

"Sara, Hiro Matsumaura." Jenna walked him to my office. I stood from my chair, walked around the opposite side of my desk, and extended my hand to him. "Wow!" I thought to myself as he towered over me. He was a nice-looking man; dressed very well, in a blue pinstripe suit. The pinstripes were so thin, they almost didn't exist. He was wearing a crisp white button up shirt and his initials were etched in the upper left hand pocket. He was wearing brown leather Louboutin loafers and he smelled like, Aqua Di Gio maybe.

"It's a pleasure to meet you. Please. Have a seat."
"Mr. Matsumaura, Sara, would you like a beverage?"
"No thank you." Jenna turned around and walked out. I sat down at my desk.

"Well. Sara, please beg my pardon, I don't mean to stare, but you are beautiful. I googled you prior to agreeing to exchange contact info with you, but there's no pictures of you online. You are very wealthy and lucrative. Why do you want an auto group?"

"Hiro, May I call you Hiro?"

"Please."

"Hiro, I have a strong love for cars; I cannot even begin to describe the passion to you. My personal collection is impressive. In addition to that, I'm a business woman and this is a business venture. Who said I can't purchase, own and operate an auto group? I googled you prior to reaching out to you with my offer to purchase this business. I know that your company finances are in pristine order. I know that you have the number 1 and number 2 BMW sales and service stores in the entire northeast and now it's available for sale; and for a good deal. I have the liquid funds and I want it!"

"Bravo. I'm impressed."

"I wasn't trying to impress you. I simply answered your question."

"You did, and you answered it with passion."

"If I don't have a passion for it, I will not acquire it."

"How's business here?"

"It's busy. Hectic. We lost an advisor a few weeks ago and turns out; he had bigger clients and projects than we all thought. It was rough pairing the clients with the right advisor. A ton of them wanted me to take their projects on directly, but as per my contract, I am no longer taking on new clients or clients whose projects I do not know personally. I prep them and the advisor and make sure the transition is smooth."

"How are you going to operate my auto group? Your undivided attention is needed here."

"Remotely. Both stores are setup with fiber optic technology. Remember, I googled you. Anyway, my office here runs on fiber optic technology. If you give me your sign on info, I could log into you ledger right now and see what your office comptrollers are doing."

"Hmm..." He scratched the top of his head. "Henderson Hill is far from here. You know that, right?"

"I was there recently. I know."

"What happens if you get stuck out there late one night?"

"Have you ever heard of a hotel? But knowing me, I'll buy some property out there. It's a wealthy area."

"Alright. I'm sold. Rita was right about you. She said you know your stuff!" We both laughed. He came prepared to sign everything over. His lawyer and my lawyer were in route to my office. He needed to square things up sooner than later. We agreed that I would go address and meet the staff at the beginning of the next week.

"I'm certain that you will like the staff and I'm certain they will like you."

"I have no concerns sir."

He spent a good part of the morning in my office. By the time he left, people were walking around preparing for lunch. Peter Silverman, from new accounts, came and tapped on my door.

"Come in Peter, what's up?"

"2 things; 1, would you like to order from Frankie & Johnnies? 2. I'm having an issue with one of Freddy's former clients."

"Yes. I would like a caprese salad with grilled chicken and come back and see me at 2pm and we will talk about the Freddy client."

"Ok cool." I leaned back in my chair.

"Seriously, Freddy, you're giving me a hard time even in death?! Rest in peace, already!" This was how I got through my days. I talked to Freddy in my office. I knew he was listening. I was sure he was standing there. It made me feel better. I had to watch my back though; I didn't want my employees to think I lost my mind. My office phone rang.

"Sara speaking."

"Hello beautiful. How is your day going?" It was Dr. Handsome face. I smiled.

"Well hello babe, my day is going. I just signed the paperwork. I am officially the dealer principal, president and CEO of BMW and Mini of Henderson Hill."

"Checkmate! Cheers!" We laughed.

"Thanks. How's your day going?"

"My day is going; I was in surgery earlier this morning. I removed a tumor from the brain of a 15-year-old. I'm BEAT! But, she will live. Life is good."

"Mazel tov! The good surgeon strikes again!"

"Thanks babe! Doesn't someone have a birthday coming up."

"Yes someone does. I have no idea what I want to do. I'm gonna wing it."

"Is your computer on?"

"Yes."

"Open your email, the one at Hotmail.com"

"Ok, open, loading, what's this?"

"Open it." I double clicked on the email from Jackson. I read it in silence.

"Wait." I sat up straight and read it again.

"OH? BABE!?"

"Yea babe..."

"Hedonism?!?"

"I heard you when you said you wanted to go. Happy Birthday! We fly out the day before. I want you to wake up nude in the sunshine on your birthday."

"Oh my! You should see the smile on my face!"

"I have my eyes closed. I can see the smile on your face. I also see that beautiful, round ass walking across the bedroom."

"Oh, you naughty boy!"

"Do you have plans after work?"

"I do, dinner with the besties. Rena wants a do over. Her ass is paying this time, too."

"I'm not touching that. Call me when you get home please, so I can come by and tuck you in."

"Tuck me in, or tuck your penis in me?"

"Which do you prefer?"

"Both, but in the opposite order."

"OW! Sexy mama!"

"Yea big daddy!"

"Baby, my lunch is here. I'll call you later." Peter walked in promptly at 2. I liked that. If I asked Freddy to come to my office at 2, he would come at 2:15 and bring a snack. I giggled to myself at the thought of him always eating.

"We have a client by the name of Robert Taylor. Freddy was his advisor. Apparently, Freddy owed him money. Something about taking a check for services that he didn't complete. I told him I would consider it and call him back, and I did. There's no record of it, which means that it went into a personal account and we can't access that. I refuse to call his mother and ask for her dead sons' bank statement."

"Yea, let's not do that. How much is that check?"

"$22,000."

"Well Mr. Taylor should provide me with a bank statement showing that dollar amount was withdrawn. He proves it; I'll cut him a refund check, but if he doesn't or if looks suspicious, he gets nothing! Wait, I can't do that, he'll tarnish our name, just make sure the shit is real before you send me a check request."

"Yes ma'am." I rolled my eyes.

"You people with the ma'am!"

"I'm sorry but we all called Brian sir. It's only right we call you ma'am."

"You can call me Sara."

"Ok. Sara. I will get right on it."

My phone buzzed on my desk. It was a text message from Jackson.

Jax: Remember when I made love to you in the shower? You should leave your office so we can relive that moment.

Me: Dr. are you horny?

Jax: Very. It's been a while.

Me: I know it has. I'm sorry.

Jax: don't apologize...

Me: I could leave early today. I do run thing around here.

Jax: you should come home early. I'll bring food.

Me: Hahahahaha! That's awesome. My man just bribed me with food.

Me: what are you bringing me?

Jax: just me. You're going out tonight, remember?

Me: oh! I forgot.

Me: Ok...meet me at my house...in 20 minutes.

Jax: Ok.

Immediately, I sprung from my desk. I didn't bother cleaning it off. I wanted it to look like I was coming back. I just locked my office door. I answer to me around here anyway. I grabbed my bag, my keys and my phone and took off down the hall.

"Jenna, I probably won't be back; but you didn't hear that."

"Ok. Good night."

I liked Jenna. That exchange happened and she never skipped a beat. She just continued doing her work. I was considering promoting her to be my personal assistant. I needed one. Then she can hire her receptionist replacement. I arrived and realized that Jackson beat me home. I parked and hopped out quickly.

"I should give you a key. How did you beat me here?"

"I was closer than I thought I was, but I wasn't waiting long."

We walked into the house. Before I could close the door, Jackson spun me around and cuffed my face. He kissed me. I melted. It was like we were kissing for the first time all over again. He had me feeling freaky but I pulled away from him and took my clothes off. I walked away; I sashayed away.

"Are you gonna make me chase you?" His accent made me wet. I felt my pussy saturate. By the time, I reached the top of the steps, Jackson was right behind me. He grabbed me from behind and I felt his erection on my bottom.

"I need that inside of me."

I placed my hand on his shaft and stroked it. He moaned in my ear. There we stood my back to his stomach. I put my hand around my back and stroked his manhood and his hand found my pussy. He inserted 2 fingers and I moaned. I stopped him and lightly jogged away from him. He followed. This time he caught me as I approached my bedroom door. He scooped me up and tossed me over his shoulder, like a rag doll. I laughed. He burst through the French doors and tossed me on the bed.

"Are you nice and wet for me?"

"Why don't you come over here and see." He did. He started at my feet and kissed all the way up my leg. When he reached my vagina, he licked it. It sent a shock through my body. I cried out. He continued licking and sucking my clitoris and I was in heaven. My legs were shaking. I was moaning. I climaxed a thousand times. My body was worn out but it was still flowing. Jackson laid on top of me and inserted himself. It went in with no pressure because I was so wet from all the previous ejaculations. He pumped me slowly and deeply. He grunted and moaned at each penetration. I held his arms and squeezed my legs tight around his back. We climaxed together and my legs shook more. Jackson was completely still. I rolled over and got off the bed.

"Sara, what's the adjective to describe what just happened?"

"Exhilarating."

"Bravo. Someone paid good money for your education."

We laughed. I needed to take a shower, so I headed towards the bathroom. I took a nice, long, hot shower. Jackson came in. Washed and left me in there. It was peaceful. I had candles burning and I was using aromatherapy wash. I was getting sleepy.

"JAAAAAXXXXX!!!!"

"Yea babe."

"Can you pour me a glass of Jameson?"

He disappeared and returned with the glass. I was still in the shower. I stuck my arm out of the shower door and he handed it to me. I quickly chugged the contents. I handed the glass back. To my surprise, he refilled it and handed it back. I peeked at him thru the small opening.

"Yup. I brought the bottle up. You haven't been the same lately. What's up babe?"

"I think I'm just doing a lot; business wise. My days are crazy and constant; I love it but I think I bit off more than I can chew. Then Freddy
leaving; now, I have to pay to fix one of his mistakes. It's like the bastard
is taunting me."

"All great things are preceded by chaos. You will be fine. Just remember
that and pray. Take deep breaths and all will balance. Now you are going
to prune. Please, get out of the shower." I looked at the clock.

"Oh, I'm gonna be late." I said it, but never picked my pace up.

"Eh, I'll get there when I get there." I took my time. I put on a pair of
multi colored harlequin pants and a fitted half shirt. It was pink. I walked
over to the jewelry armoire in my closet and pulled out a beaded waist
band. I placed it on my exposed belly. It was chilly and sent a shiver
through my body. I giggled. I put on a pair of strappy, pink peek toe ankle
booties and threw some items in a pink clutch. When I came down the
steps, Jackson was waiting for me at the front door.

"Oh my! You look fabulous! Very Sara in the 80s! Did you live through the
80s?"

"WOW! You have jokes inside of a compliment. I'll take it, old man! I was
born in 81!"

"That's the last time we mention either of our ages!" The gut busting
laughter erupted.

"Would you like to be my date to the friend dinner?"

"Seriously!?!"

"Uhhh, yea, why not?"

"I don't mind. I would love to be your date to the friend dinner; especially with you in that outfit! Damn! I'm just surprised that you want me to
meet your friends."

"I figured we've come this far, this deep; why not?"

"We are deep."

"Yea, we might be in too deep. But I will save that conversation for another day."

"Uh huh, come on, you're late."

Rena chose Kona Grille for the best friend dinner. When we arrived, the
hostess took us to the table where my friends had already convened.

"Hi guys! I brought Jackson. I hope that's ok. Jackson, my family, family,
Jackson."

"HI JACKSON!!" They all sounded like school girls; even the guys. I laughed
and shook my head. We sat.

"So...to what do we owe the pleasure of meeting Sir Jackson?"

"I'm pretty sure it's because I told her I love her."

"AWWWWWWWWW!!!!!!" Oh, my God! They were border line embarrassing.

"Hello. May I get you guys a drink?" The wait staff always had perfect timing when I was out with Jackson.

"Jameson...chilled straight for the lady and I will have my Jameson with a splash of ginger ale." I liked when Jackson ordered for me. I blushed. Javier was sitting on my left side. He leaned and whispered in my ear "I see you boo! He's hot!" He slapped me five under the table and we giggled in strict confidence. The crazy thing was, had that been one of the female besties whispering the same comment, I don't think my response would be so...accepting.

"Sara...I heard through the grapevine that you own an auto group. Uhm... are you offering discounts?"

"Do you ever discount your artwork when I buy it?"

Yea, I said it. Everyone looked down, waiting for Rena's answer.

"You could've just said no!" Everyone laughed. Thank God.

"So, I know Daniela and Arianna, you must be Rena, yes?"

"Yes. I'm Rena."

"I'm Patrick. Rena is my wife."

"I'm Javier."

"Pleasure, everyone, I've heard great things about all of you. It's good to put faces to names."

"You're a doctor, right? What's your specialty? Anything I can use?" Jackson giggled.

"I'm a neurologist. Do you have head issues, Arianna?"

"HA! Honey! She's a mental mess, but neurologists don't fix her issues!"

"Shut up! I get headaches."

"Oh yea? How often?"

"Every time Javier opens his mouth!"

We all busted out loud with laughter. People were looking at us. We didn't care. As the night went on, we got louder. I'm sure that was because we were all drinking like crazy. We sat for hours. Laughing, talking. My friends asked Jackson a ton of questions. Questions like what's your favorite color? Where did you grow up? Arianna asked him if his accent was real. She spent the evening waiting for it to disappear; It was funny. He fit in, very well. It was a joyous occasion. I wish I had the courage to introduce him to my family. My mother would love him, but she would get attached to him. I could hear her now "Make sure Jackson comes with you to dinner." I giggled to myself when I thought about a possible conversation with mom, about Jackson.

"Can I get you guys another round?"
"No. We're all set. May we have the check please?"
I knew what was going to conspire when the waitress brought the bill to the table. I think she knew also. She sat it in the middle of the table, quickly pulled her arm back and disappeared. We all reached for it.
"Sara, you know you need to pull your hand back!"
"And you know that I'm not going to. Are we really doing this, guys?"
"HMPH, y'all can fight over the bill. Ima hold onto my pennies!" Javier laughed and nicely pulled his arm away. He didn't usually offer to pay, so I was surprised he reached at all.
"Problem solved!" The entire time we were sitting there trying to decide who was going to pay, Jackson got up and paid the waitress. "I paid the bill and I also left a tip. I hate to end the night early, but, well, we're family, right? I'm going home to have sex with my woman!" He kissed me on my cheek.
"Well, I guess he told us!"
"THANK YOU, JACKSON!!!!!" We all rose from the table and started walking toward the exit.
"Rena, thank you for calling us together for this dinner. I appreciate it. I love you."
"I love you too. I apologize for ruining the first dinner with my accusation. Patrick fussed at me for 2 days over that. It won't happen again. That is why I put this night together. Oh, and I'm glad you brought Jackson. I like him. He's good for you."
"Thanks Rey!" We hugged. Jackson and I got in his car. I waved as he drove away.
"I enjoyed myself Sara. Thank you for inviting me."
"You're welcome. I think my friends like you."
"I like them too. They're good people. Just like you. I see why you all are friends."
"I remember the first day of first grade. I was so nervous; my mother homeschooled me until then. My only exposure to children was my first cousins and Hosni. I don't remember the outfit, but there's a picture on the wall at my parent's house. It was a blue dress with pink polka dots.

I had on white ruffle socks and pink and white Mary Jane's." I laughed. "Anyway, I walked onto the playground and Arianna came running over to me 'I like your dress. Let's be friends!' And we skipped off, buddies since day one. Daniela transferred to our school the following year. Her last name is Bautista, so she was in my class. I introduced her to Ari and boom! We lived in the same city; different neighborhoods, and we were always in the same public schools. I found Javier in grad school. We took an Econ class together 2nd year. He didn't know the material! I started a study group and he was the first person I invited. Turns out, he lived in the complex behind mine and, there ya have it. The girls used to come and visit all the time and I always talked about my awesome gay friend. He was the first gay person I ever knew, EVER! Anyway, Rena and Patrick are friends of Hosni's. Honestly, the memory of how we met fell into a weed pocket in my mind but what kept me in touch with them is Rena's artwork. The woman is a Phenom! She drew me at Hosni's wedding; literally sat in the audience with an 8'10 sketch pad and drew me standing at the Alter, over Hosni's shoulder. It's beautiful. That, too, is in my parent's house. They have all the good pictures."

I took a breath. I was sure I was rambling because I was drunk.

"Mmm, don't stop. I like when you speak, tell me more." He reached up and stroked my face.

"Nope, it's your turn. Tell me about YOUR wedding. Avery said he was your best man."

"Ha! If that's what you wanna call it." That accent was making me wet again. Focus, Sara! "My parents didn't want me to get married. They thought it was likely she was marrying me for the money I hadn't made yet. Anyway, Avery and I were piss drunk in Vegas for 4 days and she; my wife, met us out there, day 3. We stumbled into a chapel and boom, there ya have it. I gave her a ring pop. It was cute, but it was official." I sat silent. He kept speaking.

"When we got home, I had to keep it a secret from my mum. She would've died! So, I made up some nonsense about why I needed to move out 'suddenly' and I did, but we struggled. I worked hard; 20 hour days. Sleep for 2 and workout for 2, and back at it. I did that for years! I didn't mean to get married, therefore, I continued my life the same way I probably would have even if she wasn't with me. After, I don't know, 4 years, she finally got fed up and knocked on my mother's door to tell her we had been married. 'I knew. I was waiting for him to tell me. He must be ashamed of you. Why else would he keep you a secret?' That's what my mother said to her. They haven't gotten along since."

"See, I can't have that happening. If I ever get married, I want to love his family and vice versa. I don't want there to be any mention or question of mine or his money; none of that dignifies real love in my opinion."

"You're right. Trust me, if I ever get marri-, uhm...I just wish they didn't hate each other, is all." There he goes, being vague. I thought this would be a good time to bring up the notes that I received in Miami. It did say ask questions...

"Why does it sound like she doesn't exist anymore; your wife?"

"In my opinion, she doesn't."

"Do you not believe in divorce?"

"Both parties have to agree to it, she's not convinced."

"Convinced about what; the fact that the thrill is gone? Or that it was never there!?" I was getting upset. I had to take a breath. I didn't even realize it, but we were sitting in my driveway. "You know what, never mind. Don't answer that." I got out of the car, walked up the steps and unlocked the door. Jackson was walking toward me.

"May I come inside?" I left the door open. I put my bag down and took off my shoes. I went to the stash and rolled a blunt. Jackson poured 2 drinks.

"You drank all the Jameson before, this is Dewar's"

"I'm not an alcoholic. I drink socially."

"I'm not judging you. Listen, I know that my marriage complicates things between us. Trust me when I tell you, I'm doing the best I can to fully 'relieve myself of my duties.' It's complicated, I can't explain it yet."

"Don't walk away from your family because of me. I won't be with you if you do. Do not break up your family for a fling with your girlfriend!"

I tossed the Dewar's back in my mouth and slammed the glass on the counter where I was standing.

"Another?" Jackson grabbed the bottle and poured another shot.

"Leave the bottle; let me ask you something, If I didn't exist in your life, if you didn't know me, would you still be considering leaving your wife? If you can say yes to that, do so and come back to me when you do. Stop making me fall in love with you!"

"You're not the only one in love, Sara! I love you too! I loved you first! I can't make you stop loving me, just like I can't make myself stop loving you." I picked up the lighter and lit my perfectly rolled blunt.

"I don't like to argue, and I don't like to yell, so I'm going to stop. I am going to sit down, smoke my blunt, drink my Dewar's, and I would like to do so alone; please."

"Sara…"

"I need to sleep alone tonight. I shouldn't have asked those questions. I made myself mad. I'll be ok in the morning."

"I'm gonna call you as soon as I get up."

"I know." I smiled; I walked him to the door and he kissed me on my cheek.

"Good night babe. Sleep tight." Even when I'm angry, that accent, whew!

"Good night Jackson."

I turned around, closed and locked the door. I turned all the lights off, grabbed my bottle, my glass, my blunt and I went upstairs. When I reached my bedroom, I sat everything on the nightstand. My cell phone was in my bag. I turned it off and tossed it the drawer in my nightstand. "I'm going off the grid." That's exactly what I did.

Chapter 9

"Hi Jackson! Welcome to Total Image Salon. How may we be of service to you today?"

"Hello Arianna. I'm sorry to bother you at work, but I haven't heard from or seen Sara in 3 days. Have you heard from her? Is she alright? Can you help me find her?"

"Ok. Ok. Relax. Would you like some water?"

"No thanks. I just want my babe back!"

"Aww, you're cute! You know what, now that I think about it, I haven't heard from her. But I haven't been home, we did a 72-hour beauty-a-thon and this place was crawling with women, kids and models."

"Oh...congrats, yes? A beauty-a-thon..."

"Uh huh, it was awesome!"

"I bet it was, and Sara didn't come by and check it out?"

"No; I'm not upset nor am I surprised. I wasn't expecting her to check it out. It's not her thing. Sara is naturally beautiful. When the rest of us were getting into makeup and hair extensions, Sara was relaxing in a corner with blistex and beautiful, healthy, natural hair down to her fat a-! She's been stunning since birth!" Arianna laughed. Jackson did too, but quickly, his face fell. At that moment, she understood the love between them and was inclined to help Jackson find Sara. "The last time Sara fell off the grid, we were 26. She and Hosni had this HUGE blowout. It was nasty, but on the low; to this day, none of us know what they were fighting about. I don't even think their mom knew. Anyway, she turned off her phone and locked the doors to her house; at the time, she was living in the townhouse. She stayed in bed for almost a week and replayed the entire fight in her mind. When she felt like she solved the problem, she re-appeared. It was as if she wasn't missing at all." Jackson's eyes dropped. "Ugh!"

"Did you two have a fight?"

"Not really. It was more like she got upset with me because I was being vague; in conversation, and she put me out of her house. Her phone has been going straight to voicemail and when I call her office, Jenna says she's not in, but she's ok. You think she's working remotely?"

"I wish I could answer that Hun. Sara is my best friend, but she is vague and she's vague when she wants to be. If she isn't speaking to you, let her rock out. She will call you when she feels the problem is solved in her mind."

"That's the problem, it can't be solved in her mind. I must solve it for her."

"So, let's go over there. I don't have keys to this house, but I think Javier does. I'll call him."

"Thanks, I appreciate it." Arianna called Javier and they spoke for a few minutes.

"Yea, I have keys to her house. Let's all meet over there. If she goes all lke Turner crazy, I want her to do it to all of us and not just me."

"You're such a jerk! We'll meet you there, come on Jackson, you drive!" Jackson led Arianna to his Cayenne and opened the passenger side door for her.

"Do you always open doors? No wonder 'Sa'rah' is in love with you."

"Is chivalry dead?"

"Oh it is doc, it is! So, what was the fight about?"

"It was a disagreement. It wasn't anything major and that's why my mind is blown right now. I even called Avery to see if he's spoken to her and he said no."

"Wait, Avery; the recycling guru?"

"Yup." Jackson giggled. "Recycling guru…that's funny."

"Hardy har-har! How do you know Avery?"

"We grew up together." Arianna made a face.

"So…did you know she knew him when you met?"

"Nope, I only found out because I invited her to Miami with me and she was already going; had her own invite."

"Wait, you were with her in Miami?!?!"

"Uh…"

"I won't say anything. But why wouldn't she tell us that you were in Miami?"

"I'm not sure. She didn't tell me that she didn't tell you all. I assumed you knew."

"It sounds like we all have some things to discuss with Miss. Sara Bashir. You didn't call her mom, did you?"

"Nope, but that's only because I don't know her number."

"Yea…no…you don't wanna call Annabelle. You especially do not want to call Annabelle and tell her you can't find her precious Sara."

"Oh. I didn't know that."

"Yea man…Sara was…. well something happened when we were 16 and she was missing for like 28 hours. When we called her mom, she freaked out so badly that we had to go over there and calm her down and tell her that we found her, her phone was dead. We were 16! We didn't have phones to die. We made that all the way up, but we immediately got Sara back!"

"Huh! I wonder why I never heard that story before."

"Because this is the first time she's gone missing on you. I'm calm because I know she's fine. She's probably inside hi, drunk and unwashed, but I'll put money on it that her thoughts are clear as day!"

"Well...here's the moment of truth..." Arianna and Jackson got out of the car in front of Sara's house. Javier was sitting on the hammock chair. "When did she get that?!?" Arianna pointed to the hammock chair that Javier was sitting in. "Clearly I haven't been here in a while." She was talking to Javier at this point.

"I gave it to her at the beginning of the season. It was the remainder of a 'breakup.'"

"Hmmm, it's cool. Mi gusto mucho!" She sat down.

"Get up girl! Let's inch high private eye into this mansion!" Javier took his key out of his back pocket and unlocked the door.

"May I go in first?"

"I think you should let Javier go in first." Arianna rolled her eyes. "He's the one she gave the key to."

"True...well...go on Javi!" Javier smiled and Jackson giggled. It was cute. Arianna took a picture with her cell phone.

"It's gonna be on the picture board at the wedding. Anyone going through this much trouble for Sara, is going to marry her." Arianna was very blunt. There was no filter. Thoughts gathered in her mind and immediately came out of her mouth.

"I do love her...I would love it if she were my wife." Jackson's big blue eyes dropped. At this point, Javier was walking through the door. Ari and Jackson followed.

"SARA! SARAAAAAAA!!!!" Javier walked through every room on the first floor. It was immaculate. Not one item out of place, or speck of dirt on the floors or counters. Jackson and Arianna sat down in the living room. "It's crazy clean down here!"

Javier slipped out of his moccasins. He placed them at the front door. He ran up the stairs and made the right toward the master bedroom suite.

The French door was slightly open. He slowly pushed it further.

"Sara." He whispered and walked toward the bed. I was there, physically, but mentally I was still putting my thoughts in order. "I'm gonna get in next to you. Is that ok?" I slid over so Javier could climb in.

"Jackson and Arianna are with me. In fact, this was Jackson's doing. He's worried about you, babes. You should see his eyes. He keeps dropping them. I bet his eyes are what did you in...that, and the way he says your name. The only other person to say your name with such beauty and grace is your mom, and then here comes Jackson. He's perfect...He's perfect for you, but he's not...he's married. I get it. If you want to know where you stand...ask him questions...I bet if you ask the right question, you'll get the right answer. But I bet you're not ready. You're still trying to figure out how you LET yourself fall in love with him. You couldn't stop that if you tried. So stop trying."

Javier was right on the money. I rolled over...

"Ask him questions? Was that you putting notes under my door? What's up with that?"

"Huh?" Javier looked confused. It wasn't him. I got up. I stumbled.

"I haven't moved in 3 days. Literally. I was thinking. I emailed Jenna and she's holding down the fort. I'm going to promote her and pay her well. She's awesome."

"Are you done thinking?"

"Yea. I'm gonna take a quick shower. Can you pour me a glass of orange juice and ask Jackson to bring it to me, please?"

"Of course." Javier kissed me on my cheek and left the room. I went into the bathroom. Javier went downstairs. Jackson and Arianna were standing in the kitchen.

"Okay...so she was 'thinking'. Ari, did you tell Jackson about her last thinking moment?"

"Aye. She told me. So...what should I do?"

"She wants a glass of orange juice and she wants you to bring it to her. She's also hopping in the shower. Go tap that!" Javier, Jackson and Ari burst out in laughter. It was a good moment. Jackson poured a tall glass of orange juice and walked out of the kitchen. He quickly climbed the steps and walked down the long hallway to the French doors. When he reached them, he took a deep breath and walked into the bedroom. I was already in the shower and didn't hear him come in.

"Sara." Jackson walked into the bathroom.

"I have juice for you babe." I stuck my arm out of the glass shower door. He handed me a glass. I chugged it and handed the glass back. It wasn't quite empty.

"You can chug Jameson but not O.J? Weak!" I slid the shower door open and peeked at Dr. Cutie face.

"Hello beautiful. I'm sorry if our conversation is what made you have a 3-day hiatus. I didn't mean to upset you." I cuffed Jackson's face in my hands, exactly how he did it to me. I kissed him softly. He kissed me back with such passion. It was intense. He pushed back and quickly undressed. He climbed into the shower and continued the intense kiss. The water was running down both of our bodies. He cupped both of my breasts and pulled on my nipples. Immediately my vagina saturated and it wasn't from the shower. I placed one hand on his chest and the other on his shaft. I proceeded to pull in a swift motion. He moaned in my mouth. That was sexy and it sent a shiver through my body. I moaned. He picked me up and slid his penis into me. Deep inside. I bounced in a swift motion. It felt good to have Jackson inside of me. I didn't want to think anymore. I didn't want to ask any more questions or try and figure out hidden messages. I didn't care about the notes, none of it mattered anymore. I would rather have Jackson in my life the way he was than to not have him in my life at all. I wasn't going to tell him that though. I didn't want him to know that he had that control over me. I ejaculated numerous times on him while were in the shower. When he finally climaxed, his legs practically shook from under him. He slowly put me down. I grabbed a blue loofa off the shower caddy and squeezed Neutrogena body wash on it. I washed him. He was grateful and washed me in return. That too, was sexy.

"You are so sexy. I missed you!" Jackson giggled. It was cute. I smiled. "I missed you too. Oh, and it wasn't fully your fault..." We rinsed, turned the water off and climbed out of the shower.

"Would you like to go out for dinner or do you want to order in?"

"How did you know I was hungry?"

"Your house is spotless! You literally haven't moved in 3 days. Come on. Get dressed and I'll take us all out."

"Ok. I'll be down in a few."

Jackson kissed me again; smacked my butt and walked out of the bathroom. He dried off and re-dressed very quickly. Men! I dried my body and my hair. I brushed it into a bun on the top of my head. I washed my face and brushed my teeth. I walked onto the balcony. It was muggy outside. "Yuck!" I walked into the closet and my eyes scanned the room. I opted for a leopard print, shin length maxi dress. I slipped on a pair of leopard print sandals. I gathered the contents of my purse and threw everything into a solid black leather hobo. I turned my cell phone on and tossed it in my bag. I was sure I had a ton of messages, so I let it catch up. I took a deep breath and walked downstairs.

"Hiiiiii SARAAAA!!!! I like your dress!"

"Let's be friends!" We said it together. I missed Ari too. I walked over and she kissed me on the cheek. As I walked by, I smacked her ass.

"It's like they're 5 all over again."

"Thank you, Javier, for bringing Jackson here. You guys know what happens when I need a moment, Jackson; it was your turn to experience it. I'm not sure why it happens but it does, and when it's finished, it's finished. My dad tells a great story about the first time it happened. I was 11 and my mom went to Cairo to take care of her grandmother for the summer. Anyway, I was in a fight in cheerleading practice and when I got home, I went in my room, closed the door and sat in the closet for the duration of the weekend. No words were spoken, no movement. My dad said he was freaking out. I couldn't tell. Hosni called mom and told her what was going on. She said 'oh she's me. She'll be fine. Just leave her with her thoughts.' And that's what they did. Monday morning, I got up and carried on with my life. I don't know why guys. It's just what I do."

"Well now I know, I learned a lot about you today."

"Uh huh...I bet Ari told you a ton of stories!" I laughed.

"How come it wasn't Javier that told stories?"

"Why you always gotta say my name?!" Javier rolled his eyes. It was funny.

"We all know it wasn't Javier. It's cool...I love you anyway. Come on... we're getting in Jackson's car and he's gonna feed us!"

"Nice! Where are we going?"

"Sara...that's up to you babe."

"Let's go to see Rita!" We all got in Jackson's Cayenne and went for a ride downtown. He didn't know the route like I did, so he let me drive.

"I like how this car drives."

"You're thinking about buying one aren't you?"

"No. I like my Touareg, and I have a BMW store now. Maybe I'll get an X5 for my birthday."

"Yup! And in your family, y'all give whips as gifts. Did you know that Jackson?" Javier tapped Jackson on his shoulder.

"I think she mentioned it prior. I love that they have the means to show their love like that. I don't have it like that."

"Shut up Jackson! I'm sure that's not the case." Arianna was not convinced. I wasn't either but she and Javier were having this conversation, I was just ears in the car.

"I don't know anything about you, so I'm clearly making a statement based..."

"You're passing judgment is all..." Jackson wasn't stupid.

"Well...am I wrong?"

"What makes you think otherwise when I clearly said I don't have it like that? Listen, I make good money, I live well, I invest. I'm good. I can hold it all. I'm wealthy, but I'm not in that tax bracket!" He was laughing, I was listening and driving the hell out his car.

"They're a combination of old money and new money. Old money is long and I can't touch that."

"Ha! I 'ca'unt' touch that! I love the accent thing. It's awesome! I love it."

"It's real."

"Where are you from again?" Javier asked.

"Copenhagen."

"Oh, that's right."

"Wait, back to the lavish gift thing. Jackson, you wouldn't buy a car for Sara?"

"I'll give Sara anything she wants; anything she needs. However, I'm not in the position to spend $70 grand for every birthday, anniversary, Christmas, new year, valentine's day, Mother's Day; she's not a mum. I think she said Hosni gave her the 1958 Corvette C1 for, like Groundhog Day or something dumb!" We all laughed. Hosni gifted that car when I completed grad school. We finally arrived to Rita's restaurant and I pulled the car in the valet lane.

"I've never been here before. How come I've never been here before?" Javier was in awe.

"I'm not sure, but here you are. Come on!" We walked through the door and the same hostess, whose name I still can't remember, greeted us at the door.

"Hi Sara! How are you this evening?"

"I'm well thanks, how are you?"

"I'm good. It's good to see you. I see you'll you need a big table this evening. Would you like to sit inside or outside?" I looked at the crew and they looked at me.

"Guys, inside or outside?"

"Whatever." It was dusk...so...

"Outside is fine, thanks." We followed whatever her name was to the rear of the restaurant and up the spiral staircase. There were quite a few larger parties sitting at tables in random locations around the patio. She sat us close to the edge so that we were not in the middle of the crowd of loud tables. She knew me well. I didn't like to sit close to people. I was claustrophobic. I also didn't like it when I can hear other people conversing and vice versa.

"Is Rita here?"

"Uhm, she was before. I'm not sure if she is still, I'll check for you. I'll send your waitress over also."

"Thank you." The waitress came over and we ordered drinks and appetizers.

"They make an awesome shrimp salad here; you guys are going to love it! I hope Rita is here. She is a wonderful person. She gives me life when I see her!"

"How do you know this woman?" Javier gets a little jealous when I attempt to blend friends.

"She was a guest at L'inn the summer that I opened it. Her car was stolen when she went touring through town. She needed to get back to the city so I offered her a ride down. I felt it was the least I could do for her. She was devastated, but she was grateful. She made sure we kept in touch and we do. However, she's never been up to CT. The only time I see her is when I come to eat. It's just how our relationship is."

"Sara! Darling!!! Hello!!! Jackson!!! Hello!!!! Friends I don't know!!! Hello!!!! Welcome!! I'm Rita!!"

"We're your ears ringing?! I was just telling Javier the story of how we met." Rita looked fantastic! She was glowing...

"Rita, you're glowing! Oh, I'm Arianna, by the way. Sara and I grew up together."

"Pleasure to meet you. Are you Javier? It's a pleasure. Thank you for coming. Did the waitress tell you the specials? You must try the sea bass...Sara do you still love sea bass?"

"That's like asking if the sky is still blue! But I think I'm going to have lobster tails...so the glow? Who are you dating?"

"Oh darling! I'm not dating anyone. Who has time for that?!? Oh wait...you do! Well no, I'm glowing because it's hot, I'm menopausal and I am opening a new restaurant...in your inn!!!" She had the audacity to clap. I rolled my eyes so hard, that Ari kicked me under the table.

"Wait...what?! You can't do that; my space isn't zoned for that..."

"Well I have a plan that will work for both of us! Trust me. You will love it! I'm so excited!" I wasn't excited. First, I wasn't cool with Rita's choice of timing to spring a business idea on me. 2, I didn't like the idea.

"Rita. I love you and I'm sure your idea is great but it's not going to work. Also, I would rather you call my office on Monday and we speak then. I'm out with my friends and we would like to enjoy our meal without business deals being done. You understand, right?" Rita's eyes dropped. I honestly didn't care about her hurt feelings. She was out of line.

"Of course, I understand. I was wrong. I apologize. Please. Enjoy your meal. I will come to your office on Monday. I'll call ahead."

"Ok. Great!" Rita kissed me on my cheek and walked away. Our waitress came over and took our order. The duration of the evening was a blast! Jackson, Javier, Arianna and I had a wonderful time. We talked about world affairs, religion, television, music, everything. We all learned a lot about each other. I was full and entirely too intoxicated to drive us back home. Jackson noticed early on that I would be drunk and he was more than happy to get us home safely. We got back to my house in record time. We all fell asleep while Jackson was driving, so we had a second wind when we got out of the car at my house.

"Sara, I told Javier that I love this hammock chair!"

"Yea I fell asleep on it once. I woke up inside. Jackson carried me to bed. He's like beast and I'm beauty but he's not hairy!" I was still drunk. Everyone laughed.

"Can we smoke?" Ari asked.

"Of course, we can." I went inside to the stash and rolled a blunt. Jackson followed me and grabbed a bottle of tequila from the bar. He gathered 4 shot glasses and checked the fridge for a lime.

"Jackpot! Now we can have a party!" He cut the lime in slices and placed them on a small plate that he grabbed from a cabinet above where he was standing.

I walked back out to the porch and Jackson was close behind.

"Shots?!"

"Oh, my goodness yes! I love tequila shots!" Arianna was very excited.

"I'm glad we can stay here, if need be."

"Uh huh, You can't stay here!"

The hammock chair was big enough for all four of us to sit in a row. We were comfortable. Occasionally, Jackson would make it swing. I opted to sit on the end. There was a table on my right side. I poured shots and sent them down the line; assembly style. Jackson held his shot in the air.

"Here's to getting along with my girlfriends best friends! Cheers!"

"Cheers!" We all tossed our shots back and we all made a face.

"WHEEW! I remember when I was in medical school and being a bartender and doing this all night. I have maybe 2 more in me tonight. It's insane how the times have changed." Javier and Ari stumbled into the house and each chose a spot on the sofa to crash for the night. I never minded a friend crashing if they were too drunk to drive. I grabbed sheets and pillows out of the closet for them.

"It's drafty down here at night. I'll leave the throws out for you."

They weren't paying attention. I flipped the light switches and went upstairs. Jackson followed me. When we reached my bedroom, we stripped and climbed into my bed. He put his arms around me and held me tight. I fell asleep within minutes.

"Sara, you sleep? There's so much that I need to tell you but I don't know where to begin. I don't want to see the look on your face. I don't have the answers to the questions that I know you're going to ask me. I love you. I need you. I want to spend the rest of my life with you. I want to say these things to you when you're awake, but apparently, I'm not ready yet. I was...lost...when I couldn't find you. I never want to spend time without you. When the time is right, and I tell you my story, please don't be mad. It's complicated. I know that I cannot bring disorder to your life and I wouldn't want to. I can't lose you, so when I do tell you; you can't leave me ok? I love you."

I woke up to the smell of food. I rolled over and Jackson was lying beside me. He was beautiful. His thick black hair was tossed as if he had been tossing and turning all night. He looked peaceful; in fact, there was a slight smile on his face. I didn't want to disturb him. Instead, I slowly got out of the bed and made my way to the bathroom. I did the usual face wash and teeth brush. I put a robe and slippers on and headed downstairs. Arianna was the cooking culprit. It smelled great!

"Good morning sunshine! You should move in and do this every day."

"You don't like to have roommates, remember?"

"Touché home girl! Jackson doesn't know that I would rather live alone. However, he could be the one to change that."

"I'm happy for you Jackson is a great guy"

"What are you in here cooking, Lord!?!" Javier was awake.

"Breakfast. I'm sure you could use a meal. We took shots last night! You barely a drink, Javi!"

"Yeah, you're right. Even if we didn't drink, I would want breakfast. Cook on!"

Arianna was almost finished making a small breakfast feast when Jackson finally made his way into the kitchen. He wasn't wearing a tee shirt and his body was sensational. He was wearing a pair of sweatpants that hung nicely off his waist. Ari and Javier looked, stared. I saw it. I didn't say anything. I wasn't the jealous type. Ok I lied, I was but these were my best friends. I wasn't worried.

"Good morning everyone. Babe. I hope you don't mind. I was sweaty when I woke. I had to remove my shirt." He walked over and kissed me. Arianna handed him a cup of coffee.

"I wouldn't mind if you walked around shirtless always! Yum!" I caressed his chest. He shivered. I sent a chill through his body. I kissed his chest and walked away.

"Jackson. May I speak with you for a moment; man, to man?" Jackson and Javier took their cups of coffee and went outside. I could see them sitting on the hammock chair. The conversation seemed fine, so I went on about my business and made myself a cup of coffee. I knew Javier well and I was willing to bet he was doing the protective big brother thing with Jackson. It made me smile. These were things that I wished Hosni were here to do. It would be great if I could get him to move here, or NY, but his brute of a wife would never go for that move. Boston was her home and she refused to leave.

"What's up Javi?! Is it ok that I call you Javi?"

"I don't mind. You would be the first straight man to do so!" They both laughed.

"I want to speak to you about a couple of things. 1...Sara is like a sister to me, so her wellbeing and happiness mean more than a lot to me. I want to make sure you have a clear understanding of that."

"I'm sure she means the world to you. I understand your relationship. She told me what you mean to her. I will not hurt her. I promise."

"Yea…it sounds good, but how does Sara fit into your life? I would hate to see her develop all these feelings for you and then you walk away from her. She will never be the same. I've known her since…I wanna say we were 24; anyway…she hasn't been in a relationship in any of those years. She usually doesn't have much in common with the guys or the guys are intimidated by her."

"I love Sara. I want her to be my wife one day. And I want to spend the rest of my life with her."

"Well then…we have to get you divorced." Javier smiled; big, got up and went back inside.

Chapter 10

"Welcome back Sara. Some of the accounting staff is waiting for you in the conference room. They would like to fill you in on business."

"Good morning Jenna; Thanks, I'm headed there now. Do me a favor and come with me. You can route all the calls to the automated server for 45 minutes."

"Ok." Jenna and I walked down the hall to the conference room. Instead of facing a room of approximately 250 people; this time, I was facing 4 people sitting at a long, rectangular table. They were all familiar faces. Krista from accounting, Peter from new accounts, John from accounting and Brian Bradley. Hmm...

"Good morning Sara. Will you please take a seat?" I sat down; reluctantly, but how could I not? I was nervous and could feel the sweat bead up on my face. Jenna sat next to me.

"Sure. What's going on? Why do I feel like my life is about to change again?"

"Hi Sara, it's good to have you back."

"Peter; it's good to be back, thank you."

"Prior to your time off we spoke about an account that Freddy was handling; do you recall?"

"I do. Proceed."

"After extensive research, we discovered that Freddy was in fact working with the client off the books. The money that was supposed to be collected from the client went to Freddy's bank account. He was depositing I.O.U's to the accounting office. They were posing as checks. Anyway, the accounting office is now negative $250,000; which is the cost of the project that the client was billed for. Freddy falsified the paperwork. We called Brian in because if we do not rectify this account, the client will sue us and take us to court. He's claiming the projects were never completed. This can be tied up in litigation for years." I thought Peter was being a tad dramatic. I took a deep breath and let the words marinate in my mind.

"How many divisions are affected by this?"

"The entire new accounts department. That's the entire budget. If you decide to settle, we will have to let that department go. If you let that department go, we cannot grow. If we cannot grow...well...you know."

"Hmmm..." At that moment, I was beyond pissed! "I hate you, Freddy!" He really found a way to make sure I cursed him out daily. I wasn't going to be able to resolve this right away. I need to assess the damage.

"Robert Taylor is the client, yes?"

"That's correct ma'am...Sara"

"Who has his project now?"

"No one ma'am. He refuses to do work with us anymore."

"Jenna! Call Mr. Taylor and ask him when he can come see me or ask if I can go see him. Tell him I can personally complete his projects and have them successfully make a profit in record time. When he tells you no, remind him of his new client contract that I hope to God he signed. He signed it right?"

"No ma'am. The only thing in his client file is his contact info. We had a team of people sift through every box and every piece of paper in Freddy's office. Nothing. It's as if this client never existed."

"Brian. Any input?" Brian didn't say anything. He knew how mad I was based on the tone in my voice. My answers were short. In fact, mad was an understatement. I thought about throwing the towel in and giving up on this company but then I looked at the faces of my employees and I was determined to do better for them. Besides, I never quit; anything, ever!

"Brian. How do I fix an account that we never had written consent to work with? In fact, pardon my tone and the attitude that is about to come out of my mouth, but this is absolutely and insanely ridiculous! I will not overwork myself and stress the minds of these hard-working people over a mishap that was caused by your step son, under your watch! This is Freddy's revenge. He was mad at you for liking me and he was mad at me for being me. I will not fix this. I am requesting you pay to fix the mishap. I will lose the client and my company can move on. I refuse to let Freddy taunt me." Everyone was silent. I was silent. Did I really say that? Yea, I did. I couldn't afford to pay for mistakes that I didn't make.

"Ok. You're right, Sara. It was supposed to be a seamless transition. But it's not and I'm sorry. You all got off to an excellent start and then this happened. And you're right. This isn't your mistake. I'll go to my accountant and have him wire the funds to the accounting office by end of business today." That was easier than I thought it would be and immediately, it didn't sit right with me. My intuition was clearly telling me not to trust Brian.

"With all due respect, Brian, I don't trust you. Let's go to my office. I want your accountant and lawyer and my accountant and lawyer on the phone and we are going to straighten this out here and now. I cannot let you leave the premises. I don't trust that you will hold up your end."

"Sara. Are you serious?!"

"I am. Please, after you."

Brian, Jenna, Peter and I left the conference room and headed back to my office. The tension was so thick; I could cut it with a knife. We all took a seat but no words were spoken. My phone vibrated on my desk.

Jax: hello beautiful. I hope your day is panning out better than mine. I just got called to emergency surgery. From the looks of the CAT scan, I will be in surgery for the duration of the day. I love you. I'll text you later.

Me: OMG! I'll say a prayer for you and the patient. I am at my wits end right now. Whenever surgery is done, come over.

Jax: will do.

"Sara, did we come to your office to watch you text?"

"Brian are you really being nasty right now?! Seriously!? You owe MY company $250,000 and I want my money NOW!"

"I-I..."

"Tell me you don't have it?!"

"I have it but technically, I don't have to give it to you. This is YOUR company, right?! So, you figure it out."

"FIGURE IT OUT!?!?!"

I picked up my cell phone, scrolled through my contact list and touched send next to Anne Bradley's name.

"Hello."

"Hi Anne. How are you today?"

"Sara, I am well, thanks. How are you?"

"I would be better if your son didn't embezzle $250,000 from the company prior to death. Not to mention, I've got your husband here who refuses to pay it back. If I end up making this payment myself, I will call in a favor and your 8.9-million-dollar home that you purchased last year, will be mine. And you know firsthand that my favors always come through."

"Put me on speaker phone please." I did, with pleasure.

"Brian, enough is enough. I know that you didn't particularly care for Freddy but Sara is a good person. If Freddy cost her $250,000, it's because it was an oversight when you had control of the company. In other words, if you don't make the payment, I will. And if I do, you and I are going to have major problems! Do you understand!?"

"Anne...Sara..." Brian paused.

"I don't care what you do! I'm dying. I got rid of this messed up company because it's a messed-up company. I knew Freddy was embezzling, I'm not stupid. I just didn't want to deal with it; with him. And now you think you can sit here and bully me into giving you a quarter of a million dollars!?!? You just bought an auto group. Stroke your own check with your own ego!" I was appalled, stunned. Was he for real?! I forgave plenty and forgot a lot. However, I did not play games when it came to my businesses and my money. It was good to know different types of people. I sent a text message to a dirty mogul that had no issues getting exactly what I needed from Brian Michael Bradley. Once I received confirmation of setup, I dismissed Brian from the building. I reassured Peter that all was taken care of and not to speak to Mr. Taylor until I told him to. Peter promised that business will go on as normal and he will wait to hear from me before he made any decisions. I liked Peter. He was earning his keep around the office and I told him so. I asked Jenna to hang out for a few so we can speak.

"Thank you for everything that you do around here, Jenna. I appreciate knowing that I can trust you. Thank you for keeping my location a secret for the past 3 days."

"You're welcome Sara. I'm not sure if you remember, but Brian didn't want to hire me 4 years ago. It was to my knowledge that you asked him to bring me onboard because you saw my potential. And for that, I thank you." Jenna was humble and I loved it! I remember telling Brian 'she's young yes, but she's smart. She can grow here.' I meant it.

"Your time has come. I need a personal assistant. I need someone that can multi task on the go just like me. There will be days when I need to be in 2 places at the same time and clearly, I cannot be. I need to be able to send you to a site or a meeting and I need to know that you will reiterate the info back to me; as if I were in the meeting myself. I need someone that works well with people. Someone with an inviting spirit and presence. I have this feeling that I will be taking on a restaurant project soon, so I will need a foodie. Do you think you can handle the task of being my exceptional personal assistant?"

"OH, MY GAWD! Absolutely! I am honored. I would love to be your personal assistant. I think you are an exceptional business mogul. I like how you handled Brian today and I believe that once he is totally out of the way, this company will flourish. I accept!" We both laughed. Jenna grinned so hard, I was blinded by her smile. She had perfect teeth; white and big!

"Here's your new pay plan and new hire paperwork. You can move into my old office here. You will need the space. Immediately, I need you to hire a receptionist. I cannot have that front desk empty, so until you have a replacement, please hold down that post." Jenna graciously accepted and signed her new hire paperwork. As she was leaving, my office phone was ringing. Mind you; it was only 10:30am.

"Hello. Good morning. Is now a good time to speak? I hope so because I will be at your office in 15 minutes!"
Rita Stanton.
"Hello. Good morning. Can you please bring me a coffee and a muffin?"
"Already stopped and picked all that up. I'll see you in a few, baby!" I wasn't officially waiting for Rita, so I forgot she was coming. I was reading email from the accounting office when Jenna walked Rita to my office.
"You were closer than you said when you called, huh?"
"Yup! I was sitting in traffic and then suddenly, it dispersed, and here I am. Here's coffee and an assortment of muffins." Rita had a box of coffee from Starbucks. The muffins were muffin tops, which was even better because that was the part of the muffin that I loved. Rita knew me well. She also knew she had to come correct for this meeting and with the way my day was starting out...let's just say my fuse was beyond short.
"Ok. Let me present to you L'inn Mange. The basement in your bed and breakfast is astonishing! It is well over 7,000 square feet. It's wider than the entire house. Why can't we turn that into a restaurant? The closest strip of restaurants is 5 blocks from your inn; all with a median wait time of 35-45 minutes on weekend nights and 20-30 minutes on weekday nights. If we had quality, wholesome, good food, right in the inn, people wouldn't have to leave. You currently don't have food on site in your location. We can change that."
Rita did some real research. I was impressed. Unfortunately, there were holes in the plan.
"Ri Ri...this sounds good. You did your research and I am quite pleased. Here's the deal." I leaned back in my chair and took a sip of coffee. I had a headache. "The reason there's no food served on site is because I do not have a license to serve food. My location is for boarding purposes only. We make a killing in the winter months because of the ski resorts and we make a killing in the summer because of the summer activities. I have no issues finding a place to eat when I'm out there. The island is decorated with wonderful restaurants. I also cannot utilize the basement because

I would have to redo the entire space. As per housing law in that city, I cannot operate while under construction."

"So, then you can sell 22% of the inn to me because I have a license to serve food in the northeast. We can then close the doors for 3 months and renovate. We can split the cost." That was a great idea. But I don't want to keep giving businesses to my friends.

"Here. Call Rena and the two of you get together so she can draw your vision. You make a menu and a business plan. Then connect with Jenna and create a presentation. The 3 of you must do this right and sell me on it. If I like what I see, then we can move on to the next step. What do you say?" Rita was grinning from ear to ear.

"Ok. Ok. Great! We won't let you down. I promise." I called Jenna into my office.

"Yes Sara."

"Jenna this is Rita. I need you to get together and make a business plan. She will fill you in with the information. I'll call Rena and fill her in. You guys call her when you are ready to sit with her. I need this done within the next 2 weeks."

"Ok." They both responded and Jenna walked Rita out of my office. I assumed they went to hers. I leaned back in my chair and called Rena.

"Hello Mrs. Dr. Ellis. What's up?"

"Your cholesterol! Please, never again with the 'Mrs. Dr.' I cannot deal!"

"Ha! You're funny. What's up? Do you need artwork?"

"Uh...sure...I need you to sit with Rita and Jenna; she's my new assistant. Rita wants to recreate L'inn and add a restaurant. You know I requested a full business presentation, so they are going to get with you for the drawing. Send me a bill when you're done; I'll take good care of you."

"I want in on the business. In exchange for my drawing, I want to own 10%."

What the...!?! Why was this the answer suddenly?!?! I got quiet and pondered an answer for this. I called Jenna and Rita back into my office and I put Rena on speakerphone. "Ladies. Rena. Rena. Ladies...here's the deal. Rita wants me to accept this business plan so I need the 3 of you to work together and make it worth it to me. Rita wants to buy 22% and Rena wants me to give her 10% in exchange for the drawing. You have 2 weeks from today. Make it worth it and make it work. If I'm not sold, the three of you get nothing. Got it?" There was silence.

"I'm cool with that..."

"Me too. Rena, what's your contact info?"

The 3 of them exchanged email addresses and telephone numbers. My work with this project was done. I had to make my way to Henderson Hill to address the staff. I took Jenna along with me. She found a temporary receptionist from one of the other companies in the building. She and I got in her Nissan Rogue and she drove us to Henderson Hill. She drove well. I took a nap. It took us a little over an hour to reach Henderson Hill. This dealership was huge. 58,000 square feet of modern glass building and 15,000 square feet of garage space. All the vehicles in new car inventory were stored indoors. This made it easier for the prep department to move around when its busy during the day. Jenna and I parked in front and walked through the large sliding door at the front of the building. Hiro Matsumaura was standing at the entrance when we arrived.

"Sara! Jenna! It's a pleasure to see you beautiful girls. How is everything?"
"We had the morning from hell, but Sara is so collected. She was cool as a cucumber and now we are great!"
"Exactly what she said. Jenna takes good care of me. How's everything going over here?"
"All is well. The staff is anxious to meet you. They sold 378 new cars and 155 used cars last month. All while maintaining 100% CSI; customer survey index results. We are getting this month off to a great start; 15 sold and it's only the 5th. Your sales manager, Justin Robby, forecasted 400 new cars this month. We won't be able to gather everyone to the conference hall today, but feel free to speak to people individually."
"Ok. Great. I want to begin in the office. I want to meet the office manager; comptroller and the billing staff."
"Absolutely. Right this way." There was a spiral staircase at the back of the showroom. It lead to a second floor where there was a customer waiting area at the top of the steps. Around the corner was a long hallway that lead to the main office and the business development office. It was very clean and bright throughout the entire showroom. I opened doors as I walked along, just to see everything that was happening. We approached glass doors that slid open into the office. The girls were busy at work.

"Ladies. I would like to introduce you to Sara Bashir. She is your new boss."
"Hello Sara. It's a pleasure to meet you." The woman that stood and

shook my hand was short; maybe 5 feet and that was pushing it. She was round in stature. She looked as if she was carrying entirely too much weight for her frame, but who was I to judge. She was pretty. She was of Indian decent; dark complexion, long dark hair. She had fine features and her petite nose was pierced. There was a red dot in the center of her forehead. I was certain that meant she was married.

"Likewise. Your name?"

"Krishna Patel. I am the comptroller. I have been with BMW for 22 years and in this location for 15 years."

"You are the mastermind behind the perfect financial records. My lawyer appreciates your precision. Thank you." We laughed.

"You're welcome." I walked through the office. The way it was setup, Krishna had the front room to herself. Behind her office was a bigger space with 5 desks, a copier, a fax machine, and wall to wall filing cabinets. This was where the billing staff was located.

"Hello Sara, my name is Keiko Matsumaura. I am Hiro's little sister. Hahaha! I am also your DMV clerk. I have been here 5 years. Pleasure to meet you."

"Likewise."

"This is Jaime Harris, accounts receivable. She's been here 2 years. This is Dana Wallace, accounts payable and she's also been here 2 years. In fact, they came together from Volvo of Henderson Hill."

"Pleasure."

While we were walking, and meeting, Jenna was taking notes on her iPad mini. I looked over her shoulder and there were the names, a brief physical description and job title of everyone we were meeting. I knew I hit the nail on the head hiring her! I was not going to remember all those names. We toured the entire facility; sales and service and we individually met over 400 employees. We managed to gather everyone to the shop and I addressed them.

"Thank you everyone, for taking a moment to gather here. My name is Sara Bashir and this is my personal assistant, Jenna Mackay. I am excited to be standing here with you. I am excited to embark on this journey with you. I am not new to the automotive industry. I consulted with dealership principals and sales managers for years. I have an open-door policy. Although I do not have an office setup on site yet, you can always reach me via email, telephone, text or FaceTime. I will be making trips once a week to check on the facility. I am here remotely daily. I see everything.

I don't expect to change much. A lot of change is not needed. You are fully capable of conducting business successfully. However, if I deem it necessary, I will make a change. You guys are here every day. You should be comfortable and fully operational. If, for some reason you cannot be or you do not have the tools to do so, please do not hesitate to reach out to me and I will make it happen. I am a business woman. I own quite a few businesses; a variety. I have been successful and I do not plan on changing that. I want us to continue as the number one sales and number one service departments in the eastern region! Now let's get back to work! Cheers!"

"HERE HERE!!" The crowd dispersed. Jenna and I made our way into the parking lot.

"Sara, Sara...wait!"

"Justin. What's up brother?"

"Demos. Do you girls want demos? Any car of your choice...pick 2 and let me know what the stock numbers are. Hang out for another hour; have dinner and we'll have you riding out in style. What do you say?" Jenna looked at me with puppy eyes. They were begging me to allow her to leave her Rogue behind. I looked at her, smiled and rolled my eyes.

"Ok. Come on Jen, let's check the inventory."

"Great. I'll send one of the guys from prep to meet you inside." Just that fast, Justin was gone. Jenna and I walked the inventory lot. It was 4 indoor floors of cars. Wall to wall BMWS and Minis. They were all grouped by model and separated; real wheel and all-wheel drive. Jenna picked out an X3 diesel and I picked out a 750LI diesel. It was for my mother. I sold Jenna on diesel when I explained the fuel economy pros and the torque pros. The cars were cleaned, plated and ready for us to drive away by the time we were done eating. It was almost 4pm when we finally hit the road. I followed Jenna on the drive back to B&A.

"Today was exhilarating Sara. I am so amped!"

"I'm glad you are! I appreciate the work you did today. Good job. Can you email me the notes that you took?"

"Sure. I also have a blueprint to the business plan for Rita. I'll forward that to you as well. I want to keep you a float while we're working on it."

"Thanks, but I would rather see it when it's finished. Rita is going to know I saw it in advance. Let's keep the peace."

"Ok. Got it. I'll see you tomorrow, then?"

"Yup. Have a good night. Enjoy that car!" I was exhausted. I sat down and my cell phone vibrated in my bag. I fished it out and didn't recognize the number on my caller ID.

"Sara speaking."

"What's up ma? The situation has been handled. We're on our way to your house so we can discuss. Meet you there in...20-25. Is that cool?" I recognized the voice.

"Sure."

I hung up, grabbed my bag, my keys and sprinted out of the building. When I approached the employee parking lot, I was greeted by Saul. He was the head of the car service that is on the premises for all the account executives.

"Would you like me to send drivers to your house with your vehicle?"

"No. It's ok. I'll drive the 7 series home now. Send a car for me in the am, and I will drive my car home tomorrow evening."

"Will do ma'am."

What's with the ma'am in this place?! I got it, my people had manners and they were used to addressing Brian as sir, but I was not in the acceptable age group for 'ma'am.' I had to strongly enforce the use of my name.

"Please, Saul, call me Sara."

"Ok Sara. What time would you like your car to arrive?"

"7:45am please."

"Will do. Have a good evening."

"Thanks you too." I couldn't get to the bar in my home fast enough. I didn't park the 7 series in the garage. I wanted it to sit out with the company plate frame brackets visible to the street. I hoped that it will inspire my neighbors to send me their business. I walked up the steps to the porch, gathered the mail and proceeded into the house. I kicked my shoes off at the door, threw everything down and headed to the bar to pour a drink. I was out of everything that I wanted to drink so instead I made a fruit smoothie and rolled a blunt. I went outside and perched myself on the hammock chair. I was quite comfortable.

"Geez, girl! You are more and more beautiful every time I see you." My guest arrived.

"Cross! It's good to see you."

Crocificio Gregorio was the biggest mob boss that I've ever had the pleasure to know. He was a genuine, good guy with a 'family business' to maintain. He walked into my office when I was an intern at B&A. He was in over his head trying to become a legit business man. 'I'll still get rid of a sucker, but I need uncle Sam off my fat back!' He was my first financial setup; my very first client. It took me 2 years to get him started, but once I did, his business boomed! He owned the largest bakery in the entire borough of Brooklyn. Yup, the burly mob boss went into baked goods. They made 150 made to order cakes a week. They specialize in wedding cakes but no task was too big or too small for this bakery. When he made his first legal million, he handed me a business card. 'anytime you need a favor, call me. You're officially a friend of mine. I'll take care of you if you need it.'

I heard in a mob movie that if a boss told you that you were a friend of his, you were automatically in. So, I pulled his card today, and he held up his end of the bargain.

"It's good to see you too. This is Bobby blue. He's one of my brother's kids."

"Sara, good to meet you. I hear great things about you. Like if it wasn't for you, none of us would be here. Thanks!"

"Likewise. All I did was my job. Cross made the rest happen. Thank him. You guys want a drink?"

"Na babe. We're still working. Can we sit? Let me tell you what we did today."

Cross and Bobby took a seat on each side of me on the hammock chair. Like Jackson, Bobby made it swing in random intervals. The meeting was brief but it covered a lot of ground. Bobby assured me that no one was injured or murdered, but the point was made very clear. Cross handed me a briefcase and instructed me to open it inside.

"You know what's in there and you know what to do with it."

"Thanks. I really appreciate it."

"No problem. There's no way in hell I'm gonna have your businesses under direct fire. I set you up with 24-hour surveillance at your businesses; including the salon that you just opened for Ari. There's also a detail on your street and one that's observing the house in hidden sight. They are aware of your regular possible guests, so none of them will be harassed. You know that security comes with my work. It's not to freak you out, it's to protect you. When we feel you don't need it anymore, it will disappear."

They each took one of my hands and held them. We sat in silence for a moment. I think Cross said a prayer. That was what he did. He prayed before or after he acted like an ass.

"Alright BB, we gotta go! Sara. I love you babes. Take care. Call me if you need me."

Bobby and Cross got up and left the porch. They were escorted into the back of a Chevy Tahoe. It was all black with black tints. There was no visibility inside. I watched it drive away and when it did, I went inside. It was time to eat.

Chapter 11

It had been weeks and business was running smoothly, yet rapidly. Financially, I was making a killing! Jenna was doing an exceptional job as my personal assistant. She hired a new receptionist and she was almost as sharp as Jenna was in that position. Her name was Emma. She was tall, blonde, with green eyes, and very slim. However, her voice didn't match her look. It was deep and raspy, but she was not a smoker. It drove me crazy. I hated it, but technically she was Jenna's employee, so I did not interact with her too much. The way her voice disturbed me made Jenna laugh. It was the week before my birthday and I was late arranging my schedule. Rena, Rita and Jenna needed an extension on their business plan. I understood because I was absorbing a lot of Jenna's time. Once we cleared up the issue with Mr. Taylor, the financial consulting business soared. It was as if the public was watching us to see how we were going to handle it. We must have handled it well because the new accounts department was receiving 100 new clients a day. Mr. Taylor remained a B&A client; I personally handled his accounts. It was what he wanted. Jackson and I were doing equally well. He and Javier were becoming close also. I didn't mind. It was just guys hanging out, right? I hoped they were not up to something, but if they were, in due time, I'd find out.

"Hello, Javier speaking."

"What's up brother, it's Jackson."

"Hey man. How's it going?"

"Good, I can't complain. Remember you were telling me about your jeweler that makes custom pieces?"

"Yea, are you in need of his service?"

"Uh..."

"Of course you do or you wouldn't be asking. Are you asking Sara to marry you?"

"No. Well not yet. But I do want to get her a gift."

"Aww, that's sweet. Well lucky for you, I have an appointment there in an hour. I'm dropping off a few pieces to be cleaned and one that I broke. You wanna meet me there?"

"Ok. Where's he located?"

"2230 East Harlow Ave. It's in the brick building on the corner of Division."

"Ah! Ok. I'll see you in an hour." Jackson arrived at Harlow Jewelers before

Javier. He explained to the gentleman at the counter that he was meeting a friend that has an appointment but he too, would be interested in a purchase. Jackson walked around looking in cases while he waited for Javier. Javier walked in after about 15 minutes.

"Oh, my goodness. I am so sorry I'm late. Hi Ralph! Did you meet my soon to be brother in law in a year, Jackson? Jackson. Ralph. Ralph. Jackson."

"We met crazy man! What's up brother? You had me waiting for so long, I thought you weren't coming." The two embraced.

"Oh no! I could never stand you up. Once I did and you told Sara, she would never let me hear the end of it. Did you pick anything out?"

"Yea I saw a tennis bracelet, and a watch for myself."

"Baller!" Javier walked over to the counter where Ralph was standing. "Here Ralphie, this is what I need cleaned and this is what I broke."

Ralph needed a few minutes to fill the requests. Jackson and Javier walked next door and sat in a deli while they waited for their packages to be complete. Their conversation was friendly. They were getting to know each other. Javier was acting as a big brother and making sure Jackson knew there were people in Sara's corner.

"Jackson. I like you. You seem harmless. I'm Sara's stand in big brother. She doesn't introduce guys to Hosni. He once told her he only wants to meet the man she intends on marrying. He wants the guy to come to him and ask for permission to marry her. The rest are just playmates. I guess he's right. He's super over protective of her; mind you, her father is very much alive and well. Anyway, Sara doesn't tell much to Hosni or her father. So, don't be offended if her family doesn't know that you exist."

"I can relate to that. I have a sister. She's younger than me. I love Sara. I plan on marrying her soon."

"Uhm...yea you mentioned that...hmmm..."

"Well...I would like to marry her one day." Jackson's eyes dropped. Javier took a swig of his drink.

"Listen. Everything happens for a reason. I don't believe you found each other by accident. There's a plan for you. Who knows what the plan is. Maybe it wasn't meant for you two to be together. Maybe the reason for you meeting her was to make you appreciate what you already have."
Shots. Fired.

"Hmm...I wish I knew."

"Time will tell I guess. But listen, if she ends up with a broken heart, I'll break your jaw. In fact, the only way you won't lose your jaw is if she tells me not to break it. Got it?"

"Oh. I got it!" Jackson smiled. Javier wasn't kidding. His facial expression never changed. His face was stern, tight. Jackson stopped smiling immediately.

"Listen man. I love Sara. I understand how much you love her too. I have no plans on things going bad but like you said, 'who knows what the plan is.' if we don't end up together, I think that means that was supposed to happen. And if that's the case, there's no need to break my jaw." This time, Javier smiled.

"I'm taking Sara to Hedonism for her birthday. She's been through a lot and she's been very busy with these new businesses. She deserves a trip."

"She does deserve a trip, but Hedonism though? Don't bring her back pregnant!"

"Damn man! Don't put that in the atmosphere! Come on, let's get out of here. I have to meet her in 30 minutes." Jackson left $30 on the table. They got up and walked out. After they picked up their packages, Jackson stopped and hugged Javier.

"Thanks for meeting me on short notice brother. It was a pleasure."

"Oh, no problem man. Thanks for paying. Next one is on me."

"Aight. Cool. Take care brother."

They hugged again, then walked in separate directions. Jackson arrived at Sara's in just under 30 minutes. "Record time!" He said to himself as he got out of the car. When he reached the front door, it was locked. He walked around to the side door. "Success." Jackson walked in the house and it was very quiet.

"Sara. You here babe?" Jackson walked up the stairs and could hear me moaning as he was coming down the hall. He opened the French doors and there I was, on the bed with my legs up. I was fingering myself.

"Oh babe, let me help you." Jackson climbed up on the bed next to me. He kissed me. Deeply. The surge of passion rushed through me like electricity. Jackson took my hand away and replaced it with his. I moaned as he inserted two of his fingers inside of me.

"This is mine!" Jackson whispered into my mouth through a kiss. I reached down and fumbled with his belt. I managed to get his pants unzipped and unbuttoned. He wiggled his way out of them. I sat up and motioned for him to lay on his back. He did. Immediately, I wrapped my lips around his shaft and began to suck. My hand slid up and down behind my mouth. I forgot how much I enjoyed doing this for him. He was moaning and saying my name. I was getting excited. I was saturated. I got up.

"Go sit in the chair."

Immediately, Jackson jumped up. As he was walking to the other side of the room, I was rubbing on my breasts, pulling my nipples. He sat down and motioned for me to come to him. I didn't. I stood in front of him, just far enough that he couldn't reach me. I slid two fingers into my mouth and sucked. I slid them down the front of my body and used the same two fingers to rub my clitoris. Jackson was salivating. He grabbed his penis and began to stroke it.

"Woman! You are so sexy! Come here! Sit on me!" Instead, I walked over to him and got down on my knees.

"I wasn't done with this yet!" Again, I wrapped my lips around him and sucked. This time, I was moving very slowly up and down. I stuck two fingers inside of me and when I pulled them out, they were dripping with my juices. I put them in Jackson's mouth. He sucked. He moaned. I continued to suck. Jackson reached down and pushed me back. He stood and spun me around. He pushed my back and I reached down to touch my toes. Instead I grabbed his ankles as he spread my legs and slid inside of me. He pumped me slowly and deeply. We were both moaning. In fact, I think I was screaming. He spanked me... that was all it took. I couldn't hold back any longer. I climaxed. Just as I did, he did too. We both collapsed onto the bed.

"I love you, Sara."

"I love you too, Jackson. I love our sex!" I giggled.

"You're using me."

"Yup. Only because I think you're using me too."

"I might be."

"I think I'm addicted to you."

"I know I'm addicted to you. You light me up. You give me clear direction." I kissed Jackson on his chest. The next thing I knew, I was asleep. I woke up in bed alone. This time I didn't smell any food being cooked.

"Bummer because I'm hungry." I sat up. I was nude. I giggled. That's how I knew Jackson put me to bed. I always woke up nude. I looked at the clock. It was 8pm. It was chilly in the house this evening, so I put on a pair of sweats and a long-sleeved t-shirt. I put on a pair of fuzzy, slipper socks and slowly proceeded downstairs. From the middle landing, I could see Jackson sitting on the sofa. It was weird. He was just sitting there. He wasn't watching TV. I stood there to see if he was going to move and just as I was about to take a step, he began speaking...in GERMAN!! My German wasn't that advanced. He was speaking too fast. I stood still and listened. I hoped he would switch to English, but I wasn't that lucky. He was getting louder, but it wasn't loud enough to wake me, had I still been asleep. I was just about to turn around and go back upstairs and low and behold...

"Yea, it's important. I'm ready to move on with my life and this is holding me up. Handle it now!" Then just like that he was done. I took a couple of steps back. Had he moved, I was going to pretend I wasn't standing there the entire time. But I did wonder, who was he talking to? Was he talking about his wife? 'I'm ready to move on with my life.' I was sure he was talking about being with me. Should I ask him about this? Should I pretend like I didn't hear any of that? I didn't want to go downstairs at all. Dr. Jackson Alcott Ellis had a secret that he was not telling me. I thought I could ignore it. I went back to my bedroom and organized the thoughts that just spilled over in my brain. I opened my cell phone and scrolled until I found the name I was looking for. I touched the name and stepped out onto my balcony for privacy.

"Hey, I'm in need of your service..." I called in another favor.

My 'to do' list was insane. I had very little time to get things done before I boarded the plane to paradise. First things first, I had to take this car to my mother.

"Hey Ma! What you doing? You home?"

"Hello baby. I am home. Are you coming by?"

"I am. I don't have much time, I should pack. Jackson is taking me away for my birthday."

"Oh, that's nice. It's been a while with this man and I still don't know him. What's wrong with him?" I laughed. She had to know everything and everyone. It was killing her to be out of the loop.

"Nothing is wrong with him ma. I just want to make sure he's staying around."

"Understood."

"Anyway, I'm bringing you a gift. I'll see you in a few." I pulled into the driveway about 20 minutes after I hung up from speaking to my mom.

She was in the yard, doing some gardening when I arrived.

"Good morning, Sara."

"Good morning, Mama."

I walked over to my mom and kissed her hello. I put the key to the car in her hand.

"What do you give me your keys for?" My mother had moments when her English was broken. I usually corrected it, but I let this one slide.

"This is for you. I own a BMW store now. I couldn't let you and daddy spend money on one when I can give you one."

"Oh, my goodness! You own the store?! Praise HIM. I always tell your father that you're my special child; you're cut from different cloth. I am proud of the person you have become. I do not mind that you are not married because you are successful. A man would be a gift to your life, not a necessity." My mother always knew how to make me feel special.

"Aw mama, I am who I am because you made me and you pushed me. You taught me well. Is daddy here?"

"No. He's playing golf with some of the men from the neighborhood."

"Oh ok. Tell him he stinks and I love him. Here comes Jenna. I love you. I'll call you when I get back. Don't speed in this car; oh and it's diesel. Do not forget that"

"I drove diesel car in Egypt. I like diesel; ok, I love you too. Oh, where are you going?"

"Jamaica."

"Oooooh, enjoy! Keep your panties on! No babies until you have a wedding!" I shook my head, grabbed her and gave her a big hug. She kissed me and I walked away; toward Jenna's car.

"Hey boss woman! This is a nice house! Did you grow up here?"

"'Boss woman' that's dope; I sure did! We moved here when I was 5. Then, I went to college, came back; my brother and I still have bedrooms here."

"Ha! That's cool."

"Ok, here's here's the rundown. You ready." Jenna shook her head.

"I'm waiting for a package to come via FedEx. It will probably come while I'm away. Just leave it in my office; it's gonna come to Broad St. It requires a signature; Emma's is fine. As soon as I'm back, I need to meet with you, Rena and Rita, and get that project started. Make sure you are up to date with everything that is going on at Henderson Hill. I'm gonna be gone for a week; Hedonism for 3 days and then Santorini. Jackson went all out with this year's birthday celebration. You should be me for a week. Make decisions as if you were me. But if you are absolutely stumped on a decision, leave it, make note of it and where you're stuck and we can address it together when I get back."

I did all the talking while Jenna drove. I was certain she heard everything I said. When we arrived at my house, she parked and followed me inside. She repeated everything that I said while we were in the car and she asked questions that she compiled. We were sitting in my bedroom sized closet when Jackson came in the house and up the stairs.

"Hi babe; Sara, your door was unlocked. I locked it behind me when I came in. Hello Jenna."

Jackson walked into the closet and kissed me lightly on my lips. Then he put his arms around me and squeezed me tight. I guess that was his way of disciplining for me leaving the door unlocked. Jenna was watching him as he moved around the room. She needed to look away before I made her look away; this was the visit from my jealous side.

"Hello Dr. Ellis."

"Hi; you can call me Jackson. Sara, we're only going to be gone for a week, and it's hot where we're going. You don't need to pack this much clothing. In fact, don't pack any. We can shop for clothes as you need them. Don't you agree?" Hmmm, he had a point. I liked the way he was thinking, but...

"Don't you think we spend too much money?"

"Who are you and what did you do with my Sara?"

"I'm just saying, we eat like an army!"

"Babe; the hotel is all-inclusive in Hedonism, so we eat for free, essentially. And when we get to Santorini, my staff makes sure we eat. So technically, we're not spending on food." Jackson had everything planned perfectly.

"Ok, your flight is at 8am tomorrow morning. I'll send a car for you at 6. I would love to take you but 6 is way too early and I have a meeting with the head of HR at Henderson Hill tomorrow at 9. She wants to discuss the new harassment policy." Jenna was taking care of things that I forgot about. She really was a gem."Make sure you email me when you arrive so I can tell you not to work while you're on vacation. I will take care of everything. Oh, and Krishna called. She wants to know if the sales staff can sell your mothers demo."

"There's like 70 miles on that car; and those are the 70 miles we drove

it from Henderson to her house. Tell her to register and insure it to the dealership and hard plate it; not available for sale yet."
"Ok. Cool. I will let her know. Ok. I'm leaving. Enjoy your trip. Jackson."
"Thanks Jen. Good night."
Jackson and I finished the little bit of packing that I agreed to do. There were some items that I refused to leave town without. I fell asleep early that night; like a kid on Christmas Eve. I was so excited to go on this vacation. I was excited to be with Jackson. It was going to be a spectacular birthday week! I was certain of it.

We got to the airport with enough time for me to sit at the airport bar. It didn't matter how early the flight, I had to drink. When we arrived in Jamaica we were greeted by a private driver. He was holding a card with Jackson's name on it. It was nice. It was a long car ride; about 2 hours, but when we pulled into the driveway of this luxurious hotel, my eyes lit up in amazement. There were bright flowers and palm trees. People walking around nude or partially dressed. The water that I could see was crystal clear; pink sands. We walked through a huge glass door that opened into a lobby. A beautiful young lady and an equally attractive young man met us at the door.

"Welcome to Hedonism; the vacation of a lifetime!"
We walked around nude for three days and it was by far the best trip ever! I knew Jackson being the reason I was there and the nudity were small factors, but nonetheless, it was amazing. I ate a Papaya a day and was officially addicted.

"Jenna has to find a way to get Papayas delivered to me weekly." Jackson out did himself with this vacation. We rafted, canoed and he even convinced me to try hang gliding. Jamaica was beautiful and I could be 100% nude if I wanted to be.
"I prefer you wear a cover up please."
I smiled. Jackson was cute when he was being protective. I've never had anyone be protective over me; except Hosni and Javi. When Keith and I were together, he was more concerned about how I dressed. He once attempted to coordinate matching outfits for us to wear to a party; it didn't happen. In fact, I didn't even go to the party. The night before my birthday, Jackson and I had the most amazing, mind blowing sex! I often

wondered if our sex life was as good as it was because we have strong chemistry or is it because he really wasn't happy with his sex life with his wife and I was filling a void. I wondered if he would tell her about me. Did people get divorced after the affair is outed? If it were me that he cheated on, I would let him go. My pride wouldn't allow me to keep him around. Don't get me wrong, I loved him but I had a good name to keep up. I couldn't be known as a mistress. I finally fell asleep around 2am. I woke up moaning; and the sun was out.

"Oh, babe! Good morning!" Jackson was licking my clitoris.
"Happy birthday beautiful..." He muttered between licks. He continued this sensational motion with his tongue; he was driving me insane! I loved every minute of it! We rolled around in bed and randomly touched, kissed, licked...for most of the morning.
"If you want, we can lay here all day!"
"I wouldn't mind, but I would like to get a swim in."
"Ok. I will watch you swim, I would rather." That was weird because I could have sworn Jackson told me he was a swimmer. I could be wrong but how likely is it that a 50yr old white male doesn't know how to swim? Anyway, I jumped up and began dressing for the pool. I put on a white bikini with a halter top, a pair of flip flops, grabbed a towel and headed towards the door.
"I'll meet you at the pool. I've got to make a phone call."
That was weird too. I thought nothing more of it and went on about my business. The pool was an outdoor lap pool; which was perfect because I prefer to swim laps. There were long white lounge chairs on the pool deck. The atmosphere was relaxing. There were speakers in various corners and they were providing the sounds of the steel drum band that was playing down on the beach. It was, by far, the best swim ever! I did approximately 10 laps. Beat was an understatement for what I was feeling when I was finished. I was worn out in a great way! I laid a towel down on the lounge chair and got comfortable. The sun felt so good on my damp skin. Before I knew it, I was asleep. I was awakened by the steel drum band. This time, it felt as if they were sitting on my lap. I opened one eye and squinted. Sure enough, they were standing on the pool deck in front of me...

"Happy Birthday to you
Happy birthday to you

Happy birthday to Saraaaaaaaaaa
Happy birthday to you!"

I was grinning from ear to ear. I looked up and saw Jackson.

"Are you wearing loin cloth?!" I was dying laughing
"It's hot as hell, but I am not ready to swing in public!" Jackson winked at me.
"Happy Birthday to my beautiful angel." He kissed me.
"Thank you, thank you. This is, by far, the best birthday I've ever had."
"I'm glad to hear that. Here, this is for you." Jackson handed me a gift bag. He signaled to the wait staff and they rolled a cart over. It had a huge cake; German chocolate. They also brought over 2 chilled bottles of White Hennessy.
"Can you bring us a platter with shrimp cocktail and fruit? She needs to eat before we drink." I rolled my eyes. He was right though. Immediately, the wait staff shuffled to fulfill Jackson's requests. Randomly, people were walking by wishing me well. I was grinning hard!
"Oooooh! Look at you, soaking up all the island attention!" Jackson was extremely touchy and kissy. I was about to take advantage of him right there on the pool deck.
"Babe. Please open your gift." I opened the bag and there was a jewelry box and a key box.
"Oh, my goodness! You went to Harlow's?!" I opened the jewelry box and there was the most beautiful pink diamond tennis bracelet that I'd ever seen. My eyes lit up.
"That's the look I was hoping to get when you opened this. Here, let me put it on you." Jackson slowly placed the tennis bracelet on my wrist and fastened it closed.
"This is beautiful. Thank you so much." I opened the second box and it was a key.
"It starts something that's sitting in your driveway. I figured I could splurge just this once, but I'm not telling you what it is."
"Ah you're killing me!"
Jackson leaned in and kissed me. It was one of our deep, passionate kisses. I was lying on the lounge chair and he was sitting up next to me. He leaned in close to me and began to rub my vagina through the bikini bottom. There was a cabana nearby. Quickly, Jackson picked me up and practically ran into the cabana. He dropped his pants and I slivered out

of my bikini bottoms. He penetrated me deep. He was kissing me so he could swallow the sound that I made when he inserted himself. My vagina was saturated and he loved every minute of it. I climaxed but I wasn't finished. In fact, I was just getting started. I jumped down and spun around quickly. I bent down and arched my back. Jackson inserted himself again and began penetrating me again. This time he spanked me. I moaned out loud. I couldn't contain it anymore. I didn't care if people heard me. I imagined people standing on the opposite side of the door masturbating to the sounds of my penetration. I was such a freak, that idea was turning me on even more and Jackson was practically sliding in and out of me like a kid on a water slide. We climaxed together.

"I'll be ready for another round immediately. I'll meet you upstairs."

Chapter 12

Jackson and I cut our week-long getaway short. 3 days of hot, steamy, raunchy sex, good food, and fresh fruit was honestly enough for me. I wanted to get back to work and plan a new trip for the end of the year. "We can do Santorini later in the year. I should get back to my new offices."

"Agreed...well, not agreed, but whatever you prefer."

"Thanks for understanding."

"It's a good thing Santorini wasn't going to cost me anything." Jackson laughed. He leaned in and kissed me on my cheek.

"I know. That's why I didn't mind cutting the trip short." I laughed too. Jackson left the room to arrange our ride to the airport. There was a laptop in our hotel room with free Wi-Fi so I opened it and decided to check my email. It felt like I waited a lifetime for my inbox to load.

"WOW, a lot has been going on, huh?"

I said to myself as I checked the email addresses that were on the screen. I saw 2 from Jenna, 2 from Cross, and 2 from my investigator. That was more important to me, so I opened those first.

"Hey Sara, I have to be brief via email, but I have some information for you. Let's meet. When are you back in town?" Hmmm, I opened the second email "Hey Sara...we have a bit of a problem. I got Cross involved. I hope that's ok."

What the heck was going on? My hands shook slightly. I scrolled up the page and opened 1 of 2 emails from Cross.

"What's up Choc!? Ya investigator buddy called me. Seems like we got a situation. No worries. I'll handle it."

I thought these people knew me better than to be so vague via email, especially when I am NOWHERE near home. I opened the second email.

"I don't trust Jackson's transporter. I have a jet at the airport that is going to bring you home. When you get here, my guys will be at the gate to bring you home. Don't tell Jackson, just rock with it."

That email was time stamped 24 minutes ago. I quickly hit reply.

"Cross, I appreciate the work, the transportation. I assume you will fill me in ASAP. What time is this flight?" He responded immediately.

"Oh, thank God, you're ok. Your original flight plan says '6pm' this evening. That will still happen. When you get to the gate, you and Jackson will be walked onto a private plane. DO NOT ASK ANY QUESTIONS OR MAKE YOURSELF LOOK SUSPICIOUS." I was literally freaked out. But I trusted Cross and I trusted the investigator...

"Where's Jenna? Is she alright?"

"Jenna is fine. You have about 3 hours to get yourself together and get to the airport. Remember, play cool. You know nothing! I'll see you soon."

Here we go. I had no idea what was brewing, but whatever it was, it was about to go down! I sat and skimmed the rest of my email. The bulk of it was work related and I wasn't quite ready to deal with work, so I left those for when I return to my office. I signed off the computer and cleaned up our hotel room. I wasn't sure where Jackson was. I didn't think anything of it. While we were here, he ran laps on the beach. I assumed that's what he was doing. It was almost 5pm and I was loading our bags on the hotel bag cart so we can begin heading to the airport. I still hadn't seen Jackson. I walked around the hotel room one last time to make sure I didn't forget anything. Once all was clear, I headed to the elevator and went to the front lobby. When I stepped off the elevator a gentleman, hotel staff, greeted me.

"Sara? I have your limo ready to take you to the airport. Are these your bags? Are you ready?" I was confused. What was happening?

"Uh, yes. These are my bags, but no, I'm not ready. Where's Jackson?"

"I'm sorry ma'am..." He looked confused.

"Jackson; my man. WHERE IS HE?!?!?!?" I was officially yelling.

"Oh, I don't know. I assumed you were here alone."

"What? Why would you assume that I'm alone; IN HEDONISM?!!?"

As I was getting upset, I saw one of the gentlemen that was on the beach the day of my birthday. He too, was a waiter.

"Sir! Sir! Remember I was on the beach yesterday with a man? Have you seen him?"

"Oh, I remember the man, I haven't seen him. I'm sorry."

Now I was worried and I was frustrated. I refused to leave without him.

"I'm not going anywhere until I find him!" I sat down in the lobby, fumbled through my bag and dug my cell phone out. I scrolled through my contacts and touched send next to Jackson's name. No answer. I sat for a moment and touched it again. 42 times. I called his cell 42 times and got nothing. The tears built up in my eyes. I was shaking. I sent him multiple text messages.

Me: Babe...come on! Stop playing around. It's time to leave.

Me: Where are you?

Me: I'm devastated

Me: HELLO!!!!

I missed the flight. I refused to move. I sat in the lobby for 4 hours. My phone rang after 3hrs.

"Sara...why are you not on the plane?" It was Cross.

"I can't find Jackson. He's gone. Or missing. Or something!" We were quiet...

"Stay where you are. I'll call the hotel and rebook your room. I'm going to put Ari and Dani on a plane to you. I think I know what happened, but I'm not saying; not yet. They will be with you by tomorrow morning. DO NOT GO ANYWHERE!"

I said ok and hung up the phone. The wait staff took my bags to a new hotel suite. I was devastated. I couldn't believe my man was gone. Ghost. How did my wonderful birthday getaway turn so sour? I don't remember falling asleep but I was awakened by my best friends bursting into my hotel room.

"I wanted a vacation, but I wanted a HAPPY trip!"

"Dani stop! Look at her! She's devastated, tell me what happened?"

"Did anyone bring weed? I need to smoke."

"Luckily, Cross flew us in his jet, so I was able to bring some." Ari to the rescue; she rolled up. We sat outside on the lounge chairs, smoked and talked. I told them what I knew, which wasn't much and they told me what they knew. Equally, we knew nothing. Who knew how long Cross planned on keeping us here. My trust was with him. I knew that he would make sure we were ok, but what about Jackson? What would happen if I never found him? I couldn't recall, but I wasn't sure if Cross ever found someone for me. After the great ganja filled my lungs, my mood was lighting up. Ari, Dani and I partook in a ton of activities at the resort. As per Cross's request, we never left the resort. But since it wasn't romantic weekend anymore, Cross sent us to a more friend-friendly resort. Although I was having an absolute ball with my friends, my heart was broken. I knew that Jackson didn't disappear on purpose. He was better than that.

"Cross; please tell me you've got something."

"I've got something and I'm working on something else. Do you think you're ready to come home, or shall I keep you touring the world?"

"The world? Where am I going? Jackson may come back looking for me. I'm already in a different hotel. He'll never find me if I leave and go to another country. If I'm leaving, I'd rather go home."

"Are you ready to come home?" I paused before I answered. I wasn't ready to go home, although it may not a bad idea. I could occupy myself with work and not worry about where Jackson was.

"I'm ready to go home. I want to see my mom and check on my companies. I also want..." Before I could finish that thought, my phone beeped. "Cross. My phone is beeping...OH MY GOD IT'S JACKSON!"

"Keep him talking for more than a minute...gotta try and track where he is." I quickly clicked over.

"Babe..."

"Babe? No, it's not 'babe', but I am willing to bet you are Sara. He keeps saying your name."

"I am Sara. Who are you?"

"I think I'm going to be the one asking questions for a few, ok?" I was not in the mood to play games, but Cross said, 'keep him talking' so that's what I did.

"Ok. That's fine."

"So, I wasn't looking for Jackson; but he's somewhat predictable. Also, I wasn't trying to break your heart, but I felt I needed to step in sooner than later. He's buying expensive trips and gifts for you; and you must mean something to him, since he called in a favor to have me 'handled...'" Wait, was this HIS WIFE?

"I'm sorry. I don't follow, all I did was fall in love with a man that fell in love with me first."

"He fell in love first? Who does he think he is?" I was silent. I was beginning to feel like I was simply there to be dumped on.

"Well..." That was it. The call ended.

"Hello. Hello!" There was nothing. No sound. No more voice. Nothing. Quickly my phone rang again. It was Cross.

"I'm not sure what happened; but that call was coming from Jackson's cell phone. He's on the island. Whoever that was, is an amateur. In fact, I don't think it's a real 'kidnapper'. Stay where you are. Instead of you coming home, I'm coming to you. If your phone rings again, answer it. I have a device tracking you and your phone calls and now his too. I'll see you in a few hours." I just stood there. Speechless. What the hell was happening? Did I just speak to the disgruntled woman? What was I supposed to do? As I was pacing, panicking, Ari walked in.

"Whoa! You alright boo? You look like you just saw a ghost." I couldn't tell Ari. She was gonna ask me a million questions that I couldn't answer. I took a deep breath and went on with a 'normal flow'.

"Oh yeah...I'm fine. Cross is coming!"

"Uh oh! That could be a good thing, a great thing or a terrible thing. We can't stress it, but we can go to the beach. There's a limbo contest!" Ari began jumping up and down. She loved a good limbo contest. I laughed.

"Ok. I guess we're going to the beach!" That's exactly what we did. I slipped on a pair of soft flip flops and we walked down to the beach. It was a sunny day. Somewhat windy, but it was sunny. Daniela was already on the beach so we walked over to her. Groups were beginning to form around a man that was standing in the middle.

"Hello vacationers! Welcome to Limbo Land. Today's contest is simple. We limbo! Everyone will line up here. We'll play some music and everyone will take turns going under the limbo bar. At the end of each rotation, we will lower the bar. And this will continue. Along the way, people will fall and falter and fall out. It will be fun and competitive!"

"What does the winner get?" It was a faint voice from behind the crowd.

"Good question! The winner gets a $1,000 Amex gift card and the title 'Best Limbo-err of the beach!'"

"I'm down! That Amex gift card is mine!" Arianna was excited.

"Ok! So, all those that want to participate, please come toward me and line up over here." He pointed. People shuffled in that direction. Of course, Arianna was first.

"Whoever isn't playing, please stand on this side. You can help me judge." He pointed again and the people shuffled in the opposite direction. The music started playing and limbo was underway.

"Have fun! You better win!"

"I will!" I walked away and stood amongst the people that were 'helping the judge'. Daniela walked over to me and handed me a drink.

"It's called 'happy heart'. I figured it would help." She handed me the drink and I took a sip. It was strong.

"Whew! Yup...it's helping put hair on my chest! Thanks!"

We laughed and sat in the sand. We chose a spot where we can still see the limbo contest, but we were far enough away that the music didn't interrupt our conversation.

"I hope that Cross can find Jackson. I can tell that you are enjoying our vacation together, but I can tell that your heart is sad, it's understood."

"Cross is the man! I don't think there's too much that he cannot do. What

kills me is who would take him? Who would he willingly walk away with?"
"Do you think he disappeared on purpose?"
"I feel like he didn't because I want to believe that I know him better than that. I honestly don't know what to think."
"I think intoxication is best! I'll get us another round!" She jumped up and walked away. I glanced at the limbo crowd and Ari was still in the running. She just may win this gift card after all. My phone rang again.

"Hello."
"How did you meet Jackson?"
"He's one of my clients."
"Are you the private investigator?"
"No, I'm the financial consultant."
"Financial consultant? Why does he need a financial consultant?"
"Ask him. Aren't you with him?"
"Oh, she's feisty! Is that why you love her?"
Dial tone, and I was annoyed by its sound. Dani came back with a waiter. He was carrying a tray of fruit, nuts, meat and cheese. She was carrying a bottle and 3 glasses.
"I think you should eat. I don't think you have eaten since we arrived." My friends were always concerned when I didn't eat.
"Thanks. I'll take the liquor."
"Uh huh. After you eat."
The waiter found a small table and sat it between us. He called over 2 more waiters and they brought us chairs. I sat down and ate. The meat and the cheese was so good. The fruit was fresh. She was right. I hadn't eaten in a few days. I missed Jackson and whoever the hell was playing games with me on his phone, wasn't making the situation any better. I was anxious and couldn't wait to see Cross. Just as I had that thought, I looked up and could see men positioning themselves around the perimeter of the beach. They were all at a distance, but they stood out. They were wearing black pants and black short sleeved button up shirts. They were wearing earpieces and they were wearing full belts.
"Hmm, they're here because of you or because of Cross?"

Daniela literally never missed a thing.
"I just noticed that. I have no clue." My phone rang again. This time it was a text message.

Jax: How long have you known him?
Me: How long have you been gone?
Jax: What?
Me: Since the end of winter
Jax: I've been gone for 5 yrs.
Wait…
Me: I beg your pardon?

15 minutes passed and of course there was no answer. What did that mean? 'I've been gone for 5 yrs.' Did she disappear? Did she move? Did he have her handled? I hoped the armed security meant Cross was near-by. We needed to talk.
"And the winner of the limbo contest issss…tell us your name sweet-heart."
"Ariella"
"Ariella!" Ha! Would you look at that?! Ari won the limbo contest. Crazy girl changed her name, because she didn't want the strangers to really know her. She was weird like that.
"YAY!!!!" Daniela and I jumped up and ran over to her. We were happy for her. We went for a walk down the beach. There was a flea market close by so we checked it out.
"It's beautiful out here. May I ask how hedonism was?"
"Despite the ending, it was fantastic! Javier took Jackson to Harlow's at some point and he bought a pink diamond tennis bracelet. I opened it while sitting poolside with a steel drum band playing 'happy birthday'. It was magical." I never skipped a beat. I walked up to a woman at a booth. She had candles and incense; the aromas were hypnotizing.
"What's that wonderful scent you're burning?"
"Ah. That's Candlewood. Here." The woman stepped over and handed me a jar. I held it to my nose and inhaled the most sensational scent. I fell in love.
"I'll take it. How do you sell it?"
"Incense, a candle, bath salts and body scrub."
"I'll take the incense and the candle; thank you." The woman was sweet. She wrapped my items in loin cloth and put them in a sack bag that closed with a drawstring.
"The potato sack keeps the fragrance fresh. Keep them in here until you're ready to burn them." I smiled and shook my head. The woman

smiled and watched me walk away. When I caught up to Ari and Dani they were standing at a food stand. It had beef patties and fried plantains. I was excited. The liquor that I drank was soaked into my system and I needed more food.

"There you are. What do you want to eat?"

"I want one of everything!" I laughed. I ended up with 4 small beef patties and one fried sliced plantain. It was fantastic, succulent! We walked and watched the people move around. It was very peaceful. People weren't rushing. The ones that were driving weren't speeding or blowing their horns. I liked it here. I wanted Jackson back but I still didn't want to leave. My phone rang again. This time it was Cross.

"Where are you? Well I know where you are but what are you doing?"

"I'm sad. I'm shopping."

"I know you're sad, darling, but, I need you to stay close by. Will you please come back now?"

"Ugh! Ok. Fine! I'll turn around." I hung up the phone and stood still. I took a deep breath and turned around. "Sir Macho Italian man said that I need to turn around now."

"Well then. Let's turn around. I know he's your friend but he's a bit scary to me; I'm going to listen. Come on!" Arianna linked arms with me and we walked back to our hotel. When we arrived, Cross and Bobby Blue were standing on the steps.

"Hi Sara; ladies. Did you enjoy your shopping trip?"

"We were having a blast until my macho protector called!" I rolled my eyes at him. Ari gasped lightly under her breath. My phone rang. I stepped away from everyone and answered quietly.

"Hello."

"Why should I let Jackson live?"

"I beg your pardon?"

"Are you hard at hearing? 'I beg your pardon' comes out of your mouth a lot. What did you not understand about my question?"

"I understood the question...your hostility gives me the impression that my answer doesn't really matter."

Silence, then dial tone! I despised this woman. I needed Cross to find them and as soon as he did, I was going to break her jaw! I was utterly annoyed. I walked over to Cross and asked him if we can speak privately. I filled him in on the random conversations and he assured me that his team will find them.

"I'll have her handled on the spot, if that's what you want."
"I want to insure he's safe before I make any hostile choices."
"Will do."

The rest of the evening was uneventful. My nights were long and weary. I didn't cry but I spent a lot of time praying for and thinking about my Jackson. He was with his wife. He must've been ok but then again, she had him snatched. How "ok" is he? Why would she ask me if he should live? Of course, I wanted him to live. I was in love with him. Where was she for the last 5 years? Where were their kids? It was 6:15am when Cross knocked on my hotel room door. I let him in and room service quickly followed with coffee, fresh juice and warm muffin tops.
"Good morning. Today is going to be our day. Your investigator sent me this." Cross handed me a large manila envelope.
"Open it." I didn't take the envelope, instead, he opened it. There were pictures and articles. 'Woman goes missing.' I picked that article up first and read...

December 22, 2010
Last night, in Copenhagen, Tiffany Rodham-Ellis and her two children disappeared from a hotel.
They were last seen walking in separate directions from her husband, Dr. Jackson Ellis. Dr. Ellis returned to the hotel later that evening to find his wife and children had already 'checked out' of the hotel; according to hotel staff. Dr. Ellis was seen in town during the evening and is not a suspect in the disappearance of his
wife and children.

My heart sunk. No wonder he was so weird about his children, he hadn't seen them in 5 years. That explained why he didn't have pictures. I didn't know how to react. Cross and I continued to fumble through the information in front of us.
"Cross, I think I bit off more than I can chew with this situation. Since when do I sit on an island looking for a man that could have simply walked away from me? Who's to say he wants me to find him?"
"I don't know the answers and I don't know the guy but I do know you and I have for a long time. All of us here know that we are here for a good reason. You're in love and you need closure and if we get nothing else while we're here, we'll get closure."

"Thanks mob man!" I smiled.

"So, what do we do now?" Just as I asked the million-dollar question, Cross's phone rang. It was the investigator. Cross put the phone on speaker.

"Good morning guys. So, this is what I found out...when the other Mrs. Dr. Ellis went missing, she bought a small home in Ocho Rios. She began working as an executive director of Human Resources for most of the hotels and resorts that are strategically placed all over the island. She recently took over the accounts at Hedonism and she saw Jackson's name on the guest list. She planned to have him snatched. What's interesting is in the last 5 years, she never reached out to Jackson. He searched for her for almost 3 years and then one day he called off all searches. He moved on with his life. It was only when he stopped looking for her that she slowly began looking for him. Anyway, it looks like someone fell out of the sky and snatched him. She doesn't own a helicopter, jet or plane, but Jackson is solid. She couldn't have just snatched him. He's close by; he must be. She hasn't left the island since she got here. I have people in the village talking to people that she interacts with. If she and he are on this island, I will find them."

"She calls me from his phone. She'll ask a question or make a statement and once I answer or respond, she hangs up. She's not very patient. I think I pissed her off the last time we were on the phone."

"Does she give you a reason to think he's in danger?"

"The last time she called, she asked why she should let him live."

"Alright. It seems like our hands are full. I'll keep you posted on the developments as I get them. Also, I'm not there. I stayed in the states, but I trust my guys and you will be protected from any danger. I promise."

"Good because you are not cheap!" We all laughed but I rolled my eyes. He was charging me $700 a day! Jackson had better come home with me or I was going to kill him.

"Alright. We'll talk to you later boss!"

Once that phone call ended, there wasn't much else to be said or much else to do. We just sat there. No words were spoken. I wasn't sure what to do next or what to say next. I wanted to eat, smoke, cry and beat 'Tiffany' with a bat. I couldn't handle the barrage of emotions and just when I thought it couldn't get any more heart shattering, it did. My phone rang. Cross gave me a look. He pushed a button on a device and then signaled me to answer it.

"Hello."

"SARAAAAAAAAA!!!!!" It was faint. Like background noise.

"Shut up! Listen, Sara, let's play a game."

"I don't play games...we can fight though."

"Fight? Are you really going to fight me for a man that I'm legally married to?"

"I'll fight you for his safety. I'm sure you have him tied up somewhere. He would destroy you if he could use his arms and legs."

"I like games, I hear you're influential. I've read stories about how people will bend over backwards for you and you for them. I'm sure you have some super spies with you on the island. I would. I wouldn't be here alone knowing there's a crazy lady holding your man hostage somewhere. Let's see how good your people are. You all have 3 days to find him. If you don't, I'll kill him and leave his body on the beach. I don't want him anymore; he's a dirt bag, but I refuse to let him walk away peacefully. If you want him, you have to find him." Dial tone.

"UGGH!! I hate this woman! I want to kill her with my own bare hands. Let's go! We need find them! NOW!!" Ari and Dani heard me yelling. They were on their way to my room anyway. I heard them banging on the door. Bobby blue let them in.

"What is going on? It's too early to be yelling Hun."

"Too early!?!"

At this point, I was pacing; in fact, I was practically putting a hole in the floor from pacing. Cross was on the phone in another room. I couldn't hear him, but even if I could, he was speaking Italian. Ari called room service and asked them 'for a nice breakfast spread.' Dani made a new pot of coffee, rolled up and we all sat outside.

"Honey, I know she made you mad, but you cannot let her get you all worked up. We need your thoughts clear. We have your back, so whatever you say goes, but you cannot commit murder on this island." Dani was right, but I was mad. I hadn't been this angry in a long time. I was seeing red.

"Ok, I have some of my men in the village where Tiffany was last seen. There hasn't been any movement on her property in almost 4 days. Jackson went missing 3 days ago. I have a feeling that they're in there. SARA, WE WILL NOT BURST THROUGH THE DOOR SHOOTING, so don't ask." We all laughed. It wasn't funny, but we were high and we were all thinking it, so Cross really hit the nail on the head.

"I have surveillance surrounding the property. We'll wait for her to call you one more time. While she's speaking, we'll go inside and grab Jackson."

"Uh-huh, and bring her too! We're gonna get on a plane, and take her for a ride!"

"Sara…"

"What are you going to say to me? 'You can't kill her' why not? In fact, I won't kill her, but I want my confrontation and the money that I pay you Cross, you should respect that. Please and thanks."

"Ok."

That was the last time it was mentioned. I needed to swim. I went down to the pool and Ari and Dani hung out on the pool deck. They were laughing, reading magazines, talking. It was a very nice moment. The only missing factors were Javi and Jackson. I would be so happy if they were here too. I got out of the pool and stood directly in the sun.

"When I get Jackson back, I'm gonna send for Javi. We're gonna stay on vacation for a little while. I feel like we're going to need it."

"We need to work."

"Not anymore. I'll take care of all your expenses, I need y'all here; with me. Ok?"

"Aww, we love you. We will be here, if that's what you need."

My phone rang as I was sitting down on a lounge chair. It was Avery.

"Avery Anderson. What do I owe the pleasure…?"

"Hey Sara. I hope all is well, how are you?"

"I'm ok. "

"You're lying, but it's ok. I got a phone call from Tiffany last night. I haven't heard from her since, I can't even tell you. She was rambling on and asking me questions about Jackson's new life and I was vague with my answers, but I hope you're on this. If you're not on it, I'm gonna get on it. We cannot let this woman kill my best friend." Wow! Avery was frazzled; practically crying. I didn't want to stay on the phone for too long. I was doing a great job of not crying.

"Ave, Jackson is going to be fine. I'll bring him home. I promise." I had to hang up. I didn't want to hear his response.

"Enough of the sad nonsense. Let's climb Dunn's River Falls today!" Ari was on the money. That sounded perfect!

"Yes! Let's!" All 3 of us turned and looked at Cross. He looked away.

"Please scary mob man! We don't want to stay at the resort today." Ari put on her little girl voice and batted her eyes. Cross smiled, big! I had never seen him this cheesy.

"Alright. Fine! I'll keep some guys close by. I'm gonna work on how we're getting in that house. Be careful out there. I cannot heal broken bones!"

We jumped up and strapped on some gear; and by gear, I mean we wore real denim shorts, full t-shirts, and water shoes. We took a ride with some local gentlemen that were familiar with the Falls. Our detail was very close behind.

"Are you famous in America?" A man asked and I smiled.

"We're not famous."

"But you travel with security...is it because of the man?"

"What man?"

"We heard of a man that was going to be on the island. He's important to Ms. Tiffany. Are you looking for him?"

"Do you know where he is?"

"I don't; but I know where to find Ms. Tiffany. She's not nice to the people that work in the hotels. She's not very important, but she's important enough that no one speaks back to her." I was pissed. I did not want to end up taking over a business out here, but I had strong feelings against people being mistreated in the workplace.

"I would appreciate it if you let my security man know what you know. My friends and I would like to climb the falls and enjoy the beautiful day. I hope you don't mind."

"Not a problem, ma'am. We will make sure you have a magical day!"

He smiled. The carriage we were riding in finally arrived at the bottom of the falls. We jumped out and joined a tour group that was already in progress. They were polite and welcomed the idea of us joining them. Arianna had everyone laughing. I could tell, despite what was going on; it was going to be a good day. We climbed the falls for most of the morning. We climbed up on the actual rocks, and walked back down on the large, wooden staircase that lined the rocks. There were algae on the rocks so we slipped a couple of times. The leader of the tour group had a waterproof camera and took pictures of the event. He informed us that we can pick, print and purchase any of the pictures when we return to the resort. When we reached the top of the falls, the view was magical. The gentleman was right. Ari, Dani and I stood on the ledge of the mountain and we linked arms. "This is beautiful. Despite the other events, I am glad to have this moment with the 2 of you. I wouldn't have it any other way."

I was standing in the middle, so they each kissed a cheek. We laughed. The tour guide found us and took a picture. I was purchasing that one. Who was I kidding; I was going to purchase all of them! When we finally reached the bottom of the falls, Cross was waiting for us to arrive. "What are you doing here?"

"We found the house. You girls ready to go help her get Jackson back?" I gasped. I couldn't believe what I was hearing. Was this really going to be a magical day? I wasn't sure how to feel. It was bittersweet.

"What if he doesn't want to come with me?"

"Then you leave him here. If he cannot appreciate you and what you are doing, forget him!"

Dani was right again. I was really stepping out of my comfort zone with operation save Dr. I miss his sex. I had no idea what to expect. I wanted to go in there with guns blazing, but I had a feeling that wouldn't be very effective. We got into a large, black SUV and Cross handed each of us a black outfit; black leggings, soft black booties, and fitted black tank tops.

"I so need a shower and he's handing me fresh, Under Armor apparel."

"Ha! I know, right? What's up with that Mr. Macho?"

"I know you girls. If I let you get to the hotel, not only would there be 3 long showers but you all would be hungry, 'we need room service', or 'I need to smoke' or 'I need a drink'...it would be tomorrow before we could get here. This way, we get it done and we can all be on a plane to the next location by the end of the night."

"Next location. Where we headed?"

"Wherever Sara decides she wants to go next. She's the one that doesn't want to go home."

"Seriously? You don't want to go home?"

"I'm not going home without Jackson. And then even when I get him back, I feel like we were robbed of a great vacation, so I wanna go on an even better one. Do you want to go home?"

"Well, no, but..."

"Then speak no more of it. Let's get my Jax back and then we can talk about what's next, got it?"

That was the end of that conversation. We finally reached a gate that led up a private road. Bobby blue hopped out of the truck to open the gate. He got back in and we traveled slowly down the road. They all had guns ready, just in case. The road was about 4 miles long before we saw a house. It was a small ranch style home. It had a long driveway and an equally long walkway. I assumed there were cameras. If I had a long driveway and walkway, I would have cameras. The land that surrounded the home was very well kept. Along the far east side was a farm; cows, horses, chickens. Along the far, right side was an array of trees and flowers. I even saw a marijuana plant.

"Awe this is cute!"

"Shut up Ari. This is the enemy's palace."

"'The enemy's palace?' How 'bout you both hush." Dani was nervous and Arianna laughed. The SUV stopped and we all jumped out. We were 4 cars deep of armed detail. I dared this woman to try anything funny. We all walked up the walkway and when we reached the front door, Cross banged on it.

"Alright, alright, alright, I'm coming. Relax!" The voice was familiar. It was her, the voice that was calling me. She opened the door and quickly tried to close it shut. Bobby caught it with his arm.

"Tiffany?" I whispered from behind Cross. He stepped aside and revealed me.

"HMMM! You must be Sara."

"HMMM!"

I slapped her; right across her face! I couldn't contain myself. My hand was burning but I didn't care. She wasn't on the ground yet but I kept swinging until she got there. She didn't fight back; as if she knew it was going to happen. When I got her on the ground, Bobby blue tied up her arms and legs.

"Game over! Where's Jackson?!"

She laughed. I didn't think any of this was funny. My question triggered the men and they took off in various directions in the house, up and down steps, opening and closing doors, looking around corners. Nothing. It was quiet.

"He's not here."

"Well...if Tiffany doesn't want to tell me, then Tiffany can come with me. Grab her cell phone and any other electronics and put her in the back of the truck that I'm riding in. We have some catching up to do."

Chapter 13

We sat in the back of the black SUV and no words were spoken. I said nothing. Ari, Dani, Cross and Bobby were all quiet. In fact, the only person speaking was Tiffany.

"I met Jackson when were 24 and 22. I was instantly in love, and to him, I was mediocre. Honestly, I knew he was going to just be a 5-minute boyfriend. I took advantage of his drunk stature in Vegas and convinced him to marry me; it was a horrible thing to do, and we had a horrible marriage because I forced what wasn't there. When I found out he was looking for me, I knew it was because he was ready to move on with his life and needed to get divorced from me. I don't mind divorcing him, but I needed some revenge and some closure; he was mean to me and I can't forgive him. I wasn't planning on having him kidnapped, but he wouldn't willingly come see me. It made me mad, so, while he was doing his 5-mile run, I had him clipped at the knees by a kid on a motor bike; don't worry, he's not paralyzed. Then I had 2 of my guys pick him up and throw him in the back of my truck. I drove him to a safe location and tied him up. His cell phone was in his pocket, and you already know I snatched it and then we began to talk. Well...I did the talking, he cursed at me randomly. His accent is fading. Do you have anything to do with that?"

I just looked at her. I said nothing. I didn't even answer her question.

"Where you guys taking me anyway? Don't you think you should be looking for Jack!?"

"Don't call him Jack. He doesn't like that."

"I know girl, that's exactly why I call him Jack; always have."

"Could be why he hates you."

"He doesn't hate me, we just don't have much in common. We were better as friends. We weren't designed for marriage."

"All of that makes sense..." She just looked at me and rolled her eyes.

"Did I hear someone say something about children? You have kids with Jackson? Where are they?" Arianna chimed in.

"Don't worry about the children. Jack will never see them again. I was hoping he forgot about them, but that was the first thing he said after he was done cursing me out. 'Where are my boys?' Oh! They aren't his anymore!"

"That's messed up to keep his kids away from him. You're evil."

"Don't judge me. I raised them alone anyway. When they were born, Jackson was happy, but he still hated me. He wouldn't come home until late and leave early. He wouldn't speak to me. He interacted with the kids, but we never did things as a family. He didn't want kids with me, but he did want kids, but, I still took them away. They're safe, they think he's dead and soon, he will be!" She laughed a strong, hard laugh from her gut. I smacked her again.

"Wench!" She called out.

"Yes. That's exactly what you are. You better hope I don't find Jackson because the moment I do, as long as he says I can, I'm going to kill you."

"He won't let you kill me."

"Do you want to bet?" I looked at her with one raised eyebrow. She flinched. I laughed.

"Yea, that's what I thought. Enough of this high school, petty behavior. Cross, have you found Jax yet?"

"I'm not sure. We have a trail of hers that ends in the middle of nothing. Long Hill road. What's in the middle of Long hill road, Tiffany?"

"Hmm, I don't know. Let's go there and see."

"Well, I don't take orders from you." Cross got on his 'other phone' and called in an order.

"Now we wait." 22 minutes passed before Cross's phone rang again.

"Let's go!" The driver threw the SUV into gear and took off at a rapid speed. We drove down long, steep, hilly, dirt roads and around tight corners. We were all rolling around in the back seat. It was intense, invigorating. My heart was racing. I hoped that this was the end all be all and I could finally hold Jackson in my arms. It had been too long. I could imagine he needed to take a shower and put on fresh, clean clothes. I wondered if Cross packed any of his things prior to us embarking on this mission. I sat there and imagined seeing a happy smile on his face when I walked in to get him. I could feel his strong arms holding me tight. I could smell his scent and feel his breath. I was getting excited. The SUV pulled into another long driveway. This house was in the middle of the road, literally, and there was nothing else around it. It was weird.

"You go inside first, Sara. I'll keep some guys close behind you. I have them surrounding the premises. You will be safe."

I hopped out of the SUV and slowly took steps toward the front door of this house. It was very grungy. The lawn was dingy, disheveled and brown. The rocks in the driveway were picked over and scarce. The steps were wooden and creaky. They were not full steps in some spots and the handles looked splintered, so I didn't touch them. When I finally reached the front door, the door knob was a shiny metal; it was hot to touch. Using the end of my shirt, I turned the knob and opened the door. There he was, my Jackson. He was sitting in a chair; disoriented. His hair was a mess. His tee shirt was filthy. His face was bruised, so were his legs. He was tied at the wrists and ankles. His mouth was gagged, which really sucked because it turns out, I needed the warning that he was trying to send my way. As I took my steps toward him, I heard a click. I felt a cold circular object press on the side of my head. It was a gun. I thought it would be the end of me as the sweat beaded up around my face. What was happening and where were Cross and his people? They didn't know to come inside because I hadn't made a sound. I was certain I closed the door behind me because otherwise, they would've followed me in. I hoped this wasn't a setup. Just as I was about to open my mouth, the person holding the gun to my head spoke...

"I don't want to kill you. Hopefully this entire situation can clear up easily and quickly. All I want are answers. That's all Tiffany wants also, and then we all can go on with life. Well, you can. But I think regardless, your precious Jackson should not live anymore. Sorry."

I was shaking at this point but not because of the words I was hearing, but because of the person it was. I knew that voice. It was way too familiar.

"Avery, what is this about?"

He didn't answer. His silence was eerie. I was trying to listen closely to see what/if anything was going on outside. I couldn't tell, but it seemed equally quiet out there too. What in the world was happening? Why did I feel like I walked into a setup? The setup of all time even. I was just about to turn my head and Jackson began to make a loud sound from his belly. "MMMMMMMMMMMM!!!!!!!!!" He was straining, trying to tell me something. He was probably telling me not to move. I turned my head as the front door of the house burst open. Shots rang out and I quickly took cover. Or at least I thought I did. I had no idea what happened then or what happened next. I just remember feeling someone pull me, and then everything went black.

"Cross?! She's not moving! We should get her to a hospital. Tiffany! You better hope she' ok. If she's not..." All the guns shots ceased and everyone was trying to figure out if I was alive. Jackson was free from his shackles. However, he and Cross took the liberty of tying Tiffany and

Avery up.

"Let's go! Everyone in!" Cross knew a doctor who ran a private clinic on the island. He said it was safer going there because no one will ask questions.

"It is good to know people that owe you favors. I trust he can fix Sara." We all arrived at a state of the art facility just outside of St. Ann. The large SUV pulled in front of the building. Two doctors came running over with a gurney.

"What happened?"

"There was a situation and Sara hit her head, she stopped moving. Just check her out and fix her; please."

Arianna, Dani and Jackson sat in the waiting area in the clinic. Cross took 'the prisoners', as he referred to them, to a nearby, secure area where they were under 24/7 surveillance. Jackson called his lawyer and asked him to draw up divorce paperwork. He was determined to be rid of Tiffany once and for all. He decided to deal with Avery separately. Tiffany agreed to sign the papers, but she wanted to be let go.

"Not before we know what's wrong with Sara. If she dies, you will too. You stay here until she is out of the woods." Cross made sure she was secure. He didn't take any chances. Meanwhile, Jackson was pacing the floors in the waiting room.

"This is killing me. I need her to be ok."

"Jackson, I know that you are worried, but you must try and relax. Please" Dani tried consoling. She tried to keep everyone calm.

"Yea. We're all worried."

"Hello. Are you all Sara's family?" A short, fat doctor walked into the room. He had rosy red cheeks and a head full of red hair. He was wearing a nice suit and a white lab coat. He waddled when he walked and grunted when he spoke. He was very polite and well spoken. "Sara isn't dead. She also isn't in a coma. She appears to be in a very deep sleep. I would suggest speaking to her. Maybe if you continue to engage her in conversation, she will be more inclined to join the discussion. We have her hooked up to a heart monitor, a blood pressure monitor and we are monitoring her brain activity. Now...we wait. You may see her if you like."

Arianna, Dani and Jackson walked into the hospital room suite. It was a large room with lounge chairs and a sofa. Sara laid very still in the bed. She looked peaceful. The machines were beeping in random tones. It was very clean and well lit.

"Hey Sara, you look so peaceful. We're all here. Guess what? Jackson is here too. He's ok baby. He needs you to be ok now." Arianna sat on the side of the bed and held Sara's hand in hers. A single tear rolled down her cheek and she wiped it away.

"What happened in there Jackson?"

"I don't know. All I remember was someone untied me as the shots rang out. I tried to make my way to Sara, but one of Cross's guys dragged her out. I think that's when she hit her head."

"Who started shooting first?"

"Whoever burst through the house. In all honestly, I don't know, it all happened so fast."

"Guys. Let's not have this conversation right now. Let's be peaceful around Sara."

It was strange. I could hear everything that was being said. I wanted to be a part of the conversation, but I couldn't move. I could feel my legs, but I couldn't move them. It felt as if my body was in a state of shock. This hadn't happened before, so I freaked out. I wasn't moving but, I could feel my face get wet; like I was sweating. I couldn't pick my hand up and wipe it away. I tried to shake my head, but I didn't think that was working either.

"Dani, look, she's sweating." Dani grabbed a towel and began to pat my head dry. Ah, that felt better. I wanted to thank her.

"Her hand is sweaty too."

Arianna sat next to me all day. She held my hand and played in my hair. She stroked my arm. She told me stories. She could talk. I found myself drifting in and out while she was speaking. She told me Jackson was there, but I couldn't hear his voice. Why wasn't he speaking? Was he afraid? The nurses took turns coming to check on my vitals. I could feel them sticking and poking at me. It was annoying. I wanted them to stop.

"Ari, do you want to get some sleep?" Cross came in the hospital room.

"I want Sara to wake up. I don't want to leave her, just in case she wakes up."

Cross sat down in one of the chairs on the other side of the room. That's how they remained. After two days, Daniela and Jackson joined them. No one spoke for a few hours. Instead, they filled the room with silent love and prayer. I could feel their presence. My body was healing itself. My mind was heavy. My body felt heavy too. There was extra weight that I didn't want to carry. My body was trying to figure out what to do with it.

Day three and the doctor returned with very little update.

"It still appears as though she is asleep. Her body has no infection. She's got some swelling on the brain, but her brain is responsive. We are waiting for her to wake up."

The doctor tried to remain as positive as possible. I could tell that none of them were pleased with the waiting part. I dreamed a lot in this slumber. The dreams were mixed. In one, Jackson and I didn't know each other and when we meet at an Avery party, we didn't get along. In other dreams, we were happily ever after. While I was laying here dreaming, Jackson was out there just staring at me. How come he wasn't speaking to me? I wondered. Was he upset with me? Was he trying to separate from me? I felt hot again. My chest started hurting. I heard the doctors and nurses running over to my room. I felt pressure on my chest. Suddenly, my thoughts became very clear and everything went black.

"Hi babe. I'm sorry that it took so long for me to speak to you. I was scared. I'm not scared anymore. I know that you are in there and I know that you can hear me. I miss you so much. I am ready to spend the rest of my life with you. I need you Sara." Ah ha! There he was; my babe. He sounded sad, but God wasn't ready to wake me up yet. I wasn't ready to wake up yet.

"You know what?!" Jackson turned to face Cross, Ari and Dani.

"Maybe we should move her. Suppose she's not waking up because she knows that she is in an unfamiliar location. You know how her intuition is strong." That was a good idea. Maybe they should've moved me. Yes! I agreed! Too bad I couldn't speak. Just as Jackson's brilliance was spewing from his mind, the doctor walked in to do follow-up tests.

"Doc. I want to move her. Can we take her home?"

"I think we should wait a day before we decide to do that. The swelling in her brain has come down greatly, her blood pressure is stabilizing; she seems to be doing better. She gave us one scare earlier, but I just want to see if we can get her to wiggle toes or move her legs."

"Or wake up?" Dani rolled her eyes as she answered the doctor's response with attitude. She didn't have to say it, but she didn't like the idea of moving me. No one else knew her like I did. Therefore, that detail went unnoticed.

"You don't like the idea of moving her, huh?" Perhaps I was wrong. It appeared that Cross had been paying attention to my Dani.

"I just think we should limit risk, not heighten it." Everyone got quiet and looked at the doctor.

"Well. It would be against my medical opinion to move her now. Where would you move her to? You cannot just prop her up on the beach and hope she wakes up. Please, let's just make it through the night. Let's revisit this tomorrow."

Everyone made eye contact and shook their heads indicating that all was understood. While they were talking, I was dreaming. The dream that night was different than previous dreams. I was standing alone in a large, white room. In front of me was a table and perched on top of the table was a beautiful little girl. She was light in skin tone; like eggshell color. She had light brown eyes and dark, wired hair. Her smile brightened the room. She looked up to me. She must have been mine. "down mama." She exclaimed and then raised her tiny arms above her head. I scooped her up and kissed her numerous times on the cheek before placing her on the ground. She took off running and jumped in Jackson's arms. As I turned to walk towards them, a belly full of baby led me in their direction. I watched Jackson play with our daughter while I rubbed my belly. I was happy. I smiled with sincerity. If this were real, it would be too real. Could I deal with children? Did Jackson want more children? We were barely in a relationship, and here I was, dreaming of children. I drifted deeper in my sleep. Meanwhile, Jackson was feeling a bit bored in the hospice center.

"I want to talk to Avery. I need to ask him some questions...I'll be back. Cross, will you escort me?"

"Absolutely. Daniela, if anything changes..."

"I'll be sure to call."

Dani smiled at Cross. He and Jackson left the room. Dani stood quietly over Sara. Her eyes filled with tears.

"Sara. What's going on mama? What kind of soul searching is this? I'm scared. It's been a week. You have been laying here for one entire week. I watched you open businesses from the ground up in a week. You and Jackson fell in love in a week. I need you to wake up and give us more years of those kind of weeks."

Dani was waiting patiently for Sara to move. Nothing.

"Well then. I will stay here until you wake."

Jackson and Cross arrived at the secret location. It was a small house in the mountains; on a cliff. As they climbed the large staircase, they walked through vines and slippery mud.

"Really man?"

"I wanted to make sure it wasn't easy to escape; just in case they tried, but Bobby is here and he likes to, let's just say; they wouldn't get out alive." Jackson glared at Cross.

"I would rather keep them alive, ok?"

"I hear you, but I'm PAID to keep you safe. If your safety is at risk, I shall do whatever is necessary to keep you safe."

"Alright. I hear you brother. Just let me take the lead. I am in search of some answers."

"Your ex is a handful. If she leaps..."

"Ok, mob man. I got it. I got it."

They reached the top of the staircase and approached a solid, metal door. Cross texted ahead, so Bobby opened the door without them needing to knock. The front door opened into a foyer. The room was bare. They walked through the main room, through the kitchen and down a flight of stairs. The stairs emptied into the basement. Tiffany and Avery were individually chained to the wall.

"Oh, wow. Hmm..."

Jackson was uneasy about the chains. He closed his eyes and saw Sara lying motionless in bed. He quickly changed his thoughts on the appearance of the chains. "It's fitting." Jackson paced the room for a few minutes. He was trying to gather his thoughts. "Tiffany. Why did you disappear from the hotel in Copenhagen?" Tiffany looked away from Jackson. She didn't answer the question. "Ah. You're not answering questions. That's petty."

"I'll answer your questions, Jax." Avery sounded humble; as if this ordeal couldn't end soon enough for him.

"I'll tell you whatever you want to know."

"How did you get caught up in this?" Avery's eyes shifted. He hesitated prior to answering.

"I have been in love with Tiffany since we were young. I was surprised when you married her, but you're my friend, so I let it slide. I moved on. Then, the issues started and I consoled her; no sex though. Then she disappeared. I was upset, but I moved on. Then you show up at my party in love with Sara. I left the notes for her. I was hoping it would drive her nuts and start a thing and then maybe, just maybe, you would be hurt for losing the love of your life. But, Sara never asked questions. She's not fazed by much and she's so nonchalant about things. Then Tiffany called me; out of nowhere and it was like love reunited. She hates you. She wanted to kill you. When I found out that she kidnapped you, I came as soon as possible. I wasn't sure if I was coming to save you or to save her. I love you man. I want us to remain friends and I want Tiffany to be my wife."

"Where are my kids? Can you make Sara wake up? That's what I need. That's what I lost while the two of you are out being Bonnie and Clyde; interrupting lives. You ultimately crossed the line."

"Jax, man..." Avery hung his head and stopped speaking. He was pissed at himself. Who, in their right mind allowed a woman to destroy a friendship? "I don't really have much to say that will justify my behavior. I'm sorry, but I'm in love with Tiffany."

"That's great! The two of you couldn't just be together? You had to kidnap me, piss my girlfriend off, practically kill me and endanger her? What kills me is the two of you went through all this trouble for what? I knew you were in love with her years ago. I knew she loved you too. It was Tiffany that didn't want to give me a divorce. She thought she could make me love her. Now I am in love and who knows how much time we have together; because you people almost killed her!" Jackson was livid. His hands were shaking.

"Jackson. Don't be mad at Avery. This was my doing. I resented you for a very long time. You married me on a dare, and it was great...for a month or so, but then we started drifting apart. You tried to leave me and I wouldn't let you. Then I got pregnant and I thought the kids would change our relationship, but it didn't. Do you remember the fight we had prior to our Copenhagen vacation?" Jackson gave Tiffany a sour glare. He didn't want to travel back down memory lane, but felt he needed to make sense of what was happening.

"I remember you telling me that you weren't happy. I told you I was never happy with you. You were..."

"Subpar." Tiffany and Jackson responded in unison. Tiffany's eyes swelled with tears.

"Jackson, that was my wake-up moment. I refused to remain a part of your life since you felt that I was subpar. I called Avery and I told him I am running away from you. He tried to talk me down, but there was no reasoning with me. I left. The boys asked me for days where we were going and was dad coming. I had a friend give me a place to stay. The boys were in school and adjusting well. We lived outside of Geneva for a few years. I reached out to Avery and asked how you were doing. He told me that you stopped looking for me and you moved on with your life. Avery reached out to me and told me about Sara and how happy the two of you were. I got mad. I didn't want you to be happy because I wasn't happy."

"You were the reason for your own unhappiness. Where are my kids?"

"So, I relocated here and started my new job; almost a year ago. When I saw your name and reservation on the list, I was steamed. I wasn't thinking clearly but I knew that I couldn't let you leave the island. I wanted to hurt you, so I did. Except I wasn't expecting you to be in love. Sara is beautiful and she must love you; she stuck around and hired help to find you. I wasn't expecting to her to have such passion, such drive to get you back. I paid Avery, big bucks, to kill her. He held the gun to her head but didn't have the guts to shoot her. When we all heard the gun shots and took off in separate directions; I saw someone grab her and pull her away. I tossed a brick, and score! She fell out. I was happy. I thought she was dead but then I heard you scream. The sound shattered my heart. You were so distraught. I don't want her to die. I'm sorry Jackson. I didn't mean for any of this to happen. Please, forgive me." Jackson looked at Tiffany. Then Avery. Then Cross. He put his hand out to Cross. Cross handed him a gun. He walked a few steps closer to Tiffany. He held the gun tight in his hand and his eyes filled with tears. He remained strong and held them in.

"Tiffany. Where are my kids?" Her eyes fell low. She turned her head.

"You don't have any. They weren't yours. I lied."

"Are they Avery's?"

"They're not yours; that's all you need to know. Forget about them; you never had kids. Start over with Sara. You will never see MY BOYS again!"

"And neither will you."

Jackson fired one shot to Tiffany's chest. Her eyes were opened. She was staring right into his eyes. When the bullet hit her chest, her lips parted slightly; as if she were about to speak. The words never formed. Instead, she choked slightly and blood poured out of her mouth. Her head fell and her body collapsed. She was dead. Jackson looked at Avery. Then looked at Cross.

"Come Crocificio, let's go take Sara home."

Chapter 14

"Jackson! Are you out of your mind? You're not going to get away with this!"

"Are you planning on telling because I know Cross isn't."

"I didn't see anything!"

"You killed her! I love her! What if I kill Sara? How would you feel?"

"She's currently in a coma that Tiffany put her in! The kids weren't mine?! Are they yours?"

"I don't know. She never told me. I don't know where they are either, so don't ask."

"I don't care where they are." Cross didn't want to listen to the conversation anymore. He raised his arm and pointed a gun at Avery.

"Wait! Cross! We can't kill him. He's Sara's friend too. I think it would break her heart if we kill him."

"I'm sorry, but I don't trust him. Close your eyes so you can tell Sara that you didn't see it coming." Jackson turned his back to Avery.

"He brought this on himself." Jackson whispered to himself as he heard the shot ring from the pistol. The bullet flew out of the barrel of the gun and hit Avery in the chest. His legs collapsed from underneath him. One single tear fell down Jackson's cheek.

"I pray to God that Sara is awake when we return."

Jackson and Cross left the house from the basement door. They walked down the staircase and were met by a large SUV. Cross made a phone call to Bobby. He asked him to "take care of the house." They rode in silence for a few.

"If I let him go, he would have turned you in immediately. I don't take chances, I don't ask questions; I follow my instinct. If I have a strong feeling in my gut, then that's what will get done. When he asked you 'what if I kill Sara?', I knew he had to go because at that moment, her friendship was not important to him. Everything got out of control. That's what we say when Sara asks us. Avery was her friend. Let me tell her he's dead. She doesn't have to know that you were there when it happened."

"Thank you. Thank you very much, for everything, Sara is blessed to have someone like you; as crazy as that sounds. What am I going to do if she doesn't wake up?"

"Don't think like that. She's marinating, but she will wake up and we will take her home and spend the rest of our lives protecting her." Cross held out his hand to Jackson. They shook. The car ride back to the hospital was longer than usual. There was some traffic along the route. Once the SUV arrived in front of the hospice, Jackson jumped out and ran towards the building. He ran up the stairs and down the hall to Sara's room. He burst through the door and saw Arianna sitting on the end of her bed. Sara still wasn't awake.

"Sara. Babe, I need you. I need you to wake up. I need to tell you things. I need to kiss your lips. I love you. We can be together. Please, babe, come back to me."

Oh, it was Jackson; finally. How long had it been since he was here? He sounded sad. Something heavy was weighing on him.

"Where's the doctor? Has he any update?"

"Not yet Hun. What happened with Avery and Tiffany?"

Neither of them answered the question. Instead, all eyes were on Sara. There was finally some peace on the island because Jackson and Cross secretly handled the "prisoners" and could be focused on Sara. Shortly after, the doctor walked in.

"In all my years of practicing medicine, I've never experienced an unexplained coma. Usually we know what happened or how it happened. Sara didn't suffer a stroke. She isn't spilling any ketones. She no longer has brain swelling. She's physically fine. She could be mentally tired, but it's hard to say because she isn't awake."

The doctor was right. I was mentally exhausted. My thoughts were clear. I was simply just arranging them; trying to decipher reality and dream. I heard everything that was going on and I felt it too. Something happened but no one was saying what. I knew I could pull it out of Cross, but I had to be awake. I was not ready yet. Last night's dream was even more strange than others I had previously. A woman that I didn't recognize, showed up at my house. She was asking me a ton of questions. She asked me something about a location that I traveled to in my deeper past. She showed me pictures of some of the locals and asked me who I recognized. I didn't recognize anyone; not even the woman standing in front of me. Hypothetically, I woke up, in my bed, with Jackson by my side. He kissed me hello but I didn't move. Then a child, that same little girl, climbed into the bed. "Mama wake up!" She bellowed in my ear and patted the side of my head until I squirmed. I turned over to face her, but she was Tiffany. What the hell? "You should probably wake up now." She whispered in my ear. "You should probably wake up now."

"You should probably wake up now."

The mantra continued and slowly woke me from a trance. I wiggled my toes.

"Sara. Are you waking up?" Jackson came across the room and sat on the bed beside me. It felt like I was walking around my house flipping switches. My legs moved, then my arms and slowly, I opened my eyes. I could still hear her though. "You should probably wake up now."

"OK! I'm up! I'm up! I'm UP, shut up!"

I finally focused and Jackson's beautiful, ocean blue eyes were staring back at me.

"Sara? Sweetheart? Who you talking to Hun?"

"Jackson?!" I reached up and touched his face. He was real. I had to make sure. I took another moment to let my surroundings become reality to me. I scanned the room and saw all the familiar faces that I remembered prior to falling out. "Which one of you did it?" I whispered to Jackson. I hoped he was the only one who heard me. He was. He stood.

"May we have the room please?" Jackson walked over and opened the door. Everyone stood and proceeded to leave.

"Cross. You stay." Jackson made sure no one was nearby before he spoke again."Say that again Sara."

"I know she's dead. She came to me in a dream; I'm talking about Tiffany. She was talking to me; she woke me up. What happened?"

"Are you a gypsy? How do you know things all the time?" Cross looked at Jackson. He didn't give Jackson a chance to answer.

"She and Avery tried to attack Jackson. I had to do what I had to do."

"HMPH, if that's the story you all are telling me, I'm to believe it, right? Wait, so Avery's dead?" My heart sunk a bit. I wasn't sure why, but the thought of Avery being gone disturbed me. "No more Avery Anderson parties?!" Was it bad that that's what I was going to miss the most?

"Sara. How do you feel?"

"I'm hungry. I want to leave here. I was totally agreeing with you when you said to move me. I do not like it here. The nurses keep touching and poking me. Cross. Please. Can we please go somewhere else?"

"Where do you want to go?"

"Santorini; just for a few days, and then home. I miss my mom and my bed...and my cars. Jackson, you cannot leave me ever again! Got it?"

"I promise. I'll never leave your sight. Alright Cross, let the girls back in now." It was a reunion for the next few hours. Arianna, Dani and I were like peas in pods. I had no idea how much me being motionless worried them. Arianna expressed her fear of having to call my mother with bad news.

"I never want to be the one to tell her something happened to you."

"She would blame you; you know that, right?"

"Uh huh I know. She would say 'Sara would never be involved in things like that. It's your fault.' I would have to just eat it and blame it on grief. The years would pass and she would eventually lose touch with me."

Arianna and I were laughing hysterically. Our teasing my mother was in humor. A humor we secretly shared throughout our relationship. My mother loved all my friends and she appreciated me having good people around, however, in her opinion, I could do no wrong. I guess it was a mother thing. Cross's doctor checked me out and gave me a clean bill of health. I took a shower and changed into an outfit that Dani had on reserve. It was cute. It was a mini skirt and a decorated tank top. We all boarded Cross's plane and took off on an adventure to Greece. I was super excited. Since I slept for a week, I was wide awake the entire plane ride. I felt like it was going to be impossible to reteach my body my sleep patterns. I sat in Jackson's lap on the plane. He held me. He kissed me. He whispered in my ear. It was a wonderful moment. I closed my eyes and ingested his love. I couldn't be happier. He seemed to be in such a wonderful mood. I told him about my dreams of a baby girl. He was super excited.

"No, don't get excited. I'm not ready to have a baby yet."

"Why not? We can get married. We can buy a house and we can start a family."

"One day, yes, but not today. I have some more career plateaus I want to reach."

"Ok. Understood."

Our Santorini adventure was short; well needed, but short. Arianna slept on the beach. I had no idea that while I was in my slumber, she refused to sleep. Dani and Cross became acquainted. Jackson spent time with Cross while I was asleep. The two of them had become close also. Jackson's property in Santorini was fabulous. He had a home that was built by hand with stone. The entrance was breathtaking. Cathedral ceilings welcomed us. The floors were cherry wood and spotless. I was tempted to cook a meal and serve my guests on the floor. It was THAT clean.

"This place is beautiful!"

"Here." Jackson put a key in my hand.

"OH! When we were in Hedonism, you gave me a key. I'm not sure where it is anymore." I hung my head.

"It's ok; your belongings were kept safe. I have the key now. When we get back home, I'll give it back."

"Thank you. Now, what is this key for?"

"This house. I took it from Tiffany. I took everything from Tiffany; anything she had of mine, I took."

"Including her life?" Shots were fired; literally and figuratively and I was not afraid to acknowledge it. Jackson wasn't proud of his actions. I could tell by the change of body language." I will not judge you. I will not say a word; to anyone. Your secret is my secret too"

"I wanted to keep her alive; ask Cross. He wanted her dead from the distress she caused you. I was planning on letting bygones be bygones and let her and Avery live life far away from us. I had questions that needed answers though. That was a problem. I got answers and they didn't make the situation any better. The answers fueled an anger in me. Her words were grease to the fire. She died because it was fair; the equivalent of my anger. He died because he had to. It needed to be done. I don't want you to worry. Everything will be fine."

"I'm not worried. I was planning on killing her before we left the island." Jackson gave me a look of confusion. He smirked. I think he wondered why I said that so freely.

"When we were looking for you, and found her instead, she told me that the kids weren't yours. She also told me she calls you Jack. I wanted to shoot her right then. I braced myself solely because we didn't know where you were. I smacked her a few times also!" I smiled a big smile.

"I thought I was never going to see that smile again. I'm glad that you didn't kill Tiffany. It's hard to deal with. I would never want that to happen to you." I was kind of over having the mushy moment, I wanted to tour this castle home. I stood on my toes and kissed Jackson gently on his lips. I relaxed my feet, turned and walked away.

"Where are you going?"

"I'm going to 'Dora the Explorer' my way around this magical mansion."

"Yea, it's yours now."

"Stop saying that." Jackson extended his hand to me. I placed mine in his and he walked me through every room on every floor. It was beautiful. On the second floor, in the master suite, was a patio, with a stunning view of the Aegean Sea. It was magical. Jackson explained his love for the house.

"It's like no other home here because I refused to allow it to look like any other home here. I love it. It is probably my most prized possession." Watching his body language while we spoke entertained me. He spoke with a passion that I hadn't seen in him in the few weeks prior to our mistaken adventure. He seemed at peace; like the weight of the world was lifted from his shoulders. He moved swiftly between rooms, flipping light switches and plugging in lamps. He was speaking rather quickly. I was listening hard trying to keep up. It was as if his thoughts were spilling over a glass. You know when you're pouring water and you're simply not paying attention, before you know it there's water on the floor. Yea, that's what his thoughts sounded like. It was intense. I was feeling tired. I guess my body was finally ready to rest. I had been awake for 2 days, it was only fitting.

"Ok. Babe, I need a minute. Please, can we sit?" Jackson and I were now on the patio with the amazing view. I sat down on a lounge chair and took a deep breath. Jackson sat beside me.

"Are you feeling any pain?"

"No. I'm just winded. I think I'm ready to go home."

"Are you ready to finally sleep in your own bed and drink wine from your collection?"

"And walk around nude waiting for you to come home from work."

"I love it!"

"When we get home, will you move in with me?"

Whoa. I made big plans in one short conversation. This murder mystery getaway changed everything. We all had a new appreciation for each other. Cross and Dani were getting closer, fast, and no one paid any unnecessary attention to it. They were happy and that's all that mattered. I felt that I need Jackson to be close to me; for my nerves and his. I knew that we would be safe back home, but I also thought we were safe at a resort too. Foolish of me. Although Tiffany and Avery are gone, they are not forgotten. Someone is going to realize that they are missing and when they do, the search party is going to hit the scene. We were spotted all over that island with armed men. I was certain that someone would tie the pieces together. When they do, we have to be careful about what we say and how we act. I know that if the shit hits the ceiling, I can cover my own ass. I had abilities that my friends and family know nothing of. I knew how to work the system and I had the ability to manipulate just about any situation in my favor. Anyway, Jackson was staring in my eyes and his lips were moving but I couldn't make out what he was saying. He shook me slightly.

"Sara. Sara. You listening to me, hun?"

"Huh, I'm sorry. I don't know where I went."

"When we get home, I am going to set you up for a CAT Scan. I want to make sure all is well, really; I trust my own opinion."

"Yea. I think that's a good idea." I shook my head a bit and stretched my neck and back.

"Ok. What were you saying?"

"I said…absolutely. I would love to live with you. Then I asked if you are sure that's what you want? I know you've never cohabited before."

"I haven't but I think you are a good choice for a first."

"First and only baby. We can do whatever we want now. I don't know when she did it, but Tiffany signed the divorce papers. I sent them to my lawyer. All is done. She's gone."

Jackson pumped his fist in the air and grinned. I could tell that he was genuinely happy. I felt like reminding him that he took her out, but I didn't think it was fitting. I reminded myself in my mind. 'yea I bet you are happy!' I wondered how he was going to sleep at night. Will it haunt him later in life? I guess I'll wait and see. If something was going to change, it will change. I kept my eyes open for changes. I was getting excited about starting our lives together. How often did the mistress get the guy? Even though the entire situation was just messed up, it worked out in my favor and I didn't manipulate the situation.

"Jax, let's go home man." We stayed in Santorini for dinner that evening. While we sat, and supped, I explained to my loving friends how I was feeling about our adventure.

"I would not have embarked on this adventure with any other friends in my circle. I thank you for dropping and coming to my rescue. I will forever be in debt to you. No matter what it is, big or small, if you need it, I will give it to you, no questions asked. I am enjoying the union between friends; Dani and Cross. You both needed someone good and you are both good people. Mazel tov! Ari, don't worry baby, we'll find someone for you too." We all laughed. It really was good to be with them.

"Sara. We love you. You don't owe me anything."

"Cross, shut up man; I'm sure your tab is big dollars!"

"It is, but I'm not gonna take it. I did this because she's my friend and she needed me. I told you, you're a friend of mine. That means for life. You get it Sara? Friends for life!" Cross came over and gave me a huge hug and kiss. He was smiling from ear to ear. It brought joy to my heart. We sat, ate and socialized for the remainder of the evening. The next morning, we boarded the 30-passenger jet and took off back home. I stared into the clouds thinking about all the work that I was sure I had to catch up on. I told myself to call my mother as soon as I get home. I was going to plan Sunday dinner with her. I wanted to introduce Jackson to my parents. I thought my father would be a bit hard on him because of his age. My dad is old school. If it were up to him, my man would be my age. Men my age just didn't do it for me. Dani got it; Cross was 44. The plane ride was longer because we were traveling from a further distance. I was getting anxious. I didn't drink any liquor prior to this flight.

"Cross. Is there any liquor on this plane?"

"Yea. What do you want? I have a bottle of Kettle One. There's White Hennessy in the luggage somewhere."

"I'll take the Kettle One if it's close." He handed me a semi chilled bottle of Kettle One. I took the top off and took the bottle to my face. That was how I sat for the trip; randomly taking swigs. I got tipsy quickly. It felt good. Approximately 10 hours later, we were finally landing. When we got off the plane I stood still and took a deep breath of city air. It felt good; the pollution filling my lungs. I was really a city girl. Our car ride home felt long. I think it only felt long because I was extremely horny. It was close to a month since the last time Jackson and I held each other in a sexual manner.

Cross arranged limo rides for all of us. I was certain that Dani went home with him and Ari went home alone. Poor girl. I had to figure out how to get her hooked up. In all honesty, I would've hooked her up with Avery, but...well...

"It feels good to be back to reality." When we arrived to my house, I was anxious to get inside. I thought all my plants were dead. I didn't prepare to be away this long, so I didn't arrange to have them watered. I walked up the walkway to the front porch. I glanced at that damn hammock chair and thought about Javi.

"I should call Javi and let him know that I am safe." Jackson grabbed my hand and directed me to the driveway. Shoot, I forgot all about the gift car. As we stepped off the steps and into the driveway, my eyes lit up. It was beautiful. A bright red, 1985 Ferrari 328 GTS.

"AHHHH!!! Really Jax?!"

"Do you like it?"

"I love it!"

"I know a guy that buys, restores, and sells classic cars. You probably know him...Justin McGee. Anyway, he called me to see if I would be interested in it for me. When I got there, I thought you would look better in it. He gave me an offer and I gladly accepted. I arranged to have it delivered while we were away. It's not registered, but I'll pay for that too. Anyway, I hope you like it." Jackson smiled at me and I jumped into his arms. I was happy to be home.

"I love it and I love you. Thank you for not dying."

"Thank you for saving me."

We went inside and immediately I stripped out of my clothes. I walked around and admired my home; how far it's come in the year since I moved in. I envisioned moving Jackson here. It freaked me out a bit. "Jackson, I've never lived with a man; I've never had a roommate. I want you here with me but it's freaking me out a bit."

"No worries. We'll do what we've been doing; I'll spend time here and I'll spend time at my house. When you're ready to change that, let me know and we can have the conversation again."

"You're so understanding. Do I deserve you?"

"The question is, do I deserve you?"

"We're both questioning it, maybe we don't deserve each other."

"Hush. We deserve each other. Enough of this mushy nonsense. It's been too long since I've touched you; caressed you." Jackson walked towards me and cuffed my face in his hands. He kissed me gently. I melted. It was our first kiss all over again. The kissing became intense. I pulled away and lightly jogged around the corner and down a secret hallway. Jackson followed. This was the part of my house I didn't show others. It was my secret, special space. As we turned the corner, the long hallway ended at a door. I stopped and turned to look at Jackson. He glanced a devilish glare at me that turned me on. I giggled and opened the door. This room was all white marble. There was a rose gold chandelier hanging from the ceiling. It hung over a marble Jacuzzi. I flipped a switch on the wall and the Jacuzzi filled and bubbled. In the far back, right corner of the room was a bar.

"Would you like a drink?"

Jackson shook his head. I opened the bar and took 2 glasses out. I opened the chilled bar door and pulled out a bottle of Macallan 18.

"How come I've never seen this room?"

"I don't tell people it's here because it's not open territory. This is a secret space; for me only." I giggled. Jackson held his glass up and chugged his drink. I followed suit. I walked over to the Jacuzzi and stepped into it. The water was hot and it felt good under my butt. I flipped another switch that turned lights on in the water, It also dimmed the light from the chandelier. The mood was perfect. Jackson went back to the bar and poured 2 more drinks. He walked over and followed suit into the water.

"You never cease to amaze me."

"My life is one surprise after the next."

"I love it."

I scooted over closer to Jackson. He grabbed my waist and I climbed into his lap. He ran his wet hands through my hair and he pulled it slightly; it fell into the water. I cuffed his face and kissed him intently. The passion surged though my body and I felt my vagina saturate. Jackson inserted his hard shaft in me. Immediately, I yelled out in pleasure. I rode him in a swift motion while the water smacked my bottom. He whispered in my ear, kissed and sucked on my neck. Periodically, I would stop moving, but I never got up. I rode Jackson, in the water for the remainder of the evening.

I didn't remember getting out of the water. That meant he carried me. I woke up nude in my bed. I could smell food. I was happy, but I couldn't move. My body was stiff, tight. It was weird. I opened my mouth and attempted to yell. "Jackson!" The sound was low. It was as if my voice was removed from my body. I laid still trying to figure out how I was going to make a noise so Jackson would come check on me. I picked my arm up and it fell back down. I could feel the sweat bead up on my forehead. I had to relax. I couldn't move. Just then, Jackson came up the steps. I could hear his feet walking toward the bedroom door. He slowly opened the door and walked in. He was tip toeing but there was no need.

"Sara. Oh good, you're awake. I called the cater club and they delivered breakfast. Come on, let's eat." I couldn't move. I opened my mouth to respond.

"I, can't move babe." That one sentence took the life out of me. I cried.

"Ok babe, Relax. I'm going to dress you and take you to my office. Don't worry. I'll take care of you. I promise." Jackson called his practice manager and warned her that he had an emergency. He walked into my closet and gathered a pair of grey fleece sweats and a white t shirt. He pulled out a bra, panties, and fuzzy socks, walked over to me and dressed me. He massaged my legs and arms. I regained feeling in my arms and legs and slowly could speak after a few minutes.

"Thank you for being here."

"I wasn't planning on leaving. I'm glad you can move, but I still want to take you to my office. I want to do a CAT Scan. The paralysis thing is not normal, contrary to what you want to believe." I rolled my eyes at him. Those still work. I knew paralysis wasn't normal, but since I regained motion, I was prepared to continue with life as normal. I wouldn't have gone to a doctor had Jackson not been there. Well, maybe I would, but It was hard to say. I managed to get off the bed and take a few steps. My cell phone started ringing. It was my mom.

"Hello Mama."

"Hi, How are you?"

"I'm well thanks, how are you?"

"You're lying. You are not well. I can hear it in your voice. What's the matter?"

"Nothing ma. I have a headache, but that's because I'm hungry. I think Jackson went downstairs to make a plate for me. What's up ma??"

"When do I get to meet Jackson?"

"Soon. I promise. Maybe we will come for dinner this weekend. I need to ask him what's on his schedule."

"Ok. Good. Listen, your father needs to take vacation. Can you send him somewhere??" I laughed. The mixture of broken English and the thought of why she could possibly be asking me, were rather funny to me.

"First, ma, I cannot make dada do something he doesn't want to do. Why does he need to take a vacation?"

"If you said 'pa, I want you to go on vacation with me' he would so."

"Mama, I'm not going on vacation for a while. I just came back. What's wrong with dad? Why does he need a vacation?"

"He is working long hours, still. He's too old. I tried to plan a trip to Cairo and he told me no. He said he doesn't have time. He barely eats, sometimes praying, he's a mess these days. I think if he spent some time away, he would..."

"He would be thinking about all the work we took him away from." I had to cut her off because she was sounding a bit crazy. My father always worked long hours. He went on vacation twice a year and he was fine. I knew there was no reason to worry. My phone beeped. It was Megan. I trembled slightly.

"Ma. May I call you back?"

"Please do." I let Megan's call go to voicemail. I didn't want to know what she wanted. I was hoping she would say so in a message. I stood up again and walked out of my bedroom. I walked downstairs and to the kitchen. I followed the smell of the food.

"Wow. You look fine. How do you feel?"

"Hungry!" I sat down at the table and Jackson handed me a glass of cranberry juice. Reluctantly, I drank it. It was good. Refreshing.

"Ok. Now food."

"Ok. Here." Jackson sat a plate in front of me. It smelled so good; mixed veggies and chicken breast. I enjoyed it as if it was the last meal I was eating. Just that fast, I forgot about Megan's phone call. However, she didn't forget that she was trying to reach me. I could hear my phone ringing repeatedly.

"It's Megan."

"You have to answer. I'll go get it." Jackson handed me the phone. 6 missed calls. Before I could return a call, she was calling again.

"Hi Megs."

"Sara…Avery is missing. Have you spoken to him?"

"No. I haven't."

"I spoke to him last week. He said he had to leave the country for business. His secretary called me on Monday when he was a no show for an important meeting. His phone is going straight to voicemail and the box is full. His house is spotless except for party plans and something isn't right." I sat silent for several reasons. Not only because I knew what happened but because I was curious to know why Megan would ask me about his whereabouts.

"Megan, I only interact with Avery in a business setting, except for the annual party. I wouldn't know his whereabouts. I wouldn't know how to find him; I don't know him personally."

"Oh. I didn't know that. I'm sorry to …wait, what about Jackson. Has he heard from Avery?"

"Not to my knowledge. I'll ask him. Listen, we were traveling; in fact, we just returned. I hate to rush you off, but I need to wind down. The time zone change is killing me. I'm sorry."

"Oh. My apologies. I didn't mean to disturb you. Thank you for listening." I hung up the phone as quickly as possible. I didn't want to even think about the agony that Megan had been dealing with. I looked up and Jackson was staring back at me.

"What are you thinking about Sara?"

"Nothing." I cleared my mind and ate my meal. That was the last time it bothered me. The rest of the evening was uneventful. I stayed in with Jackson watching movies.

"Are you going to work tomorrow?"

"Yes. I need to make sure I still have a company." I was laying on the sofa with my feet in Jackson's lap. He massaged them.

"There's a lot of tension in your feet. You need to lay off the high heels sometimes."

"No. I'm too short for that. People don't hear me when I wear flats. I appear weak I think. I will be more than happy to accept foot massages from you on a regular basis."

I winked. Jackson laughed. He rubbed his hands up my legs and thighs. He positioned himself on top of me and scooped me into his arms. I cuffed his face and pulled him close to me. We kissed. I ran my fingers through his thick, dark hair. He moaned slightly into my mouth. He took one hand and rubbed it down my body. He caressed my breast in his palm and squeezed my nipple. I moaned. It was pure ecstasy. I pulled his shirt over his head and exposed his muscular, hairy chest. It was beautiful; like looking at a piece of artwork. He wasn't a man, he was art; a statue. A possible vision of him shooting Avery flashed in my mind and it turned me on more. He was shirtless and sweaty; holding a shotgun. I grabbed his belt buckle and tugged it. I managed to get it open and he wiggled out of his pants. He slid them off and tossed them aside. His erection was exposed; he was turned on. I placed my hand around his shaft and proceeded to stroke. He placed his hand around my neck and pulled gently. I moaned.

"Hmm...you like that huh?"

I did. It was sexy. I couldn't contain myself any longer. I pushed myself back away from him and slid my mouth down his hard penis. He moaned my name. I sucked slowly. My mouth was salivating with excitement. I sucked for a moment then got up. I turned around and walked away from Jackson. He smacked my behind as I walked by him.

"Our sex is intense. You drive me absolutely insane!"

"Agreed. I dreamed a lot while I was in super sleep. In one of our dreams, we were struggling with the passion. It was gone; as if someone blew the flame out. I'm sure I cried in that dream."

"Our passion won't burn out. It goes hand in hand with our love. If we are in love, we will have passion. If the love dies, then the passion flame burns out. I thought you would wake up angry with me."

"I was curious to know why it took you almost a week to speak to me." Jackson's eyes hung low. "I didn't know what to say. My words always result in an exchange with you. When I finally did speak, it broke me that you couldn't move or answer to me. Which reminds me, we need to do the CAT Scan. I still want to know what's up with your brain."

I was hoping he forgot about that. I was sure the CAT Scan was not a bad idea, but hospitals and doctor's offices made me apprehensive.

"Don't look at me like that. You will be safe. I'll take care of whatever it is. Come on. Let's go."

"Right now?"

"Yup. Right now." Jackson and I hopped in my TDI Touareg and he drove us to his office. As we pulled up to an elaborate office building, I noticed Calla lilies out front. I stood still for a moment and gazed at them. I smiled and continued walking. The main entrance of the office building was simple; long hallway, elevators and a staircase. We got in the elevator and Jackson pushed 20.

"Of course, your office is on 20!"

"Scared of heights?"

"Eh. Not really..."

"So, then what's the problem?"

"Nerves."

I rolled my eyes and hung my head. Jackson walked up to me and slipped his hands in mine.

"I love you. You will be fine." He kissed me. The elevator doors opened into a beautiful, well-lit office. A beautiful brunette with bright blue eyes greeted us at the door.

"Hello Dr. Ellis. Hello, you must be Sara. It's good to finally meet you." I thought to myself, 'who was this woman?' She was insatiable!

"I am Angela, Dr. Ellis's practice manager. He talks about you randomly, but he has been worried since the paralysis began. Please follow me. I'll get you setup." I smirked and followed Angela down the hall. When we reached the end of the hall, Angela opened the door and we walked into a large white room with a large white machine. I assumed this was the CAT

Scan room. I stood still while Angela maneuvered around the room.
"Please, have a seat here, Sara." I sat in a large, cushioned chair.
"Have you been feeling any pain?"
"Hmmm, well, I haven't felt any pain, but I do not feel like myself. Does that make sense?"
"Sure. Would you call it discomfort?"
"I call it; uneasiness."
"Ah. Got it. Ok. According to Dr. Ellis's timeline, you were asleep for 12 days and 8 hrs. Do you have any recollection of that time-period?"
"I heard the conversations that commenced around me. My intuition stayed in tact, oh and I dreamed. A lot."
"Were the dreams clear?"
"Very."
"Did you want to react to any of the conversations being held?"
"Yes. Especially when they suggested moving me. I could feel my ligaments, but couldn't make them move."
"Tell me about the day you woke up from the super sleep. Do you remember something unusual happening?"
"No. I was dreaming. Someone started talking to me and their words willed me awake."
"Do you know who it was?"
"Yes."
"Do you know them personally? Is it a family member or friend?"
"No; to all the above."
"Tell me what you felt earlier when you woke from a nap."
"I was numb. Paralysis set in. I couldn't move."
"Was your brain functioning?"
"Yes. My thoughts were clear. I could speak; it was faint, but I could speak."
"Were you dreaming then?"
"I don't remember a dream, if one was happening, so I'll say no." Angela jotted her thoughts onto a notepad.
"Ok. We are going to do this CAT Scan because Dr. Ellis is insisting. However, I think the concern is psychological." Did she think I was crazy!?
"I don't think you're crazy, but there is a connection with the person that woke you. A CAT Scan won't show us the connection. It has to be uncovered in therapy."
She continued to set up the CAT Scan machine. I watched until she

motioned that she was ready for me. I laid down on a surgical table and a large box shaped device slid down from above and fixated itself on my head. I sat still for 5 minutes. The longest 5 minutes ever!

"Ok. I have all I need. I am certain that Dr. Ellis is going to rush me for these results. Let's rejoin him in his office and see what he's thinking."

I followed Angela back down the long hallway. When we reached Jackson's office, Angela knocked and opened the door. Jackson was sitting at a large, mahogany desk. The wood was so smooth; like new. For a split moment, I envisioned him having me sprawled out across it and I licked my lips. His credentials hung on his office walls and my eyes examined every word. 'National Association of Neurologists; President', 'Tau Delta Omega National Honor Society', USA Today News articles; He was featured in Time Magazine, Medical International, and Business Insider. His undergraduate, and medical degrees hung behind his head. He was on the phone when we walked in, and signaled for us to sit. I wondered who he was talking to but as he continued his conversation, I gathered he was talking to the doctor that treated me on the island. He finished the conversation and hung up the phone. He sat for a moment; no words were spoken by any of us.

"Ang, may we have the room please?"

Oh, this couldn't be good. Angela got up to leave the room. I batted my eyes at her and mouthed 'thank you' as she walked out. She smiled and closed the door tight behind her.

"Sara..."

"Jackson..."

"You have scar tissue here." He pointed to a spot on a floppy image that he was holding in his hand. It was a dark, hollowed space. "There's a mound of scar tissue building around the frontal lobe. It's contracting and causing the immobility. I can fix it, but it means brain surgery. If I don't fix it, the paralysis will continue. What scares me about it continuing is we never know when the paralysis will happen. It cannot be foreseen. We were lucky that you were home and I was with you when the last one happened. Can you work from home until we can schedule surgery? I'll pay Dani and Ari salary to hang out with you. You shouldn't be alone, but I have to report to my office every day this week." I pouted. It was too much for me to handle. Jackson performing brain surgery on me?!?!

"I appreciate you not wanting me to be alone, but I spent too much time listening to Ari talk while I was in super sleep. I would rather..."

"Alone is not an option, so take it out of your mind."

"Well then, I would rather Jenna be the one to watch me."

"It's not like you need a babysitter, but I need to make sure my baby doesn't hurt herself when paralysis hits."

"Ok. When do you plan on cutting into my brain?"

"Sooner than later. These are the scans from when we were on the island. This is today." Jackson laid the 2 scans on the light table for me to view. I could see there was a significant difference. I sat back in the chair and exhaled.

"How long do I have to be in the hospital for recovery?"

"Of course, that's more important than the recovery process." Jackson rolled his eyes and smiled.

"I trust that the doctor will take great care of me."

"Oh Sara. I would like to keep you in the hospital for a week. I'm sure you will invite the option of turning your bedroom into an ICU but I don't want to take that chance. Let's say a week and see how you progress."

I rolled my eyes and smirked.

"Fine."

"Come. Let's go to your office and brief Jenna. I think next Monday is a good day to take out some scar tissue."

Jackson cleared his desk and led me out of his office. When we reached the nurses station, Angela stood to greet me again.

"Sara. We will take great care of you when you become our patient. Please don't worry. I'll make sure your room is filled with your favorite things."

"Thank you, Angela; I appreciate it."

She really was a sweetheart. I was still nervous, but she contributed to putting my nerves at ease. Jackson and I headed over to my office. When we walked in, there was a new girl at the receptionist desk.

"Hi. Welcome to Bradley & Associates. How may I assist you?" She was pleasant, but obviously, no one showed her my picture.

"Hi. My name is Sara Bashir. This is Jackson Ellis and this is my company. What's your name?"

"Hi OH MY GOD! Ms. Bashir. I am so sorry. I wasn't expecting you until Monday. My name is Natalie." Jenna came around the corner just as my facial expression was changing.

"I thought I was going to have to come get you off that freaking island! Welcome back beautiful. Hi Jackson." Jenna hugged and kissed me on the cheek.

"Oh Jenna. You have no idea."

"I have a little idea. I spoke to Cross a few times while you were gone. Are you back to work today or tomorrow?"

"2 more weeks. Let's go to my office so I can tell you why." Jenna and Jackson followed me through the large glass doors, down the corridor, down the hallway, and around the corner to my office. We walked in and we all took a seat.

"Should I have Natalie bring us drinks?"

"No need. So, Jenna...what did Sir Gregorio tell you."

"He was vague with the details, but he told me Jackson was kidnapped; it's good to see you back. He told me you were sick and that's why your flight didn't come back on the rescheduled day that was on my calendar."

"Yea. That's the gist of it. The deeper details are, I hit my head and now I have a scar tissue abrasion that is building on my frontal lobe. It causes brief moments of paralysis. Jackson is going to fix it. My surgery is scheduled for Monday. I need you to spend this week with me at home. Jax doesn't want me to work, because the paralysis can/will happen with no warning."

"Absolutely. I am confident that Natalie can keep things running smoothly while we are out."

"Yea what happened to the girl whose voice I can't stand?"

"Emma. Emma answered the phone one day and told Hiro Matsumaura that you were gone and no one knew if you had any plans on returning. After I snatched the phone, I fired her; stupid girl."

"What did Hiro need?"

"He was calling to check on you; on the stores. I sent him a spreadsheet of progress from the start of your takeover. Year to date, we have already doubled revenue in sales, service, parts and accessories. Things look good. He asked if you would be interested in owning a piece of an international business; a trucking company. I told him to send over a proposal. He said he will." Wow! Jenna was on point! I love this girl. Promoting her was the best thing for my company's progression.

"Ladies. We are no longer discussing the reason we are here."

"Oh. That's right. Sorry. Jenna, you can fill me in this week while we're shacked up in my house. Dr. I'm over protective would like to take me home."

Jackson rolled his eyes. Jenna and I laughed. She understood me and I loved it. I was looking forward to spending my week with Jenna.

"Ha! Ok. I will stay here for the rest of the day and get Natalie situated. I will come over tomorrow. What time would you like me there?"

"Eh, whenever. I don't care. I'll be home all day!"

"I'll come early and bring you breakfast. Let's say around 9?"

"Perfect. I will see you then."

Jackson and I left my office. As we reached the car, my cell phone rang. It was Megan. Here we go again.

"Hi Megan."

"Hi Sara. If Avery is missing, what happens to his company?"

"Uh, I don't know, but I'm sure his company has a will. His lawyer can assist you with detailed instructions. Are you declaring him missing?"

"Yea. It's been too long. It's difficult because he didn't leave much of a trail. It's almost like he planned to disappear. Anyway, I was asking about the company because I need to know who to give it to. I don't want to run it; it's too complex. If I need, will you help me find a buyer?"

"Absolutely. Keep me posted, just give me two weeks to rest; I'm having a minor procedure done next week."

"Oh. I hope all goes well. I'll let you rest. We'll speak soon." Jackson gave me a look of confusion and disgust when I hung up the phone.

"Why are you advising Megan on what to do with Avery's company?"

"Because I know him on a business level. My job is to manage his company. That's what I am going to do. Furthermore, I don't know what 'HAPPENED' to him; I need to make sure that remains true." I stared into Jackson's beautiful, sea blue eyes. He didn't break the stare and that's how we sat for a moment.

"Have you done this before?"

"Have I done what babe?"

"Covered tracks. Hidden a crime?"

"Ha! I can't answer that. I would have to kill you."

Chapter 15

Jenna arrived bright and early on Monday; ready to begin her biggest task yet, "entertaining Sara." She came in with a huge fruit salad and muffin tops. She brewed a fresh pot of coffee and made mimosas. She set my outside table and came to wake me with a smile.

"Good morning sunshine. Let's begin our day!" I was not a morning person; not like Jenna. She was uber happy in the morning.

"Where's Jackson?"

"He's downstairs. He asked me to wake you."

I rolled my eyes. Of course, he asked her to wake me. He didn't want to run the risk of me whining about not needing a babysitter. Meanwhile, I wouldn't complain. Jenna was the best choice. I rose from bed and stumbled to the bathroom. I washed my face and brushed my teeth. I brushed my hair into a bun on the top of my head. I slipped my feet into fuzzy slippers and proceeded to the kitchen. Jackson was drinking a cup of coffee and Jenna was making a plate.

"There she is! Good morning sweetheart." Jackson stood and kissed me hello. "I have to get to the office. I am due in surgery at 11. Be a great girl for Jenna. Jenna, don't let her work too hard. If she has a paralysis moment, massage whatever ligaments are stiff and it should pass in minutes. If it doesn't, call my office immediately."

"Really?! Babe, I'll be fine."

"You better be! We have a lifetime ahead of us." Jackson headed out of the house and Jenna and I remained inside.

"What would you like to do first, Sara?" I sat still for a moment thinking. "Sara. You ok?"

"Yea. I'm fine. I want to smoke and I want you to fill me in on business." I walked over to my secret stash spot. I rolled a blunt and made a cup of coffee. Jenna and I went outside and sat on the hammock chair. Jenna opened her iPad and handed mine to me as well.

"Ok, business is going well at Henderson Hill. Mini is currently sitting at 132 new cars sold and 80 used cars. BMW is currently sitting at 141 new cars sold and 90 used cars sold. CSI is still well over 98%. Hiro sent over the trucking company proposal. He wants you to buy into 52.5% and you will receive that percentage in earnings. The only thing is it will be based overseas. You will have to travel to Amsterdam once a month."

"Hmm...interesting. I mean...that's...we'll get back to that. What's happening at Bradley?"

"Things are good there. New accounts is still booming; in fact, 32 new accounts opened last week alone. There are a few doctor's offices in the building that are late on rent and have received eviction notices. I will follow up on those at the end of the week. Uhm..." Jenna hung her head. "Rena is pulling out of the L'Inn project and Rita is having a fit. I told them they couldn't bother you because you were still away, so they have me in the middle of it. All I know is Rena told Rita 'Sara can't be trusted'. I'm not sure what that is about, but now Rita is going crazy looking for a new designer."

I rolled my eyes and grabbed my cell. I scrolled to Rena's name in my phonebook and touched her name. She answered with what sounded like a smile...

"I was beginning to think you weren't coming back to the states."

"What's this I hear you're telling people that I can't be trusted? What problem do you have with me now?"

"I don't want to do business with a woman that keeps gangster degenerates on her payroll." I laughed. Clearly, she was talking about Cross and how I had him handle the Brian Bradley situation. "I thought you were a new person now, Sara. You were supposed to be over the manipulating people and situations phase of your life. I thought you got rid of those contacts."

"I don't expect you to understand."

"What's there to understand? You paid a man to take money from another man."

"Says the outside looking in."

"Well whatever! I am done with you as a business partner and friend. I don't want to be near you when karma gets back at you!"

"Let's see how long your career lasts when I stop buying your artwork." That was low, but I meant it. Rena hung up on me. I sat for a moment and let Rena's words sink into my brain. Maybe she was right. I was doing a lot out of my character, but I was doing what I needed to do to protect my investments. If she didn't like how I handle my business, she didn't have to be around my business.

"Sara. Where did you go? You still with me?"

"Oh Yea. I'm here. I was just...what was I saying?"

"You weren't saying anything. You were just sitting there. Is this one of those paralysis moments?"

"I'm not sure. I'm learning it as it happens, but I don't think so."

I had to calm myself down. I wanted to punch Rena in her throat.

"Uhm...ok. Well...you were on the phone with Rena."

"AHHH!!! I'm done with Rena! She doesn't want to work with me anymore because she thinks I'm a hoodlum. Mind you, I used my 'hoodlum' connects to help her out of a tough situation once. Whatever! I know another designer. He costs more, but he's better. You get what you pay for, and he can care less about my 'hoodlum' tendencies."

I rolled my eyes. It was crazy to me how much people judge and then tell you 'I pass no judgement.' Lies!

"What did you do that was so hoodlum?"

"The Brian Bradley thing..." My eyes fell low.

"Oh, you mean making him pay you the thousands he owed you? Listen, if it were me, he'd be dead. I applaud how you handled him." Jenna high fived me and my mouth opened slightly. I was impressed by her candor.

"Close your mouth babe. Yes, I have a feisty side."

"Oh yea?! Is there a freaky side also?"

"Every classy lady has one she keeps encaged until it's time to unleash it." Jenna winked at me.

"Touché."

"So, tell me about this designer? How can I reach him?"

"Jen, are you single?"

"I am."

"Hmmm...ok. Good to know, for future reference. You never know who I may meet. The designer's name is Nate Airless. He's got an office in midtown. He is best reached via email. Make my name the subject line, and he'll answer right away."

"Clout!" Jenna fist bumped me, got up and went inside. My phone rang.

"Hello."

"Hi babe. How are you feeling?"

"I feel fine."

"Ok. Good. What are you doing?"

"Sitting outside on the hammock chair. Jenna was filling me in on my business world. She just went inside."

"What's her story? She single?"

"Why? You interested?"

"I think she's interested in you."

"Oh?"

Guys. They always think women have secret crushes on each other. It's called respect. It takes a real woman to compliment and respect another woman; an even stronger woman to recognize if it's jealousy, or not. Jenna respected me, as I respected her.

"Eh. You never know; but none of this is the reason why I called. There was a message on my desk this morning from Avery's lawyer. Apparently, he left his company to me in his will. Megan is convinced that he isn't coming back and she's settling his estate. Eh! I guess I own a recycling company now. I gave his lawyer my lawyer's contact info and they will discuss and keep me posted."

"I'm not sure what to say."

"I didn't know what to say either. I just sat and let the lawyer speak. When he was done, he asked if I understood. I said yes, and that was the end of it. I'll be over there in a few. Do you need anything?"

"No thanks babe. I'm fine."

Jackson hung up the phone. His demeanor was different. I needed him to get over it; the killing Avery & Tiffany thing, what was done was done and it couldn't be undone. If he let it wear on his conscious, it would've worn him out. I learned that when the result was taking a life, chances are the life wasn't worth saving. Apparently, he felt the same way, hence him taking the lives of people he once loved. I was beginning to feel restless. I decided to go find Jenna and convince her to take me shopping.

"Jenna! Jenna!!" Instead of being lazy, I got up and went looking for her. I found her sitting in my closet.

"Sorry. It's just peaceful in here."

"I know what you mean. No windows, just seclusion and about a million dollars worth of high end fashion!"

We both laughed. Turns out Jenna did some research and tracked Nate Airless down. She sent him the draft of the project and asked for his expertise.

"You were right. I put your name in the subject line; he must've hit reply and send at the same time! His response time was crazy fast. Anyway, he's on board. He said he owes you a favor and he will be doing this project pro bono. Sara, a TON of favors are owed to you. It seems everyone I speak to owes you something. I don't ever want to owe you a thing! No offense, but it's costly to owe you a favor." Jenna and I both laughed but there was truth to what she was saying.

"Jenna. It's not easy being me. I'll tell you pieces as time goes on. I think I can trust you. Come on! Let's go shopping."

Immediately Jenna and I gathered our handbags and headed to the front door. We jumped in her car. It was easier and I didn't want anyone driving my cars. We spent a good portion of our afternoon going back and forth with stories from our childhood; life in general. Jenna was more interesting than I thought. She graduated Magna Cum Laude from Oberlin with a degree in physics.

"My dad paid for my tuition out of pocket which meant he got to declare my major. But the rules were, 'no matter the concentration, you must excel at it'. I worked my tail off for that physics degree that I didn't want. When I graduated, he landed me an internship and I was supposed to go work for NASA. I didn't want to do that. I took out student loans in my name and obtained a second degree in fashion merchandizing from St. John's. I want to start my own brand; I can sew, very well, but my dad is... adamant in his ways and beliefs. I haven't spoken to him since you promoted me. 'why work for someone that you have the potential to beat?' He always says not to work for someone because they never fully care about your well-being."

"I care about your well-being."

"That's because you're genuine."

"Eh. Rena doesn't agree."

"She's not really your friend. Every time you turn around, she's passing judgement. I've always admired you. You do your own thing and your work is always done. Now that I work for you, I see how truly magnificent you are. My father is a hater hence why none of his children converse with him. It is what it is."

My talk with Jenna made me think about my father. My father always accepted me and what I chose to do with my life. 'Sara, are you happy?' That's what he would ask. 'if so, then do whatever keeps you happy.' He never passed judgement. Even if I were to tell him about some of the things I've done to get ahead in the business world, I think he would still ask me if what I did made me happy. I do not fret when I need to get things done. I simply get them done. Our day out consisted of light lunch, shopping, coffee, and a visit to Javi's office. I figured we should stop by, since I hadn't seen him since before the island adventure. I didn't share many details. I told him he should come by later. Jackson and I will tell him the details. Not that I didn't want to tell Jenna, but I know from experience that she shouldn't know much just in case questions were asked. When she says, 'I don't know', I wanted there to be truth to the statement. I wanted her to be able to sleep at night. I knew she wouldn't judge me, but I didn't want her to cringe when she looked at me, or Jackson. I had a strange feeling while we were in route back to my house. I knew we would get there before Jackson; I didn't want him to worry. I had a feeling like someone was talking about me. When Jenna pulled into my driveway, Rena was sitting on my hammock chair.

"Don't you think you insulted me enough today?" I said as I climbed the steps to the porch. I did not want to deal with Rena and her foolishness. She rolled her eyes at me.

"Can we speak alone?" Jenna moved slowly and disrespectfully, she walked up to Rena and bumped her shoulder when she walked past. Jenna whispered something under her breath. Only Rena heard her. Jenna rolled her eyes and walked into the house. Rena and I sat on he hammock chair.

"Well I see she is learning all of your qualities; good and bad. She's got your permanent stank face down to a science, huh?!" Rena had her big girl panties on; talking trash!

"I need a backup. I am training her to be my stunt double."

"Really???"

Rena rolled her eyes. I wasn't sure why she was surprised by my smart comment. She knew my mouth was a loaded gun, especially when I was provoked.

"Why are you here, Rena? You made it clear that you don't want to have anything to do with me or my business."

"I am just trying to understand who you are becoming."

"Becoming?! No! This is who I am. This is who I've always been."

"Since when are you a hit man?"

"I'm not a hit man, but I know where to find one when I need one."

"Brian GAVE you his company. Do you think you were owed that? Do you think you really deserved it?"

"I deserved the truth. What I got was a setup. What wasn't going to happen was me paying for an oversight that I wasn't in power to oversee. You have no idea what you are talking about when you come to me with these open accusations. You assume that Anne Bradley is telling you the truth when she speaks to you. Let me be the first to tell you, she is not." Rena sat and shot me a glare. She was about to start speaking when I cut her off. "And furthermore, Anne Bradley is NOT broke; under any circumstances. She was left with her home, and her investments. I gathered what I needed from Brian; solely Brian. Are you here on his defense? In fact, even if you are, I don't want to hear it.

"I wanted to tell you that I will finish the project because it's not about you. Turns out, Rita is a good person and she deserves great things. I may not agree with some of the ways you do your business, but I do think you are the best business woman alive. I am willing to complete the project free of charge."

"Thanks, but I already hired a new designer."

"What!? It's been like 4 hours. Who did you hire that quickly?!"

"I'm a business woman first. There was no way I was going to let any more time rest on that project. Nate Airless is taking care of it for me. No worries. Do you need anything else Rena?" Tears gathered in Rena's eyes. Had this been 6 months earlier, I would've been upset at this moment, but, I wanted to add insult to injury and put her off my property. Instead, I got up to get her some tissues.

"I guess my mind is blown because I didn't know that you would take any and every measure for your business. My business isn't as big as yours or as detailed, so I guess that's why I don't understand. I just don't want you to get hurt. What if someone seeks revenge on you for something that you did? Recent or past, and they take you out. Then that means we lose you. We, I cannot lose you. You mean too much to me."

"I appreciate your concern, but forgive me for thinking that it is only concern because you think you know firsthand that I may be in danger. Don't think about it anymore because it's making you offensive and I don't have much patience for people offending me, especially on my property."

"You're right. I am sorry. Please forgive me."

"I'll forgive you, because I am a Christian, but I will not forget because I am a human."

"That's understood. I guess I'll go."

Rena slowly walked away. I sat for a moment and scratched her off the list of people that I do not need to keep around. It broke my heart a bit but it had to be done. If I kept her around, she would ask questions and when I did not answer the questions, she would cause problems. I did not even try. I was cool with her walking out of my life. Everything happens for a reason, right? Jenna came out and took her seat back on the hammock chair. She laid her head on my shoulder. It was only fitting that I laid my head atop hers. That's how we remained for a few minutes. I didn't mind the silence because it was giving me a chance to reflect and feel the energy coming from Jenna. As I sat there re-evaluating myself, my life, my business, I could not help but think about my good intentions and my hard work. Rena criticized the decision that I made to ensure the lifeline of my business. Did she think she wouldn't do the same? She didn't understand. Her business was based on a talent. My business was based on my knowledge, networking skills, and efficiency. If I was challenged with the same situation again, I would've make the same decision again; hands down! I looked up and Jackson was pulling into the driveway. He was so beautiful. I still got a warm and tingly feeling when he arrived; he touched me, kissed me, and I melted.

"Hello ladies. How are my beautiful girls?"

"Hi Jackson!" We bellowed in unison; like little girls. We blushed.

"Jenna. How is our patient doing today?"

"She is fantastic. We spent some time out today. She's eaten, drank, smoked, worked, put Rena out of her life; I'm sure she needs a hug." Jenna patted my knee. We shifted so Jackson could sit between us. He did and placed a hand on each of our legs.

"I'm ok. Everything happens for a reason. There is a reason why Rena confronted me in such a manor. There is a reason why she isn't here and Jenna is. There is a reason for everything, but I cannot dwell on looking for answers that aren't meant for me to have yet. Or at all, for that matter."

"When I first met Rena, I thought she was jealous of you, remember?"

"I do. I told you you were crazy."

"'We're good friends' you said. 'She has no reason to be jealous of me.' Silly rabbit!"

"Tricks are for kids." Jenna listened to the exchange with a look of confusion. She interjected.

"What kills me is, every time we sat down, she was praising you. 'oh she's doing so well', 'I'm so proud' blah. Turns out, it was a façade!"

"No. She probably felt that way until she spoke to Ann. Lately, Ann has been feeding her with negative connotations about me. Eh, I don't care. Mark my words; she will need me before I need her."

"Yea, well; forget her!! I'm hungry. Let's eat." Jackson got up and walked in the house. Jenna and I got up and followed him.

"Let's order sushi."

"Jenna doesn't eat sushi."

"How about I cook?" Jenna walked in the kitchen, opened the fridge and cabinets and tried to put a meal together. I walked over to the wine cellar and chose a bottle of Shiraz. We all sat in the kitchen with a glass of wine; I also rolled a blunt. We talked about everything. Jackson must have asked Jenna 1,000 questions. Questions like "what's your favorite color?" Or "democrat or republican?" My favorite was when he asked her why she was single.

"Have you ever fallen in love with someone that didn't love you back? Once you get over something like that, life goes on and it goes on better alone."

"Not everyone will love you back, but when you find someone who does love you back, life goes on without ever wanting to be alone again. Trust me. It's not your time yet. Look at me, I'm 50 and just found the love of my life."

"Dude! If I have to wait till I'm 50 to find true love; let's just say I pray I won't have to wait." Jenna made chicken breast stuffed with spinach and feta cheese, wild grain rice and a salad. We all sat at my large dining room table. We would've eaten outside, but the skies opened with a torrential downpour. Jenna was an amazing chef. We laughed, joked, practically almost cried. I shared stories with Jenna that even Jackson didn't know.

"I remember when I first started working at Bradley. The lead analyst was in my class at NYU, but did not hold honors. She was messing up big time and Brian was tired of reprimanding her. She stormed into his office; tried to throw me under a bus and said I faked my Magna Cum Laude and my degree is a fraud. Turns out, she never completed her degree. She lied; she lost her position at the company. That night, she called herself 'meeting me outside like we were going to fight. She stood in front of me and swung. She missed. I didn't; let's just say she will never smile again!"

"WOW! You do have a napoleon complex!"

We all laughed. It was that infectious, gut busting laughter.

"I have a question, how long have you been a weed smoker?"

"HA! That's a good question. I guess I was, 27 when I started."

"Wow! Why so late?"

"I did everything late. I lost my virginity at like 24. Had my first drink at, well that doesn't count; I'm Egyptian, we come out the womb with a golden chalice. HA!"

"Better late than never, I guess."

It was a good evening. As we began winding down, I poured all of us a shot of Sambuca. It was a chilly evening, so we sat by the fireplace on the porch. It was a wonderful, liquor filled evening with good company.

"Can I ask you guys a crazy question?"

"I'm listening...I'm not sure if Sara is coherent." There was no doubt. I was drunk, like drooling on myself drunk. It felt good to be THAT drunk.

"Suppose I said, 'let's have sex' what would you say?"

"I would prefer to watch the two of you have sex. That's hot!"

"Yea, you have a better chance of staying alive if you don't touch Jackson."

"That's scary because I know it's true."

"Why do you ask, Jenna? Do you want to have sex?"

"Not right now. I'm too drunk!" Jenna laughed out loud. Her face was red. "I'm not a Sambuca drinker, normally. But Sara, you are ridiculously sexy!"

"Isn't she!?!?"

"So, wait, are you only drinking Sambuca because I'm sexy?!" It was silly. I laughed.

"Uhh...possibly. If you were ugly, or less attractive, I would've asked for something stronger. HA!" Jenna laughed and slapped her own leg hard! She managed to speak through the giggles. "I just want to make sure that if I cop a feel, I won't be hit in the face."

"Oh Jenna!!" I leaned in and kissed her softly. "You're fabulous and I am so thankful for you. Just keep being amazing! Maybe you can rub on me later in life." I smiled big. Jenna did too. It was getting chilly, so we made our way inside the house. Jackson locked all of the doors behind us. His cell phone rang. It was Cross.

"Dude, it's late."

"I know. I'm sorry. We have a situation. Can you come to my office?"

"You have an office?!"

"Yea, jerk! I have a legitimate business, so..."

"Yea. I'm coming." "Sara. Cross is requesting I come to his office. He wants to talk about something, and you know how he feels about speaking on the phone."

"Ha! My crazy Cross. Do you want me to come with you?"

"No. I want you to get some rest. I would like you to be with me tomorrow when I accept the key to Avery's company."

"Aye Aye Sir!" I stood and saluted Jackson. He smiled big and kissed me hard on the lips.

"What's the secret emergency?"

Jackson walked into Cross's office suite.

"Megan McBride. She's been poking around trying to figure out where Avery is. There's no trace of him because I'm flawless but she's..."

"Being annoying."

"Exactly."

"Yea...We grew up together. What does she know?"

"She knows he was out of town for a night. She's now trying to figure out where he went and how he got there. He flew to the island on his own private jet. I couldn't let his pilot return, so that's what's peeked her interest."

"Are you asking me if it's ok to take Megan out?"

"Asking?! Jackson, c'mon..." Cross laughed wholeheartedly. Jackson knew he wasn't asking, but he was hoping.

"I guess my emotions went out the window when I started shooting 'loved ones'. I think if Megan is causing a problem or begins to pose a threat, then do what you gotta do. But if she's simply trying to find her brother, then."

"Don't tell me you are thinking about telling her what really happened?"

"No. Don't be ridiculous."

"So, what's the problem? I'm sure if my options are keep you out of jail or help put you in, Sara, would opt for the first."

"Avery left his company to me in his will. I take over as President & CEO of A. McBride Recycling Corp as of 2pm tomorrow afternoon. I still can't wrap my mind around it."

"Congrats! The recycling business is a good business to slip and fall into. Listen, I'll see how much poking Megan continues doing and I'll handle it accordingly."

"Great. Thanks man. I just don't want to raise any suspicion. How do I justify it?"

"it's not for you to justify. Honestly, you have no idea what's in a will until a will reading. Prior to the things going haywire, how often did you speak to Avery?"

"Not often. We fell off when I stopped looking for Tiffany."

"Then there's no reason why you would have killed him." Cross winked at Jackson and he chuckled.

"Touché man. Alright...Sara and I are kind of dealing with enough with this brain aneurism thing. If Megan gets..."

"No worries. I got it. Go take care of Sara, please. I like you and you're a friend of mine, but if she dies, I will kill you!"

"I know." As Jackson made his way to his vehicle, his cell phone rang. It was Megan.

"Megs! What's up Hun?"

"Were you in Jamaica with Avery recently?"

"No. Why do you ask?"

"He's missing, his pilot is missing, his jet is missing and tomorrow afternoon, you are going to officially own his company. What did you do?"

"We grew up together and you are mentally unstable. I am not surprised that he left his company to me in his will. Remember, you are the one that declared him missing. I wouldn't be surprised if Avery is fine; simply revamping his life somewhere and doesn't want to tell you about it.

"Jackson. Something isn't right. I am determined to find out what it is and why it isn't right. If my search leads me to you or to Sara, you both will go down for the disappearance of my brother. If you know anything, you need to tell me now."

Megan sounded so pissed off. Jackson believed with his entire soul, that she was determined to find out and that was a risk he wasn't willing to take. He continued talking to her. He tried to comfort her with stories from their childhood; traveling back down memory lane.

"Do you remember that time we pretended that Avery cut his leg on that rusty fence in the backyard? You were so grossed by the fake blood, you started throwing up! Then we got in trouble for making you sick."

"Ha! Those were good times. Our mom was mad at you guys for a long time. I remember being in our 20's and you and Avery had a huge fight. You stopped speaking for a while and no one knew why. He confided in me that was the worst moment in your friendship history. He said he couldn't trust you."

"Hmmm, well, our friendship was full of good moments and bad moments. I lost trust in him when he fell in love with my wife."

"The one he forced you to marry? I probably would've been mad at that too."

"The only wife I've ever had. I should've seen it. They were close. I was always at work."

"Did you kill him?" Jackson was extremely quiet. He didn't want to lie or tell the truth.

"No."

"I hope that's the truth." Megan hung up. Jackson had a feeling that she knew he wasn't telling the truth. Instead of worrying about something he couldn't do anything about, he turned the radio up in his car and continued to drive into the night.

Chapter 16

"Hey, Sara…wake up Hun. We have to get you ready."

Jenna walked into my bedroom at 5am on surgery day. I wasn't excited, but over the past few days, the paralysis moments were more frequent. I rose from my bed and went to the bathroom for a shower. The hot water felt so good on my skin. It was refreshing. The last week of events were invigorating and informative. My businesses were doing so well and I was apart of everything; via Skype. Modern technology allowed me to successfully work from home. I considered doing this all the time; going into offices on an as needed basis. Jackson and I were even closer. I was concerned about his feelings toward performing brain surgery on me. He assured me that it was a simple procedure and he wouldn't have any other doctor perform it because it was me. He was certain he was the best man for the job. This was the first time I had surgery. I didn't tell my mom, dad or Hosni. I didn't want them to go out of their way to make a spectacle about it. I told Jackson to make the call if I die, otherwise, we didn't need to worry them. He didn't agree but he respected my wishes. Sometimes, I just preferred to do things alone. I was always like that and it drove my mother insane. I believed she tapped into my spirit and knew something was up. I was prepared to answer any questions she had for me the next time we spoke. I got out of the shower, washed my face and brushed my teeth. I figured I didn't have to be too flashy, but I did want to be comfortable. I grabbed a pair of black, Victoria's Secret sweatpants and matching hoodie. I brushed my hair into a ponytail and threw on a pair of moccasins. I was annoyed though. I had been awake for 3 hours and I couldn't eat or drink. Jenna and I arrived at Jackson's office slightly after 8am. He was already there, since he had to prep for surgery himself. Angela came down and greeted Jenna and me with her warm smile. All the paperwork had been done prior to me getting here. I laid down on the bed in the hospital suite and tried to relax. I took a deep breath and scanned the room with my eyes. I said a prayer; asking for God to do His will, whatever His will may be. Jackson walked in shortly after my Amen.
"Are you nervous?"
"Yes."
"Don't be. I won't let anything happen to you."
"Isn't this a conflict of interest?"
"Sara, seriously? I need you to relax. I love you. I am going to quickly and

effectively remove the scar tissue from your brain. You are going to recover with flying colors and then we are going to spend the rest of our lives together. Understood?"

"I understand. Ok. Let's get it over with; please. I desperately need a cup or 2 of coffee." Jackson kissed me and the nurses rolled me down the hall. We arrived at a large, open, operating room. It was intense, so I closed my eyes. A nurse injected me with Propofol and asked me to count backwards from 100. I successfully made it to 97!

"Ok guys. This is my life laying on this table. We have 40 minutes to successfully remove this scar tissue or she will never function again. Are we ready?!"

"Yes. Proceed Dr. Ellis." Jackson took a deep breath and recited a prayer in his mind. He grabbed a blade and proceeded to cut. Exactly 40 minutes later, he closed the incision, having successfully removed all the scar tissue.

"Now. We wait..."

"It went well. I got all the scar tissue. There was no damage to the frontal lobe or any surrounding areas. Now we wait for her to wake up and we check her motor function, memory, things like that." Jackson called the "crew" as he liked to call them; Javi, Cross, Dani, and Ari. Jenna was already there.

"Round 2 of 'wait for Sara to wake'. I'm starting to hate this game."

"At least we know what the issue is this time." Dani sat down with her work and got comfortable. "Just in case we have to be here for a few days."

"I'm sure she is ecstatic that you all are here."

"Na honey...she's gonna wake up, see us all looking at her and she may have a royal fit."

"Javi, you are the only person in the room that will ever have a 'royal fit'."

"Don't tease me. I know Sara and she is going to wake up and..."

"Wonder what you all are doing here?!" I woke up just in time. Everyone had a look of pure relief on their faces.

"Oh, it is good to see you awake."

"And we didn't have to wait a week for you to wake."

"Try 12 days. Hi guys! Jax, babe, I'm ready to go home." Jackson leaned in and stared into my eyes. He kissed me.

"Hello beautiful. You cannot go home yet, but let me check you out. Then we will feed you." Jackson took out a flashlight and shined the light in my eye.

"Follow my finger." I did as I was asked. Jackson removed the stethoscope from around his neck and listened to my chest and lungs.

"Take a deep breath, please." I did.

"How do you feel? Any pain? Stiffness? Discomfort?"

"Hunger. Thirst."

"The usual." Jackson completed his exam and left the room for a moment. He returned with Angela and a nurse whose name tag I couldn't read.

"Hi Sara. This is Rebekah. She will be your nurse."

"Does she get to be my nurse at home?"

"Are you going to ask to go home every day?"

"Yes." They had no idea the agony that came with me having to be in a hospital for longer than I deemed necessary. I had to be bleeding profusely or ignited in flames to get me to remain calm in a hospital.

"We actually suggested that Dr. Ellis take you home tomorrow. Please allow us one night of observation."

"She doesn't have much choice. All of the people sitting in this room will attack her if she thinks she's leaving against doctor orders." I rolled my eyes.

"Will someone please bring me a glass of orange juice, a cup of coffee and a muffin top?"

"I'll do it." Jenna left the room in search of the items I requested.

"Besides wanting to go home, how are you feeling?" Arianna stood next to my bed and ran her fingers through the hair on my head that wasn't covered by bandages.

"Ari. I love you Thank you for being here."

"I love you. There is nowhere else I'd rather be. Hopefully there won't be a next time, but the next time you request to have your boyfriend cut you open like a dead fish, will you please give me the forewarning phone call?"

"Don't worry, there won't be a next time. Jenna, how's business?" She walked back in, just in time.

"All is well. When you're home, we need to discuss Hiro Matsumaura's truck proposal. It looks good from first glance. Nate Airless came by and had a meeting with me and Rita. His prints are fantastic! He just wants you to say ok and they are ready to begin building. The papers were drawn yesterday. You should be able to sign them tomorrow."

"That sounds good. I am on board with building at the inn. We should notify the staff that we will be closed during renovations but they will all receive a salary. Get the payroll info for me so I can figure out how to pay wait staff that survive on tips. We may also need to revise the pay plan for the start of the new inn. I'll worry about that later. I want to read Hiro's proposal now. Will you obtain it for me?"

Jackson rolled his eyes. Angela picked up on the look and interjected. "Sara, I think it is a good idea to let your brain rest today. Please. We don't want to have to go back in there. Once the swelling comes down, I will allow you to read any long drawn out document of your choosing. Right now, I want you to drink herbal tea, eat clean veggies and fruit, listen to classical music and relax for 2 days. Can you do that for me, please?" Angela smiled hard and looked around the room. Everyone was on edge awaiting my response. I rolled my eyes, but she was right. I just had brain surgery and my head was swollen. I didn't even want to know what I looked like right then.

"Ok. Fine. I will relax for 2 days, but i to at home. I will pay you and a nurse to be in my home. You will love it. I have a wrap-around porch and a wine cellar."

"Hahahaha!!! Ok Sara. You got it. We can't drink wine while on call though."

"Oh well. Sucks for you. I have amazing wine. So, may I go home tomorrow?" I looked at Angela and she looked at Jackson.

"Ok. I don't think that will be a problem. For now, you need to get some rest. I have to empty the room." Jackson shot a glare at everyone standing around the room. Ari and Dani stood simultaneously and gathered their belongings. They waked over to the bed and each kissed a cheek at the same time.

"I love you stink bomb! Get well soon."

"Bleh! Wench! I love you too." They all walked out and Jackson closed the door behind them. He flipped a switch on the wall and the lights dimmed.

"Sara. Are you feeling any pain?"

"Didn't you ask me this already?"

"Yes, and I haven't gotten an answer. Show me where it hurts."

Jackson knew me too well. I had a slight pain; a throbbing sensation. It felt as if my bandage was too tight. I raised my arm and showed Jackson where it hurt. He placed his hands on my head and slowly began to massage it. It felt good and the throbbing subsided. I felt my eyes closing and before I knew it I was asleep.

Jackson went into the waiting room where Ari, Dani, Cross, Javi and Jenna were sitting. He took a deep breath and slumped down in the chair next to Jenna. She caressed his leg slightly and looked deeply, into his sensual, blue eyes.

"Somethings not right, is it Jackson?" Jenna whispered

"She fell asleep, but she's got pain. When she wakes, I'll check her out again." They all sat quietly. Waiting. 15hrs later...

"I can't believe she's still asleep. I think we should wake her up." Ari was getting annoyed. It was island adventure all over again. "I did NOT sign up for this again."

"Ari, do you think the rest of us 'signed up' for this? Sara is our friend. We MUST be here for her. She would be here for us."

Javi was getting annoyed. He was learning the island adventure story for the first time and angry on all counts.

"Why didn't y'all call me when y'all boarded private jets to go save her the first time!?"

"That's my fault Javier, I didn't know how to reach you. We were moving so quickly, I had to grab them and go; all in one motion."

Whew! Cross saved everyone from Royal Meltdown of the year!

"Uh huh, you're frightening, so I'm gonna just eat that."

Javi rolled his eyes and sucked his teeth. Meanwhile, I was in super sleep again. It felt...well I couldn't decipher how it felt. Nothing was happening. No dreams, no thoughts. I was just in deep sleep. My friends were getting annoyed. There was nothing wrong with me; but how come I couldn't wake myself up? I moved my legs. I moved my fingers...

"Sara...Sara..." That was Angela's voice. Oh man, I hoped she continued to speak..."Sara. Wake up. You're moving. Go ahead and open your eyes. C'mon..."

Her voice was so tender. Ok. I can do it. "Sara open your eyes!" I had to say it to myself.

"Hey...welcome back. You slept a very long time dear. How do you feel?" Angela was standing next to me, caressing my hand.

"I feel..."

"She wants to go home." Jackson walked in the door and rejuvenated me. He gave me life.

"Jackson!" Like a child, I squealed with exuberant joy!

"Yes, please Jackson, may I go home and will you come with me?" I looked in his eyes and pouted. Again, like a child. He reached down and kissed me. As he grasped my hand, he held it up to his face and kissed it. "Ang... get a nurse and whatever you need. You're hanging out with us for a few days. That's the only way you're going home." I smiled and Jackson left the room. Ari was watching me sit up and try geting myself together.

"How many times do I have to ask you to stay alive?"

"I'm alive babe. I'm not going anywhere. I am going to rest and let this thing heal and then back to work!"

"Make sure you stay alive. I don't want to live without you, Ok?"

"Ok. I got it. I love you."

"I love you too."

I was quite content on the ride home. When we arrived to my driveway, Jackson parked the car and motioned for me not to move. He got out of the car and unlocked the front door. He came back to the car, opened the passenger door, scooped down and picked me up. He carried me inside the house, up the stairs, to my bedroom, and gently placed me on my bed.

"For a split second, I thought I was going to lose you. I don't ever want to lose you."

"I'm not going anywhere. I promise."

Jackson cuffed my face with his soft hands and pulled me in for a soft romantic kiss. I melted for this man, this marvel; that's what he was, a true gem. He stood before me and a barrage of emotions filled my soul; like water filling a glass. He kissed me and it felt like the first time we kissed. It was magical. Jackson pulled me away slowly.

"I think you should rest. I hate myself for even thinking that right now; nonetheless, saying it, but as your doctor, post-surgery, get in that bed and tell me what I can bring you." Jackson smiled at me. I couldn't help but smile back. I agreed, against my will, but he was right; I should rest...

"I would like to smoke."

Jackson shot me a glare, then walked over to the stash box in the bedroom. He handed it to me. He sat on the edge of the bed watching me. I smiled at him in random intervals; knowing he was watching.

"Megan is looking for Avery." He sighed.

"Is she the only one looking for Avery?" He gave me a look. It looked like confusion. "If she's the only person looking for Avery, we already know what the answer is. If there's a plethora of people looking for Avery..."

"When I addressed the staff at the Recycling company, they cheered. When I sat one on one with his assistant, she told me that she's not worried about where he is. 'He was a disgusting, pig!' And she rolled her eyes. I kept the same team of advisors running the company and raised their pay slightly. They send me detailed reports and all is well. They're all happy. Megan on the other hand..."

"Is his sister and has a difference of opinion."

"She knows something."

"She thinks she knows something. She will find something if you allow her to continue snooping around. What does she know already?"

"Ahh, let's see, she knows he boarded his jet to Jamaica and she knows his pilot did not return. She asked me what I know, if anything at all and I denied any and everything."

"I'm sure she read right through you. Listen, I don't know Megan very well. I know her from a business standpoint and I don't benefit much from her business. Therefore, if she's in YOUR way, then you know what you have to do."

"Hmm..."

"I'm not a murderer..." Jackson walked over to me and cuffed my face; like always. His eyes were heavy; as if he was going to cry. It broke my heart. He probably thought I was a terrible person. "But if my option is to get rid of one to keep you with me...Have you spoken to Cross about this?"

"Ha! Yes, and for all we know, Megan could be handled already. Cross has NO patience."

We both laughed. We laughed because we knew it was true. Just because Cross hadn't left my side since the surgery didn't mean his Sicilian worker bees weren't hard at work. The next few days were uneventful; which was pleasing and peaceful to me. Angela and I had become close and Jenna earned herself a raise. She sent the IT department to my home to hard wire my office. She turned my home office into a workable space. While my main concern was getting well, Jenna was busy making me a mogul.

"I ordered new furniture for your home office. Now that the installations are complete, I can finish my task at hand. Since the room is so big, I made it a convertible space. You have your boss side and your chill side. The sofa, love seat and end table will go here. This way if you need to have an informal meeting, you may do so. You can log into the database

of your businesses; even Ari's salon. Did you read the truck proposal?"
"I did and we need to go to Amsterdam. I want to tour the facility and meet the staff. Hiro said he will contact you and you can arrange my travel for some time next month."
"Absolutely."

Four Weeks Later...

Jackson was multi-tasking his career; being an amazing doctor and learning the ins and outs of the recycling company. Megan hadn't bothered Jackson in a while. He was thrilled; I wasn't moved. I took her silence as a sign of potential danger to us, but I let it play out. The Inn was coming along nicely. Nate Airless's team worked faster and harder than ever. Nate and I still hadn't seen each other. I made it clear that he was to deal with Jenna and Rita. I want to teach them how to make it without me; I wasn't going to live forever. It was also giving them a chance to get acquainted. Arianna's business was booming. She had every chair in the salon rented. She was open 6 days a week for business and late nights. Dani and Cross kicked it up a notch and I was planning Thanksgiving dinner at my house.

"Mom. I don't want you to cook a thing. I want you to come and be a guest in my home. Let me serve you."
"I always cook for thanksgiving. Now you tell me no! I don't like change."
"Yea I know you bat crazy lady! What would you like to cook?"
"Zee entire meal! I will make it here and bring it there."
"The...you can cook in my kitchen. I will stay out of your way."
"Tank you. So, tell me who will be there."
"You, dad, Hosni and family, Jackson, Jenna, Dani & Cross, Ari, and Javier."
"You didn't invite Rena?"
"No. Rena and I no longer socialize. She passes judgement and I just can't deal."
"Are you misconstruing observations with judgement? Have you looked at you through her eyes?" My mother made a point. I never really looked at the situation as Rena. Instead, I was instantly insulted because she basically called me a hoodlum.
"She's supposed to be my friend. Why does she deem it necessary to judge how/what I do?"

"Maybe what you are doing is wrong and that's the only way she knows how to tell you it's wrong. Perhaps you should reevaluate it." Without even knowing the situation, my mother was right. "Sara, I know that you have your hand in a lot of things. You know a ton of people and you have no problem making things happen. However, you need to be aware that things do backfire! You cannot embark on a journey without evaluating every possible outcome."

"Yes. I know. Everything has a reaction, a consequence, a repercussion. I'll sit and evaluate what happened; our exchange, and I may consider going back and apologizing."

"I think that is a wonderful idea. Rena loves you. I am sure that you over-reacted to whatever it was she was trying to show you."

What made that conversation bad was the fact that I couldn't tell my mother the real story. I had to be vague. What made that conversation worse was the fact that my mother was right. I sat and I listened to my mother's wisdom, I listened to her opinion on life and how people should address one another. I listened to her memories of me and my friends growing up. I listened to her tell me how good of a friend Rena was to me and our entire family.

"Don't forget, her daughter is your God child. Do you want to miss her grow up because your feelings are hurt?" Of course, I hung my head. She was right about the baby. It wasn't her fault. I didn't want to miss her life. "I am hanging up now. Call Rena and make some peace. I love you."

"Ok, I will. I love you too ma."

I said I was going to call Rena, but who was I kidding, I was not calling her. I had too much pride. I didn't want to admit that she was right. I thought space was well needed. My mind was fixated more on Megan and her snooping than on Rena and her judgement. Even though I did not know Megan personally, I had an idea how she felt. If Hosni disappeared, I wouldn't rest until I had an answer. Megan and Jackson knew each other. He grew up with Avery. I knew that she knew that Jackson was lying about knowing Avery was in Jamaica. I also knew that Jackson taking control of Avery's company with no fret, could've raised a suspicious eye. I laid in bed at night thinking about the year since I've met Jackson. My life was relatively peaceful, with the occasional flair ups, but for the most part it was uneventful. Life changed when we embarked on a journey that we didn't see coming. Then our lives changed drastically. Planning thanksgiving dinner gave me joy. I was finally planning an event that I held dear to my heart. In the past, my mother always cooked thanksgiving dinner and it was always hosted at my parents' home. Meanwhile, I was a home owner long enough to have hosted at least one thanksgiving dinner. In the past that wasn't happening. I was sure it was because I was never involved with a man of my own. It could've also been because I had no patience for Monica in my house. Today, all of that changed.

"Rise and shine! Your sister in law arrives today! Are you excited?!" Jackson deemed it necessary to wake me early. Hosni said they would be in around noon, but in Jackson's mind, if I wasn't awake from 7am, then I would be unbearably rude to my house guests. I pouted because he was right. He was always right. I got up and made my way to the infamous coffee pot. I went to the front door to gather mail and check the weather. I already knew it was cold out, I just wanted to know how cold it was. '22 degrees.' I shook my head. I love warm weather and for the life of me, I could not understand how I ended up living adulthood in the eastern region. Winters made me want to kill small children and summers made me want to bring them back to life- it was daunting. I hated winter.

"Babe. Can we move for the winter?"
"Yea. After Avery's Christmas party, we can go spend the rest of the winter in Santorini." I stood still and mouthed the words he just uttered.
"Wait. What?"
"What? What?"
"Avery's Christmas party?"
"Yea, Megan called me yesterday to say the party is still going to happen. She has gifts and an announcement and she wants us there."
"Both of us?"
Jackson laughed and shook his head. He then turned and walked out of the room. 'I guess we're going to the dead man's party.' I said to myself in a haphazardly tone. It just didn't seem right. Of course for the next few days, hours, weeks, I randomly daydreamed about what could possibly come from dead Avery's Christmas party. Suppose he wasn't dead? Imagine if Jackson didn't actually shoot him. I knew that was not the case, but it sure did feel good to dream it. We were still a few weeks away from the infamous dead mans Christmas party and business was booming. The year end crunch was at an all time high and my staff at Bradley was hard at work.
"I spoke to new accounts this afternoon and they were at 50 new ac-

counts for the month. BMW can't keep cars in stock; which is fantastic. The manufacturer sent a large payment to the store."

Jenna and I were sitting at the island in my kitchen drinking coffee.

"Sounds good to me. Sounds like I'm making money. I'll take all days in the black."

"Absolutely. How are you feeling physically?"

"Physically, I'm fine. I'm a bit tired but we have been burning the midnight oil. When is the grand opening for L'Inn?"

"Saturday. We should drive up Friday night."

"That's tomorrow."

"Yes. It is…"

"Aww man! Me and my last minute-ness. I'll throw some stuff in a bag tomorrow. Are you driving or am I?"

"Well, you have a FaceTime meeting with Hiro tomorrow morning at 10. I will be in route by then. I can set up car service to bring you up."

"Ok. I'm cool with that. I'm a tad nervous. I hope my Inn looks good; better than I remember."

"I'm sure you will love it. When I saw the finished draft, I was elated. If it popped up on my search for a hotel, I would immediately book a room."

Jenna's flattery was always appealing. She knew how to use her words. I looked at her and smiled. She smiled back, looked at me and walked out of the room. My phone began to ring.

"Hello…"

"You didn't RSVP." It was Megan.

"I'm sorry, what?!"

"You never RSVP'd to Avery's holiday party. Are you coming?"

I felt a little special. Megan sounded like she was too calm. I was hesitant to answer her question, but I was anxious to know what direction this conversation was headed.

"A lot has been going on. I'm not sure where the RSVP card is; and Avery usually calls to ask me if I'm coming to his parties."

"Funny how he hasn't made any phone calls lately, huh?"

"It's not funny to me." I lied through my teeth and shook my head. It was all in a days work; lies, cover-ups. It was all in MY days work.

"How come it's not funny to you?"

"I told you; business related or party related is the only way I speak to Avery."

"So you don't know that he's been missing since August?"

I gasped for the affect. "Oh no! What do you mean he's missing?"

"I was able to trace his steps to Jamaica. I have a team of people looking for him on the island. Apparently, he was spotted with a woman who's description doesn't sound familiar. Do you know who it might be?" I hated repeating myself with a passion.

"Megan.."

"I know. I know. You don't know Ave on a personal level. I got it. Anyway, in good faith, I am still hosting his holiday party. I will put you on the guest list. Will Jackson be joining you?"

"You're doing it wrong. Avery's invites were never a plus one invite. He always invited people individually with the hopes that his party will unite different people. Just make sure every individual person is coming."

I wanted to make sure I threw Megan off her game. If she thought I was innocent, then I was innocent. This phone call had the wheels spinning in my mind. I had to get one step ahead of Megan. If she had word that he was spotted with Tiffany, there was no telling what else she knew. I was going to handle this mission alone. I believed we were where we were because too many people got involved. That was definitely my fault. Oh well. You live and you learn and then you make shit happen.

Hosni and family arrived promptly at noon. I watched his wife's Cadillac Escalade pull into my driveway. Immediately, the doors flew open and children came pouring out of the backseat.

"Auntie!!" They bellowed as they ran up the walkway.

"Hey! Stop running!"

I could hear my brother yell from the driver side of the car. Monica got out of the car last. To my surprise, she was carrying a baby bump.

"Well I do believe congrats are in order."

"Yea. Your mom knew. You would too if you called…" Monica rolled her eyes. I turned and walked in the house.

"Please take off your shoes. Monica leave your nasty attitude on my front steps. We're not doing this this weekend, especially not in my house. Got it?" I'll teach that rude wench. Pregnant or not, she will not be disrespect-ful this weekend.

"Ladies. Please calm down. Hello my beautiful baby sister! You are amaz-ing!" Hosni scooped me into his arms and spun. I giggled. I forgot how much I loved him and missed him until that moment. Jackson came around the corner and waited for Hosni to place me back on the floor. Hosni turned around to look at Jackson.

"You must be Hosni. I've heard so much about you; Jackson Ellis."
Jackson extended his hand. Hosni embraced him.
"It's a pleasure to meet you man. Welcome to the family. This is my wife,
Monica." Monica waddled into the room and flashed a fake smile.
"Sara. The kids want to swim. Is your pool indoor?"
Did she really just snub my man?!? I wanted to slap her! I needed to find
some inner peace. She knew that I had an indoor pool; hence why she
packed the kids bathing suits.
"Uhm, yes. Yes they can swim. I'll be back. COME ON GUYS!!"
Hosni had beautiful children, despite what my mother thought. His oldest,
a girl, Abigail, she was 7. His youngest, a boy, The Second Hosni, or Tish,
as we call him; he was 4. I was going to ask Monica if she knew what she
was having, even though I knew the answer was going to be no or 'we're
not telling.' Ugh! Anyway, Abigail's hair was extremely curly hair and
Monica didn't know how to maintain it. I decided I would teach her. I
started combing my own hair around her age. The patter of their little
feet followed me down the hall and to the basement door. We walked
downstairs and they two-stepped to the bottom. It was cute. I flipped the
switches on the wall and the wall separated to reveal an indoor/outdoor
pool. In the summertime, the roof opened.
"Oooo!!! Auntie the wall is moving!"
"I know. It's cool, right?"
"UH-HUH!!" Abigail's eyes opened wide. She smiled equally large. It was
moments like these that made me wish I spent more time with them.
They were truly a blessing. Abigail tip toed over to the edge off the pool;
at the shallow end, of course. She squatted down and sat on the edge.
Her legs fell into the water. Tish was more daring. He leapt into the pool
and proceeded to swim. I was impressed.
"Tish, baby, who taught you how to swim?"
"We go to take classes. Mama makes me do gymnastics, dance, swim and
tennis. Tishy does swim, fencing, and tennis. I hate classes." Abigail
pouted. She was kicking her legs, so the splashing water made her giggle
a bit. She was so cute!
"Abby, hun, don't say you hate anything. Hate is a strong word."
"Mama said it's ok to hate because people suck." What kind of nonsense
was that to tell a 7yr old? Monica really was deranged. I didn't have a
chance to respond because Hosni, Monica, and Jackson joined us in the
pool room.

"Nice. I think I'll hop in too. Sara, the house looks fantastic! You look great! I read Business Insider, so I know how your businesses are doing. Jackson is wonderful. Life is good for you. I am proud of your blessings. I cannot wait to see all of your friends."

"Well you won't see Rena." Jackson interjected. I shot him a glare. I wished he hadn't said anything at all.

"I talked to Rena and in her defense, she just doesn't understand. She is oblivious and thinks the world is all roses and palm trees. I told her you would be right here when she's ready to let bygones be. "

"Thanks and thank you for the compliments. Your children are beautiful and I love them. I just wish Monica wasn't filling my nieces head with obscene thoughts about people and society. Please do not allow her to teach the children to hate. That's how violence in schools gets started."

I didn't mean to go off like a righteous tyrant, but something needed to be said. I watched the news stories on these kids killing kids and shooting the schools up and the journals always depict these dark thoughts on hatred and views of the world.

"You know what Sara, when you have children you will understand. The world is a scary place. They need to be aware."

"Aware yes, but you are breeding them to be the problem. All I'm saying is, don't be surprised if she shoots up her high school; at that rate, she might shoot up the dance school now!"

"Well. We'll make sure the reporters don't come and ask you questions. You're gonna make me look bad."

"You are bad. Your thoughts are bad."

"You're the murderer!"

'Drop the mic' was all that popped in my head. The record skipped and stopped. The room was silent. No one moved. No one spoke. All eyes were on me and Monica.

"I'm not, but there's one on my payroll. I can have you handled, all you have to do is continue disrespecting me in my house."

I was livid. I turned and walked out the room. I traveled through the halls of my home and made my way to my bedroom. I walked in and sat down next to my stash spot. Of course I was going to roll a blunt. I should've poured myself a drink. I knew for certain that Hosni was the reason why she made that comment. He knew I was pissed because before I knew it, he was knocking on my door.

"I don't know why she said that."

"She said it because you gave her the info. She found it in her memory and boom! What kills me is, I didn't think I had to tell my brother 'make sure you don't tell your wife.'"

"She's my wife!"

"She's not blood!" We were yelling at each other at this point. I heard the footsteps of Jackson and Monica coming down the hall. I moved closer to close the door. Jackson stepped in front of it. He and Monica walked in past me.

"Sara. You are who you are. I am just making it obvious for you because you seem to have forgotten who you are. You don't agree with what I chose to teach my children, but who taught you to kill?"

"Perhaps, I would like them to become better than me. That's what you should want for your children; to be better than you. At this rate, they will be beneath you and that's lower than Hades."

"Ok. Wait. You two need to relax. I cannot have this. This cannot happen tomorrow when mama and pop arrive. Monica, what we discuss in the privacy of our home needs to stay there. Otherwise I cannot trust you."

"Seriously Hos!?! And what about you?! You are my brother; my blood. You telling my business to anyone is unacceptable! Wife or not!"

"I don't think there is anything you can do to stop me from communicating with my husband. If you speak, then I will know. Point blank period."

"Uhm...may we have the room please?" Jackson was swift with his thinking. "Jenna came in before we came up the steps. She can get you all situated in bedrooms and with food if you are hungry. Right now, I need to speak to Sara." Hosni and Monica left the room and Jackson closed the door behind them. He walked over to me; I was standing in front of the large window in my room. He stood behind me and placed his arms around my waist.

"You cannot have her handled. Your brother would never speak to you again."

"I don't think I care much. Monica was never personable with our family. She speaks to my mother, but in a hostile tone. She never spoke to me much. When Hosni said I was going to be in the wedding party, she threatened to cancel the wedding and was arranging to elope. When I asked them about possibly moving closer; a few years back, she looked me dead in my face and said 'I don't want to live too close to your family.' Hosni bought a boat for the summer home in Newport. She made him sell it because 'we don't live like Sara. We need to have something to leave to our children.' She is judgmental of me and she is biased to my family and she is just spiteful and evil."

"You have to find a median where you both can tolerate each other."

"She doesn't care to. The first 5 years of their relationship was spent trying to figure out what her beef is with me. I just don't get it. If she gives my mother a hard time…"

Jackson kissed me hard. He stopped all thought from continuing to form in my mind. It felt so good to take my mind off the 'murder' conversation. This happened when people were told things. I used to move swiftly and no one knew what I did or what I was about to do. Hosni and Rena called me one night with a proposition; 'we need someone to turn up missing. There's something in it for you too.' Once I got the details, I handled business. No one asked any questions, no one made any statements. Two days later, they put an envelope in my mailbox. $5,000 cash. That is where it began. I was an on-call hit woman. I made sure business was handled. My one rule; if someone asked, you knew nothing. Got it?! I almost got caught once, shortly after that, I met Cross, it was a blessing in disguise. I told him my story and he told me his. We exchanged info of contacts and compared notes. It was hit man love at first sight. If someone placed a bet that Hosni told that to anyone, I would've just lost my bet. If I couldn't trust my Irish twin, who else was there to trust?

Chapter 17

"Good morning Sara." It was 7:30 Thanksgiving morning. I was standing in front of my coffee pot, awaiting 16 cups to brew. I despised having house guests; it was too early, so I was nice.

"Good morning."

"Do you hate me?"

"Never, I do not hate you. Am I angry with you? Yes, I am! I do not hate! Our mother taught us not to hate." I rolled my eyes.

"I didn't tell her the story like 'oh Sara killed a man.' Rena called me crying. She said having the conversation with you brought back a barrage of emotions. The man we asked you to handle back then, was a guy that hurt her. She never told me the details. Anyway, when I was finally able to calm Rena down and hang up the phone, Monica was standing behind me trying to fill in the blanks."

"So she doesn't have details?"

"No. She speculated an ending. It was by pure chance that she was correct. I tell my wife a lot of things, but the relationship that you and I have cannot be touched. It killed me to know that you questioned my loyalty to you. I know now that it was based on her pure dislike for you. I'm sure she did it on purpose. What I don't understand is why she hates you so much. When I ask, she says 'I just don't like her.' I'm sorry sis. It's hard on me that she doesn't get along with the most important people in my life, but I love her, She makes me happy. She's a good mother; despite the hate thing. My kids are beyond healthy. I just question why she's with me since there's so much she seems to hate" Hosni looked as if he was being plagued by this for a long time. I felt pain while we were speaking. Not my pain, his pain. I couldn't imagine loving someone and questioning their love for me.

"Hos. Ask her, talk to her. Tell her what this relationship is doing to you. If she cannot listen to your words and stand in your shoes...."

"Then what? He should kill me?" The wicked has risen and it was eavesdropping in my kitchen. I rolled my eyes and left the room

"I'll be back when my coffee is finished brewing."

You know I loved my brother if I left a room with fresh coffee. I should've made them walk out, but I promised Jackson that I would be on my best behavior this weekend. The doorbell rang as I was walking through the house. I shuffled to the door. It was all of my friends, and boy was I happy to see them!

"Happy Thanksgiving!!" They bellowed as I opened the door.
"Happy Turkey day!! Please, come in." I stepped aside and let them all in.
Javier was carrying a turkey. Ari and Dani had grocery bags.
"Javi fried a turkey last night. We brought food to make breakfast. No one gives much thought to Thanksgiving day breakfast."
Dani pushed her way into the kitchen. I smiled and followed. Immediately, Dani opened a bag and began emptying the contents onto the island. Hosni and Monica shuffled into the living room.
"Is Jackson here, boo?"
"Yea, he's asleep. It's early. I didn't want to wake him."
"If you are out of the bed, he's awake. Trust me. Go see."

Javi shot me a glare. He was annoying when he was adamant about something. How did I become the one doing as I'm told, in my own house? 'I despise house guests.' I muttered as I strolled through the living room and up the steps. I approached my bedroom door and opened with caution; to my wonderful surprise, Dr. Saved his girlfriend was still asleep nude, and I was instantly excited. Slowly, I pulled the sheets back and slid into the bed beside him. His body was so warm and in immaculate shape. He was laying on his back with one arm perched above his head and the other, sprawled across his chest. 'How does he sleep like that?' I wondered. It really didn't matter. I felt like giving him head so I slowly ran my mouth down his shaft while I salivated. He moaned out of his sleep and looked down at me...
"You're amazing...!" He muttered from under his breath.
"Do we have house guests?" I stopped the motion for a moment.
"Jackson, seriously?! I just want to give you head right now, don't worry about our houseguests." He nodded. I continued. We stayed in bed, engulfed in ourselves, totally not concerned with the array of people that were in my house.

Meanwhile, downstairs...

"Hosni. I do not like your sister. I do not like your mother, however, your mother is easier to deal with than your sister. She's a hypocrite. She's a spoiled brat!
"SHE'S MY SISTER! SHE'S MY MOTHER! Who do you think I would be if it weren't for them? How many men would marry the love of their life

despite the fact that SHE doesn't like his family? My sister and mother respond to how you treat them. You were rude from day one. You frowned in 45% of our wedding pictures. You wanted to move, I moved. You wanted kids, we had kids. I want peace, can you give me peace?"

"Oh, screw you, Hos! I didn't want the kids. We had them to make your mother like me. 'she'll feel better about you once she gets grandkids.' Remember, you said that! She still doesn't like me and she thinks the kids are ugly." Hosni realized yelling in defense of his sister and mother was getting him nowhere. He sat down and took a breath....

"Where do we go from here?"

"We suck it up and endure this blasted meal this evening. Then we pack our stuff, get in the car, back to Boston and have no dealings with these people until next year!" Hosni was torn. Torn between his first loves; his mother and sister, and the woman that he dedicated time, love, years and children to.

"Yea, that's not going to work for me anymore"

"What? Are you leaving me because I don't like your wretched sister and mother?!" In a fit of rage, tired of her disrespecting his family, Hosni rushed toward her. He raised his hand to hit her, but didn't. instead, he clinched his fist and yelled..

"You are a disgrace! Never in my life have I met anyone with such disrespect and such hate! What has anyone in this family done to you to make you hate in such way?" Monica's eyes fell and a single tear fell from her face.

"Do you think you can raise 3 children alone?"

"I'll move back here and have FAMILY SUPPORT! That's way more than what we got from your family when we moved to Boston."

Monica left the room. Hosni sat down and he felt a bit calm. Was this the beginning to the end? In the back of his mind, he knew it was something that he needed to say. He pondered. He wondered if Monica would really leave, or if she was going to simply lay down and wait for dinner. Dani heard the commotion from the living room where Hosni and Monica were talking.

"Ari. Will you watch this pot? I am going to check on Hosni. I think its safe to assume that Sara is doing nasty things to Jackson." They laughed. Dani walked into the living room and Hosni was sitting on the sofa, staring into space.

"The answer isn't going to appear on the walls, even though I know you think this is a magical mansion." Hosni giggled.

"I should've stayed with Ari when we were in college. She would've given me peace. I thought Monica was the one. We meshed so well in the beginning. She holds way too much anger and animosity towards my mother and sister and I just can't have it anymore. Also, she stands before me carrying our third child and she says 'I didn't want children.' I just don't know her anymore. This isn't new either. It took me way too long to get her to agree with this trip. She gets here and day 1, Abby repeated something about hate that Monica told her and Sara had a fit. From there, the war began. In all fairness, they were both right, but Monica super screwed it up because she was out of line with her words. She repeated something that she shouldn't have heard in the first place."

"Hmm, well I think you may still have a chance with Ari. She doesn't want to bear children, but is all for adoption, so you're good with the that!" Dani laughed from her gut. Hosni giggled, but didn't seem amused.

"In all seriousness, there must be a way to save what you have with Monica, but it cannot be done if you aren't on the same page. I can't imagine all these years were for nothing. In regards to Sara, we all know she's strong willed and we all know she says exactly what's on her mind, but I am certain that if there were a genuine apology, all bad words could be forgotten."

"Monica would never apologize. She doesn't think she said or did anything wrong. Let's see how dinner goes. She may answer the mystery question for me." Hosni smiled at Dani. She reached for his hand. He grabbed and shook it. She leaned in and kissed him on the cheek. "Thanks. I love you Dani-bell."

"Ah. You're welcome. I love you too HosDi." Childhood nicknames. As adults they just seemed ridiculous, but as children, they were so awesome. Hosni and Dani got up and joined everyone that was in the kitchen. Immediately, Dani began looking in pots.

"Hey woman! It's all good in here. I got it under control." Ari glared at Dani while she was clattering pot tops.

"Stop! Mira! You're gonna wake Sara and Jackson!"

"Oh honey. Has it been that long? They're not sleeping..."

"Oh. Then what are we doing?" Jackson joined the crew in the kitchen. Dani grabbed a cup and poured him a cup of coffee.

"Hi Jackson! Good morning. Where's Sara?"

"She's watching the news. I'll take a cup up to her."

"Is she alright?"

"She will be. I'm sure the last 24hrs with Monica haven't been the most joyous for her. I know they have been tough for me." Jackson took a sip from his cup. His eyes skimmed the kitchen in hopes of finding something he could grab and take upstairs.

"Is she hungry? Here. Take this to her." Ari handed Jackson a plate. There were 2 deviled eggs, a sliced avocado, and a steamed dumpling. Jackson gave a look of confusion to the combination of food on the plate.

"It's one of her favorite snack meals. Her mom made it every year for thanksgiving. She calls it the 'keep the kids busy' meal or something."

"Ok, whatever you say!" Jackson went back to the bedroom to join Sara. He sat beside her and placed the small tapas style plate in her lap. He handed her a cup of coffee and got comfortable beside her.

"Did Hosni make this?"

"Nope. Ari did. She called it the keep the kids busy meal or something."

"Hahaha!! She's awesome. My mother used to make small plates so that she didn't have starving children at the kids table. It was just enough food to make you sit down and shut up, but it wasn't enough to make you play in your plate later."

"Your mother sounds amazing. I can't imagine not liking her."

"Right?! And you haven't even met her yet." There was a knock at the bedroom door. It sounded like tiny hands....

"Who is it?!"

"It's me, Abby."

"I could only imagine what she wants. Come in sweetheart." Abby slowly opened the door and walked into my bedroom. Her eyes opened wide as the door fully opened.

"Hi Auntie! Hi Uncle Jax. Auntie, can I live here with you?" She smiled so brightly. I hated thinking no, nonetheless saying it. I was more concerned with why she was asking.

"Aw sweetheart. I would love to have you live here with me, but your mama and papa would miss you too much."

"They can come visit." She nicely wandered into my closet. I could hear her rummaging. It was becoming more clear to me that she adored her Auntie.

"Auntie. Why is your house so big if you don't have kids?"

"Because I need a lot of space for all my crap."

"I don't think you have crap. Our house is boring. You have a pool; we

don't have a pool. You have a lot of cars, we don't have a lot of cars.
Mama doesn't let me watch TV…ooooo what's this!?" Immediately, I
jumped up. There was no telling what this child found, and she wanted me
to let her live here! I walked in the closet to see that she found a Rubix
cube. Immediately she sat down and twisted all the colors around.
"I'm 'posed to make all the colors match, right Auntie?"
"Qui." She looked at me with beautiful light brown eyes. My heart melted.
I would keep her but Monica wouldn't let me.
"I'm going to check on the rest of my guests. Are you ok in here by
yourself , Abigail?"
"Yes." I stood there for a moment. I couldn't imagine becoming a parent
to a beautiful, innocent child and teaching her how to hate. I shook my
head. Monica had no idea how great of a blessing children were. I could
hear my house phone ringing; which was weird, so I shuffled into my home
office to answer.
"Hello."
"Where is your cell phone?! I have been calling you for days."
"Rena?"
"UH, yea! You kicked me out my life, now you don't recognize my voice?"
"You walked out the door on your own. Happy Thanksgiving. How are
you?"
"I'm good. I miss you. I have been trying to figure out a way, and I just…I
miss you. I'm sorry I was so mean and defiant."
"You've been defiant since the first day I met you, but I never passed
judgement. Do you have dinner plans? I think some of our conversation
should be held in person."
"I'm coming to your house. Your mother called and insisted I come. She
said you have a big head."
"Yea, she would say that." We laughed. I was shaking my head.
"I was calling to see if you need me to bring anything."
"I have no idea. I am providing the home to sup. My mom, Dani and Ari are
cooking and Javi fried a turkey."
"Did anyone bring you the keep busy plate yet?"
"HA! Yup! Just finished it. Can you bring pie? I want to eat pie!"
"I will make pie. I'll see you soon."
Rena coming to dinner made me feel a bit more at ease. I knew, for a fact
that Rena respected my mother, so if Monica tried her usual stuff, with
her tone, Rena would have my back if I had to shut it down. Unless this

was a sick intervention. I quickly laid that thought to rest. I hung up the phone and realized Rena was right. I hadn't seen my cell phone in a few days. I stood and shook my head. 'It will pop up', I muttered to myself as I glided down the hall. I could smell food and I heard an abundance of conversations throughout the house. Moments like these made me want to gather family more often, but then it was moments like Monica and her rude attitude that made me wanna slap myself and change the tape. I stepped softly into the guest room where I put my niece and nephew. Tish was still asleep. I stood for a moment; watching his tiny chest move from his beating heart. He, too, was truly a blessing. "they're cute kids." I said to myself as I was thinking about the conversation I had with my mom. Having my family here brought me joy, but I was anxiously awaiting for the moment they all exited.

"SARAAAAAA!!!! SARA VE'RE ARE YOU?!?!" My mother and her accent arrived. Quickly, I closed the door and shuffled closer to the steps.

"Shhh, Tish is still asleep. Hello Mama!"

"He's a boy! Stop calling him Tish!"

Happily, I hopped down the steps and into my mothers arms. Her embrace was like smooth silk pouring over my body. I felt a calming peace when she held me. She must've known I needed her because she held me for a few minutes. I felt like 7yr old Sara and not 34yr old, destructive Sara. Lately, I was careless. I was a danger to myself and others. I needed to go back to work, sit in my office and stay there until the building closed at night. When I did that, I stayed out of trouble. I didn't have a man, prob-lems with friends, or murder. I've always had problems with Monica, so that was normal and Avery would still be alive too. While in my mothers arms, I felt remorse. I felt like I put a dagger in my own heart and turned it. In the same regard, I was selfish. I would never admit to any of these faults; for fear of losing everything and everyone. I needed to redo my mask. I realized I was most concerned with me, in love with others sec-ond. Megan could never find out what happened in Jamaica. I felt bad thinking that, and sobbed quietly into my mothers chest. She rubbed my back and she sang...

"Ohhh Mary don't you weep...Oh Mary don't weep no more...Oh Mary don't you weep no more. Pharaoh's army got drowned, oh Mary don't you weep! Now old man Satan, he done got mad, missed that soul that he thought he had, Pharaoh's army was drowned...ohh Mary don't you weep."

She pulled me away and kissed me on my lips. I felt lifted. She was exactly what I needed, and at that moment, I found some peace.

"Ok. Ok. Who is cooking now? Your time is up. I have chutney and curry sauce to make. Your fah-zer is in bringing the food and the burners. He should be here soon. He went to serve at the soup kitchen with some of his Mason brothers."

Ari and Dani cleaned the messes they already created. I set up serving tables on the side porch, where it was covered and still inside. For extra warmth, Jackson turned on the fireplaces. It was feeling warm and fuzzy in my home and I was enjoying it. I sat with my mother while she shuffled around my kitchen. I caught her attempting to rearrange some of my cabinets, but I smacked her hand. I opened a bottle of Prosecco and orange juice and made Mimosa's. We sat, laughed and talked. She had a lot to say to Ari and Dani; we even brought Abby in the kitchen. All of the women were accounted for, with the exception of the wicked witch. She made a few passes by the door to the kitchen, but never came in. She never addressed my mother. It irritated me, but I said nothing. She was content with being in her negative emotions and I was content with being engulfed in the blessing of family. She had no idea how bad an idea it was to disrespectfully not address my mother. We all sat down at my dinning room table around 5pm. I sat at one end. Jackson sat to my right. Arianna, Dani, Cross, Javier; my mother at the other end. Then my father, Rena, Patrick, Jenna, Hosni and Monica. We set a kids table in the family room and allowed them to watch a movie while they ate. I looked around the room and smiled at the blessing of family. I blessed the table before we indulged.

"Please. May we all grab hands." I took a deep breath…"Heavenly Father, Thank you for this beautiful blessing of family and food. I am grateful to you for blessing me. I am thankful for this day. I am thankful for my life; for the life of others. I ask you to bless the many hands that prepared this beautiful meal for the nourishment of our bodies. I ask for peace. I ask all in your name, Amen."

"AMEN."

"Lets eat! Dad, will you carve the turkeys?"

"We have 2 turkeys, lamb, fish, duck, chicken, who all are you feeding? Za army?"

My dad had a rough, raspy voice. His words sounded like pain when he spoke. His accent faded; as if he really lost it, but, my thoughts were he mimicked it because my mother just sounded new to the country. It was mean, but it was true.

"Honey, just cut whatever you cut. We will eat it all anyway."

"Dad. We all know you will put everything on your plate. Eat it. Digest it, and do it again."

He laughed. His belly moved up and down like Jello. He stood, stretched his arms, then grabbed the machete style knife. He cut with grace and patience. My mother handed him a large serving plate and assisted with the loading of it. Meanwhile, the rest of us were busy passing the large plates of sides around the table. Macaroni and cheese, mango chutney, string beans, candied yams, tomato and mozzarella, cranberry sauce, stuffing, kale, peppers and onions, fresh salad, sushi, and calamari. It was feast fit for royalty.

"Sara. I am so happy that you decided to do this. We should make it an annual event."

"Yea, lets not do that." Monica muttered under her breath in between bites.

"You have been sour all day. Perhaps you need a nap." Oh boy. My mother's mouth showed up…"Monica. You think that I did not notice because I didn't say anything, but you didn't speak to me when I entered the home. You were raised differently, but in OUR family you speak when entering a room. You speak when you are younger and elders walk in the room. You speak first thing in the morning and you always say good night. When we were all gathered in the kitchen, you walked past the door 22 times and did not enter, did not speak. You must tell me now, why you are so rude?!" The room was quiet. I was certain that everyone stopped breathing.

"I don't fit in this family, and you know it. You never accepted me because I'm not Arabic."

"Do you love my son?"

"Yes."

"Then I do not care that you are not Arabic. Take care of my son. Take care of his home. STOP BEING DISRESPECTFUL TO ME AND MY DAUGHTER. Take care of his children and we are fine."

"I'll show you respect. I apologize for not having done so in the past. But Sara is another story." I rolled my eyes and sucked my teeth.

"What have I ever done to you, Monica?!"

"Sara…YOU ARE SPOILED…YOU'RE SELFISH. YOU are only concerned with you first, your tight crew, and then your businesses. You do not care who is affected by the decisions that you make, as long as YOU ARE FINE. People think that you are so helpful and so loving and so caring and they are blinded by the façade. Their minds are jaded; in a trance, put on by your methodical methods. This thanksgiving dinner is a mask. YOU, SARA KARINA, are a disgrace!" I was stuck. Monica belted out years of anger and disgust towards me. The first thing that popped into my head was her demise; after the baby came. Women died during childbirth all the time. I stopped my thought process because that was actually exactly what she is talking about.

"So, who was it?"

"My best friend."

"What year?"

"May, 2006."

"Would you believe me if I told you that none of it is personal?"

"You don't know these people?"

"I know the people that were hurt by the people."

"So none of it was personal?"

"Nope." I shrugged my shoulders. "Monica. If you want to hate me, that's fine, you can. Plenty of people do. But look around you, no one else at this table feels the way that you do. I am totally cool with that. 1 out of 12 ain't bad."

"So if you can't beat them, join them?"

"Yup."

There were a ton of things wrong with this exchange, but it was comforting knowing that she was holding a grudge all of these years. It was comforting to know that she had a legitimate reason to hate me instead of an unknown. No one questioned the exchange, as if they all knew the real words behind the hidden ones. Rena was bold enough to break the silence. Fitting...

"Monica. We all know that Sara does things that we don't always agree with, but the amount of good she does outweighs the bad she does ten fold. We don't dwell on the bad things that she does because we all know that it was for the greater good."

"Rena, you weren't speaking to her prior to today. How do you expect me to believe that?"

"I wouldn't be sitting here if I didn't believe that."

"All of you people are crazy, just like her!"

No one moved. No one responded. Instead, we continued our meal. In peace and quiet. It was funny because there was no tension. Just peace and quiet.

"Auntie! Auntieeeeee!!!"

"Yes Abby. What's up mamacita?"

"The movie is finished. Can we watch another one?"

"I don't mind. Did you finish eating your meal?"

"Yes. I licky all the chutney off my plate and fingers." I laughed. She was too cute.

"You licked your plate and fingers; that's cute. Let's go wash your hands and face. Come on." I got up from the table and walked my mango sticky niece down the hall to wash her hands and face. When we returned to the family room, the other children were sprawled nicely across the sofas. I assumed they sent Abby to get me, since she was the oldest child in the room.

"Julissa, Tish, are you guys finished eating?"

"Uh huh." I walked over to the table and sure enough there was not one morsel of food left on any of their plates.

"Do you want more food?"

"I wanna watch frozen!"

"Frozen?" I was confused and Rena walked in the room in a nick of time.

"Hahaha! You need to have a kid. Frozen is the Disney Pixar movie about the ice princesses. Do you have a blue ray player? I have it in my car."

"Ah Ha! I do have blue ray and if you have the movie, then we have a movie night! Guys sit here. We'll be right back!"

"Okay!!" Rena and I quickly shuffled out of the house to her minivan. She pushed a button on her keys to open the front doors to the van. We hopped in and closed the doors. She leaned over and pushed the button on the console. The blue ray player opened up and out popped the movie.

"I'm mad there's a blue ray player in your minivan. I think I'm more mad that you have to play movies while you drive a massive minivan. Is this really life as a mama these days?"

"Hahahahaha! Children still freak you out huh?"

"You know, not as much as they used to. However, I was a tad freaked when Abby asked me if she can live with me."

"Awww, that's just be a little girl's admiration for her auntie that she doesn't see a lot. I'm sorry that Monica is so sour towards you. Was that a 'handle' she was asking you about at the table?"

"Yup. The one I did for you and Hos that night."

"Oh well, I definitely don't feel bad. Having you to handle that situation for me, uplifted me. It gave me peace. It allowed me to move onto greater things. If it wasn't for that; for you doing that for me, I don't think I would have Patrick and Jules right now. I thank you for that. Seriously. I love you Sara. Thank you so much."

Rena hugged me and kissed me on my cheek.

"You called me in dire need. I didn't know you as well then, but you were Hosni's friend in need. No questions asked. I'd do it for you again and again if you needed me to." Rena and I didn't need to discuss the harsh moment we shared. We knew, in that moment of her defending me at the table, that all bad blood between us had been squashed. I didn't need to know why she was upset prior; she wasn't upset anymore. I didn't realize how much I missed her until she was back.

"Come. Let's go back inside. Any moment, Jules is going to begin that fit." We hopped out of the minivan and sprinted back to the house. The temperature was really dropping outside, but the temperature inside heating up, ALOT.

"I DON'T CARE WHO YOU THINK YOU ARE! YOU WILL NOT DISRESPECT ME OR MY DAUGHTER IN HER HOME! Hosni, you need to teach your wife manners and respect. Otherwise, she will be exiled and disowned by me." We were gone for ten minutes; literally. What happened?!

"You're going to exile me? You're ruthless just like Sara."

"Yes. Exile. You will go or you will be escorted out."

"You can't do that!"

"Oh yea? You think Sara is ruthless, yes? Where do you think she got it? It's in our genes. Your daughter will be zee same. Embrace it." Rena and I set up movie night for the kids. There was no need for them to witness to the screaming horror that was taking place in my living room.

"Hosni! Let's go! NOW!"

"I'm with my family and this is where I'm staying. My kids are staying also. You can leave if you don't want to be here. You are the only miserable person in the room. You are bringing the night down. The kids are comfortable. I am comfortable, please. Just go."

Monica's eyes filled with tears but none of them fell. My mother used to call those crocodile tears. You're not really crying, but you are upset, so you make faces for attention. Hosni turned his glass up to his face and finished the brown water. He slammed the double shot down on the table and rose from his seat.

"Enough of this nonsense! Sara, turn on some music"

I did and we partied for the duration of the evening. I don't remember going to bed, but I woke up next to Jackson, so I was content. I rolled over and kissed his chest. Again, he was asleep on his back with his arm in the air. He shuffled around but didn't open his eyes. I kissed him again. He smiled and it was gorgeous! I was like a schoolgirl all over again. Finally, he opened one blue eye.

"Wow! Your family can partyyyyy!! We were up till like 4:30 smoking hookah and drinking liquor. Amazing. I had a ball. Your dad told me stories from his childhood. Did he really have a pet Lion?"

"Oh my gawd! I cant believe he told you about his lion. Yes. His Lion died when I was like, I don't know 13, maybe. Anyway, we had to go to Egypt for the funeral. I was like 'dude, really?' When we arrived, we were treated like royals. We raised not one finger for 3 days. Women bathed me. It was insane. I would go back now for that same treatment."

"It's so cool listening to your life. I fall more in love with you everyday. I even like the secret boss lady in you. It's sexy!"

"It's sinister."

"Don't make it a habit. Leave the danger to Cross. He's better fit for it. I want to make you a stay home mommy." I couldn't believe he said that. However, I hadn't been feeling the same scary way I was feeling about children in the past.

"Uh huh. Right. After. We. Get. Married." I leaned in and kissed Jackson on his lips in between each word. I rolled over and out of the bed and head toward the bathroom.

"Wait. What time is it?" I bellowed from behind the partially closed bathroom door.

"Uh..11:47. Why?"

"Wow, we slept late. How likely is it that the house is empty??" Wishful thinking.

"I'll go check.." Jackson got up and walked slowly out of the bedroom and down he hall. He approached the first guest bedroom door. He opened the door and saw Jenna asleep. He closed it and moved onto the next room. He opened it. Abigail and Tish. He proceeded down the halls and down the steps. He found everyone in attendance at dinner with the exception of Cross and Monica; he watched mom and dad leave around 5am. Jackson panicked. He fumbled around in the drawer at the kitchen island. He remembered tossing his and Sara's cell phones in there a couple of days ago. He opened his phone and scrolled to Cross's name in his contact list.

"Jackson, brother."

"What's up brother? Where are you?"

"Uhhh, I'm around. Watching some live action. You know?" That was Cross for he can't talk right now. Jackson picked up on it and hung up. He grabbed Sara's cell and went back to the bedroom.

"Here babe. You should check your messages." I stood still and skimmed through all of the bubbles of missed emails, text messages, voicemail messages, and missed calls. Most of it was business. Some of it was happy thanksgiving texts and memes and then the missed calls from Rena. There was one voicemail message from an unknown number.

"Hey Sara. My name is John Thompson and I would like to ask you some questions regarding Avery McBride. Will you call me back after the holiday? My number is 212-345-2201 ext.550. Thanks. Bye."

I opened google on my phone and entered the telephone number. It belonged to an investigation firm. I debated returning his call then, but I opted to wait and see if anything else was going to happen. My thoughts thought too soon and my cell phone practically rang out of my hand. It was John Thompson.

"Sara speaking."

"Oh hey Sara. Its John Thompson. You got a moment?"

"Sure John. How may I assist?"

"Uh yea. Megan McBride-Haynes hired me to find her brother. I was able to back track him to Jamaica. Turns out, you were there at the same time he was. Did you see him on that trip?"

"No sir, I did not."

"Do you mind me ask why you were in Jamaica?" I giggled.

"I was in Hedonism."

"Oh. That's uh, that's nice. Did you know a lady by the name of Tiffany Rodham?"

"No. I can't say that I do."

"Well apparently she was on vacation with him except no one knows who she is or where she came from and now she's gone. How well do you know Avery?"

"Not well at all. Just business related."

"Hmmm, ok. So I wonder why Megan thinks you know more than you claim."

"I don't know. You have to ask her."

"Will do. Thanks for your help." John Thompson hung up the phone. My blood boiled. I took a few deep breaths to relax. I didn't want to tell Jackson who was on the other line. He, too, was on the phone now, but he was in my office.

"Jax. Are you still at Sara's?" He was talking to Cross again.

"Yea. You coming back?"

"Yup. See you in a few." Jackson made his way to the coffee pot and brewed a full pot; 16 cups. Abby came down to join him.

"Hi Uncle Jax. Good morning…do you speak Arabic?"

"Hi Abby angel, good morning. I am not fluent like you, but your Auntie is doing her best to teach me. I speak German."

"German!? That's cool. I have a German friend and he speaks to his mom in German and it always sounds like he's anger and yelly." Jackson laughed from the incorrect grammar.

"You mean angry and yelling. It's a rough language, that's for sure."

"Do I have to go home today?" A bit confused, Jackson hesitated prior to answering sweet Abby.

"Don't you want to go home today?"

"No. I like it here."

"Aww we like having you here, but I think at home with your mama, papa, brother and soon to be sibling is the best place for a young girl like you."

"I know. They need me, huh?" They both laughed. Jackson a tad harder than Abby. The coffee was done brewing and Jackson grabbed a cup.

"Are you old enough to drink coffee?"

"Uhh…no! Juice please." Abby smiled at Jackson and melted his heart. He dreamed of the day that this exchange would be happening with his own daughter. Sara walked into the kitchen…

"Good morning, Auntie. Jackson asked if I'm old enough for coffee."

"Good morning; your Arabic is beautiful, Abbigai. Good job. Abbigai was an acceptable, Hebrew version of my sweet nieces name. She will answer to just about anything I call her. I gave Jackson a glare.

"She's 7 babe. No coffee." I smiled and kissed him on his lips. "Good morning. Are you guys getting acquainted in here?"

"I want to live here and I got even less of an answer from Uncle than what I got from you, auntie." Oh little miss "I think who I am" was giving me attitude. She even crossed her arms. I needed to get to the bottom of this wanting to live in auntie's house.

"Angel, is there something going on at home that makes you not want to be there?"

"It's more fun here. Can daddy stay too?"

"You, daddy and Tish can come visit me anytime you want. I'll give you a key and the number to my car driver. You can call him and ask him to come get you anytime you need to get away. Is that fair?"

"It will work for now, but when the baby comes, I'm moving in. Being big sister is hard." Abby's sweet brown eyes fell slightly and she hung her head.

"Aww baby. Being the oldest is a lot of fun. I'm older than all of my brothers and sister. When we were kids, I got to be in control. My parents depended on me to help them out and my brothers and sister depended on me to be their friend, to keep them company, to teach them what I already knew. Being the oldest is hard, but it's rewarding. You will always be needed."

Jackson was amazing. I was younger than Hosni, so I really couldn't relate to how Abby was feeling. I imagined that Monica put a lot of responsibility on Abby; it was fitting for her demeanor. I would've really loved it if Abby were mine, but she will always be my niece and I will have my own baby girl one day.

"Yea. I guess, but I still wanna live here."

"What if we moved close by?" Hosni joined the conversation and Abby's eyes lit up.

"Really daddy, can we?!"

"Yea. I don't see why not. Sara, do you have a realtor that I can bother today?"

"Absolutely! Yay! Hosni's coming back!"

Abby and I jumped up and danced around the kitchen. We were so happy with Hosni's sporadic decision.

"Abby, hun, will you take your juice to the living room? I need to discuss somethings with auntie and uncle."

"Ok daddy." She grabbed her cup and ran out the room. Jackson closed the kitchen door. I poured a cup of coffee for Hosni and we all sat down at the island.

"Monica called me last night ranting about the words that were said to her over dinner. Mom is pretty sneaky, someone followed Monica back to Boston last night. She said when she got to the house, someone walked up to her and told her she had 22 minutes to get all of her belongings out of the house. She was allowed an opportunity to call me, but she has officially been exiled from the Bashir family. When she and I got off the phone, I called mom. Mom said she didn't do it. I watched you drink yourself to sleep last night. Who banned her?"

"I have no clue. It wasn't me. I'm sure it was mom, she just didn't want to tell you. Mom is like that. She has a ton of Thawb wearing relatives that we don't even know, walking around waiting for orders."

"Strange. Well, my wife has been exiled. Apparently, someone is going to bring the new baby to me. We come from a very particular, over bearing, over protective, family of dangerous women. None of the men do this. What's up with that?"

"Don't you remember when we were kids hearing the stories of the women in the family? They all have this protective energy. It comes from the eye of Ra; at least I think it does. Anyway, they take care of the home, the children, and the 'light work.' The men provide the roof, the food, the money; that's it. You heard mom, it's genetic." Hosni accepted the explanation that I provided. It was enough for him to not bring it up again, but I could tell that it bothered him.

"OK, so back to me needing a house…"

"Yes. I'll call Jane Lunden. She helped me find this house. Granted, I was looking for almost a year but I'm sure she can help you with something quick."

"That would be great. It will kill Abby if I tell her we're going back to Boston. She hates Boston." I rolled my eyes. She was not old enough to hate anything.

"She doesn't like Boston. She's not old enough to hate anything." Cross walked into the house and joined us in the kitchen.

"Sara. Why wasn't the front door locked?"

"Hey Cross. I'm not sure. This is as far as I've made it since I came down the steps. Would you like coffee?" I grabbed a cup from the cabinet and poured a cup for my macho, scary friend.

"Thank you for dinner last night. The food was so good. Is there any chutney left? Your family is amazing. I had no idea that you come from a family of dangerous Arabs!" We all laughed, especially Hosni.

"You're welcome Cross. You are welcome here anytime. You're officially not a guest, so feel free to check the fridge for chutney." Cross made his happy way to the fridge. He flung the door open, stood with his hands on his hips and browsed the selections. He finally made a decision and grabbed a container; to his surprise, it was chutney.

"What do you suggest I eat this with for breakfast?" I laughed. My macho Italian friend was eating traditional Indian food and loving it.

"You can eat chutney with whatever you wish. What were you planning on eating?"

"Uh...chutney!"

"HA! Ok then eat the chutney."

"Cool. Now let me tell you why I'm here. By mistake I found a man that is looking for you. I got rid of him. I have someone watching whoever was hired to watch Monica. I think the person is Arabic. They were hooded. I assumed it was per request of your mother; I have my guys watching from a serious distance."

"Cross, you always make me not feel so bad about the money I pay you. I need to work today. Can you's stay out of trouble for a few hours?!" I pointed my finger at the guys standing around me. I trusted them, but I had to make it clear; no trouble.

"What makes you think we will get in trouble?"

"Javi isn't awake yet. There's no telling what kind of mood he is in when he gets up!" They all laughed. I laughed too, meanwhile, they just didn't know. I grabbed my cup and left the kitchen. I went upstairs to check on Jenna. She was awake but not out of the bed.

"Hey boss lady. We need to go to Bradley today."

"Alright. I'm going in the shower. Meet you downstairs in 40?"

"Sweet!"

Chapter 18

Jenna and I arrived to Bradley shortly after 1pm. We walked in immaculately dressed. I was wearing a tight fitted grey sweater dress with over the knee black boots. Jenna was dressed very similarly, but her dress was pleated and swayed when she strut down the hall. We opened the doors to the building and there was a new receptionist.

"Good morning ladies, my name is Lily. Welcome to Bradley and Associates. How may I direct you?" She was pleasant, but she didn't know who I was. Who kept hiring receptionists without me knowing? How come they never knew who I was?

"Lily, is it? I'm Sara, this is mine, the company, all of it. I sign your paychecks. This is Jenna. Jenna is going to explain to me why we keep getting new receptionists and how come they never know who I am."

"Sara works from home most of them time, but when she's here, she's royalty. She'll give you instructions for her phone calls, and you must be quick; she needs you to think on your feet. Got it? Please, don't forget."

I rolled my eyes and walked through the glass doors. I walked swiftly down the hall to my office. For some reason, the new receptionist thing really bothered me. I needed familiar faces. Change freaked me out!

"Sara, I'm sorry. I'm not sure why they forget who you are."

"We should hang my picture up on the wall so there's no mistakes. We have work to do, you said? Let's do it." We walked into the conference room and joined a meeting that was already in progress. Someone passed the notes around to what we missed already. There seemed to be yet another issue with Brian Bradley.

"Wait...according to these notes, Brian Bradley is filing for ownership again?"

"Yes ma'am."

Apparently I didn't do enough to Brian, now he was back for more. I sat quietly and listened to the rest of the meeting. I had an excellent staff and they were going above and beyond with the legal team. They made it clear that as long as I have the original contract that Brian drew and we signed, then he didn't have much to stand on. I shook my head. Karma was really getting me for being a mob boss who shouldn't be a mob boss. I was sure that the women that came before me in the Bashir family didn't go through so much thinking when they handled situations. Why the hell did I feel so much remorse? The meeting went on longer than I planned, or wanted it to. The lawyers decided to handle it on their own and they will notify when they needed me. I wasn't happy with that but it was all I could do. I walked back to my office, sat down in my chair, took a deep breath and decided to text Jackson.

Me: hey Dr. Sexy face. Wyd?
Jax: hey babe. I am sitting in your home office; doing some charts.
Me: oh nice.
Jax: what's up gorgeous?
Me: Brian is trying to take the company back.
Jax: Hmm...
Jax: I wonder what that's about?
Me: I don't know, but I was instructed by my legal team, to stay out of it.
Jax: You can...Cross and I don't have to.
Jax: What time are you coming home?
Me: within the hour. Why? What's up?
Jax: I want to take you on a date.
Me: Yay! Date night!
I was so happy to read that. I was long over due for a date night with my man.
Me: Ok. I need to finish up so I can come home. See you soon. :-)
Jax: Ok babe. See ya soon. :-*

I placed my phone in my bag and waved Jenna into my office; she was standing at the door.
"Hiro called. Can we board a flight to Amsterdam tomorrow evening?'
"Pack your bags. We're going to Amsterdam. What's going on? Is it bad?"
"He didn't say. But he didn't sound worried. When I asked him how things were, he said 'all is well.' So I guess we shall find out together."
"Hmm, I guess so. Tell me, Jen, what do you think of Brian trying to take this all back?"
"I think he's a jerk. I was tempted to meet him outside, but I think allowing the legal team to handle it is a good idea. I looked into his finances and he's been gambling; like crazy! Anne won't let him spend any of her money and she's trying to get him into an addiction program. It's not looking good for him. When the lawyers come across that little bit of info, your boy Brian is going to be in for it. I learned a lot about you over the last few months. Do not move on this. You have to focus on Megan. Avery's party is next weekend. Make sure you're ready for that."

I sat back in my chair and took in Jenna's advice. All of it was smart thinking. That was a good play, on her part, looking into Brian's finances. When did she find the time to do that? Jenna was truly worth having by my side. I must have trusted her, she dined with my family. I was tired, It was getting late in the day, so I sent Jenna home and I made my way to the parking garage. When I got home, Hosni and kids were gone and my house was clean and quiet. I smiled. It was refreshing. I closed and locked the door behind me. I took off my shoes and tiptoed across the cold, hardwood floor. I made my way up the steps and down the hall to my bedroom. Jackson was in the shower. I quickly disrobed and opened the door to the bathroom. I opened the door to the shower and climbed in behind my massive, statured man. His chiseled back was saturated, I stood behind him and placed my hands across his broad shoulders. I kissed the center of his back and he moaned. I continued to rub his back, shoulders, and arms. He turned around to face me. He kissed me gently on my lips. Every time he touched me, it felt like the first time. The passion sent a sensation through my body that was unlike any other. He held my arms and slowly pushed me under the streaming water. I closed my eyes and exhaled. He grabbed my breast and began to suck. I moaned out loud and he sucked harder. My legs trembled. My vagina was saturated. He ran his hand down my body, down one leg and up the center of my legs. He slowly pushed a finger inside of me and I moaned out loud again. I grabbed his shaft and began to move my hand up and down slowly. He scooped me up and pushed my back on the wall. He slid inside of me and penetrated in a swift motion. He felt so good in me, I cried. I cried tears of joy.

"May I put a baby in you?" Ugh. What a way to kill the moment. I just was not ready to add a child to the mix. I didn't want to be a baby mama. Jackson had been on this child thing since Tiffany told him the children weren't his. I didn't want to carry the void filling child. It killed me to say no..
"I, I'm just not ready babe. I can't." The motion stopped. He slowly put me down. He ejaculated into the tub and washed himself clean. He turned around and kissed me. He opened the shower door and got out.
"Hurry babe. We have reservations in 45 mins." He walked out and closed the door behind him. I was sad. He seemed upset although, I was not sure why he was upset. Why could I not be ready yet? What was wrong with that? Why wouldn't he ask me to marry him first? Why would he just jump to children? Was it because of Abby wanting to live here with us? I

washed my body and my hair and got out of the shower. I dried and moisturized my skin. I walked into my large closet and stood there staring. Jackson walked in.

"You should wear a black dress. We're going fancy tonight."

"Are you mad at me?"

"I'm a little let down, but I'm not mad. I understand that you're not ready. I want to be a gentleman and marry you first. I was out of line for asking and especially in the moment; I apologize babe."

"No need to apologize. I love you."

"I love you too."

Jackson left me to get dressed. I wore a long, black, suede dress with long sleeves. It sat off of my shoulders and was tightly fitted all the way to the bottom. I wore black lace stockings and a pair of red Louboutin shoes. I grabbed a small red clutch and filled it with a handful of essentials. I walked into the coat closet and grabbed an equally long, black fur coat. I walked out of the closet, down the hall to the top of the steps. Jackson was standing at the bottom and as I appeared his eyes brightened.

"Amazing. You are absolutely amazing!" I walked slowly down the steps and he extended his hand to me. He pulled me in closely and embraced me. His strong arms felt so good around my body. I inhaled his sweet smell. It was intoxicating. He pulled me away slowly and we walked arm and arm out of the house. We hopped into his Porsche Cayenne and he drove us into the night. We pulled into a driveway and rode all the way to the top of a mountain. "Chateau D'Ellis" was written in fancy white lights across the top of the building. It was massive with large, white pillars and large front steps. It was very similar in style to an old southern plantation home. It was magical. Two men walked over to the car; one on Jackson's side and one on mine. They opened the doors and escorted us out of the vehicle. Jackson walked to my side of the car and grasped my hand. He walked me inside. A young, short girl greeted us when we came in.

"Hi Uncle Jax! Hi Sara. Welcome Welcome." Jackson laughed and kissed the shorty on the cheek.

"Sara, this is my cousin Pamela. Pamela, Sara. This is my parents place. Well they own it. It's managed and run by various other family members."

I was amazed. The vaulted ceilings were so beautiful. They were designed like the night sky; Orion's belt and various other stars. We were escorted to a private dinning room. There was a medium sized, round table in the center of the room. The light was dim and there was an orchestra playing in the far back corner. We sat down and we were greeted by a server. "Good evening. My name is Thomas and I will be your server this evening. May I start you with a drink?" I sat and pondered. What am I going to drink tonight?

"I'll have Merlot tonight."

"We'll have a bottle."

"Absolutely." The waiter walked away. I sat and looked around the room. The walls were pure white and there were live vines scaling the walls. The floors were beautiful cherry wood. They reminded me of home. Jackson looked at me with admiration. I couldn't understand how he could look at me the same way after discovering all of my flaws. I was blessed to have such a wonderful, trustworthy, non judgmental man in my life.

"What are we celebrating Dr. Surprise?"

"We are celebrating life and life together. We are celebrating your beauty; how wonderful you are. We are celebrating happiness."Jackson reached for my hand. He held it up and kissed it. I melted. "Sara. I love you. Do you know that?"

"I do. I love you too." The waiter arrived with our bottle of Merlot and 2 glasses. He opened the bottle and poured us each a glass.

"Oh. I forgot to ask, do you want to go to Amsterdam tomorrow. Hiro requested Jenna and I come for an in-person meeting."

"Tomorrow? Sure. Why not?"

"Cool. We're only going to be gone for the day."

"Whatever. I don't mind. As long as I'm with you. I don't mind."

I smiled. The remainder of the evening was magical. We laughed and talked about a ton of things. It was our first date all over again. We ate a meal of fresh baked duck with steamed carrots and hearts of palm. It was served with wild rice and mint jelly. It was amazing. A combination of foods that I would never put together, but great, nonetheless. I excused myself to the restroom at the end of the evening. I was tipsy. I definitely drank the entire bottle of wine. I think Jackson had one glass. When I returned, Jackson was standing; awaiting my return. He assisted me into my chair and proceeded to kneel in front of me.

"I don't want to live life without you. Will you marry me?"

Jackson opened a red velvet box and revealed the largest diamond ring I'd ever seen. It was perched on a solid diamond, platinum band. He carefully slid the ring on my finger. It fit perfectly. I was amazed; astonished. I

couldn't believe it.
"OH MY GOD YES! YES I WILL!!!"

I was loud and I didn't care. I jumped up and leapt into his arms. I was so excited. The waiter brought over a bottle of champagne and chocolate cake. We drank and ate cake. We danced. We laughed. We smiled. We took pictures. I was looking forward to finally becoming Mrs. Dr. Jackson Ellis. Sara Bashir-Ellis. I like that. We were out until well after 1am. I fell asleep in the car on the ride home.

I don't remember getting home, but I woke up the next morning nude in my bed. Jackson was nowhere nearby. I rolled over and extended my arm. I gazed at my engagement ring and smiled. I reached for my cell phone; it was on the nightstand next to me. I grabbed my phone and opened my camera. I snapped a picture of my well manicured, recently jeweled hand and sent it as a group message to Javier, Dani, Ari, Jenna, Hosni, and Rena. No subject or comment, just a picture. I laughed, placed my phone on the nightstand and got up. I smiled all the way to the bathroom. I could hear the phone vibrating off the nightstand. I was basking in the new glory; all in the midst of preparing for a quick trip to Amsterdam. After 20 minutes, I finally read the barrage of messages.

Jenna: OMG!!! Clearly you said yes! Congrats!
Ari: YESSSSSSSS!!!!
Dani: I'm literally in tears. I am so happy for you!!!
Javi: please don't be a bridezilla. I will slap you!
Javi: Congrats boo!!
Rena: oh I cannot wait to draw this portrait. YAY!!
Hosni: Congrats baby girl. I am proud of you. Jackson is good people.
Hosni: I'm staying at mom and dads with the kids. I'm looking at a few houses over the next few days.
Jenna: I'm omw to your house. I need to brief you before we board the plane. Is Jackson coming?
Me to Jenna: ok. Ok. Yes.
Me to Hosni: Good. I hope this is a decision that you are happy with.
Hosni: It means more to me that Abby is happy. She loves being down here. She asked if we can come over tonight.
Me: Aww. I love her. I'm going to Amsterdam for the night; business. I'll come by when I return.
Hosni: Ok. Be safe. I'll let her know.

Jenna arrived within 30 minutes of our conversation. She came upstairs and found me getting dressed in the closet.

"Apparently the truck company is doing really well and needs to expand. We are traveling to view the new facility and listen to the proposal for the new locations; worldwide. Hiro would like to be in 10 cities by June, so he sent the slides to the presentation that we are going to sit through. He suggests we browse it in advance."

"That sounds fantastic! I love that Hiro is handling the major points of this business and is filling me as time goes on."

"I must admit. All of your business are doing well. All the people that you are in business with are on top of things." Jenna fist pumped me. I continued packing and getting dressed. We were finally leaving the house to go to the airport. We arrived to the tarmac and boarded a private jet. Hiro sends nice planes. Immediately, I searched for the bar.

"Score! Vodka and cranberry." I poured myself a cocktail and had a seat in a plush, leather seat. Jackson sat on one side of me and Jenna behind me. "You ok babe?"

"I am now."

We traveled. It felt as if we traveled more than anything. It was an 8 hour flight to Amsterdam. Hiro had a limo pick us up from the airport and bring us to his office. Jackson toured the city. Jenna and I sat in meetings all day. We accomplished quite a bit. The truck company was going to open offices in London, Paris, Austria and Copenhagen by the end of the following June. The Amsterdam location was already shipping over 100,000 packages daily. Hiro recently moved to Amsterdam. His wife died in Japan. He said 'she's with God. She's no longer suffering, therefore I am at peace.'

It was bittersweet; listening to him tell us about her health journey. He also decided against taking the truck business to Japan because his wife asked him to leave their homeland. He did as per her request. We finished our meeting and Hiro took us to dinner. We sat outside on the edge of a cliff; at least that's what it seemed like. The air was crisp and clean. Hiro knew I was a weed smoker so he chose a restaurant that has an extensive smoke menu. I was able to package some to take home since we were flying privately. A very long 24hrs later we returned home. I was pleased with what we accomplished with Hiro. He informed me that he will do the bulk of the traveling. He will send for me as needed, but I have access to the private jets whenever I needed them. I received 47% of the profit. I had to put a call into my accountant's office on Monday.

I needed to know my new net worth.

"We accomplished a lot today. Did you enjoy touring Amsterdam?"
"I did. How's business? Is all well?"
"All is extremely well. Despite the rocky thanksgiving conversations, I am content." I looked at my hand and smiled. "And now I'm engaged."
"Would you like to set a date?"
"Uh, during nice weather. June maybe, July."
"Big wedding or justice of the peace?"
"I have to stand before God."
"Understood. Big wedding or small?"
"Intimate. Friends, family…"
"Home or away?"
"Home. It's easier. We can go away for the honeymoon. Are we still going to Santorini for the rest of the winter?"
"If that's what you want to do, absolutely."
I truly loved this man. He amazed me. There was never a question asked when I wanted something. The remainder of the evening was uneventful. I was a tad jet lagged, so sleep was imperative. Jackson held me while we slept. His arms held me like barricades. I had no nightmares when I laid beside him. In the past, events would visit or haunt me while I slept. Since we've been home from Jamaica, I successfully accomplished getting full nights of wonderful sleep. We were awaken the next morning to the sound of both cell phones ringing. I let mine ring, Jackson answered his.
"Hmm.."
"Jax. It's Hosni. Is Sara asleep?"
"She is. What's up? Is everything ok?"
"I'm at our parents house. Mom and dad took my kids to 6 flags for the weekend. I stepped out for take out, I come back and there's a baby on the doorstep. He's beautiful. He looks like me, but the crazy thing is that Monica wasn't due yet."
"Relax. I'm going to wake Sara and we'll come there. Do not call anyone else." Jackson rolled over and kissed me. I moved slightly, but not enough for him. He shook me lightly.
"Sara. Sara, wake up. We need to go to your parents house now. Hosni called frantic."
All I heard was 'parents, Hosni and now.' I jumped up and stumbled into the bathroom. Quickly, I washed my face and tossed back some mouth-wash. I was already wearing panties; that was good enough for me and

I jumped into a pair of grey, fleece, sweatpants. I ran back through the bedroom and grabbed a t-shirt that was on the bed. It was Jackson's. I didn't care. Jackson was already downstairs when I came running. He opened the front door as I flew through it. I felt like I was running on bolts of electricity. Jackson drove. I never asked any questions, so I didn't know what to expect. Jackson pulled into the driveway and it seemed very peaceful, quiet, serene. I flung the passenger door open and ran down the driveway, sprinted up the steps and burst through the front door. I saw Hosni sitting in the living room holding the most precious baby I'd ever seen. As I walked toward him, he extended his arms and handed the baby to me.

"I stepped out for take out. When I got back he was on the front steps. There was a note. 'Congrats! It's a boy.' He came with a birth certificate. He was born 4 nights ago. He seems healthy. But Monica wasn't due for another 3 weeks. Sara, is she dead?!" Hosni's eyes filled with tears. All I thought was 'he better not cry.' I wouldn't be able to compose myself if he cried. I couldn't answer the question because I honestly didn't know the answer. This time I didn't do it.

"I didn't want her dead, Sara!"

"I didn't kill her, Hosni!" Hosni always resulted to yelling and yelling wasn't getting us anywhere. I took a deep breath and attempted to relax. I was nervous. I realized I had no idea where our parents were. "Hos...where's mom and dad?"

"They took my kids to 6 flags. Say they will be back this evening."

"So, I doubt mom had her killed. Maybe she legitimately gave birth and died. Is there a hospital name on the birth certificate?"

Hosni just stared at me. He was absolutely useless when he wasn't focused. I just shook my head and grabbed the certificate off the table. 'Greenwich Hospital.' Great. This should be easy. I opened my cell phone and dialed the main number to the local hospital. After a few moments of going through the prompts, I was finally connected to a human.

"Thank you for calling maternity and delivery. How may I assist?"

"Hi. I'm looking for my pregnant sister. She went missing thanksgiving eve and she's 9months and beyond pregnant. I am just checking hospitals for her because I'm worried."

LIE LIKE A RUG, SARA!

"Sure ma'am. What is your sisters name?"

" Monica Levy-Bashir."

"Please hold."The pleasant female placed me on the longest hold ever in the history of holds. She finally returned. "Ma'am, I'm sorry but no one here by that name."

"Any unclaimed or missing baby boys born within the last 4 days?"

"Please hold." Again...FOREVER ON HOLD! I was becoming more and more impatient. "Ma'am. No baby boys unaccounted for; none left behind"

"Ok. Thank you for your assistance."

"You're welcome. Good luck finding your sister."

I hung up and joined Hosni on the sofa. He was still stuck; in a daze. I sat beside him and held the pretty baby. We all fell asleep.

"SARA! HOSNI! SARA?!?!" Mom was home in her loud glory. I didn't realize I was still there. I was still on the sofa and the baby was still asleep in my arms. My mother came in the living room with the kids. I opened one eye and made a face. The children remained quiet.

"Abby, Hosi, please go upstairs." The children pouted and walked out of the living room.

"Mom. Here, this is your grandson; not my child, obviously, but the one that I will assume was pried from his mother's womb because her where-abouts are unknown. Do you know anything about this?"

"Honestly, I may have something to do with her leaving in the night. BUT, I did not know anything of this."

"I believe her."

Oh Hosni, thanks for joining the conversation. We spent the rest of the weekend with my mom and all the kids. Jackson enjoyed himself; mean-while I was exhausted. I would rather be at home reading documents or watching the news. How bad was I? My mother was basking in the joy of having her kids, grandkids and no Monica.

"Sara. You know I missed my boy! I am glad that she is gone. My Hos-ni-poo is home."

"You do know he's 36 and you cannot call him that anymore."

"I birthed him. You will understand one day. Having unnamed baby here does not make you want babies?"

"It makes me want eternal sleep. Children are a lot to deal with and they have too many too close in age for me."

"After the first one comes, you will change your mind. I wanted more ba-bies, but your fazer say 'we have one of each. Now we just repeat? No.' I guess he was right. Once you and Jack Jack marry and have one, you may change your mind."

"Mama. Please, let's refrain from calling him Jack Jack, ok?"

My mother was cooking a meal in a crock pot. The smell was divine. It felt good to be home. I would come back to stay here if I were pregnant. Jackson would just have to understand. There was something about my mother that was so calming. Being in her presence made bad thoughts and dealings disappear. Hosni walked into the kitchen where we were sitting.

"Sara. I just realized that I have no job down here. I need to report somewhere on Monday morning. Can you help me find something?" I stood for a moment thinking. I grabbed my cell and called Jenna.

"You told me I was off till Monday" I laughed. I had been wearing Jenna out.

"I know babes. I just need a fraction of your brain power."

"You turn me on when you tell me I'm smart."

"You're invigorating!"

"Please, continue." My mother was staring at me trying to figure out who I was in exchange with.

"I need a lawyer position for Hos. Do we have space on a legal team somewhere?"

"Yes, actually. I glanced at an email I wasn't planning on answering until mid day Monday; something about needing a legal advisor to sit in luxury car showrooms at all times for all financial transactions. Apparently something happened somewhere and BMW and Mercedes are making changes. I'm not reading it in full detail until Monday, but if that's what I think it is, we will probably need Hosni starting Tuesday. He would have to be in Henderson Hill daily, or at least a few days a week. That can give him something to do until I find a more suitable, stable legal spot for him. Or we could assist in the startup of his own firm. This way it's full circle; you would get a percentage off him for the upkeep of his surroundings. Kind of like what we do for Arianna." Was it possible that she gave me too much info? I just laughed to myself.

"Ha! You gave me a lot. Listen, I am surrounded by kids and would not mind a reason to disappear to a room in this grand castle. Will you forward that email to me? And that firm idea, let's address that first thing Monday morning. I will be in the office at 8:45. Enjoy the rest of your weekend." I made a kissy sound and hung up the phone and as soon as I sat my phone down on the counter, it vibrated from the emails that she sent over.

"Are you really going to do work now?"

"Yes ma'am I am. I will send Jackson in the kitchen to entertain you. I'll be back."

I kissed mama on her cheek and left the room. I walked all the way down the dark, mahogany wood hallway to the library at the back of the house. I turned the large, cold, golden door handle and walked into my favorite room in mom and dad's house. The wall to wall book shelves were filled with the greatest novels of all time. Every collection of encyclopedia, dictionary, bible, any literally work you could ever imagine; was housed in those shelves. There was no carpet on the floors. Instead the hardwood shined ever so brightly. The letter 'B' was engraved in the center. There was no desk in this room. Instead there were two large, plush captains chairs with matching ottomans and they were separated by a rectangular shaped glass table. In all honesty, this room could use a makeover, but if I suggest it, before I know it, my mother will have me spending 100's of thousands of dollars remodeling their entire home. I just wasn't going to do it. I opened my iPad and read the email that Jenna sent. Apparently, there had been complaints about finance directors taking advantage of customers and illegal, improper paperwork had been sent to the banks. The result was thousands of contracts had been bounced or simply not funded. The banks were practically begging the dealer principals to take each situation into their own hands and fix them internally. For the dealers like mine, that hadn't been hit with the illegal activities, we are asked to place law individuals on staff anyway. "Be ready, even if you are never subbed in.' Who's quote was that I wondered as I read. It was tacky, but I got it. I got what they were telling me to do. I made my plan. I'll hire Hosni as my legal, finance director of the Henderson Hill BMW and Mini stores. He could oversee all the legal stuff and I will consult on the financial stuff. This would allow him to get his feet wet and stay busy until I was able to complete his firm. He specialized in corporate law, so I thought about getting him started in my office building. I vaguely remember Jenna saying we had some of the doctors offices not paying any rent. I asked her to check on that again. As I read the rest of my email, I saw there was one from Rita. She was hosting a New Year's eve bash at my Inn. I gave Rita all responsibilities to that location. I simply collected the money and stayed for free when I was in town. She was the official overseer of that business and she loved it. I knew because there were no issues and I hadn't heard from her. I loved the relationship we had. I made money, she didn't bother me. I'll take it. I would love to go to L'Inn for NYE and NYE fireworks. I knew Jackson would love it too. I sat for one uninterrupted hour reading email and making arrangements. Hosni found me.

"Didn't realize how big this house was until I went looking for you just now. It took me 20 minutes."
"Awesome! Mission accomplished." I grinned.
"I know what you mean. This place was big when we were kids, but for some reason it seems significantly bigger now."
"Your mother started talking about you possibly remodeling it for her. I think she's gonna ask." Hosni grinned.
"She should spend your money on this."
"I have to buy a house." He stuck his tongue out at me.
"I have a house you can rent. It's in the Henderson Hill section where you will be working for a little while starting on Tuesday."
"What?! For real?! I asked you about a job an hour ago. You found one already?"
"How do you feel about working for my dealership as a legal, financial advisor? I'll need a few months to get a firm started for you; that's our big project. The intent is that you can hold it down in the dealerships for a little while and begin hiring your own handpicked advisors. You can still run that, if you want, because all of my companies can be accessed anywhere in the world, and then you can begin your corporate law firm as soon as I secure a place to place your firm. What do you think?"
"I think you are the smartest person I've ever met. You are so thoughtful. You should've been the older sib." Hosni hugged and kissed me on my cheek. He reached into his pocket and pulled out a letter.
"This came in the mail for me today. I haven't read it yet. I was looking for you. Will you read it?" He extended his hand and sat down next to me. I opened it and began to read.

"My dearest Hosni,

I'm sorry that I allowed my grudge to separate me from your family. I heard stories of the Bashir family and their strong love; that's how come

I sought you out. I needed to feel that love, and you gave me that love. What I didn't realize was that I had to share that love with the ENTIRE family, otherwise, they are not happy. My ill feelings toward Sara go back before I even knew you. I don't know if she did it herself or if she had it done, but she assassinated my best friend; someone that I knew from birth. Someone that I loved before I loved myself. She, Sara, showed no remorse. All she knew was what's done was done. What I didn't know was that you were the one that asked her to do it. Again, it was before we were established, but I cannot spend the rest of my life in a family that took away the most important person in my life. My water broke the Monday after Thanksgiving. I gave birth to this baby boy all alone. I gave specific instructions on what to do with him. Hopefully you have him. Tell my babies that I loved them before they knew what love was. Tell them that they are with better people. Sara was right, I want my children to be better than me, than her. I pray they will be. In fact, I know that they will be if they remain with you. Please do not look for me. In fact, let's assume that if you are reading this, I am gone. Tell the children that I am dead; when you are ready. This way they don't spend their teen years driving you crazy trying to find me. Thank you for loving me and showing me that love is real. Thank the Bashir women for showing me that all cannot be forgiven. Remember, you are a brilliant man. Do not let your sorrow for losing me hinder you from greatness. The stars are aligned for you; for the kids. Make sure Abby knows that hate is a very bad thing and her mama was ignorant for telling her otherwise. I love them. I love you. 'Ay me! For aught that I ever could read, could ever hear by tale or history, the course of true love never did run smooth.'"

'Hamlet.' I said to myself as I folded the letter and handed back to Hosni. We spoke no words. We sat together and let the words of the assumed dead woman linger in our minds.

Chapter 19

It was the week before Avery's holiday party and I was not concerned about a party in the slightest. I managed to get Hosni settled into the dealership and his new role. He took to it naturally. I thought about leaving him there as my financial director. We spoke briefly about him hiring and managing all of the finance personnel of both dealerships; naming him finance director. With that decision being made, I held off on starting a firm for him. He seemed to enjoy the change of atmosphere. He also enjoyed the loot. He opted to buy a home in between my and our parents home because Abby enjoyed being around us so much. The kids go to school nearby and my mother took care of the baby during the day. We also hired an Egyptian nanny that only speaks Arabic, so the kids will learn the language. Life around the Bashir households was coming together nicely. Jackson and I were slowly pushing the wedding subject along, but not in full detail. We assumed the wedding had already happened with our behavior. We address each other as Dr. Mr. & Mrs.

"Mrs. Ellis have you decided what you're wearing to Avery's party?"
"A bulletproof vest and a 22 strapped to my thigh." Jackson didn't find humor in my joke. It was unfortunate because I was hysterical. "I'm sorry. I haven't decided. It's a holiday party, so I may wear red and gold. Why do you ask?"
"You haven't discussed it and normally you are excited about an Ave bash."
"Ave is dead now, so it's not the same." I pouted. Jackson walked toward me and kissed me on my forehead.
"I have to go. I promised Hosni I would come over and help him set up the entertainment center in his living room."
"Boys will be boys. Ok. Have fun. I'm going to do something, I just don't know what yet."
Jackson laughed and left the house. I sat still and thought about the exchange we had. He was right. I had no idea what I was wearing nor am I excited about the party. I decided to see what Dani and Ari are doing.

Me: Hiiiiiiiii!!! I wanna shop! What are you's doing?
Dani: nothing. I just got out of the shower I'm not sure where Ari is. Are you picking me up?
Me: I can. How long do you need?

Dani: Idk...15 mins maybe.
Me: Ok. I'll see you soon.

It was cold out; bitter cold. I put on a pair of fleece lined leggings and a long sleeved t-shirt. I also put on an oversized, wool cardigan and a pair of tall leather over the knee boots. I went to the closet and grabbed a long North Face bubble. I was going from home to car and then car to mall but was dressed for a hike across the mid Atlantic. I went to the garage and stood at the door. 'What am I going to drive today?' I thought to myself. I have that kind of luck that I will jump into a rear wheel drive coupe thinking there is no chance of snow and then be blind-sided coming out of the mall to storm of the century. I played it safe and hopped into my BMW 5 series with x drive. I headed to Dani's. We shopped for a few hours and had a ton of very interesting conversations. Dani enlightened me to where she thought Ari may be.

"Don't get upset. She wants to tell you when she knows what it is."
"Huh?" I was standing at a jewelry counter in Sacks and Dani attempted to have a conversation with me but failed to setup the conversation.
"Ari has been spending time with Hosni. She doesn't want to tell you, because she claims it's nothing; she's just helping with the baby."
"I don't care that she's spending time with him but he's sensitive, so they both need to be careful. The reason; to help with the baby, is a bold face lie. I hired a nanny. She lives there. All I know is I don't want to hear it if things don't go the way she wants it to."
"I hear you, sister. I told her the same thing. Of course I didn't know about the nanny."
"She does. Why is she lying? Well, it doesn't matter. I don't have enough space in my memory to add this."

We spent about 4 hours in the mall. It was refreshing. I found a red gown for the party and I bought a white fur coat. I wasn't kidding about the bulletproof vest and 22 on my thigh. I had a seamstress that created an armor to place inside of my dress. It wouldn't be too big; she's made them for me in the past, but I never kept them. They reminded me of who I fought so hard to hide. Jackson wasn't home when I got there, so I took advantage of the solitude. I carried my bags upstairs to the closet and hung the gown. I took my clothes off and made my way back downstairs. I rummaged through the fridge and found just enough leftovers to make the best thanksgiving sandwich. I walked into the cellar and pulled a bottle of Sauvignon blanc. I carried my sandwich and bottle to my bedroom and got comfortable. I opened my laptop and began reading the news. There was press coverage to the Avery Anderson holiday party.

"What the...?!" I couldn't believe it. What was Megan doing? The party was still days away and I was anxious beyond belief. Why did she feel the need to have this event covered on the news? I called her and to find out.

"Sara! I was just talking about you; how if it wasn't for you and your financial assistance, Avery wouldn't have all of this to share with the world. Thank you Sara."
"You're welcome?" I was confused by the exchange and was hesitant with the response. "Why is the event being covered on the news?"
"Why not? Avery always wanted his events to be shared."
"Events yes. Hence why there are cancer benefits and carnivals hosted by him annually. His PARTIES are always private."
"You seem offended by my decision."
"You seem selfish with your decision. You are making a spectacle of what should be private for family and close friends. Do what you want. I'll see you on Saturday."
I hung up the phone. I was upset. She pissed me off. No worries. I ate my sandwich and drank my wine. An entire bottle later and I was knocked out. I didn't know when, but Jackson came in and cleaned the space around me. I woke when he sat on the bed.
"Hi babe. I'm sorry. I was trying not to wake you."
"There is no such thing as not waking me. I sleep light."
"Ha. Yes I know. In advance, I apologize for the lack of sleep when we have kids. I sleep like a rock."
"It's cool." I rolled my eyes at the 9,000th mention of children.
"Megan has press coverage at the party."
"Man, that's gonna make it harder to kill her."

Wow! I was surprised to hear him say that. He had a plan also, I see. I hadn't made mention of any of my thoughts. They're sacred. Mine only. Talking is a sign of weakness. It was sloppy. 'Don't talk about it, be about it.' Point blank period. I didn't say anything else about Megan and the party. I was calm after eating and drinking and I was ready to sleep for the night. I took off all of my clothes and climbed into the bed. I dreamed of life after the party. Jackson and I in Santorini wearing very limited cloth-ing, walking along the beach. I had to run away for the winter; there was too much happening here. I thought it was fair to give things a moment to calm down and just when everyone was getting back to normal life, I would come back. I did it every so often; disappear. The last time was about 7 years ago. I went to Bora Bora. I lived in a high class tiki hut and I dined with natives nightly. It was relaxing, reserved peace. I was allowed to be myself. I took my mask off and sat among those who were less fortunate than me. This time, the hiatus was different. This time Jackson would be there. He didn't realize that was what I was setting us up for, but I was. I was still Jackson's financial advisor and I monitored his earn-ings. He and I had enough available liquid funds to disappear and never return. It crossed my mind, but I thought to play the timeframe by ear. I didn't remember falling asleep, but I did. I woke up alive and refreshed. Jackson was already gone when I rose. He left a note on the mirror in the bathroom.

"Dinner at Baang. 7pm"

Ok. I guess we're going to Baang tonight. It had been a while since we were there. I had no plans on doing anything today; not even working from home. I made my way to the infamous coffee pot and brewed a Sara sized pot. I heard something slam against my front door. After I caught my breath from it scaring me to death, I walked over and opened the front door. It was a newspaper.
"Hmm.."
I've never had a paper delivered to my house. I watched the news and I read online magazines. I bent down and picked up the paper. It was for-eign. There was only one page and one article. It was tied around a brick, hence the startling noise.
"Man goes missing...found with mistress?" I was so confused. I went back inside and closed the door. I poured a cup of coffee and sat down on my living room sofa. I opened the freaky, one page, horror mystery paper and proceeded to read.

August 24, a man arrived via private jet to a small airport on the island of Jamaica. He was greeted by an unidentified woman and they climbed into the back of a large, black SUV. The man remained assumed unharmed, in a remote location. 'Jane Doe' proceeded to move swiftly between hotel resorts. Jane Doe returned to the same remote location after 3 days with a second, unidentified man. Sources say the 3 were stalking a guest at a resort close by. The first man to arrive by private jet never returned to his jet. The unidentified woman disappeared as well. 4 days later, a third unidentified man arrived to the small airport and loaded the private jet onto a larger private jet. He climbed on board and that jet flew away as well. The original, private jet was registered to Avery Anderson McBride and witnesses say he made mention of taking a quick, weekend trip to catch up with old friends. It's been 4 months since Avery Anderson McBride has gone missing and this weekend, you find out where he went."

'I'm over Megan'; was all that came to my mind when I read the self printed news article. She was trying to shake me and it wasn't going to happen. I must have egged her on. When I saw the news coverage, I shouldn't have called her. Instead, I should've acted as if I didn't know. When I called her and expressed my attitude, I dropped the ball. This time, I didn't call Megan on it. Instead, I tossed the newspaper in my recycling bin and made my way to the stash spot. I managed to get an entire morning of uninterrupted peace. It was awesome! Jenna showed up sometime after 1pm to make sure I was still alive.
"Baas lady! Wah g'wan?! Why weren't you in the office this mawnin'?!"
I was taken aback by Jenna's very bad accent. She would've been better off trying to mimic my mother. I laughed.
"Uhm, because my name is on the building and you gave me a world class home office and I didn't want to be a grown up today." I pouted and hung my head. Jenna rolled her eyes and brushed by me. She walked into the kitchen and opened the fridge.
"Grocery shopping is on your list of things to do tomorrow. Shall I add cooking?"
"You're such an excellent planner."
"You need it since you don't want to be a 'grown up' today; whatever that really means. Anyway, let me tell you why I'm here." Jenna pointed and led me to the living room. We laid across from each other on the sofas. She didn't find food, but she found coffee and a muffin top.
"Megan called the office looking for you today. I picked up the call and I asked how I may assist. She asked me if you left the country yet. What is she talking about?"
I sat for a moment and let Jenna's words sink into my brain. Megan knew more about me than I thought. I wondered where she was getting her

info. Could it be she was a super mob boss also? Could explain why she always seemed to have so much free time. This was getting serious. Jenna didn't wait for an answer.

"So anyway, I told her you have no plans on leaving the country. She asked me how was I so sure. I told her she's asking a lot of questions and not giving up any info. Mind you, the entire time we're speaking, I'm running her identification, she thinks she's the only one that knows how to spy. She started asking about your trip to Jamaica. She wanted to know if I knew what happened there. I told her I didn't because I wanted to know what she would say next. She says 'I think Sara or Jackson, or both of them killed my brother but I can't prove it. I need your help.' She's trying to get me to sell you out; do you want me to kill her?"

"OH GOODNESS NO! I want you to stay out of it. Keep playing dumb if she calls you again. She is trying to ruffle my feathers. I fell into her trap once this week; I'm not doing it again. The party is tomorrow night. Let's just see what happens."

Would you look at that? I had a team of hired assassins that I didn't even hire, they signed up willingly. I couldn't allow this satanic behavior to rub off on my Jenna or my Jackson. When I was ready to leave, I had to leave Jenna here. She had to run my businesses. I would keep her in the loop though. I didn't want her to falter. After spending the entire day in pajamas, I got ready to meet Jackson for dinner. After an intense, hot shower, I climbed out and decided to air dry my body while I blow dried my hair. I made my way to the bedroom sized closet and pulled out a pair of dark denim jeans. I paired them with an ivory cashmere sweater that fell off one shoulder. I pulled out a pair of brown ankle booties and there completed my winter casual date night outfit. I was dressed slightly before 6:30. I grabbed a small, brown Louis duffle and tossed some belongings in it. I grabbed a brown leather coat from the closet and made my way to the garage. I drove the EOS just to complete the nostalgic moment. I pulled into the parking lot and to my surprise, Baang was officially out of business.

I rolled my eyes as I dug through my bag and pulled out my cell. I scrolled and touched Jackson's name. It didn't ring. It went straight to voicemail.

"Well, I guess I'll sit here and wait for him to show up." Jackson pulled in shortly.

"What the!?? It's out of business?!"

"I called you. It went straight to voicemail."

"Piece of crap; it didn't even ring. I did ride through a dead zone. Look at you driving the EOS. I remember when I first saw you driving an EOS, I thought I was going to have to introduce you to luxury cars. You quickly informed me that that was incorrect thinking." I smiled at the memory and the bit of information that he shared.

"My thoughts were 'I'm never going to see him again. He's married.' I too, am glad that I was incorrect with my thinking."

"My second thought was 'I'm never letting go of this amazing woman.' Anyway, I could tell you all of my positive thoughts about you all night long. Instead, come, I know where we can go." We left my car in the empty lot. I hopped in on the passenger side of Jackson's car. We arrived at a place called Collar's. It was very plain at first glance. We walked up the front steps, through the large front door and into a large open space. There was a podium and at the podium was a young girl; 22 maybe.

"Welcome to Collar's. Entertainment for 2?" Strange, I thought to myself. Why did she say 'entertainment' and not dinner?

"Yes please."

"Follow me please." The young girl walked us down a black, spiral staircase. When we got to the bottom, the room was very dark, black. There was a large stage and various round tables surrounding the stage. Each table was small; 8x10 maybe, and they were dressed with black tablecloths. Each table also had a red tea light candle. My eyes skimmed the room and I put two and two together.

"Doctor. Are we at a Burlesque show!?"

"We are. The food is to die for; top shelf liquor and the girls, you would appreciate the girls."

"MmmMmm!"

I didn't mind gazing at a sexy, good looking female, I just wouldn't touch one. An older, attractive woman was our waitress. She had light green eyes and heart shaped lips. She wore her hair in a very neat bun. It was tight too. I was certain she had a headache. If she did, she played it off well. Although, she had a tendency to stumble. She was tall as hell. I made sure that I did not stand close by while she was in my presence. She emasculated me! She was soft spoken and I wasn't sure how it was going to work once the music began. She handed us a drink menu and pointed to the specials. Jackson and I ordered Bourbon; it fit the atmosphere. We ordered steaks and family style sides. We ate like royalty in this place. The food really was to die for. The show began with the handout of cigars.

"I wish this was weed."

Jackson rolled his eyes while I rolled with laughter. The show was entertaining. I probably wouldn't come back; it just wasn't my cup of tea. It felt good to be out with Jackson. We were so caught up with everything else, that we weren't giving each other the necessary attention.

"Let's go on dates weekly. I don't want us to slip away from each other." For a moment, I was worried about the health of our relationship.

"Babe are you worried that we will fall out of love?"

"I am worried that we are going to get to involved with keeping each other alive, that we will forget to live."

"I will never forget to live as long as I am living with you." Jackson held me close while we walked back to the car. He opened the passenger side door and I slid into the car. He hopped in on the opposite side.

"I think we should run away after the party." Jackson was looking directly into my eyes. It was as if he was taking the thoughts from my brain and speaking them with his voice. How many girls really meet their better half and have the pleasure of spending the rest of their lives with him? I couldn't be happier with my soulmate. Hosni called my cell as we were traveling home.

"Hello Hosni, how may I assist?"

"Sara, I think I know what I'm going to name the baby."

"It's been 2 weeks, I'm pissed he still had no name. What's the reason for the wait?"

"Monica and I never spoke about names, so I didn't know where to begin, but I've got it!" There was a pause. I think it was because I was supposed to respond.

"Well, what's handsome baby's name?"

"Hasani Khalil Bashir."

"I like it. It fits with the other names. How is little Bashir?"

"He's beautiful; fantastic. It's weird though, the older kids haven't asked for or about Monica. Should I be worried?"

"I'm not sure, Hos. That's something you should ask mom about."

"Yea."

"How's Ari? Tell her to return calls. If she doesn't want to call, she can text. But she doesn't restart dating my brother and then avoid me." Hosni got quiet. I could hear him fumbling.

"Is she there? Did you put me on speaker?" Neither of them said anything. "I don't care that you are rekindling, just be careful. You both are sensitive and Hos, you are more sensitive than Ari. Take care of the children, but don't be pertinent in their lives if you don't plan on staying with Hosni. I have my own relationship to pay attention to. I will talk to you black bastards later. I love you." There was no need for me to wait for a response. I said what I needed to say and I hung up the phone. I was slightly upset because Ari felt the need to keep that a secret from me. However, I was not surprised. She didn't tell me when they were dating the first time. Instead, I walked in on them kissing. It was awkward. Jackson and I were finally home and I couldn't wait to take my clothes off. I was unbuttoning and unzipping as I was walking around the house.

"You never answered me when I said lets run away."

"I was planning on us doing so after the party. I had no intention on leaving Santorini anytime soon." Jackson smiled. Just then, the decision was made. Jackson and I were leaving on Sunday morning; after the party, and it was going to be a while before we came back. It felt good knowing that the upcoming hiatus will not be endured alone. Bora Bora was beautiful; the experience was life changing, but I hated doing it alone. As I stood in my closet, completely nude, I was debating on just packing and leaving, but I was dying to see what was in store for us at the infamous Avery Anderson party. I needed to also fill Jenna in. I called her.

"Hellerrrr!!" Lately, Jenna was testing the waters with her accents.

"Jenna."

"Ma'am?"

"Remind me to shake you when I see you again; shaking my head at today's accent. What's on your agenda for tomorrow?"

"It's Friday so I plan on setting up the next work week, working and going home to get drunk. Then Saturday is the party, so I guess I'll see you Sunday?"

"I'll need you here while I'm getting ready for the party. I am going to be shouting instructions to you."

"Ok. No problem. Are you coming in the office tomorrow?"

"No. I have no intention of doing so. If you need me to, I will."

"Nope. Enjoy your day off." I hung up the phone and turned around to see that Jackson was already in bed.

"Sucker. You didn't wait for me?"

He laughed. I climbed in beside him and snuggled under his arm.

"How did you know that I wanted to run after the party?"

"I didn't. But the idea popped when you asked if we can go away for the winter. Then all the hoopla with your brother and Monica; who knows what's going to happen at the party; I figure, why not go away till summer?"

"You were staring into my eyes and pulling the thoughts from brain. It's mind blowing how well we sync."

"And you're worried that I will forget how to live." Jackson kissed my forehead. I remained quiet. I wasn't asleep, but I was reflecting. I was reflecting on what I had, how far I had come and where I was headed. A year ago, I was laying here alone. Two years ago, I didn't live in this mansion. I didn't own multiple businesses. Now look at me. I had a beautiful, loving, warm hearted, gentle, intelligent man. I had my health. I had my wealth. I was happy and I was nervous to attend a holiday party because I feared I wouldn't live. I always embarked on a journey with a clear mind; no expectations. Now, I was embarking on a journey and my mind wasn't clear.

Chapter 20

It was the morning of the party and I slept late; super late. It was 12:20 when Jenna walked into my bedroom. I was in a deep sleep. I didn't even hear her. She shook my legs.

"Rise and shine. We have things to do before you get dressed for the party."
"MMmmmm..." I rolled over and squinted at Jenna. I felt like 16yr old Sara being awakened by mom for school; except today was not a school day.
"Oh, and Hosni is on his way here with the kids. Apparently Abby wants to swim."
"It's December."
"Your pool is indoor. Come on! Up!" Jenna and her morning perkiness. She really was my mom.
"Where's Jackson?"
"Jackson still had no tux for the party. He called Javi and they went to Brooks Brothers."
"Oh Lord. My gay bestie took my man suit shopping, I'm afraid to see what he comes back with. What all do we have to do before I get ready?"
"Well you need to eat. I'm sure you wouldn't mind smoking. You have a nail appointment in 1 hour; you need a fill-in and Ari will be here at 3:30 to do your hair."
"How were you able to get Ari to call you back?"
"Oh. I went to the salon and dragged her out of there. I told her all about herself; and how she shouldn't hide from you because she's in love with your brother. I also explained to her that you are not childish and what you said about them needing to be careful was totally right. Anyway, I made her cry; you're not surprised and she promised she will be here to do your hair and to talk to you like a grown up." I shook my head and smiled. I made it out of the bed and into the bathroom. I really didn't feel like moving; especially because Jenna didn't mention coffee anywhere in her speech.
"Jen, coffee."
"There's a fresh pot on downstairs. Come on, I even rolled a blunt for you." I walked out of the bathroom and kissed Jenna on her cheek. As I strolled by her, she smacked my butt. I giggled. She was my newest best friend. She had a warm, inviting spirit, an excellent personality and she was open minded. She will retire as the richest personal assistant ever! It

helped that she got along with Jackson, my family and my friends. Sleeping late may have been a bad idea. I rushed through my shower to make my nail appointment. Then I sped home to meet Ari. Of course I walked into a home full of people and children. The last few weeks were so quiet around here, so I guess I could endure one random, noisy evening. Immediately, I picked Hasani up and held him close to me. He was so fat and I loved the smell of babies.

"Auntie!!! Hiii!!! Look!" Abby came running and her hair was straight and flowing.

"Oh my goodness, Abba, you look beautiful!" I put the baby down. I scooped Abby up into my arms and hugged her tight. She kissed me on my cheek and played in my hair.

"Ari combed it for me. Auntie do you comb your own hair?" I laughed.

"I do. But tonight I'm going to a fancy party, so Ari is going to style my hair for the event."

"I like Ari. She's better than my old mama. Do you know what nana said?" She placed both hands on my face and turned my head so she can whisper in my ear.

"Nana said mama is dead now. She went to live with Jesus, but not to be upset because she left a baby." I was shocked that my mom told her that. My eyes filled with tears.

"Don't cry Auntie. I'm not sad. My mama made me sad sometimes. I hope Jesus can fix her soul." WOW! Talk about a grown 7 year old! She was wise before her time. As the night went on, Jenna, Ari, Abby and I had a ball being girly and getting me ready. She was sad when I said it was time for me to go. I think it took Jackson 40 minutes to shower, shave and dress. Me, more like...well let's just say he was waiting for me at the bottom of the steps once I was fully ready. I took Jenna aside and filled her in on the plans.

"After the party, Jackson and I are going to come back here change, and leave. We have our bags packed and we are going straight to the tarmac where Hiro's jets are. I have one loaded and ready to take us to Santorini. We're not coming back." Jenna opened her mouth to speak. I covered it with my hand. "Don't worry. You run everything and you can reach me whenever. I need you to hold it together. You have to make sure I do not plummet. I trust you Jenna and I know you can do it, but if you have doubt, tell me now."

"Are you leaving as a result of what you already know is going to happen tonight at the party?"

"Somewhat. But Jackson and I don't want to spend winter in CT."

"But you said you aren't coming back."

"We aren't coming back anytime soon."

"I've got it. Ok. So I'll continue doing what I'm doing. When Hiro needs us to come..."

"Yup. I'll meet you wherever he's sending us. We are going to do business as normal except you will be in Connecticut and I will be in Greece."

"What about your family?"

"They know the deal. They expect it to happen. I'm surprised no one has asked me actually."

"Ok. Cool. So what else do I need to know or do?"

"Stay around and stay in touch with my family. Learn them. They aren't going to come flat out and tell you things, but you are sharp and observant, so I know that you will pick up on things."

"Absolutely. Is there anything that needs more attention than others?" I looked at Jenna and she was giving me a look as if she already knew what I was going to say. She snatched the words right from lips. "Ari, Hosni and the kids. I got it. I'm on it. Can I stay here?"

"In my house? Uh, yea. I guess. But you can't sleep in my bed."

"That's fine. I ask because your house is the perfect distance between the office, Hosni's home and your parents home. If I have to keep my eyes open, it's easier to do it on this side of town."

"Agreed. We should look into new housing for you before I come back."

"Whenever that is."

"Exactly."

For a millisecond I didn't want to leave, but then I remembered what this was really about. It was about me feeling like I needed to step back and reflect. When the mob in me came out, this had to be done. The difference between this time and the times in the past, was, the amount of harm was significantly greater now but in a smaller package. I felt more upset when I spoke to Abby. Hearing her accept her mother's disappearance as death was a bit heartbreaking. My mother telling her that she went to be with Jesus took guts and glory. I was glad she didn't ask me where her mother is.

"Sara. Saraaaa...come on daydreamer. We have to get you to the ball." Jenna assisted me down the steps. Jackson stood at the bottom with a corsage and pinned it to my gown. He leaned in and whispered to me.

"Are you wearing a vest mama?"

"Don't judge me, I don't trust Megan."

"Touché. Shall we?"

Jackson assisted me into my long, fur coat. He extended his hand and walked me out of the house. We climbed into the back of a limo that was waiting for us and we drove into the night. Avery's mansion was over an hour away from where I lived. We seemed to get there in a much shorter time frame. The driver turned the corner onto Avery's street and the amount of people out front was insane. There were news vans, reporters, and photographers. As the driver pulled into the driveway, I began to feel hot. Something wasn't right.

"Driver. Can you pull up on the side over there?" I noticed a desolate area where I could get out of the car and into the house without being noticed by cameras. Megan met the car as it parked.

"Welcome Sara, welcome. Hi Jackson. Welcome to the party. I take it you didn't want to be photographed or interviewed."

"Not really. Just want to enjoy the party."

"Oh you will. You will love the announcement that I have to make. Here's some reading material. You may want to prepare your statement."

What was this girl talking about? Megan handed me a manila envelope and walked away. I opened it. There were pictures of Avery and Tiffany on the beach, at a home, with kids. The pictures looked as if they spanned years. Tiffany and Avery built a life together and Avery continued to be Jackson's friend. Just then, I figured out what happened. Jackson knew that Avery was sleeping with Tiffany he just couldn't prove it. Once he received his proof and the end result was kidnapping and harm done to me, Jackson took Avery's life.

"Megan, wait." I followed her into the house. She led me down a long hallway, and down a dark staircase. While we were walking, I sent a text message to Cross.

Me: Here's my current location. Pine sol in 10.

I followed Megan into a semi lit room. She turned to face me.

"Sara. Sara. Sara. I'm glad that you are semi predictable. I knew I would be able to lure you; and here you are. Silly rabbit! I have the press here because I need the world to see your facial expression when I out you and your dangerous dark side. Its unfortunate because when I first met you and you helped me get my finances in order, I thought you were such a sweet, innocent, savvy, intelligent business woman. It was impressive how you maximized my small business. I asked Avery how did he meet you and he said that you did a favor for him a few years prior. So when you tell people that you don't know Avery on a personal level, you are in fact lying. But why do you lie about something as small as that? You lie because the truth hurts. I went in search of the truth. I needed to know what your real deal was. I found out that Avery actually created you. You met Avery in your 20s and he saw something in you that you didn't even know was in you. You didn't see it in yourself. He took you under his wing and taught you EVERYTHING. He had no idea that you were going to master the trade and use it against him. As soon as you learned 'the trade' you went off on your own and Avery lost all of his connects and contacts. You finished college and started your financial thing. You felt bad and reached out to Ave. You 'fixed' his finances. Then, I'm not sure what happened. All I know is he's dead and I'm sure you did it but I can't prove it. You were never seen on the island, but Jackson was. Jackson was there. What I can't figure out is why would Jackson murder his own best friend? What did you do? In fact, I don't care to know what you did. You are a horrible person, Sara Bashir. You kill for fun and steal money for a living. Well that ends tonight."

She reached under her clutch and raised her hand. She had a small 22 caliber handgun, similar to the one under my gown. I reached under my gown and pulled my gun. We shot at the same time. One quieted shot rang out from my pistol and hit Megan in the forehead. I managed to duck; her shot missed me and hit the wall.

"You should have left me alone, wench; you'd be alive right now." I whispered to myself as her limp body fell back and hit the ground. I slipped my gun back to its private location, turned around and headed toward the door. As I exited, Cross entered and took care of the rest. I moved swiftly and rejoined the party. No one knew I was missing; well almost no one.

"Is the deed done?"
"I was looking for the restroom; and yes, I handled some business along the way." Jackson looked at me and smiled; a handsome, devilish smile.
"I saw Cross head in the back of the house."

The night continued and more guests gathered. It turned out to be a beautiful, magical evening. There was a live orchestra that played various holiday tunes. The press reporters were speaking to people at random; asking them their thoughts on the party. The food was amazing. There was duck, turkey, chicken, bison, veal, fish, lasagna, various fruit salads, various garden salads, various grains, herbs, rice, pasta and everything was buffet style. There was wait staff carrying trays with appetizers and trays with champagne. I grabbed a glass and walked calmly through the rooms looking for familiar faces. There were a few people I recognized from other Avery Anderson parties, they acknowledged me, smiled and said a few words. A reporter walked over because he recognized me.

"Sara? Sara Bashir, right?"

"Hello, yes, and you are?"

"Robert Moses. I write for the Tribune."

"Chicago? What brings you to Connecticut?"

"Ironically, you. I was invited by Avery's assistant; she and I know each other through mutual friends. Anyway, I read about you and your automotive acquisition from Hiro Matsumaura and I always wanted to pick your business savvy brain. She told me that Avery knew you and she was certain you would be at this party. She invited me and said she would introduce us. It's a wonder you were standing alone." I laughed. For some reason I was flattered by Mr. Moses and his tenacity. He had spunk. It's rare. I assumed it was because he was new to the press world. "How long have you been on that side of the microphone?" He laughed. He knew by my question, that I had him figured out.

"Just 2 years but I have some pretty impressive interviews already under my belt. Here's my card. I won't talk shop with you now, because this is a pleasure event, but when you go back to work, look at my site and reach out if you're interested in sitting down." I took his card. I'll look him up.

"Thank you. I appreciate you knowing that tonight is not the right night. I appreciate your positive thoughts, compliments and comment. Please, enjoy the rest of the party."

I walked away. Slowly, I could heard some of the reporters saying my name and taking my picture. I had no idea that I was THIS well known in the business world. I glanced at the time and realized this was usually when Avery would make a speech. I made my way toward the orchestra; I saw a microphone over there.

"Good evening everyone. May I have your attention please?"

I tapped the top of the microphone slightly. People quieted down and all eyes were on me.

"I appreciate you all being here this evening. My name is Sara Bashir and I am Avery Anderson's financial advisor. I'm sure you all are wondering where Sir McBride is. Well, Avery has been 'missing' since August. There seems to be no foul play. He boarded his jet and flew away. I don't know him very well on a personal level but I know his person. He is very determined. He's fun loving. He works hard and he is extremely quirky. I'm sure he is sitting some place warm with his feet up and a glass in his hand. I remember him telling me when he's ready to retire, he is just going to do so; no questions asked. It helps me feel better to think that's exactly what he's doing. He's comfortable in his own land. He's watching his money increase. I have all intentions on still running his business and making sure he is in positive financial standing. I will make sure the mogul has a standing empire to return to. Avery Anderson events will still happen annually and so will the parties. However, going forward, no more press coverage at parties. They will be private. Charity events and fundraisers can have press coverage. I think Avery would prefer it be that way. Avery is flashy, but it's downplayed for privacy. On behalf of The Avery Anderson McBride foundation, Bashir Enterprises, myself and Avery, thank you for joining us in this holiday celebration. Please, enjoy the remainder of the evening. Eat, drink, dance, socialize and enjoy Avery's money."

The crowd roared. Avery always told his guests to enjoy the money he spent when he addressed them at parties. I may not have known Avery all that well, but I knew how to deliver an Avery Anderson speech.

"Please sign the guest book as you move around the party. Please fill in your name, address, email address and telephone so you will receive updates and invites. Merry Christmas. Happy Hanukkah. Happy Kwanza. If I do not see you, Happy New Year! Enjoy. God bless. Good night."

They all clapped and cheered. All I could think about was leaving, getting out of that gown and getting on that plane. That's exactly what I did. Jackson and I left the party before it was finished. People were shaking my hand, waving and speaking as we were moving around the room. I enjoyed the fame; the attention, but the real secret was no one knew what actually went on in that party. That night I upgraded from feisty female mob boss, to heartless, selfish, money hungry mother. I made it official that I had taken control of Avery's business. I took his sister out and I didn't hesitate. I couldn't hesitate. If I stood still and let Megan take another shot, I would be dead, she would've told my secrets and everything that I worked so hard for would be gone; my family would be shamed. 'Bashir's don't get caught.' My mother told me that when I was in my 20's. Tonight, I learned exactly what that meant and I couldn't get caught. Jackson and I walked to the limo arm and arm. The limo driver got us home in record time. I think he knew that I was in a hurry. Jackson and I rushed inside and as I was walking, I was undressing. I slipped on a pair of fleece leggings and an oversized hoodie. Jackson wore sweats and hoodie also. We grabbed some last minute things , locked all the doors and turned on the alarm system. I sent a text to Jenna with the code. We ran back outside and hopped back into the limo. The awesome limo driver got us to the tarmac in no time flat. We boarded the plane. Jackson handed me a bottle of Woodford.

"Bourbon?"
"One of the best on the list."
"I always fly with Vodka."
"You deserve to fly with something better for this flight."
"Do I deserve anything good?"
"You deserve the world, the moon, the stars..."
"Why do I feel so bad?"
"For some reason, you have a conscious."
"The only Bashir with one."
"Maybe that's for good reason."

I took that as Jackson's way of telling me that I should be the one to end generations of treachery. The Bashir women were dangerous. I knew I was but it didn't become clear until recently. I knew I couldn't continue like this; ending lives. Jackson was right, I indeed, had a conscious.

"I do what I do in order to protect what I have."
"Then don't stop, but that also means that you have to find a way to cope when bad things happens. You can't feel remorse. If you are going to feel remorse, then you have to find different means of protecting what you have."
Just then I received a text message from Jenna.

Jenna: I came to your house. I was trying to catch you. Please tell me you are on the plane.
Me: I am. What's up? Is everything ok?

Jenna: John Thompson is looking for you. He's being annoying; totally not hearing me when I speak.

Me: Oh yea?

Jenna: Yea, but I'll take care of it. Let me know when you land.

Me: Will do.

I put my phone away and smiled. Jenna was who I needed to converse with, to clear my conscious. She seemed to be content with going above and beyond for me and my business. I think she had some closet mob boss in her also. I think she can handle handles without a blink of an eye. The rest of our flight was peaceful and quiet. Jackson slept. I sat and reflected. I also drank the entire bottle of Bourbon. Intoxicated was an understatement for what I was. We arrived in Santorini the next morning. We were driven to 'our' home off the coast of the Aegean Sea. It was beautiful, breathtaking and quiet. Once settled inside, I showered and put on a sundress. I took a walk around to familiarize myself with the area. It felt comfortable; like it was the right decision. I remembered I needed to reach out to Jenna. I reached for my cell and called her.

"Hello. Hold on." She was whispering. I waited. "Ok. Sara. Have you landed?"

"I've landed, showered and now I'm standing on my beach. What are you doing?"

"I am...well, Cross and I are getting rid of something...." I knew what that meant.

"How'd you end up with Cross?"

"He reached out to me. We are going to take over all of this, for you. From now on, you call me or you call Cross. Let us do it. We need you to stay out of the way.""

"I don't mind but what's going on specifically? You can handle whatever handles you want, but I need to know everything."

"Have you watched or read the news since you've landed?"

"I'm in Greece, looking at the Aegean Sea. Guess what I have not done?"

"Touché. Well...let me fill you in. The Avery Anderson McBride Memorial Holiday party; as it is now being called, was the greatest event in the history of the business world. You had no idea but CEOs of Pepsi, Microsoft, Mercedes Benz, Facebook, Apple, and Time Warner were all in attendance. Your name is number one googled item. John Thompson reappeared and Cross had to make sure he didn't ever again; he was asking questions shooting out threats. But,the fame is yours. Everyone wants an interview. You spoke to a reporter that evening. I just emailed his article to you. It was short, but it was good. Here, I'm excited. I'll read it to you."

A Lady in Red: Last night was the first official Avery Anderson McBride Foundation Memorial party and it had the most invigorating host; Sara Bashir. In a very modest, polite manner, Sara gracefully walked the room with a pleasant, beaming smile on her face. She was cordial, professional and impeccably dressed. Sporting what looked like vintage Versace, she mediated and marveled a room full of executives. I heard whispers, questions, "is she royalty?" "where'd she come from?" Sara was little known until a string of fortunate business ventures landed in her lap. Now, the owner and CEO of a top financial firm, the owner and dealer principal of the fastest growing automotive company and she just became a recycling guru; with the assistance of her fiancé. She made a wonderful speech; short and to the point, and hosted the hottest party of the year. The food and the drinks were astonishing and the atmosphere was a spectacular winter wonderland. Business owners watch out! Your toughest match just entered the ring and she's wearing $3,000 Louboutin shoes!

"Your hiatus is a hit as well. No one saw you leave the party. It was almost like you vanished. It sounded amazing! I wish I could've seen it."
I was beaming! I couldn't believe that I was famous. I wanted to run back and bask in it. Instead I allowed Jenna to give an official statement.
"That's amazing. What are people googling?"
"Just you; in general. Who you are and what you do. At some point, Forbes is going to want to speak to you. I looked at your net worth...I'll update at end of business and send you an email of the financial statement. You reached a financial plateau. I'm not sure if it's what you were aiming for, but it happened and it's great. Congratulations!" I beamed.
"Thank you Jenna. Thank you very much for being here and helping me get here. Listen. You can be my voice to the people; until I return. Give an official statement thanking everyone and let them know that this is only the beginning. Let them know that I am willing to assist any small business in need. Tell the business world that we all achieved financial greatness. What matters is what you do when you reach the top. What happens next? I want you to do a focus group with the staff at Bradley. Find out what matters to them. What's important? What do you live for?

What charities do you support; if any? I want to help them reach their plateaus also. We are a full circle company. What we give, we get." I felt good speaking to Jenna. We were on the phone for hours. I sat on the beach while she moved between homes and offices. I asked her about her dreams and aspirations. I told her that her main purpose in life was definitely not to help me run my life. She understood and assured me that I will be the first to know if/when her career goals change.

"I can imagine that when you and Jackson have children, I will be phased out. My services will not be needed around the house with the kids. Although, I must admit, your nephews and niece are pretty awesome kids. I think having Hosni and no Monica was a blessing for them."

I enjoyed hearing her praise my wonderful family. She was getting familiar with my mother and my mother was definitely making Jenna earn her spot with the family. Jenna was tough. She can handle anything. I wasn't worried. As I sat on the beach and thought about my blessings, my life, my accomplishments, I knew that I owed it all to God. I knew that my pure and sole existence was from Him. Jenna and I finished speaking after 6 hours. I hung up the phone, got down on my knees and prayed.

"Heavenly Father, thank you. Thank you for waking me up this morning and starting me on my way. Thank you for the constant blessings that you send my way. Thank you for my struggles. I know that I am not good and I am not always diligent and I know that I often go astray. I beg of you, Heavenly Father, please forgive me, for I know not what to do when I get into a moment. I need your continued assistance. I know that's why you sent Jenna to me. I thank you for her. She is my glue. I thank you for Jackson. I ask that you keep a hedge of protection around him; around me while we lay here in your paradise. I know that he wants children and I ask that if it is your will, that it be your way. I have faith. I believe that all things come of thee, oh Lord. I thank you for my mother and her strength. If it were not for her carrying me in 90 degree heat, I would not be here today. She thanks you for the strength to have done so. She thanks you for the strength that you gave her to raise such a strong willed individual. I ask that you keep a hedge of protection around her. Thank you for my father; for my brother; for the nephews and the niece. Thank you for allowing me to forgive Monica and she me. I ask that you keep a hedge of protection around her. Heavenly father, I cannot thank you enough for everything. I am not worthy, yet you still bless me. I am forever grateful. As I lay low in your paradise, please help me search within myself and find what makes me. Please forgive me for the wrong I've done and recognized. I ask all of this in your precious name, my eternal, great, father, Amen."

The End....

Made in the USA
Middletown, DE
26 June 2018